RUIN

DARK ISLAND SCOTS, #1

Jolie Vines

WWW.JOLIEVINES.COM

Editing by Emmy Ellis at Studio ENP.

Proofreading by Zoe Ashwood.

Formatting by Cleo Moran / Devoted Pages Designs

Cover design by Natasha Snow.

Cover model photography by and copyright of Wander Aguiar

Cover model: Chris Lynch.

To all you readers who fall for the antihero

BLURB

I wanted him. He wanted to ruin me.

It was the blood I noticed first. Running down the neck of the man on the ferry.

Then his bruised knuckles, dark eyes, and arrogant smirk.

The handcuffs came last.

No one else paid him attention, but I couldn't look away. Or deny my instant lust.

I had no idea he was being imprisoned on the remote, dark Scottish island I knew well.

Or that he'd been kidnapped, not arrested.

I went from that naïve girl on the boat, dreaming of stolen kisses, to the one who held the key to his prison cell.

When heat turns to hate, all that's left is ruin.

--

Ruin (Dark Island Scots, #1) is a new adult romantic suspense with dark themes, including angst, lust-to-hate-to- love, and lost innocence. This series will be deeply interconnected, so expect the occasional wicked cliffhanger. It'll be well worth the heart palpitations.

Lose yourself in *Ruin*.

READER NOTE

Dear reader,

Thank you for picking up Ruin, - the first in my new series. Get ready for dark delights.

Please be aware that this series contains darker storylines, such as domestic violence and threat of sexual assault. An up to date list of trigger warnings can be found on my website.
https://jolievines.com

You can listen along with the swoony audio, narrated by Zachary Webber and Zara Hamption-Brown.

If you're new-to-me as an author, I have three other series set in scotland.

The third - *Wild Mountain Scots* - overlaps with Ruin, with a few of the characters appearing in each other's stories. If you spot the McRae family, be ready to fall in love with them too.

Happy reading!
Jolie

1

Thea

It was the blood I noticed first. A red streak trickling down the man's neck, blending with his black hair. The stranger sat upright on the boat's bench seat, glaring out, his jaw locked tight, and his hands linked behind him so his biceps popped.

Anger poured off him, hot and unhidden.

Stalling in my footsteps, I stared at him, all that intensity...fascinating.

A light sprinkling of rain fell, but the man made no effort to shelter himself. Nor did anyone else on the ferry pay him any attention or tend to his injury. The others who filed over the ramp kept their gazes elsewhere.

At my back, my father propelled me on, muttering about the weather. Summer rain wasn't unusual here in Northern Scotland, but it made the ferry trip to the islands less than fun. I'd know—we'd been taking this route twice a year since I could remember. Except today, I wasn't supposed to be here.

I skittered on, my bag banging into my legs. In my

other hand, I clutched my umbrella, probably useless against the stiff sea breezes.

One by one, the other passengers filtered into the cabin, and Dad followed. I hung back, reluctant to sit on the wet metal seats but somehow stuck outside.

With a clatter of chains, the ferry moved off, easing into the harbour.

Our sea journey began. I grabbed a rail and steadied myself, trying to look anywhere but at the man.

Yet my focus drifted his way once more.

At nineteen, I was a late bloomer, never really interested in guys. Definitely not ones like this man who screamed *bad boy* with every aspect of his appearance.

At a guess, I'd put him a little older than myself. Maybe twenty. Sharp cheekbones. Torn black shirt. Attitude. The sort of boy your mother warned you about.

Well, not my mother.

I wished she'd take that level of interest, but I couldn't dwell on that, or the last time I'd seen her. It hit on something deep inside I couldn't handle.

Instead, I stared at the stranger and tried to forget my traumatising visit.

Tattoos scrawled over one arm, visible under his sleeveless t-shirt. I traced the unfinished ink down to his wrist.

Metal glinted.

I did a double-take. Handcuffs? God, yes, they constrained him to the seat. He was a prisoner.

My heart thumped wildly.

Without turning my way, the stranger lifted his chin. "Take a picture, sweetheart. Use it when you're alone in bed tonight."

Heat flooded my face, though no one could hear us. "Sorry. I didn't mean to—"

"Aye, ye did."

He was Scottish, hardly surprising, but that gruff edge to his accent compelled me all the more.

A squall of rain lashed the boat, and I huddled deeper into my anorak. "Why are you chained out here? You're going to get soaked."

He didn't answer, and I drifted closer.

"You're hurt, too."

Again, no reply came. But he angled his head to watch my approach.

The drizzle amplified to heavy drops. They clung to his black eyelashes and darkened his jeans.

A few minutes in this and he'd be drenched. The crossing to the islands took almost two hours, and the skies darkened in our direction of travel.

"Who are you here with?" I tried again. "I'll go fetch them so they can take you in."

This earned me a smirk. "You'll waste your breath. No one's going to care if I get wet."

"It isn't right."

"I'm handcuffed to this boat. Nothing about this is right."

Making a decision, I snapped open my umbrella and perched next to him. If anyone needed kindness, it was this man.

His expression changed to incredulous.

"Where are you being taken?" I held tight to our flimsy shelter, the wind buffeting me. Was there a jail out on the islands? I'd never heard of one.

"Fuck if I know. Where does this ferry go?"

"North Uist, then on to Torlum. But you won't be going there. That's a tiny island, and the boat's only going there to drop off me and my dad. You'll get off before."

"Torlum," he repeated.

A tremor ran down my spine, some sense of foreboding at hearing the name of that place on his lips.

At his neck, more blood ran.

"Did you fight when you were arrested?" I asked. "They shouldn't have just left you bleeding."

"I wasnae arrested."

"Then what happened?"

His eyebrows merged. "Why do ye care?"

I swallowed under the weight of his stare and realised how I sounded.

As a girl, I'd been obsessed with detective stories. I adored Enola Holmes and the ancient Nancy Drew books. Mysteries were my constant interest. My curiosity had got away with me.

"I...don't know," I stuttered. "That cut behind your ear needs treatment—"

"Theadora," Dad's voice rang out.

I leapt to my feet, half dropping the umbrella. "Yes?"

"What the hell are you doing? Come inside at once."

"But, Dad. He's locked up here. He can't be left like this."

"I said now," my father demanded. His attention flitted over the man, and his lip curled.

Embarrassment washed over me. I turned around. "Tell me who to talk to inside, and I'll get them to come out."

"Don't bother."

"Theadora," Dad commanded once more.

I knew how it looked. I was the idiot hanging around a criminal, thinking they needed me. After the visit with Mum, I was determined to be better for my father. Calmer, smarter, and everything a daughter should be.

I suppressed my curiosity and my need to help, obeyed, and walked away.

Yet other emotions rushed.

Darker ones that liked how the bad boy looked.

Inside the cabin, my father produced his phone and

stabbed at the screen.

"Will you do something about him?" I asked.

"No. And neither will you. Have some sense. Leave it alone." Dad stomped away, starting a conversation with whomever he'd dialled.

I sank into a warm, dry seat and peered out of the rain-splattered window. The lone person left on the deck only watched the sea.

Maybe twenty other people milled around inside the cabin.

With heated cheeks, I raised a hand. "Is somebody taking care of the man outside?"

At my voice, a few exchanged glances, but nobody stepped up. They went back to their phones or chats, and the prisoner was left to wait it out in the rain.

I took my knitting from my bag—my work-in-progress an infinity scarf made from the loveliest blue merino yarn—but my concentration kept slipping. Therefore, so did my stitches.

At North Uist, most of the passengers departed, but the handcuffed prisoner stayed on deck. At the next stop, a small island, the couple gingerly walked the ramp, and two men remained in the cabin.

I stared daggers at the people who were obviously the jailors. Nothing about them suggested they were police. More thugs, with thick muscles and unshaven faces.

My imagination ran riot.

Finally at Torlum, the ferry docked at the tiny harbour, and we exited. Puffing with the effort, my father hurried me up the slope on the single road that led into the island.

One tiny village and scattered individual homes, mainly crofters living off the land, made up the population of Torlum. A hundred people at most. I peeked around at the prisoner being dragged off the boat and in the opposite direction to us.

"Why is he here?" I questioned. "Where are they taking him?"

Dad made no reply.

I knew the reason for his mood. He hated our trips here, always had. Once, after a few too many whiskies, he claimed the island held a darkness. Something evil which delighted my overactive imagination.

But that's all it was—make-believe. I had a plan to help with Dad's grumpiness, but I had to wait to see if I could put it in place.

A few minutes on, and we arrived at Granny's gloomy and forbidding house.

A large Victorian, it was entirely out of place in the landscape. Most homes on the island were single-storey, plain and functional, or weather-beaten farmhouses. My relatives of a few generations ago had built this as a hotel, but now only my grandmother lived here.

"Smile and be quiet," Dad ordered. "I don't know how she'll be this time, and we have business to attend to. With any luck, we'll be able to leave tomorrow."

"We're not staying for longer?"

"Not if I can help it."

He let himself in, and I hovered on the doorstep, twisting to take in the wide-open landscape.

Water sparkled in pools here and there. Acres of flat-land and beach begged to be explored. Steep slopes rose into the island's interior. A lonely lighthouse perched high on a cliff.

I'd wanted to use the time here to relax. Seeing my mother had shaken me more than I'd ever say, and I needed to take a breath before returning to university in September.

Except I was anything but calm.

No small part of it was how my mind had gone away

from the ferry dock and followed after the too-intriguing prisoner.

Something was wrong in his treatment, and I wasn't sure I could let it go.

2

Struan

My kidnappers marched me along the road, silent and smug. With my hands still cuffed at my back, I was chained to Goon One's wrists, Goon Two tailing us.

I glowered at the ground, mind churning over what the fuck I was going to do. After they'd grabbed me from the streets of Glasgow last night, checking my ID before tossing my wallet and phone, I'd been thrown into a van.

Cuffed. Gagged.

I'd smashed into the sides. Bellowed from behind the tape over my mouth. The wheels kept rolling.

It had already been the worst night of my life, those final words called after I'd stormed out of my home haunting me.

Don't ruin this.

Yet I had.

This was the cherry on the fucking cake.

Finally, the van had stopped and daylight flooded in. I'd been allowed to take a piss, smacked upside the when I tried to escape, then led onto the boat.

To the first set of passengers, I'd yelled that the ugly fuckers securing me to the seat weren't cops, and that I needed help. Not one person glanced my way, and I'd earned another punch along with the threat of being knocked out cold.

Only the English tourist girl who got on later felt bad enough to talk to me.

Which meant she had less sense that she should. Pretty little thing like her would get eaten up by this world and spat out.

Even locked up, I'd been all too aware of her. Her pert face, cheeks flushed from where I called her out for staring at me. Red lips. Brown hair, wet from the rain. Back home, a lass like her wouldn't look twice at someone like me. Not for anything more than a quick fuck with a boy who scared her.

Compared to her, or against anyone else, I was obviously trouble.

I'd been arrested in the past, more than once. Mostly for fighting. The police had to give the same old speech each time, about rights and their process. But if these men weren't cops, I had no fucking clue who they could be. Aye, I lived on the wrong side of the law, but I didn't mess around with gangs. No reason why any of them would take me.

Besides, if anyone wanted me dead, they were doing a shite job of it.

Whatever. I needed to make a run for it. If I could get in a lucky punch on the man behind me and KO the arsehole, I could choke the man I was cuffed to with his own chain.

Find the key. Steal a wallet. Back to hop on a boat.

"Chill the fuck out, kid," the rear guy suddenly said. "Can hear your brain whirring from here. Try anything, and I'll be delivering you to the place unconscious. Got me?"

"What place?" I muttered.

"Wait and see. We're almost there."

Up ahead, a white-painted building came into sight, L-shaped with a single floor and low roof. A half-fallen sign outside read *Torlum Youth Hostel*.

Sharp fear stabbed at me. In its isolated spot, the place was something from a horror movie. One where the dumb teenager wanders in and ends up murdered.

I couldn't go in there.

"What the fuck is this?" I asked.

Neither man answered.

The second took my shoulders and kept me moving. At the entrance, the run-down exterior gave way to a grim reception. I stalled at the door, jamming my heels against the step as I took in the dark space. From an office, a woman emerged. Bobbed grey hair and a square frame. Fuck me, she looked tougher than the men who'd brought me here.

Her cold-eyed gaze slunk over me in the doorway. "I only heard about this one today. Age?"

The man to my right shrugged. "Just the delivery guys."

She huffed then jacked a thumb at a chair. The two yanked me to it and forced me to sit, unchaining me from Goon One though leaving my hands behind my back.

The woman approached, something in her hands. "Hold his legs."

The men did as she asked, and I surged against their restraints.

"Who are ye? What is this?" I demanded.

She ignored me and stooped. Grabbing my ankle, she raised the damp leg of my jeans.

"Get the fuck off." I bucked and kicked out, but the goons clamped down harder.

A cold lump of plastic snapped into place around my leg. A green light blipped on.

"A tracker," the woman spoke my thoughts, her accent maybe English. "Number four on the system." Then she straightened and finally stared me in the eye. "Listen up. You belong to me now. You'll do as I say when I tell you."

"Fuck ye," I bit out. "If I've been arrested, there's shite ye need to tell me. I have rights."

She lifted her grey eyebrows into her hairline. Then the bitch laughed.

"My name's Struan Gallagher—" I started.

"I couldn't give half a shit," she said, then yelled, "Sin."

What the fuck did that mean?

Footsteps came from down the hall, and a huge, shaven-headed lad appeared. Behind him, another younger man followed. Both maybe late teens or early twenties.

They gawked at me, something calculating in their stares.

"Boo," I said.

Neither blinked.

The woman grumbled, retreating to her office. "Take the cuffs off him. Sin, he's yours now. You know the rules. Don't kill him."

Goon One yanked me to my feet and removed the hard steel from my wrists. Instantly, I dropped into a fighter's pose and threw a punch at his head, connecting with a sweet smack.

The dumb fuck dropped to the floor with a howl. I wheeled around right as the other hooked me around the throat and lifted me off my feet.

"Fuck," I wheezed, wrenching against the chokehold.

But his other arm banded around my chest, locking down my arms. Dude on the floor grabbed my legs, digging his fingers in.

Even overpowered, I wasn't going to let them take me down a second time. Not if I had to fight until I was bloodied.

With a gleam of pure evil in her eyes, the woman emerged once more. This time, a needle glinted in her hand.

"There's always one who has to start like this," she complained.

No pause, she jabbed the needle into my neck, pressed the plunger, and everything went black.

I woke on the scratchy carpet of a bedroom. Bunk beds lined the wall, and the second of the two lads who the woman had called watched me from a lower bunk.

"Awake?" He tilted his head.

I blinked, my eyes gritty. My head weighed a ton, but I forced myself up to sitting. And retched.

The boy winced. "Yeah, that shite will mess up your

gut for a couple of days, so I hear. When was the last time ye ate? Better to have something in your stomach."

"What did she inject me with?" I managed, my tongue thick like I'd been chewing cotton wool.

"A sedative, I guess? No clue. I didn't fight so didn't have the pleasure."

I blinked again, and the room came into better focus. Six beds in three bunks, a few pieces of furniture, and a single window at the end.

Darkness hid the view.

I'd been out of it for hours.

The lad leaned in, the bare overhead light bulb casting shadows on his pitying gaze. His t-shirt had the slogan *Boys Get Blue Too.* "There's a few things I need to tell ye about this place. First, forget freedom. If you're here, it's for a reason. Ain't no getting out. Full prison is probably the alternative."

"Fuck that," I spat. The tracker on my leg pressed in, and I wrenched at it, the block one thick strap with no obvious break points.

"Yeah, ye won't get that off. We've all tried," the lad continued. "They are waterproof, knife proof, and we even hacked at one with bolt cutters. No go. They can deliver an electric shock that'll knock ye down, so make sure to only keep a low charge on it when you're told to juice it up. Second rule, we all share the work."

"Who's we?"

"You're the fourth. Sin's making dinner. Burn was the last. I'm Scar. I mean Camden. Keep doesnae use our real names, so we got used to the nicknames she comes up with."

"Keep? That the woman who jabbed me?"

"Aye. Our keeper. She's never given another name."

Now I looked closer, I picked up the ridge of a scar running down the side of Camden's face. It cut into his dark hair, then was hidden by the messy lengths.

"How old are ye?" he asked.

"Nineteen. Twenty in a few months. What is this, like a young offender institute? Some kind of fucked-up therapy camp?" All kinds of suggestions hit my brain, but nothing fit.

Scarred Camden only stared in response, taking a moment to process something I'd said. "What month is your birthday?"

"December. Why?"

"I need to talk to Sin. Rest up, and I'll be back to clue ye in on how to handle tonight. Then we'll get ye fed. You'll feel better soon."

Screw that. I wasn't about to sit around and obey their rules. Whatever the hell this was, I wouldn't live it.

I dipped my head in pretend agreement, and the lad stood from the bunk and left the room, the door snicking closed behind him. Stumbling to my feet, I paced after him, half falling onto the metal-framed bunk.

"Shite," I mumbled, my head swimming.

I made it to the door, but the arsehole had locked me in. For a moment, I let new panic wash over then through me.

My life was no bed of roses. Ma and I had sofa surfed or lived in single rooms when she didn't have the money or the right needs for a place of our own.

More than once, we'd had to run.

Last night had been different. She'd come to me with her fucked-up news, and I'd walked out on her without saying goodbye. Ruined it all. Had I really meant to let her final evening go down like that? What the fuck was wrong with me?

Except everything she'd told me buzzed in my head, loud and more nauseating than the drug.

I had to get free.

I'd been born a fighter and wasn't about to sit around and wait to be murdered in my sleep.

A locked door meant nothing.

Sucking in a breath, I forced my body to work, then hefted the wee table from the corner. It weighed enough that I staggered backwards.

Throwing it was going to be a challenge.

Nae problem. I had another way. With a second to centre myself, I held it out in front of me and, putting all my power into it, ran at the window.

3

Scar

Sin leaned over a cooking pot, glowering at the stew. "Are ye sure?"

"Told me so himself. Twenty in December. Which means—"

"I know what it means." He tossed the wooden spoon into the sink with a clatter. "Too close for comfort. We need to get into the office and change those details."

A shiver of anticipation ran over me. "Don't ye think Keep will have already seen his record?"

"No chance. At the earliest, she'll print it out tonight. We need to do this now."

"Ye mean I do."

He eyed me. "As the only one of us any good with computers, aye, it's your job. But you're part of a family here. Want to see the new boy hurt?"

I swallowed, humbled. Sin did more for me than any person in my life had ever previously bothered. If it wasn't for him, I wouldn't have shoes, good food, or have been saved from regular beatings.

He took it all on his broad shoulders and, when we were free, I wouldn't forget it.

"No, sorry," I mumbled.

He ruffled my hair, but his gaze sharpened, his attention going to the door. "Now or never. I'll cause a distraction. Go do what we need done. If ye fail, that scrappy fucker willnae survive the month."

"Got it. What are ye going to do to distract Keep?"

At my words, an enormous crash came from down the hall. Glass, shattering.

Ah Christ.

Sin and I both snapped our heads to the sound, and my friend barked out a laugh.

"He's gone through the window. Wait here until she comes out, then I'll keep her busy."

There was no door to the kitchen, and Keep thundered past down the hall, her Taser sparking in her hand.

"Break my window, did he?" she snarled.

"Go," Sin silently urged, following her.

I dove the other way and got on with faking the history of our newfound friend.

*I*n the office, I powered up the ancient laptop, tension stringing me tight. It whirred and chugged to life, pale-blue light falling over me but the system not yet online.

Desperation filled me.

I had no time to do this. Keep could return any second. I'd cop a punishment worse than ever if she found me here.

Still, I had to wait it out.

Sweat broke out on my forehead. I kept my senses trained on the sounds from deeper in the hostel, tracking every crash and bang. Every shout. Sin would work to distract her until he saw me return. I had faith in him.

Still, my skin crawled with the need to get out of here.

"Come on, you piece of shite," I muttered at the machine.

The screen blipped, and the desktop loaded.

In a heartbeat, I was in the file system and finding Struan's record, my fingers flying wildly over the keys.

His data stared back at me. Stark and undeniable.

A clatter came from the reception area outside the office. I froze, then Sin's booming voice followed.

Fuck. I had to work faster.

In short order, I made a permanent change. One Keep would never know about, but that made all the difference to Struan.

I didn't know this guy. Had no clue what kind of man he was. But we'd all agreed to Sin's plan. None of us would let our newest member be hurt like had happened in the past.

Too much rode on handling this our way.

Saving took another age, the machine whining. The second it was done, I powered it down, resisting the urge to scream with the time it took. It clicked, the blue light died.

Finally. I closed the lid and crept to the door.

Outside, Keep strode out of the front exit, snarling orders at someone. Sin stood purposefully behind her, blocking sight of me.

My chance.

I eased the office door open and slipped out, keeping low to cross the floor. Almost stumbling, I made it back into our corridor then threw myself into the bunk room.

Against the wall, I sucked in air, too panicked. Sin returned and caught my eye. A single nod communicated all we each needed to know.

It had worked.

Thank fuck for that.

4

Thea

In my narrow bed, I huddled in my blanket, knitting needles lightly clicking. It wasn't late enough for sleep, but we'd already had dinner, and I'd escaped to my room for space.

My grandmother's place was a house of horrors. On our arrival, Dad had an argument with her home help. They were supposed to live here and care for her, plus either clean up or bring in a cleaner if they needed it. Little of that had been done.

Dust covered every surface, the taste of it in the air. Dirty dishes sat in piles in and around the sink.

Granny was thankfully cared for, but my father had flown into a fury, and the carer had fled.

I'd got to work cleaning while Dad called his lawyer who was apparently coming here tomorrow. My father wouldn't talk about it with me, but I suspected he was trying to get legal rights over his mother so he could be of more use to her.

All of which I could help with.

I'd spent an hour working on the infinity scarf, the repetitive action meant to be soothing. I was knitting it flat, intending to block it out with a seam to make it round. But I'd been staring into space for a good ten minutes, not watching my stitches.

I wasn't all that relaxed. Instead, my nerves jangled.

Setting aside my knitting, I grabbed my phone then typed out a message to my favourite person here.

Thea: Hey, are you home?

My childhood friend wrote back immediately.

Lottie: Don't tell me you're on the island. I'll choke on my dinner.

Thea: We are. Just for a night or two.

Lottie: Bestie! Meet up?

I jiggled my legs. Dad had expressly told me to stay in. But the rain had held off, and I needed to talk to a friend.

Thea: East Beach. Half an hour. I'll need to sneak out, so don't leave if I'm late.

Off the bed, I silently padded to my door, knowing the pressure points on the creaky old floorboards. Downstairs, Dad talked on yet another call.

There were few good things about Granny's place, but two staircases made the list. With my shoes and bag in hand, plus a bottle of water from my bedside table, I snuck down the concrete back stairs and out of the kitchen door. Then I slipped on my flats and fled to the scrubby garden wall, scrambling over.

A quick peek at the house gave the all-clear. In the yellow light from the window, my father paced, too busy talking to listen out for me.

The cool night welcomed my exploring. By faint moonlight, I traipsed down the path to the road, then followed it past the harbour and to the east side of the island. Torlum was tiny, and I entered and left the village in a minute. There were few cars here—no point when the only way on and off was by boat and the island barely measured four miles in length—and I saw not a single other person out.

Lottie's family lived in the far north of the island, so she'd take a little longer cycling over. I stepped onto the sands and stared out to sea. The rain and wind from earlier had gone, replaced by a calm evening. Waves dragged on the shore in a rhythmic pull, and the tang of salt in the air speckled my lips.

Birds shrieked overhead, an eerie sound, and I peered at the cliffs. Above was the lighthouse, the light shining out across the water. I knew these bluffs well. I'd climbed all over them as a child and made dens in the high-up cave.

Everything was black and white. Ghostly lamplight, silvered sands, dark water, and ominous rocks.

The pale face and dark hair of someone coming my way.

I hesitated, my pulse skipping.

It wasn't Lottie. She was short and curvy. This person was much bigger.

A man.

Then I spotted a new colour in the greyscale. Red. Blood, sticky and wet down his arm. The second lot I'd seen today, and on the same person.

"Oh my God." I jogged over to the prisoner from the boat.

Out of his restraints, he seemed larger, more...dangerous. Yet that didn't stall me. He'd been injured then, and I'd wanted to fix him. Now, my breath caught at the sight of his new wounds.

Other parts of me woke with bright and keen interest.

He stopped in his tracks. "The lass from the ferry."

I opened my mouth to give my name, but he continued speaking, weaving on his feet.

"Theadora."

"You remembered."

He gave a hard laugh. "You're the only person I know here."

I swallowed and snapped my gaze to the arm he cradled to his chest. "What happened to you?"

"Glass. I escaped through a window. Badly."

I had no clue why, but I laughed. Some kind of squawk of shock. "Let me see."

He shook his head once. "I have to get off this island. If they find me, I'll never get away."

"Who's chasing you? Your guards?"

"No, they're gone, I think. And they weren't guards, or not legit ones. They picked me up from the streets. No one knows I'm here."

A tiny inkling of fear broke through my concern. I wasn't entirely sheltered—a shitty upbringing plus a year at university in Edinburgh had sorted that problem—but this was more than I knew how to handle.

"Why would strangers take you? Why here?" I asked.

He gave an exasperated groan, staggering past a few feet. "If I knew that, I'd be a lot fucking happier. Listen, ye dinna have to believe me, but I still need to go."

"Wait, what's your name?"

"Struan. Not that it'll do ye any good to know. Better for ye if ye walk in the other direction."

From up the beach, a shout came. Struan—for I now

had a name to go with the face—wheeled around, grunting with pain from the move.

"They're coming for me."

I made a decision. Probably a stupid one, but I owned it. "There's no way you'll outrun them. You can barely stand. Come with me."

"No, I have to keep moving."

"There's no ferry now. No causeway. We won't make it to the harbour. What are you going to do, swim? We're miles from anywhere. You'll drown. Let me hide you until they pass."

Another shout came, and torches pierced the dark. Struan's features compressed, fear plain. Then he gave a short nod.

Irrational pleasure rose at having his trust, and I led the way to the dark cliff. From here, it appeared impenetrable, but there was a path over the rocks and up the face.

"Stay close," I whispered, then reached out.

Struan took my fingers in his bigger, calloused ones.

Excitement thrilled through my veins at his touch, and I moved on, navigating our path over the slippery rocks and ascending. Before long, we were high above the beach and almost invisible to passersby. Loose pebbles rolled under my shoes, but I kept going, and Struan stayed close, his breathing ragged.

More voices called out, and by the time we reached the cave, they'd arrived directly below.

A light flashed up the cliff.

With a gasp, I ducked, and Struan dropped to his haunches. But we'd made it, the cave a dark void to our left.

Under the lip of rock, I crept, taking the prisoner with

me. Inside, we were safe, our hiding place invisible unless you knew the exact spot. For a long moment, we just sat on the dry, sandy ground, catching our breaths. Struan's leg nudged against mine, and I didn't shift, enjoying the sharp stabs of that new feeling.

This was a stupid thing to do. Help a man who others hunted.

The sense it gave me, of being alive, useful, *needed,* was utterly addictive.

The voices passed by, and I took a deep inhale.

"How badly hurt are you?"

"I don't know," he murmured back. "I was drugged, so everything feels numb."

"I'm going to use my phone light to take a look. It won't be visible from outside, I promise."

He didn't reply, so I found my phone, silenced it, and used the dull glow to see with. The blood on his arm was worse than I'd thought, and I shone it higher until I found the cut, just above his elbow. An inch wide, it oozed glossy red when I put pressure on it.

"I can't see any glass stuck in there," I whispered. "I'm scared of touching it more in case I put germs on it, but we need to stop the bleeding. You should see a doctor for stitches."

"No doctor. I'll tear my t-shirt to make a bandage."

I eyed the strips of material he called a shirt. It would leave him half naked, but it was that or start shredding my clothes.

Heat swirled in my belly.

"I'll help you take it off," I replied through a tight throat.

Struan sat up, and I lifted his hem and carefully

pulled the shirt away, trying not to gawp at his bare torso. I failed, soaking in the sight of cut muscles and lean, hard man.

He wrenched at the material, tearing it in two. "Clean me up with the first then tie the second on tightly to stop the bleeding."

"I have a bottle of water. I can rinse the blood off, too."

"Fuck. I've naw drank anything since yesterday."

I goggled at him then snatched up my bag and found the water, handing it over. Struan uncapped it and gulped half down in one go.

His throat muscles bobbed in the faint light.

He swore and held the bottle to him, his eyes closed. "Do ye have any food in that magic bag of yours?"

"Probably. Let me check." I fished around and brought out a granola bar.

Struan took it and had bitten into it before I could blink. Chewing, he gave up a laugh. "You're an angel. I'm hallucinating ye." Another couple of bites and his humour died. "Why are ye helping me?"

"Honestly? I've no idea."

"But ye believe me that I'm naw a criminal." He worked his jaw. "Don't answer that. I'm not a good guy. I've been arrested more than once. But this shite is next level."

I kept my mouth shut, and Struan's gaze connected with mine, the scrutiny intensifying, like he needed to get into my head.

Inexplicable delight ran through me, a fizz of...chemistry?

Struan's look turned predatory, raking over me with raw heat and a hunger I barely understood. It scared the life out of me, sharpening my senses.

Suddenly, he lurched up and into my space. I gasped and dropped back onto an elbow. He prowled up my body, forcing me to lie back. One hand landed next to my head, supporting his weight.

His body didn't touch mine in any place, yet I was still pinned down.

"I repeat, why are ye helping me?" he growled. "What's in it for ye? Are ye part of this place?"

"W-what do you mean?"

"Small island. A lass who isnae from around here. Ye landed at the same time I did. Is your da my jailor?"

"No! He works in politics in London. We're only here to visit Granny."

My phone dropped to the cave floor and shut down, leaving us in perfect darkness.

Struan's warm breath ghosted over me. "A lass like ye shouldn't be anywhere near someone like me."

I shivered, unable to answer.

"Which only means ye have another interest. Name it."

The weight of him grew palpable, pressing down on me though his body still hovered an inch above mine. The deep scent of man filled my lungs.

Lust sliced through me, shocking in the fast rush of it.

Never once had I felt that. The dark and delicious taste of it on my tongue.

"What is it?" he continued in a taunting drawl. "My mouth, my dick? Does the bad-boy thing get ye off?"

Brand-new desires broke over me. Not to touch him. Not at all. I wanted the opposite. For this complete stranger to grab me and make me do stuff.

God, I couldn't admit that. Instead, I swallowed and

said the first thing that came to mind. "I've had a terrible summer, and this is putting everything into perspective."

Struan waited for a beat then eased himself back, taking his heavy dose of magnetism with him. "That's it? I'm a distraction for a bad day?"

"A bad month," I muttered, too hot, and woke my phone to give its scant light once more.

Something like disappointment flashed over Struan's expression. "Whatever. Fix my arm and tell me what happened that made ye risk this to take your mind off it."

"My story is nothing to yours."

"Ye don't know shite about my story, sweetheart. Talk anyway."

Sweetheart. No one but him had ever called me that, and I liked it. I also missed his body so close to mine. The flare of dominance he'd shown.

I'd be remembering that for a long time.

"I'm going to brighten my phone torch so I can see your cut better. The voices have moved away outside."

From his sprawl on the ground, he picked up the rest of the granola bar from a rocky shelf without objecting.

I focused in on the slice in his skin. The blood flow had eased. I had a pack of tissues in my bag, so I used one to dab at the wound, feeling for the hard edge of any hidden glass. Finding none, I took the rest of the pack and held it to the wound, ensuring it had stopped bleeding before tying on a strip of shirt.

But as his biceps flexed, the bandage shifted. I snared my hairband and slid it up his arm, holding the edge of torn t-shirt in place.

Struan watched the tumble of my hair over my shoulder then slammed his eyes closed. "For fuck's sake, talk."

I jumped and started a nervous babble. "My mother lives in the US. She moved out there a few years ago to be with her new husband, and they now have twin boys. I went to stay with them over the summer after I finished my classes. I'm studying at Edinburgh."

He listened while I quietly filled the silence of the cave.

"I'm happy that Mum's happy, but I'm also very aware that I'm not a big part of her life anymore. Which is fine. I'm nineteen, so not a kid."

"Thought ye were younger," Struan said. "But either way, that meant she left ye when ye were young, aye?"

I pressed my lips together, adjusting the bandage around his arm. "It was a few days off my fourteenth birthday that she announced her plans. Dad agreed to the divorce without any issues, she moved, remarried, and the rest is history."

"Why didn't ye go with her?"

"That...wasn't an option."

He opened his eyes, startling me from where I'd been idly staring at his face. Struan had such interesting features. High cheekbones and an angular, stubborn-set jaw. Two blond streaks lined his shaggy black hair as if he'd bleached it. But those eyes were such a powerful dark blue, vibrant even in the shadowed cave.

And though he stared at me now, he didn't interrupt again.

"This trip was a big deal for me. I'd never met my brothers before, apart from on video calls." I swallowed regret at the memories. "They're lovely, super cute, but Mum has changed. She's a free spirit, and they live in an artists' community. I guess I just didn't fit in."

I stopped my telling, unsure of why I'd even started.

"What was the killing point?" Struan asked

"The what?"

"The moment it all went to shite."

"You don't need to hear everything."

"Don't tell me what I need. Out with it."

I glared at him, this stranger I was sharing secrets with. Whose sticky blood decorated my fingertips. "Mum had a couple of her friends over with their kids. I'd been checking on my brothers who were down for a nap and came back to the kitchen. Sitting on the porch, one of the women made a joke about me."

"What did she say?"

"Something along the lines of how I'd obviously not had a rebellious stage. Meaning my clothes and the way I acted, I guess. Mum replied that I'd always been a meek and obedient little thing. Then one of her other friends asked if she meant boring. Mum laughed."

I'd waited thirty seconds then stomped around the kitchen like I'd just arrived, and the conversation had changed like they hadn't been laughing at me. I'd never felt like I belonged anywhere—Dad was from an old family with wealth on both sides, but he'd picked a wife who was so far from suiting him it was unreal. Mum had been eighteen and starting an art degree when she fell pregnant. She hated Dad's family, life, and friends, and they looked down on her.

They'd argued constantly. I was always in the middle. Not in either of their moulds but trying to be enough for both of them.

Now I knew how my mother saw me, I only really had Dad.

Struan's stare intensified. "Did it hurt?"

"What do you think? How would you feel if your mother thought you were a joke?"

"My mother isnae thinking much about me anymore."

That stalled my pity party. I set aside my hurt feelings and held out my phone. "She'd be worried though, surely. Want to call her?"

Struan's lips twisted, more emotion passing over his gaze. But darker now. "She doesn't have a phone now."

"Find her on social media? I'll DM her."

"What I need is a way off this island."

Voices came from outside, above us now. I stiffened and killed the light.

Struan groaned. "Too late."

"They'll pass by, I'm sure. They can't know you're here. I've never seen another person in this cave, and they already searched the beach."

In the complete, velvety darkness, his fingers touched mine. I hitched a breath, and he clasped my hand then brought it down until I was touching his ankle. And something hard attached to it.

"Tracker," he whispered, releasing me. "I wasnae sure if it worked until now. Ye need to go or they'll blame ye for helping me. Or blame me for letting ye. Either way, we cannae be found together."

Harsh reality pressed in. Others would take one look at him and assume the worst. I believed him. There was plain honesty in everything he said.

"At least give me a way to help. I can talk to my dad. We'll call the police."

"They won't do shite. I'm fucked."

He was dismissing me. I didn't want to go.

My cheeks heated, and I stood on shaky legs and gave up one last piece of information, the final act of kindness I could deliver. "We have a boat. It's tied up in the harbour, the last on the walkway that runs to the right from where the ferry docks. The code to the lock is three-two-three-one, and it's well maintained, even if we never use it. If you can get out to sea, head south towards the next island then follow the ferry. It runs there a few times per day. Let me know if you manage it. I'm easy to find online. Theadora Stewart."

A pause came, then Struan stood in a rush of air. He palmed my cheek, his fingertips gripping hard under my jawline

I wanted him to kiss me.

"I don't understand ye, Theadora Stewart, but I will-nae forget your name."

Then he dropped the hold and there was nothing for it but to leave.

Outside the cave, I crept down the rocks, keeping low. Torches crossed the beach, merging then flicking away.

A shout challenged me the second my shoes touched the sands. "Stop there."

"Why? Who is it?" I called back.

The man swore. "It's just a girl." He moved closer, squinting at me. "Haven't ye heard there's a dangerous criminal on the loose? Get yourself home. Now."

My heart skipped a beat, and I hid my bloodied hands behind my back. "A criminal?"

"A murderer. Killed his own mother. Wait up, I'll have someone escort ye back. You're Augustus' lass, aye?"

Augustus was my father. They all knew him here. What was stranger was the lie told about Struan. He hadn't killed his mum. He'd worried about her. Unless... No. He hadn't lied to me. I was sure of it.

But I couldn't help him now.

Instead, I kept my head down and fell in with an elderly fisherman, tasked with delivering me home.

5

Struan

A jarring *thud, thud, thud* reverberated inside my skull, my brain swelling, or some shite like that.

Too easily, I'd been caught trying to climb the cliff from the cave. Staying still had been pointless, with the tracker broadcasting my location, so outrunning them to reach that boat had been my only choice. They'd laid in wait and grabbed me before I could react.

I'd expected a beating, but three guys had held me while they took turns. Fucking cowards.

Dragging me, because hell was I going under free will, they delivered me back to the hostel. My right eye had already swollen up, but I still made out Keep's grim features at the door. The main man holding me dismissed the others then hunched over to speak to her.

"This isn't meant to happen," he hissed. "Your job—"

"Don't tell me my job. This new one's a problem," she argued back, then stepped up and slapped me upside the head.

I let my head loll then laughed at her.

"You've got lazy," the man continued.

He dropped me. He'd zip tied my arms behind me, so I hit the concrete path hard, jarring bones.

"It won't happen again," the keeper said. "He'll fall into line. It's that or the big house, hey, lad?" Her toe to my ribs barely moved me.

I laughed louder, not able to see but sure I was pissing her off.

Then another smack to my head sent everything spinning.

Next thing I knew, I was flat out on the lino in a tiny room, empty aside from a bucket in the corner. Not the dorm for me with the comfortable bunk beds.

The zip tie had been cut, the ends still around one arm, digging into my skin. Not that I could move far.

New metal cuffs chained me to the floor.

My whole body ached. From being kidnapped and brought here, to the window break and beating I took on the beach. I could deal with the pain. What I couldn't handle was the lack of freedom.

I'd got out once but wouldn't get the chance again.

In misery, I remained slumped on the floor, letting the situation catch up with me. I was fucked. Well and good.

The door swung open.

"Oi," the person said. One of the other inmates. "Wake up."

I stayed down.

He sighed, a scratching sound following. "Thanks to ye, we're all grounded for a month. Surf's fucking amazing right now, and I have to sit it out because of your dumb arse."

Cracking open my good eye, I peered at him without interest.

At first, I thought I was looking at Camden. Or Scar. Whatever his name was. This guy was younger, though. Seventeen, perhaps. The same messy dark hair, but he was more of a pretty boy.

If there were four of us, the huge, shaven-headed, evil guy had to be oldest. Then probably me, Scar, and this guy last.

And the scratching sound? The Zippo lighter in his hand. He flicked the wheel again, a spark flaring but with no flame. *Burn,* Scar had given his nickname. No surprise why they didn't give him lighter fuel.

He continued without needing an answer. "The one joy in this soulless place, and ye had to ruin it."

The wry humour in his tone couldn't make me smile.

He sat cross-legged beside me. "I get it. I fought, too. Not like ye did, with the broken window and all. Sin is still pissed off about that. We have a board up in its place, but it's naw airtight. The bedroom's going to be fucking freezing over winter."

I tried to sit, but pain lanced through me.

"If ye think Keep will replace the glass, think again. She wouldnae care if we froze half to death. So long as no one actually died." He punched my shoulder. "So fuck ye for that. I only came in to bring ye water. If you're lucky, we'll find a way to get a meal to ye later. But Keep's intention is to break ye. You'll be locked in here, light on, until she says otherwise. If you'll take my advice, cool your fucking engines. Learn to save your anger for when it matters and listen to us, the people who know, aye?"

Replies formed, my instinct to tell this wee scrotum

where to go, but I couldn't summon the energy to speak. He wasn't worth it.

He left me, and I stayed down, sensing attention on me still.

A long while passed before I budged. Slowly sitting up, I ignored spikes of pain, then checked myself over. Bruises marked my skin, ugly purple and dark red. Dried blood stained my arm and torso.

My bandage had gone, but a dark brown piece of elastic still held in place around my elbow. It looked like a strip of leather.

Theadora's hairband.

Even barely conscious, I'd been constantly aware of the slight constriction. Touching it now gave me hope.

If the keeper saw it, she'd take it, just to be vindictive.

I slid it off then dragged it over my foot, concealing it on the opposite ankle to my tracker. A counterweight, reminding me that not everyone was evil.

I couldn't do shite to see the lass. Take the kiss I should've stolen. But I could recover. Get my strength back.

The next time I made a run for it, I wouldn't fail.

6

Thea

From the living room bay window, I watched the ferry slice over the water towards our island. Last night, I'd barely slept. Struan had been caught not long after my return. Dad had come to my room to tell me, reiterating his warning about not wandering at night. Presumably some islander had filled him in on the drama.

He had no clue about my run-in with the very man he feared. How, in the shower, I'd scrubbed his blood from my skin.

Fought the urge to touch myself with him in my mind.

Someone appeared on the pathway, and I jumped.

Lottie waved and danced up to the front door. I flung myself into the corridor to answer, then we hugged it out on the doorstep.

"Oh my God, finally we get to see each other. Can ye believe we nearly met in the middle of a manhunt?"

She entered, and I gestured for her to go into the kitchen. I'd spent the morning cleaning, and at least now it didn't smell of rotten food.

"I know. How crazy was that?" My pulse fluttered. I wanted to tell Lottie about Struan. But Dad was in hearing distance. Soon enough, he'd be occupied. The ferry was bringing his lawyer, who I needed to sneak a chat with, but if I didn't grab this chance to talk to Lottie now, we wouldn't be able to do it face to face.

No mystery should be solved over the phone.

Dad had set up an office in a backroom, so I gestured for Lottie to follow me and knocked on his door.

"Dad? Lottie and I are going to take a walk."

With the supposed criminal captured, he couldn't object.

The door swung open. "Hello, Violet," my father said, using her full name. He frowned at me. "Stick to the harbour and the town and you may. What about Henry? I'm sure he'd rather talk to you while his father and I attend to matters."

I waved a breezy hand. "Send him down to the beach to find us. I need the fresh air, and it's safe now that all the drama is over."

He gave a grunt and disappeared once more, so I snatched my jacket and led the way outside.

Lottie jogged after me. "What's the rush? And who's Henry?"

"Dad's lawyer's son. I need to talk to you and he'll only interrupt us." I set our path in the opposite direction to the beach entirely, locking my arm into my friend's. "Yesterday, there was this man on the boat."

As fast as I could, I shared the story of meeting Struan, including our run-in at the cave. I saved the part where he'd asked if I wanted his body.

And how I really had.

That needed unpacking before I could explain myself.

"What I don't get is why he's here. Half the village turned out last night to search for him, but I don't believe he's a criminal. And even if he was, why bring a dangerous person here? It doesn't make any sense."

Lottie stopped dead in the middle of the path. "How do ye not know this?"

"What are you talking about?"

She clucked her tongue. "About a year ago, everyone in the village was warned about a scheme they're trialling here. It's this kind of rehabilitation camp for bad boys. I mean the really wild ones. They bring them here to re-move them from their lifestyles, with the alternative being jail, which would only expose them to worse criminals. It's meant to be a kind of healthy intervention to give them a better future."

That...didn't sound too bad, except Struan had made out that he'd been abducted.

"Where do these men come from?"

Lottie raised an easy shoulder. "Beats me. Dad made a fuss about it, but I'm pretty sure he and the other people who complained were paid off. All of a sudden, we had money to spend on the house, and that doesn't appear by magic."

We started walking again. The road that circled Tor-lum was mostly flat, with the sea on one side and the hilly interior on the other. I was curious over where Struan was being kept.

"You said a camp. Do you know where it is?"

She dipped her head, her fair hair braided against the ever-present island breeze, and her tone singsong. The Outer Hebridean accent was more rounded than general

Scottish, with touches of Danish. Many of the islanders spoke Gaelic, the words alien to me.

"I mean camp because of the activities they have them do, but they live in the old hostel building."

I knew exactly where that was. We'd explored the place one summer, and it had long been empty.

I chewed my lip, debating on how much more to share. Except, I trusted Lottie. I'd known her forever. "Mind if we scout it? The guy I met definitely wasn't treating this as a rehab thing."

"Would ye if ye were taken away from your family? When we get close, I'll let ye in on a secret I've never told another soul."

On that tantalising note, she linked her arm with mine once more, and we continued on.

Farther up the coast, the hostel came into sight as a speck in the distance.

Lottie pointed at it, then to the expanse of bright ocean beyond. "A couple of months ago, I cycled out this way late at night after everyone else had gone to bed." Pink flooded the apples of her cheeks. "I mean, nothing interesting ever happens here. I was bored out of my mind."

I clued in to her embarrassment. "You came out here to spy on the boys?"

She giggled. "I did. Dad would kill me if he knew. Anyway, I saw them. I was hiding just here, and three figures crossed the road carrying surfboards. They were silent until they hit the water. Then I picked up on laughter. Each of them had a tiny flashing light, presumably to see each other in the waves. Different neon colours."

I gazed at the sea, picturing the scene. "Is surfing part of their therapy?"

"Doubt it. There were surfboards and gear in an old shed at the hostel, though, remember?"

I didn't, but my mind ticked over. If the boys could get out at night, Struan could, too.

Except I wouldn't be here this time to help any further escape attempt. Dad had said this morning that after he'd met his lawyer, we'd be leaving.

"Tell me more about the new one," Lottie asked. "Is he pretty?"

Again I poked at the part of my memory that contained how Struan had made me feel.

But Lottie's information on why he was here had taken some of the urgency from me. Struan didn't need my help. He had to fall in line with whatever the aims of this place were for him. They'd help him, even if he didn't realise it at first.

My shoulders slumped. There was no mystery after all. Just two different sides to a story.

I heaved a sigh. "Oh, you know, dark and dangerous."

Lottie waggled her eyebrows. "Sounds hot."

She had no idea, but my heat had gone off the boil.

An hour later, and we were back at Granny's. Lottie gave a cheery greeting to Henry, who waited in the doorway, then set off for home.

I trudged up the path. "Hey."

"Hello to you, too. Why so miserable?" Henry gave me a perfunctory hug, patting my shoulder.

Try as I might, I couldn't rouse myself from the slump I'd fallen into. "No reason. Well, I'm stressed about next term."

"Esme is as well. Total bitch mode has been deployed."

He launched into chatter of his sister's anticipation of her third year at uni. Despite being a year ahead, Esme sometimes hung out with me. Henry was only six months younger than me but a school year behind. This autumn, he'd be starting at uni, too, but a different place to me and his sister.

We entered the kitchen, and I subtly looked him over. He'd changed since I'd last seen him. Bulked up and styled his floppy blond hair differently.

Yesterday, on the way here, I'd categorise myself as not being into boys. Henry was the epitome of the kind I *should* like. Nice manners, an easy smile, and bouncy, fun conversation.

He was a Golden Retriever to Struan's Rottweiler.

I couldn't be less interested.

Clearly something had gone wrong in my wiring. Maybe from the shock of the sight of blood and the drama of the chase last night. My imagination had got the better of me. Lottie's information had proved that true.

The office door swung open, and my father appeared. Grumbling to himself, he stormed outside, probably to light a cigar. I watched him go, and my stomach contracted.

I hated how stressed he was.

When I'd been sitting with my grandmother earlier, he'd glowered from the door, seeming unable to handle being around her. Which brought me back to my other big thought in coming here. My *make-Dad-happy* plan.

Excusing myself from Henry, I entered the office and closed the door.

"Mr Charterman? May I speak to you?"

The lawyer peered up from his hunch over the desk,

unsmiling.

I pressed on, needing to get this out before my father returned. "Dad's been really stressed recently. I don't know what about but I'd like to take some of the pressure off him. I'm old enough now to take on responsibilities."

Charterman narrowed his eyes but didn't interrupt.

I inched closer, my cheeks warm. "Here's my thinking. Dad worries so much about Granny. He's so far away in London and hopeless when it comes to talking about care. Can I take that off his shoulders?"

"You want to look after your grandmother?" the lawyer intoned.

"Well, it'll have to be from a distance while I'm at university. But at least I'm in the same country. I can get here faster, or just be the point of contact. The one her carers call. I can handle the day-to-day stuff so Dad doesn't have to. Is that possible?"

For a long moment, the lawyer just watched me, and I willed him to let me help. Dad still saw me as a child, but I wasn't.

Something registered in Mr Charterman's gaze. Almost as if he hadn't seen me properly until this moment. Maybe realised I wasn't a little girl anymore. "Let me see what I can do."

"Thank you," I whispered, right as Dad clomped back into the kitchen, and I slipped away.

Henry and I had lunch, and I showed him around the village, the afternoon wearing on.

When we returned, the two were still in the office, but the door swung open fast.

Mr Charterman appeared but looking back and still speaking to Dad. "We'll have her cosign it, and that'll be enough for now. It'll all work out in time, you'll see." His gaze switched to me. "Theadora. We need your help."

Deliberately, he winked.

My breath caught. Whatever they'd decided, this felt like a secret dealing between me and him. I skipped into the office and placed a hand on Dad's shoulder.

Mr Charterman followed and pointed at the tablet. "Sign here and here."

I lifted my eyebrows but moved closer and took the proffered stylus. Under the device, several piles of paper-work littered the desk, and a map of the island peeked out from in between. I gazed at the signature box beside the lawyer's finger. Underneath, someone had already typed out my full name and the date, so I didn't have to.

It was the final page of a long document. A kind of pressure built around me. An awareness like the one last night when I'd realised I was in over my head.

It felt wrong to sign something I didn't understand, but equally, I couldn't ask. Not if there was a provision included that allowed me to take some of the burden I wanted.

"Come, child," Mr Charterman urged. "The boat will be leaving soon. If we aren't on it, we'll all be stuck here tonight."

"We'll talk it through later," my father added with a sigh.

Guilt had me scribbling my name quickly on the screen.

The lawyer took back the stylus, and I was dismissed.

Outside the kitchen, I darted upstairs to pack the few things I'd brought. Placing my knitting carefully into my bag, I pieced over my memories of the other big deal part of my trip. Struan.

Was telling him about the boat a mistake? I pondered mentioning it to my father so he could change the code or alert the people who ran the rehab place. If Struan needed to be cut off from his old life, I risked undoing that hard work.

Something stopped me.

He wouldn't try to escape again, not once he realised what kind of place it was. I ignored the tiny hope that he might contact me, then finished packing, ready to return to the mainland.

In the hall downstairs, I paused outside my grand-mother's room.

"Can I meet her?" Henry said from the kitchen door-way.

I jumped but gestured him over. "I'm going to tell her we're leaving, so you can look in, but she's very frail."

"Sorry about that."

I was, too. Years ago, she'd been a lovely, sweet granny who I'd adored visiting. She cooked, told stories, and was always ready with a hug.

She was the one who'd taught me how to knit, though we'd been laughed at for the old-fashioned habit by my parents.

Dad said her dementia meant she wouldn't recognise me again, but I didn't want to leave without saying good-bye.

Tapping at the door, I listened, but no answer came. The home help had returned this morning and was proba-bly keeping out of the way until we left.

"Granny?" I twisted the knob and slowly opened the door.

Her room was out of a time warp, something from the old days. Brown furniture with skinny legs. Net curtains at the windows. Faded flower prints on her bedspread, framing her body.

I took a step in. "It's Theadora. My friend Henry is here to say hi, too. Sorry we can't stay longer, but I'll be back soon. Thank you for letting us stay."

My grandmother mumbled something.

My heart thumped, and I crept closer. "What was that?"

She muttered again, and I kept moving until I reached the bed. Nerves gripped my stomach tight. Until now, and on our last visit, I'd remained quiet around her on Dad's orders.

My grandmother faced the window, her fingers clutching something half hidden.

"He's a thief," repeated the old lady.

"Who?" I breathed.

"Father."

The poor woman. My great-grandfather must've been dead fifty years.

I reached to stroke her arm. "Hush now, it's okay. No one has stolen anything."

Jerking around, she peered up at me with watery eyes, feverish in her movements. "You're the only one I can trust."

She grabbed my hand with strength I didn't know her to have, then placed the object she'd been holding onto my palm.

A small, gold key.

With my back to Henry, I blocked his view of the exchange.

"No, Granny." I tried to give it back.

"Ye have to keep it safe from him," she croaked.

"Keep what safe?" Henry asked.

"Theadora?" my father called from elsewhere in the house.

"Quick, Stella," Granny instructed.

I shouldn't have obeyed, definitely not when my grandmother had confused me with someone else, yet I shoved the key into my skirt pocket, the weight of it foreign against my thigh.

"Coming," I called, then swept out, ignoring Henry's curious expression.

Dad waited by the front door. "You shouldn't be in there. She's not in her right mind, and you're only going to excite her. Come, we're leaving."

I hustled along with him, taking leave of the place that had too many mysteries around it.

On the boat, I put one of my many questions to my father. "Granny called me Stella. Who's that?"

"Her sister. Long dead. Dementia does that. She's away with the fairies."

And that was that. He didn't want to talk more, and university beckoned. I'd hold on to the mysterious key until my next visit, then I'd place it back in my grandmother's room somewhere.

At least, with the powers I now had, I could help Dad. That was the better direction of my overeagerness to help. Not the island's newest inhabitant. Him, I needed to forget about entirely.

7

Struan

A scrabbling noise woke me from my half sleep. For almost four weeks, I'd been in this room. The first had been torture. Our keeper had done exactly what the lad threatened. The stark overhead light had remained on constantly, to the point it featured in my dreams.

Tormenting, sickly, never letting up.

With no furniture in the room, I hadn't been able to reach the flat panel to smash the fucker out. I'd tried endlessly to reach it, to break my chains, bawling my frustration at my failure.

The whole while, I'd sensed eyes on me.

Then one evening, without warning, everything went dark. I'd assumed that meant someone was coming for me, but nothing had happened. After that, it was a regular thing.

Lights out became my new centre of gravity.

Three times a day, one of the lads brought me food and removed my bucket. Sometimes, they'd stop for a wee chat. In my solitary confinement, I'd begun to rely on those conversations. The other option was to go batshit crazy, and while that could be fun, I still had stuff to live for.

They took care, though, not to talk about anything important. Scar repeated the rules of place. The younger good-looking kid, Burn, talked surfing until I knew enough to go out and jump on a board.

The leader of them, Sin, never entered my room.

I heard him talking to the other boys, though. The big fucker was a sadist. He barked orders at Scar and forced Burn to read to him every night. Word after painstaking word filtered down the hall to my prison cell.

Of our keeper, I saw little beyond one savage visit. One morning, she'd entered with an electric hair trimmer in her hands. Grabbing me by my neck, she'd sheared my hair, tearing off chunks until it fell around me. At the first cut, I'd lashed out, but she'd shocked me with her Taser.

The pain floored me, seizing my muscles.

I'd let the rest happen. Since then, I occasionally heard her, but she never came near.

The scrabbling sounded again, followed by a series of thumps.

Then someone tapped on my window. Unlike in the dorm, this room only had one tiny, high-up window that I couldn't see through. At a guess, I was probably in the store cupboard.

Lifting to my feet, I moved to the window. My chain wouldn't reach to allow me to tap back, so I cleared my throat instead.

"It's Scar," a voice hissed. "Listen up. She's going to let ye out tomorrow, so ye can live with us."

A few weeks ago, I would have laughed at the optimism in his tone. But I needed out of here. My body had slowly healed, but my muscles had wasted. Staring at the same walls with only my imagination had broken pieces of me.

Relief rushed in my veins where only anger used to live.

"Good to know," I muttered in reply.

"Aye, see you on the other side, brother," his voice returned.

Brother.

I'd never had much family other than Ma. Her old man had died a few years back, and her mother a long time before. My own da had been a waster with no interest in me.

Friends had come and gone, or left behind when I got kicked out of school for fighting.

No one had ever called me brother.

The following morning, I was ready when the door swung open.

Keeper loomed in the frame. In her hand, that fucking Taser crackled. I stared at it, keeping my head low. Not a challenge with weak-as-fuck muscles.

"You get a do-over, kid. This time, if you slip, you'll be locked in here until the day I die. Got it?"

"Got it," I mumbled back.

She waited for a second, as if to see what I'd do, then reached to unlock my restraints and trudged away.

Sin replaced her, his hulking form blocking the door. "On me," he ordered, his voice low and deadly.

Fuck this guy.

The minute shite went down, I was taking him out with me. No matter how much it hurt.

Still, I followed, and we crossed the hall to the dorm room. I squinted around, too much to examine after a month of four walls.

"Pick your bed." He pointed at the last set of bunk beds along the wall. "Mine is there, and no fucker is sleeping above me. Scar and Burn share the middle one."

"Why don't ye use their real names?" I challenged like an idiot.

I didn't even know Burn's name. Only that Scar was Camden. Sin was probably a biker name like Sinner or some bollocks.

The huge man stilled, and I got a proper look at him. I was a shade over six foot, which made this guy a beast, at least six inches taller. Under his tight grey t-shirt, muscles bulged, surprisingly clear of ink.

I'd never trust this man. Not with a single thing. He was made for hurting others.

And he was glowering at me. "Pick your bed," he said, slower.

There was no point, but I gestured at the lower one on the last empty bunk.

Sin lifted his chin. "Your days will go like this. You'll work in the house until I'm sure ye willnae run again. Then you'll come out with the rest of us. Can ye cook?"

"I can chop and fry stuff."

"Good enough." He pointed to a door off the bedroom.

We entered a bathroom complete with a urinal, a stall, and a shower. Sin hit a button, and hot water ran, instant steam rising from the tiles.

Fuck. My skin crawled where I needed a wash. Over the past weeks, the best I'd managed was to scrub bottled water over my bloodied arm. The rest of me, I'd not bothered with, so I stank. I was lucky none of my cuts had got infected. I'd probably have lost a limb.

"Wash up. Shave if ye want. Towel's on the hook. Clean clothes on the shelf there," Sin ordered, then he leaned in, as if giving over a secret. Under the cover of the running water, and with evil in his eyes, he spoke so low I could barely hear. "Whatever ye hear and see late in the evenings, don't react."

I furrowed my brow, but the big man walked away. And I didn't want to wait for something to interrupt this. I tore off the shirt I'd been given to wear in my cell and yanked my jeans and boxers down, tripping over in my haste.

Bare-arse naked, I stepped under the spray.

Hot water sluiced over me, and I stifled a groan, pressing my palms on the tiled wall. My skin broke out with goosebumps, and I closed my eyes against the rush of sensation. For a long minute, I could do nothing but soak up the warmth.

I'd been so cold, so alone.

I wanted to run. Yet if I tried it, I'd be back in the hole.

The thought of spending the night in that dorm room with those three psychopaths was too much. I couldn't believe them normal, no matter the kind gestures and amusing chat. The short conversation I'd had with Sin added more mental weight. The prickling needles raining down on me was also too fucking much.

My leg muscles trembled, and I clamped my knees to stop it, my breathing coming hard. I'd worked out as best I could over the past month, but it was nothing to my normal life. A few more days in there, and the damage could've been permanent.

Everything ached.

I stooped and ran a finger under the wee elastic band on my ankle. All this time, it had remained hidden. An opposite pressure to the tracker and my reminder of good things. When I touched it, I recalled the pretty brown eyes of the lass who gave it to me. The last person to give a fuck.

Who'd had a lucky escape from messing with me.

All of a sudden, the heat disappeared, and icy water beat down on me.

I gave a startled gasp, opening my eyes.

From the doorway came a cackle of a laugh. Burn stood there, delight in his expression. "Ye looked like ye were enjoying that a bit too much. Thought ye might need a cold shower."

"The fuck?" I managed but couldn't move from the chilly deluge.

Then a meaty hand landed on Burn's shoulder, and he was yanked back. Sin marched over to the sink, turning off the fast-flowing tap I hadn't noticed interrupting the water pressure. He glowered at it and then sliced his gaze back to the boy.

"Don't hurt him," I spat. God only knew why. I didn't give a shite or want to be friends with anyone here. Prankster or not.

Warmth returned, and steam billowed.

The giant's expression remained sour, but I didn't hear screaming once he'd returned to the bedroom.

And I needed not to care. Reaching for the flannel hanging on the hook, I forced myself to methodically clean every inch of my wasted body. Shave. Cut the chunks of my hair until it resembled me again. Fuck understanding this place or getting to know my cellmates. I had to be prepared.

If I was ever to escape, I needed to bide my time.

Once I was dressed, Sin directed me to the kitchen and put me to work on food prep. Potatoes to peel and cut, onions to slice. He worked alongside me, silently preparing some kind of soup or stew.

I'd been fed basic meals in my cell for the past month but figured the others ate better. Now, I wasn't so sure that was the case.

Chopping board after chopping board of vegetables went into a big, bubbling pot. Sin didn't criticise my slow progress or my attitude when my strength left me and my hands wouldn't work right. His pace wasn't much faster.

"No meat?" I broke the quiet.

Sin gave a single shake of his head.

"Keep wants us weak and easy to manage." Scar entered the kitchen.

I hadn't seen him since my release, and his curious gaze skipped over me. With only three of them in this fuck-awful place, I was the novelty.

He dropped his voice and sidled closer, dirt on his hands. "We sometimes have ways around that."

Sin hissed, and Scar shut his mouth.

Another person appeared in the doorway. The woman who ran the place strolled in, and my grip on the stubby, half-blunt knife tightened. From the way the two men stood taller, I guessed her appearance was a surprise.

Her focus wasn't on me. She curled her lip, directing her words to the man beside me. "It's your lucky day."

Sin downed tools and stared back at her.

Keep waited for a second, her beady eyes all over him,

but if she wanted him to ask a question, she was disappointed. "He'll be here Saturday night. Be ready." Then she gave a dirty laugh and left us.

"Who'll be here?" I asked.

But the atmosphere shifted as if the room darkened around the edges.

Scar had skittered out of the way at the keeper's appearance. Now, he watched Sin with rounded eyes. "It worked."

Sin only braced himself on the sink, his knuckles white. "Can't be sure until he's been and gone."

"She was talking to ye, though."

He cut a look my way. "Aye, she was."

"Will one of ye tell me what the hell is going on?" I asked.

Sin's expression lost all emotion, and a hard light shone in his eyes. He took up his knife and brandished it in a warning. "No. Get back to work or you'll be returned to that cell."

Scar sucked in a breath and dove from the room, presumably returning to whatever his job for the day was. I glowered at Sin's back, briefly considering burying my knife in it.

His threat wasn't idle. If I was honest, the big man scared me. He and the others acted like a tight unit, which only meant bad things for me, the outsider. I knew his type, and I'd never trust him, which made him the enemy, too.

I'd get one shot, but I was a brawler. I knew how to make it count.

Except I'd never attacked someone blind. And beyond that, killing him alone wouldn't do any good. Getting out of here was going to take more cunning than my first attempt, and so long as the person coming here on the weekend wasn't after me, I'd find another opportunity soon enough.

8

Thea

The lecture theatre buzzed with students clamouring to escape, our sociology discussion over.

I hung back, slowly packing away my laptop and notebook.

The second year of my political science degree already felt twice as hard as the first. I was drowning in classes and study, barely time to breathe in between. The only part that really interested me was the sociological side of it and how government policy changed people's lives.

Such as how intervening in the lives of young offenders could break the cycle of criminal activity.

So far, I hadn't found any case studies similar to what was happening with Struan, but the man was never far from my mind.

Not just for the mystery of him. The savage darkness in the man called to me. Woke me in the night with my hand between my legs, confused over what I was doing.

"Professor Layton?" I called.

The woman lifted her head from her papers, focusing on me. "Theadora. Is there something you needed?"

With my cheeks warming under the attention, I rapid-fire asked whether she knew of any modern-day interventions like the one Struan was undergoing. I added only a few details, but the professor gave a tight shake of her head.

"There are many examples in history, even up until recent times. But you will not find something like that happening now, not in the UK. The key word you're looking for is consent. Without that, the kind of action you are describing would break numerous human rights laws."

"Even if it was an experiment designed to help?"

"The only examples I can think of where decision-making is taken away is when there's a risk to life. And that would have to be proved through a court with visible and fair steps taken. It could not be hidden."

I mumbled thanks, and she hefted her briefcase and left the theatre.

I trailed after, only more baffled over Struan's abduction. Maybe he'd misunderstood what was happening or misrepresented it to me because he didn't like it.

But the blood. The violence.

The whole vibe had been threatening and scary. *He'd* been scared. No, no matter what Lottie's family had been told about why the boys were there, something definitely wasn't right.

"Hey, my little bitch."

On the steps outside the hall, I sought the familiar voice.

Esme, Henry's sister and daughter to Dad's lawyer, clipped along the street, her yellow-blonde hair styled in sleek waves and her autumn fashion on point with a maroon dress and fitted blazer. I envied her style hard. Since starting back at uni, I'd only seen her a handful of times, though I'd messaged her often.

Happiness flooded me. "Hello to you, too. You look lovely. How are things?"

She flapped a hand at my irrelevant conversation starter. "Can't stop. I'm glad I ran into you as I've been meaning to issue an invite. Daddy's friend is throwing a party on Saturday night. I'm going. You are, too."

I opened and closed my mouth. "Do I know the friend?"

"Doesn't matter. The old man is as rich as Croesus, and Daddy wants to impress him. Your father will be there, too, hence why you need to go. The old man heard they had pretty daughters, so we're on a charm offensive to help persuade him to seal a deal."

"What kind of deal?"

"No idea." She tottered on, blowing out a plume of vape smoke. "Talk to Henry if you need more information. He'll pick you up at seven."

"Henry's going, too?" I called after her, but my friend clearly had somewhere to be.

My next lecture was at a different building, so I put my head down against the cool October breeze and headed out into the Edinburgh streets. As I went, I found my phone and texted Henry.

Thea: I heard from your sister that we have plans for Saturday.

Henry: I heard that, too. Did she blindside you?

Thea: A little. But that's okay. I just need to know what kind of evening it is.

By which I meant dress code, but Henry would get that.

Henry: Go smart. Always the better option.

He was right, and I mentally ran over my wardrobe.

I hadn't spoken to my father directly since we'd left the island and he'd returned to London where he worked as a political adviser, but that wasn't unusual. Dad had a tendency to slope off, sometimes for weeks on end. Golf courses, day drinking, and heavy schmoozing were his bread and butter.

At the corner of two streets, I ducked into a shop entrance and tried to dial him. The phone rang a few times, but the answerphone kicked in. I didn't bother leaving a message. He wanted me there on Saturday, so I'd be there. He often invited me to such occasions so it wouldn't be strenuous to handle. We could talk then.

The rest of the week passed in a blur of note-taking and late-night reading. By the time Saturday night came around, I was worn out and not in the mood for a party. Still, I had to go for Dad's sake.

In my apartment, shared with three other women, I took a fitted purple dress from my wardrobe, paired it with nude low heels I was sure Esme would approve of, and pinned my hair into a roll. Then I waved a cheery goodbye to my flatmates and left to meet Henry.

Double-parked on the busy road outside my building, he hopped out to open the car door for me. His floppy hair bounced and gleamed under the streetlights. "Hello, Thea. You look very...proper."

I hid a sigh and settled into my seat. Not that I wanted compliments from Henry, but no woman wanted to hear *proper.* My dress wasn't on the sexy side, but I thought it pretty enough.

We drove north out of the city. I'd texted Dad to ask about the evening but heard nothing. Likewise, Esme had no time to fill me in with a better answer. Henry was my next best bet.

In the driver's seat, he practically buzzed with excitement.

"Tell me more about this party," I asked. "Who's the guy, and why are our fathers trying to win him over?"

Henry sucked his teeth. "I'm in the dark on this, too. I think my dad persuaded him to give a dinner, and we're invited as our fathers' plus-ones. Probably to make them seem like trustworthy family men."

"What about Esme?"

"Cried off, so she won't be there."

Disappointment curled inside, but Henry didn't notice, continuing on with his chat.

"She and Dad had an argument. He's been arguing with everyone recently. You'd know."

"I would?"

"After the blazing row our dads had on your island?"

"I'm sorry, what are you talking about?"

We queued at a junction, and Henry twisted in his seat to peer at me, his brow consternated. "Seriously, how did you miss that? On the ferry, I thought they'd tear each other limb from limb. Almost from the minute we got to the house, they were at each other's throats."

"I wasn't there then," I said faintly, but my mind was away trying to remember all the details I'd somehow missed. Dad had been bad-tempered when he'd spoken to me, and so had Mr Charterman, but that felt fairly normal. They'd seemed resigned in the office at the end.

How on earth had I not noticed the kind of tension Henry described?

Because I was meek. My mother's criticism of me returned with a vengeance, and I cringed, turning to the window to hide my heated face.

"Do you know why they argued?"

Henry made an off noise. "Something Dad's working on that your father disagreed with. Or maybe the plan they had couldn't work. I wasn't paying attention. Both blamed the other."

As far as I knew, Henry's dad worked for mine whenever he needed lawyerly tasks carried out. This sounded more like they were in business together.

After an endless car journey through dark countryside up to the Cairngorms National Park, where Henry entertained me with stories of the antics he and his friends had got up to during freshers' week, we finally arrived at our destination.

The most enormous mansion appeared at the end of a drive, illuminated with exterior spotlights and clearly designed to make an impression.

"Whoa." Henry whistled in appreciation.

"Are we meeting royalty?" I brushed my hands over my skirt.

My driver jigged his knees in excitement. "This is the Great House, and the owner's name is McInver. Well, current owner. He's pretty ancient from what Dad said. Probably why our fathers are so interested in him." He gestured with his head to the house then drove on to the parking area.

I didn't like the implication that my father was somehow hunting this guy for his wealth. I knew he did that as part of his fundraising, where rich people gave political parties cash to help bring laws around that would benefit them, but that was never personal. He did it to serve his party.

I kept my thoughts to myself and, on Henry's arm, entered the expansive lobby.

Mr Charterman was already inside, checking his watch.

But before we approached him, Henry stalled me with a hand to my elbow. In a fast move, laced with urgency, he bent low to my ear. "Whatever you do, don't let the old man get you alone."

I didn't get a chance to ask why, as his father was on us and giving us the once-over. "You're ten minutes late. I've had the caterers delay the meal."

"Is my dad here?" I asked.

He shook his head. "Go to the dining room, and I'll find old man McInver and bring him down. Smile, the pair of you, for God's sake."

He wheeled around and walked the other way, and Henry pulled a face then guided me on down the semi-dark hall.

Though chandeliers shimmered overhead and lamps shone brightly from side tables, the mansion had an eerie feel to it. Not least because no one else could be seen.

I leaned into Henry, my heels clicking dully on the marble floor. "Isn't this meant to be a party? Where is everybody?"

"Don't know. I'm starving. Hope we don't have to wait around for food."

Ahead, doors lay open to a dining room. The huge table, with a pristine white tablecloth and silver cutlery, had only been set for four.

A lone waiter guided us to our seats, opposite each other across one end of the table, and a strange sense of occasion caught my tongue.

Likewise, Henry remained silent, his gaze all over the oil paintings surrounding us and a display case of shiny objects at the end of the room. "Esme's guess was right," he said to himself.

I could only imagine what that meant. As far as I knew, Esme hated her younger brother. They had different mothers, and she resented how close she and Henry were in age. For his half, he tolerated her snark and ordering him around with his ever-present grin. The idea of her sharing some insight with him seemed unlikely. Which meant it probably happened at a family discussion.

All of a sudden, the walls closed in on me.

Esme had told me about this party, stating that my father would be here. Except he wasn't. Nor was it really a party with only the four settings. Presumably for me, Henry, the homeowner, and Mr Charterman. I'd expected to sip wine and make polite chat, but as one of four, my role had to be much bigger.

I pulled at the collar of my dress and flicked a look at Henry. "Why am I here?"

"Asking myself the same question," he answered out the side of his mouth.

"Seriously," I hissed,

"I don't know what to tell you."

At the end of the room, his father entered, a jovial smile on his face as he spoke to the man behind him. My pulse sped, and I shrank in on myself, both eager to see the person who owned this place and wanting to hide from him.

I almost felt as if I'd been brought here *for* him, particularly after Henry's comment about not being alone with the man, but that was my imagination running riot.

Behind Mr Charterman, a hunched-over elderly gentleman followed.

My breath left me in a rush. He didn't seem scary. In fact, quite the opposite. His face was somehow familiar under his thatch of black hair, only greying around his temples despite his advanced age. At a slow shuffle, he leaned heavily on his stick.

"Naturally, you can't break up the estate. The grounds pay for the house, and inheritance tax is a bitch," Henry's dad spoke. "Such a pity you never married. Waiter? Bring out the meals."

I let go of my silly notions and stood, ready with a smile.

"I should've married," the old man muttered on a wheeze. "Should never have taken no for an answer." As they neared, the old man spotted us and suddenly halted. "Not mine," he shouted.

I kept up my pleasant grin. "I'm Theadora Stewart. It's a pleasure to meet you, Mr McInver."

"You're trying to pull a fast one on me." He ignored me and pointed his walking stick at Henry.

My friend suppressed a smile and ducked his head. "How are you, sir? I'm Henry Charterman."

"Yes, yes," Henry's dad said soothingly. He guided the man to the place at the head of the table, right next to me. "If you'll sit here, I've ordered in a good dinner for you."

"On my coin, I bet. Bloodsucker," the old man blustered.

He reminded me of my poor grandmother, and I subtly sent Henry a wide-eyed glance. Henry returned it, his face pink.

Murmuring niceties, Henry's dad tried to help McInver into the chair. The waiter arrived back with a large tray, silver domes over the plates.

Wobbling around, the old man raised his stick at him. "I don't want this. I never ordered it and I won't pay. Take it away. Go now."

He flailed his stick at the tray, but the waiter swung it out of the way, narrowly avoiding disaster.

"Serve the meal," Mr Charterman ordered.

The waiter set the plates down and beat a hasty retreat.

"A hearty meal will set you up," Henry's dad continued. "Then we can talk. There's so much to be done, and you aren't getting any younger."

"I bet you'd poison me if ye had your way," the elderly man ranted, his eyes wild. "Sign the papers, kill me off. I won't have it. Not the way ye want, Charterman."

"I wouldn't—"

"Aye, ye would. Ye think I'm too old to see your scheming? I told ye I have my own irons in the fire. How do ye like that, ha?" the man interrupted. He swung around and poked his stick across the table at Henry, knocking over a wine glass. Red bloomed on the tablecloth. "Not this boy. Not him."

But then his crazed gaze set on me and turned leering. "Is she yours?" he asked Henry.

Henry choked. "No, sir."

"Good lad. Women are inconstant bitches. But I thank ye for bringing me a prize. Leave her and close the door on your way out. I might be old but I can still have her."

My bemusement shifted to embarrassment. The man was deranged. I shot another look at Henry. He grimaced but didn't budge.

His dad moved from the old man's side to behind me, and I was glad for the literal backup.

McInver didn't break his lustful stare. "In my day, I had them all lined up and waiting on me. I like 'em chubby, big titties. Something to dig my fingers into and pull on." The ancient man licked his lips. "This one is all skin and bones. But her face... She'll do. Give her to me."

Sweat peppered my back. "Um..."

"Stand up, Theadora," Mr Charterman instructed at my back.

He drew my chair out, and I rose to my feet, grateful but ready to leave. I felt bad for him, as this evening was going entirely wrong, but more, discomfort crawled over me.

I'd grown up around Dad's cronies—ancient, over-privileged men who talked about women like they were pieces of meat—but this was the first time I'd been the piece of meat in the firing line.

Mr Charterman's hand landed on my shoulder.

McInver set down his cane and gripped the table. "What, Charterman, do ye intend to stay and watch? Help out, man. Get that ugly dress off her. I want to see what's underneath."

That was more than enough for me. Panic replaced my uneasiness, and I squirmed under the restraining hand. "Henry, we need to go."

But Henry only waited on his dad. Pressure built even more. Neither spoke.

"Henry, I need you to drive me." I peered up at his father. "Is it okay if we leave?"

I hated myself for asking, but it was instinctive. I was a guest, so manners dictated I wasn't in control here. But from the start I'd been uncomfortable, and the nasty words from the mansion owner felt all too threatening. He couldn't hurt me, not in his state, but that didn't mean he didn't want to.

McInver gave a high laugh, his gaze roaming my body. "Come on, boys, she's skittish. One of ye will have to prime her. Let me see her tits. Lay her out amongst the plates. I don't mind if she screams."

With surprising speed, he rounded the corner of the table then arrived in front of me, sandwiching me against the lawyer. He leaned in until his bloodshot eyes were all I could see.

"Pretty little thing, now I look properly. Young. I understand why ye chose her. Now, girl, spread your legs. I'm going to take that virgin cunt."

His gnarled hand snatched me between the legs, and I screamed and wrenched away, shoving aside my chair with a clatter as it fell.

Mr Charterman swore, sidestepping my chair. "Stop."

I didn't know if he meant me or the old man, but I stifled a sob and kept moving.

"Thea." Henry snagged his keys from his pocket and threw them to me. "Wait for me outside."

They landed on the floor with a crash, and I stooped to grab them then ran, unwilling to wait to see what happened next.

In the car, I locked the doors and hunkered down, breathing too hard and at a loss to understand what the heck just happened.

The caterer left soon after, but it took another ten minutes for Henry to appear. His dad marched out first, sparing no glance for me in Henry's Porsche, and sped away with an angry roar of his engine. Then Henry traipsed down the steps.

He waited for me to unlock the door then fell heavily into his seat.

I'd rehearsed too many conversations and overflowed with questions, but Henry cut me off with his odd expression.

"I don't know, so don't ask," he ordered.

"But—"

"I said don't, Theadora," he shouted.

Never once since I met him at ten years old had Henry raised his voice to me. He'd always been so sweet. To everyone. Yet he'd sat there and listened as the man said those vile things then tried to assault me. He'd *warned* me in advance.

Trying not to cry, I sank into silence for the long drive to Edinburgh.

At my building, Henry caught my fingers, preventing me from flying from the car.

"This is the truth. Dad didn't know what the guy was going to do. I'm sorry you were caught in the middle of it. That was freaking weird."

"I don't care. I want to go inside." My skin still crawled.

The muscle at Henry's jaw ticked, and he kept up his tight hold on me. "I'm not the bad guy here, Theadora. We're friends."

There was so much wrong in that. He was hiding

things, and I just wanted to get away.

"You're hurting me," I tugged my hand, and he released me.

I dove from the car and into my building, clattering up the stairs. Intense and utter vulnerability threatened to overwhelm me before I could hide away in the safety of my bed.

Dad didn't answer my call, and nor did Esme. An hour later, in my room, my phone finally dinged. I picked it up and read the screen, too disappointed to see Henry's name.

My initial hope had been inexplicable.

For all the weeks since I'd met Struan, I'd hoped he'd find a way to message me. I checked all my social media accounts regularly, waiting for him.

But he never sent a thing.

On the drive this evening, heading farther into the north of Scotland, I'd liked how much closer I was to him. I'd pictured the rest of the journey to Torlum Island. Compared the image of the mansion to the sight I'd had with Lottie of Struan's basic home.

With him, I'd felt my very first kick of lust.

His effect on my body had been startling, and something awoke that I couldn't work out how to explore by myself.

I'd thought it his violence, his dominant move.

But tonight, the awful, vile McInver had taken worse action. His touch burned away the need I had for Struan's.

Now, I wanted nothing.

Henry: Dad asked me to apologise on his behalf. None of us expected the drama tonight. See you soon.

They wouldn't. Not if I could help it.

My mother was right. I was an obedient, naive thing. Closer to a girl than a woman, despite my age.

And I had no idea how to change.

9

Struan

I paced the bedroom, my energy returning the more my adrenaline rushed. All week, I'd been confined to the house. I'd cooked, cleaned every room I'd been ordered to, and wallowed in the space. Sin and the others left for long hours and came back dirty and exhausted. Sometimes injured. They were doing some kind of land work, but I still didn't ask questions.

If I didn't know, I couldn't care.

But today was Saturday. Someone was coming. The visitor Keep had warned us about would be here this evening.

Darkness fell outside, and my heart sank.

Sin hadn't eaten or bothered showering. Instead, as midnight closed in, he sat on the bunk room floor and ordered Burn to pick up a book from the few on a shelf.

"Start where ye left off," he muttered.

The younger man trudged back to his bunk, the heavy old book in his hands. "Fuck this."

Sin glared at him under hooded eyes. "Read the damn

know.

Like I didn't want involvement in this scene, or awareness of whoever the hell was coming and what they intended to do. Pressure built within me. I had to get out. Except I couldn't.

Burn opened the book and squinted at the words, then painstakingly read a sentence. His face reddened, and he slapped the book closed. "I can't, okay? It's too hard. What's the point?"

Sin drew himself up and towered over the boy. "You'll do it because I told ye to," he gritted out.

Burn glared back, but whatever he saw in Sin's eyes killed his protest. He picked up the scene once more.

This was a joke. I knew that book. *Little Women.* My mother had read it to me when I was wee. For how shite our lives had been, she'd loved reading to me. But the troubles of the four lasses in the story were nothing compared with ours in the hostel.

Burn's stumbling, hesitant reading drove nails into the coffin of my imprisonment. His fingers kept up the flick of his Zippo wheel, the spark both too close to the book and not close enough.

I couldn't handle it.

Bursting from my bunk, I stood before Sin. "Why the fuck are ye forcing him? Read it yourself."

Silence fell in the room.

"Seriously," I continued, my blood too hot. "He doesnae want to do it. If you're lacking entertainment, tough. That is just cruel."

"No, Struan, wait," Burn said from behind me, something gripped in his hand.

But I was too far gone to divert my attention. If they'd hoped the slow death of solitary had broken me, they'd be disappointed. All I'd needed was food and exercise to heal some of the damage.

Worse, it had torn away even more of my restraint.

I turned and snatched the book then hurled it down the room, hitting the board where the window used to be. Loose pages fluttered. It only angered me more.

"Don't do it again. You're fucking evil," I growled at Sin.

From his great height, he gazed at me.

Danger danced in my veins, and I flexed my fingers, ready for a fight.

This, I knew. Slamming my fists into another man's body. Breaking bones. Bloodying flesh. I'd missed the anticipation, the adrenaline, the antagonism. All that energy needed release.

Sounds came from elsewhere in the hostel.

The click of a lock. Low voices.

Without pause, Sin left me and walked to the door. He put his hands behind his back and turned around.

"What's happening?" I asked, my anger simmering. I took a step after him.

Together, Burn and Scar jumped to stand in front of me.

"Sit down and stay quiet," Scar murmured, his hair falling forward to hide his scar.

"Why?"

"Do it."

They pushed me to sit on the bunk, and I let them, waiting to see what played out. Obviously the visitor was here, but what did that mean for Sin?

The light overhead suddenly extinguished, plunging us into dark. Either side of me, Burn and Scar gripped one of my shoulders each. Holding me back.

The door opened. Light sliced in.

From the angle, I couldn't see the stranger's face. But the shiny shoes were definitely a man's. Something metallic clicked, *handcuffs,* then, without a single word, Sin followed them into the hall. Our door was locked once more.

"Who was that?" I broke my no-questions rule.

Neither answered.

A grunt came from elsewhere in the hostel.

It sounded again, along with the thud of something hard being hit. I stiffened, only too aware of how the two boys with me cringed. Sin was being attacked. Scar pressed his hand to his mouth and, even in the dark, panic shone in his eyes.

Maybe we were next.

Shouting began. A male voice ranted, indistinct at first, then louder and clearer. I strained to hear the words.

"You are nothing. Worthless. A piece of shit. Do you understand? Nothing."

He didn't sound Scottish, whoever he was.

"Repeat after me."

Hit. Grunt.

"I am nothing."

Smack.

"Nobody cares. I have no value. No rights," the stranger recited.

Sin's tensed, low voice repeated the words, pain in his tone.

My heart dropped my boots. I had no problem with

brawling. Missed it. Needed it, probably. A fist connecting to my body jolted me out of myself, forced me to live in the moment in order to survive. It woke my blood like almost nothing else.

But this wasn't a fair fight. Sin couldn't hit back. It was fucking sadistic.

"And do you know why?" the stranger continued. "You were born that way. Born useless. Worthless. And you'll die the same."

A crunch came, and Sin growled in anguish.

The abuser's voice got louder, repeating the message from the top. With every line, the hits resounded.

Sin's sounds of pain turned to a yell. Then a scream.

The words ended, and then there were just thuds. Ominous. Sickening.

All the anger I had iced over.

"What the fuck happens now?" I demanded. "More? Worse? Is he going to rape him?"

Burn jerked. "Shut the fuck up."

Scar raised a hand as if to stall him. The lad batted away the attempt at comfort, his whole body tight and his expression fierce.

I didn't move, heavy on the mattress and pinned down by all that was unfolding. The realities this place brought.

All too easily, it tapped into dark places I'd been in the past.

My life had never been easy, and I'd witnessed things I wished I could unsee. My mother's line of business exposed us to an underworld of bad people. They were everywhere.

Against the backdrop of Sin's suffering, I reeled at an onslaught of memories. Ma held against our door with some guy gripping her by the throat as he yelled abuse to her face. A five-year-old me battering his legs until he smacked me aside. Then later, after he'd gone, my mother curling around me in the narrow single bed, singing me to sleep with a bruised face.

That one stood out, probably because it was the first I remembered. But it wasn't an isolated incident. Before I'd even learned to read, I understood that men were only interested in women for two reasons. Either to fuck them or to hate them.

It had taken a long time for me to see that there were other types of families out there. Kids at school talked about what their da was cooking for tea that night, or sleepovers with grandparents. Hot meals for me came from fast-food counters, and only when we had money. Sleepovers were when I was stashed in the corner of one of Ma's friend's bedsits, hoping and praying she'd come back to me.

I despised hearing about those gentler versions of life.

I'd desperately wanted it for my tiny family of two.

In the cliff cave, Theadora had offered to contact my mother. She'd held out her phone. I should've taken it. Should've found out what had happened to Ma after I'd left.

The thought of knowing scared the shite out of me.

A particularly hard hit resounded, followed by a deep groan. Then the sounds of the attack ceased. I listened hard, but all I could pick up now was my own breathing and the thrum of blood in my ears.

"Talk to me," I asked again. "Tell me something, any-fucking-thing about what I just heard."

Burn shot up and strode away to stand with his back

to the wall, gaze fixed to the door.

Scar took a shuddering inhale. "Sinclair takes the beatings because he says he can handle it but it might kill us. He isn't the bad guy ye think he is. He protects us. Reads with Burn because how else will he learn?"

Sinclair. A third unwanted name.

"That was a beating, not worse?" I gritted out.

"Isn't it bad enough? Sin never talks about it after. All I know is that bastard needs to die, and one day soon he will."

"Who's the bastard?"

"How would we know that? Not like he introduced himself."

"Ye must have a theory."

Silence still held in the hostel, no more screams or smacks of flesh. The tension in the room didn't shift.

Scar watched the door. Emotion played out in his voice. "Aye. Several. None are fact. Maybe he gets off on it. Maybe he's Sin's father and hates his guts. All I know is what Sin told me: he gets his goodies in what you heard."

He shifted his weight, and I caught another glimpse of the item he'd been holding, now shoved beside his mattress.

A phone. All this time, and they'd had a motherfucking phone hidden away. My anger boosted once more, mixed up by all that had happened tonight.

Footsteps echoed in the hall again, and we all jerked to stand. The door opened, and Sin entered. With his head down and his jaw tight, he moved directly past us to his bunk and climbed in, the stiffness of his limbs giving up his pain.

Scar and Burn seemed to hold their breath, staring

at the back of the big man as he laid down. For a second, I was right there with them, rearranging my thoughts on the guy. Understanding more than I wanted to.

But then something else demanded my attention.

The door had been left ajar.

Every night, we were locked in. Only able to use the bathroom, not access the hall that led to the kitchen and other rooms.

The centimetre gap screamed at me.

I took a deep breath, blood rushing and readying my limbs. I was still weaker from my isolation than I wanted to be. Tonight had given me an insight in what it was to stay here. To live like these men. I pitied them. Knew all their names now. Sinclair. Camden. Jamieson.

I hated that.

The hostel had almost broken me, but not entirely.

Faster than I'd moved in over a month, I leapt to the middle bunk, snatched the hidden phone from the mattress, and darted out the door.

10

Struan

Patches of moonlight carved up the dark hall, coming from the kitchen and the tiny window of the cell I'd been kept in. I crept along to the glass door that led to the lobby. Nothing moved beyond. No one pursued me. Yet.

With an unsteady grip, I turned the handle. The door opened, and my pulse raced, the beat of my heart so loud it had to be announcing my escape attempt.

This was my one chance, and I couldn't fuck it up.

Stealing through the shadowed room, I made my way to the front exit. A light was on in the keeper's office, and voices came from inside. The dangerous stranger was still here, and angry from the sound of the argument he was having with Keep. Presumably why she'd made her mistake with our door.

The disruption of his visit had given me this opportunity. But I couldn't be glad for the beating Sin had taken.

A flash of regret hit me that I wouldn't get to apologise for the assumptions I'd made about him. But he'd never been straight with me, and more importantly, I'd be free.

I was almost at the exit when a glint of metal registered at the edge of my vision. I squinted at the reception desk, and my already too fast heart gave an almighty thump.

A set of car keys sat on the counter.

I didn't hesitate or debate the waste of a couple of seconds. Scooting over, I plucked them into my palm, clamping my fingers around them to silence the jingle. Then I bolted for the door.

It too gave, and I was out in the night air and flying down the path.

Shite. Shite, shite, shite. Free.

I couldn't think about my luck. There was no car here, so I pocketed the keys and ran flat out until my lungs burned. In the months I'd been here, I hadn't forgotten the route back to the harbour. Scattered houses turned into the tiny village, and the tang of seaweed and salt built. Then the long wooden dock came into sight down the hill.

Just as I'd never forgotten the route, I had Theadora's boat location and lock code laser cut into my brain. *Last boat on the pontoon to the right. Code three-two-three-one.*

But the harbour wasn't empty.

I crouched behind a low wall and scoped it out.

The brightly lit ferry waited at the end of the dock, the ramp down, and two men stood talking.

Several conclusions hit me.

The man who attacked Sin came by boat. Not only was he responsible for our jailing, he was powerful enough to demand transport out here when he needed it. Which also meant he didn't live here.

And that arseholes like these guys would probably

jump to obey him.

Every second I'd ran, I'd kept a sharp awareness for my surroundings. For any people who might see me.

Walking past these guys to the row of smaller boats was going to get me caught.

A month ago, I would have considered rushing them. Knocking them out and stealing the boat. After everything I'd been through, I doubted my strength.

By stealth, I slunk down the concrete expanse and waded in along the rock wall, just out of the pool of light illuminating the shallows. The cold rushed into my boots, soaking my jeans. The phone I'd stolen was at risk of a soaking, but there was nothing I could do about that. Ducking, I waded out deeper to the dock, moving fast.

The ferry loomed ahead, one of the figures now in the cabin window. At the corner of the walkway, the other arsehole smoked, the red end of his cigarette glowing. I had to pass him to make it to the second length of dock.

Floating in the water, I panted silently. If I swam, he'd hear the splashes. If I crept by, I risked being seen.

The crackle of a radio reached me with a low murmuring. The smoking man swore then tossed his cigarette, the red light flaring right in front of my eyes before extinguishing. His footsteps led away, and I held my breath. This was my chance.

I pulled myself along on shaking arms until I reached the corner of the second walkway then, without pause, continued down to the end.

A line of boats waited on the other side, but I ignored them all for the final one.

Theadora's.

Gripping the side, I tipped into it, a trail of water following, waves lapping. On the boat's floor, I froze.

Nothing happened. No shouts. No alarm.

For a long moment, I closed my eyes and tipped my head back to the wooden boards. I'd fucking done it. But shite, maybe that was the easy part.

Theadora's other warning played out—not to get lost at sea. I had to follow the ferry, which meant waiting for it to leave.

The minutes ticked on. I listened then peered out of my hiding place. The autumn air chilled my wet clothes. I'd live with pneumonia if it got me off this fucked-up island.

Shuffling, and still keeping low, I moved down the boat and found the heavy padlock securing the motor with a rubber-enclosed chain. My shirt made a blocker for the phone's screen light, luckily still working, and with flicks of my thumb, I entered the code.

The lock clicked open.

Yanking the chain free would make a racket. I needed to wait for the ferry to rev up and drown out the sound.

So I sat there. Iced over and catching my breath.

A second glance at the phone showed me the late hour, then the battery died in front of my eyes.

The minutes wore on. The boatman took regular cigarette breaks, and the captain joined him for one, their low voices not carrying far enough for me to hear their words.

Maybe they weren't here for the abuser. Maybe it was a regular ferry for people to go to work or some such shite.

Just as despair hit hard, the thunder of steps came down the dock.

"Cast off," a man snapped.

Holy fuck. It was him. Sin's attacker.

I didn't dare take a look, huddling deeper in my shadows my end of the dock. The boat clanked, the engine roared, and the thick scent of diesel fumes washed over me. Finally, they were leaving.

I rolled up and hauled on the chain. It fell free, and I squinted at the engine. I'd never driven a boat, but the joystick control and on/off button was simple enough.

Rope held the boat to the dock, so I climbed off and uncoiled it. Then I jumped back on and hit the button.

The engine started with a shuddering cough.

A thrill ran over me, and I pushed the lever, needing to chase the ferry before it got too far ahead.

My stolen ride jumped forward, smacking into the next boat along. I swore then shoved away with my hand so the nose faced the harbour entrance, then yanked on the direction control. The rudder? Tiller? Whatever.

I slid out into the black water, tailing the bigger boat. With no lights, I was invisible in the murky water, my noise drowned out, too.

Then it was just a case of staying on course.

Waves rocked me, and sea spray soaked me further. Wind drove a chill into my bones. I kept my focus on the bright ferry guiding me in.

The journey out here had taken a couple of hours. This return trip seemed much faster, probably because we weren't making multiple stops. Yet by the time lights appeared in the black—the mainland, I hoped—pink dawn rose on the horizon.

My muscles ached, cramped from the position I held myself in, hunched over the controls. Daylight was a problem. There would be no hiding for me.

Just like at the hostel, I'd need to choose my moment

then make a run for it.

The ferry's engine sound changed, and the boat slowed. Voices called, and it landed at wherever the hell we'd stopped.

A dark thought crawled over me that this could be another island. But I had to take my chances.

Lurking out in the sea, I put the engine into neutral and waited it out.

The cabin door clanked, and I faintly picked up the sounds of the passenger leaving. Presumably to go home to his wife and family after his night of fun. The boatmen tied up the ferry. Car lights shone higher up the rise. Then there was nothing.

I remained in place for long minutes, biding my time. Waiting until I was sure no one else was around.

All the while, the sky grew lighter, morning settling in.

People would be searching Torlum for me. Maybe calling the ferry company when they found the stolen boat, requesting any sightings.

The dock—larger than the island one we left behind—was empty right now, but in a minute, the two boat workers could be back. Or fishermen, or even the cops.

There was nothing for it. I flexed my muscles then sailed in hard. At the wooden walkway, I killed the engine and scrambled off the boat, leaving it adrift.

"Hey, use the slipway," someone called.

I didn't wait around to see who. At a sprint, I bombed down the harbour path and straight into a car park, then snatched the keys from my pocket with only a small hope that they'd still work after their dip in the sea in my pocket, and that the owner would have parked here.

I hit the button.

Lights flashed on a crappy old Ford.

I gaped at it and forced myself to keep moving. Then I opened the door and fell into the car.

Shutting myself in, I fitted the keys to the ignition, sending up a prayer to a God I didn't believe in. The engine turned over then rattled to life.

I'd done it.

I had no fucking clue where I was. I still had the wee treacherous tracker around my ankle. But a laugh rolled out of my damp, frozen body. Let them try and catch me now.

I eased the car out of the parking space and exited the car park, flying down the empty road. My soggy boots squelched on the pedals. On the boat, I hadn't dared take them off, but now I reached down and dislodged each in turn, seawater dripping onto the rubber mat beneath the pedals.

A cable trailed around my feet. I pulled it, following it back to a unit plugged into the cigarette lighter.

A multipoint charging device.

In my pocket, the phone poked into my side. Without letting up my speed or taking my eyes off the winding country road, I fished out the phone and messed with it until one of the charging heads slid into place.

The image of a battery flashed on-screen.

My mouth dropped open, and I wheezed out a laugh. Of all that happened during the course of the night, my escape, the boat ride, the heart-stopping moments, this one socked me in the gut.

I had a car, and the phone, and a nightmarish last month behind me. Nothing could stop me now.

*T*he sky lightened the longer I drove. Wide-open countryside with views to the sea skimmed past my window. I passed a just-opening café, and my stomach growled, but food could wait. I sped through little towns, still no clearer whether I was on an island or mainland Scotland.

The signs, some in Gaelic, didn't help. Then the road took me past the town of Portree, and finally I saw something that clued me in.

Skye tours, scrawled on a poster.

My geography was sketchy as fuck, but I knew that the Isle of Skye was linked to the mainland by a long road bridge.

Smirking, I put my foot down.

Thirty minutes on, and the end of the island was in sight. I grinned, eyeing the span of quiet bridge over the water. Fuck yeah, I was alive and free.

The whole time I'd been on the run, I hadn't really considered where I wanted to go. Once, home had been Glasgow. Before that, Aberdeen. Edinburgh. Wherever my mother was.

But I couldn't follow her now.

Fierce emotion crested inside me, and I stamped on the accelerator. I missed her. I never wanted to stop protecting her. As crap as she'd been at most areas of parenting, my love for her had never been in doubt.

Mixed in with that came guilt. That I'd somehow let her down, though I was in no way responsible for what happened to her.

If I was a better person, I'd also feel guilt about the men I'd left behind in that hostel.

Sinclair, Camden, Jamieson.

Sin, Scar, Burn.

They'd been broken by that system far worse than I could imagine. They'd had the same chances I did to run. None of them had taken it.

Wondering why could drive me nuts.

Then last night... Anger ran through me. Sin had taken a beating, apparently on behalf of all of us.

To the tune of the sputtering engine, I pieced over all the ways in which I could help them. If I went to the police wearing an ankle tracker, they'd have questions I couldn't answer. Maybe deliver me straight back. An anonymous tip-off might work. But who'd take me seriously unless I was standing in front of them and insisting on it? Providing the evidence myself.

They weren't my problem, but I had to do something.

Ahead, the Skye bridge entrance loomed.

The engine made a guttural, choking sound.

Other than getting it to go, I'd barely paid attention to the car I'd stolen. But one glance at the dash killed my mood. The fuel tank arrow sat right on empty.

I smacked the steering wheel with the heel of my hand then bit out a string of swear words.

The engine choked, and the car shuddered. My peace of mind did the same, breaking apart. This piece of junk was about to die on me, and I could do nothing about it.

I had no one to call, and no clue where to go next.

I'd slowed, and another vehicle cruised by and moved onto the bridge, a man about my age driving.

He cut me a look as he passed.

My anger broke. I had to do something to get this fucking ache out of my system. I floored the accelerator, burning through the gears and the very last dregs of fuel.

Then I chased the other car.

On the wrong side of the road, I drew level and glared daggers at the arsehole inside.

Fuck him for having a purpose today.

I needed to race him, though it would achieve nothing. The man glowered back. His car, an old but decent 4X4, was more powerful than mine, and he could have easily put me in his dust.

Instead, he kept pace.

I glanced ahead to be sure I wasn't about to kill anyone, but I wasn't pulling out.

Around me, the old Ford shuddered and rattled. We rolled down the hill off the first section of bridge, landing at the wee island where it connected to a flatter second section.

Just one more stretch and I'd make it to the mainland.

The engine cut out altogether.

"Fuck," I yelled and punched the seat next to me.

The car cruised to a halt, whining, and I stamped on the brakes, stopping at the side of the road. Then I slid on my damp boots, smacked open the door and climbed out, ready to throw myself in the damn sea.

The car I'd been racing roared ahead, but the driver stopped and reversed.

"What?" I yelled. "Want a second go? Too bad."

He parked in front and exited his car. Redheaded. Tattoos. A year or two older than me. The guy would've fitted in well at the hostel.

He shucked on a leather jacket and scowled. "What

the fuck are ye playing at?"

I glared back, pissed off and not needing an audience.

"Do ye have a death wish? You'll kill yourself like that," he continued.

"I'd do the world a favour."

His focus left me and skipped to the car. "What's wrong with your heap of scrap?"

My adrenaline drained into pure exhaustion. I'd have to walk the last segment of the bridge, but then where would I be? All I could see was mountains, and I had no idea what the nearest town was. Even if another car passed, no one would pick up a lad like me if I hitch-hiked. Glasgow had to be two hundred miles away, if I even wanted to go back there for the measly possessions I'd left behind.

"Dead." I gestured to the car, closing my eyes. I sensed the fucktard nearing.

"Need help with it?"

"No."

"I'm Max McRae. Weird coincidence, considering ye just broke down trying to run me off the road, but I'm a mechanic. I can take a look if ye want?"

"Are ye fucking with me? I'm not going to suck your dick in return, so don't bother."

To my surprise, he laughed. "Christ, man. The attitude on ye. I'm offering to help with your ride, ye wee dipshit. Go stand somewhere else if you're scared."

I wheeled around. "Scared? Fuck ye."

"Then ye willnae mind if I take a look?"

Time was against me, but I had no other choice than to let him help. If he got it going, it would be a quicker getaway than on foot. "It's your funeral. Start with the fuel."

I snatched the phone from the charger and marched away, ignoring the steam that rose as the man popped the Ford's bonnet.

Desperate for something good, I brought up the browser and searched for Theadora Stewart. Just like she said, she was easy to find, her pretty face beaming out with the same shot used on multiple sites.

I made an account under the name @islandboy. Followed her.

In a heartbeat, she followed me back.

Fuck.

Twice already, she'd tried to help me. I bet if I asked now, the lass would leap to offer herself up.

I stared at her photograph and recalled her body under mine. Her soft intake of breath. The fear that came off her mixed with lust.

Then a message landed.

@theadorastewart: Hello?

My blood rushed south. If I went to her, I'd abuse that naivety right out of her. I hovered a thumb over the reply button then backed out of the app.

"Want the bad news or the bad news?" Red asked me.

Max, he'd called himself.

"Don't ye mean good news or bad news?"

He pulled a face. "Nope. This car is fucked up. I can list ten things that will fail your next MOT."

"Can ye get it going?" I palmed my forehead. "All I need is petrol. It was fine until it ran out."

Max the mechanic stared. "Fuck's sake. I thought ye meant the fuel lines. Well, aye, you're welcome to my spare can. But seriously, this willnae get far. It isn't safe."

I raised a shoulder, trying to force gratitude. He had

no reason to help me. "I'll take my chances."

"Do ye live around here?"

"Aye." If four hours by stolen boat and car counted.

For a moment, he just stared at me, then made some decision and strode to his car, collecting a petrol can. He waited on me then sighed and moved to fill up the Ford himself.

"Appreciate it," I muttered when he was done.

Max put away the things he'd brought out of his car. "Listen, I occasionally do outreach work round here, hence why I have the borrowed off-roader and not my usual motorbike."

"What does outreach mean?"

"Helping teenagers fix up their rides for free. It's why I'm here on Skye. The Highlands and islands are a lonely place if you're without transport. I'd know. I live in the Cairngorms. The outreach office usually has a list of kids who are in trouble and might need help. We could've had your name from the police already if you're doing community service or on a youth offending scheme."

"Youth offending," I muttered. "That's a fucking joke. My brothers wish it was like that."

Brothers? Where the hell did that come from? Screw those guys.

He extracted a little white card from his pocket and held it out. "The printed details are for the office, but I wrote my number on the back. Can ye read?"

"Of course I fucking can."

He whistled, his grin instant. "No shame if ye couldn't. My da struggles. That's life sometimes."

That's life. Pure shite unless ye were lucky. I pictured Burn's slow reading. He'd probably missed more school than even I had.

He and the others at the hostel could use this man's help better than me, if they ever got free. They were open to it where I was a shut case. Accepting nothing from no one. Only causing harm.

Still, I reached and took the card.

"Good lad." Max patted the Ford's roof. "Should run now. Take her to a garage when ye can. Or just call me and I'll come out if I'm around. I'm used to heading out on rescues."

"Why?" I bit out.

"You're out in the middle of nowhere, probably in a car ye stole from your nan, and wearing an ankle tracker." He thumbed at himself. "Been there, done that. Minus the nan. I bet ye assume everyone who looks at ye thinks you're a fuck-up? Not everyone."

I glanced down to where my still wet jeans hooked over the tracker and swore. "I need to go."

Max shrugged, tapped the car, then walked away, calling over his shoulder, "If ye text me, call yourself joyrider or something so I know who it is."

My race buddy sped away.

Enough time had been wasted. I needed to move. At least now I could get farther south.

I leapt back into the Ford and turned the key in the ignition.

Nothing happened.

Engines roared farther up the bridge, two cars speeding over the brow.

A chill ran down my spine.

I messed with the gears and tried again.

Nothing.

"Come on," I yelled at the Ford, repeating my actions. The din closed in.

Without any sign, I knew whoever was in those cars were here for me.

One passed and skidded to a halt in front while the other did the same behind, blocking me in. Trapping me.

I'd gone from high to low once already, but when I spotted the first driver, my stomach tightened to a ball. My capture at the cliff had been led by one thickset ugly fucker of a man. He'd taken pleasure in every punch he'd thrown at me, two other men pinning my arms so I couldn't fight back.

The bruises had barely faded, but he was back.

Three men climbed from the cars and closed in. I stood from the open door and edged around it, ready to sprint.

A wall lined the bridge, and I eyed it, unable to see the drop to the land or water.

"Don't do it," Ugly Fucker demanded. "If ye come in easy, we willnae hurt ye. We're under orders to take ye back."

"The fuck ye will."

"Listen to him," a second man said. "Sin said if we find ye, he wants ye brought in unharmed."

I stopped moving. "Sin? Sin sent ye?"

How was that even possible? He was a prisoner.

Or maybe that was a lie.

Either way, I wasn't about to find out.

I bolted and leapt over my bonnet, sliding on the still warm metal. A short grassy verge led to the wall, and I fell over it, gripping the stone to check the fall before I committed.

A hand grabbed my arm. I fought it, but another reached and took hold of my shirt. The stones scratched my chest and face as they hauled me back over and pinned me to the grass.

I twisted and kicked out, but I was outnumbered and beat.

Ugly Fucker puffed, his hands on his hips. "Ye had to make it difficult. I said I wouldnae, but ye deserved this."

He lined up and swung his meaty fist into my temple.

This time, on my return to the prison island of Torlum, I did it unconscious.

11

Sin

Out of routine, I strode back into the hostel, worry and frustration mixing up my blood. My flesh burned from the beating I'd taken last night, and I didn't need this bollocks.

Keep stepped out of her office, her Taser in hand. "Why are you here?"

It was lunchtime, and we'd normally all be out working.

Except I had a runaway to handle. If I got this wrong, he'd be fucked. Permanently. Our vicious keeper would see to that.

"Forgot lunch," I muttered, not making eye contact.

She grumbled but returned into her space, locking the door.

I moved through the hostel to the rear door, opposite to the store where we kept our food. And where we could sneak out at will.

Or we had been able to until Struan had pulled his stunt, putting us all on lockdown for almost a month.

I stood in the doorway, glowering at the expanse of island and the empty road.

The smartest of us, Scar, had begged me to bring Struan into our confidence, but he wasn't ready. Last night had proved that out.

Movement on the road caught my eye.

Struan marched along with Jenkins holding his biceps.

The other two men Jenkins had taken with him fell back, which suited me. Keep would be less likely to see.

I stepped from the shadows, showing myself. Jenkins adjusted their path until they arrived in front of me.

The islander lifted his chin. "Got him. We also brought back the boat he stole. And the car. Took a while to get it started again."

He tossed me Keep's car keys, and I pocketed them. I'd toss them into the reception later. Make her think she'd dropped them. Then he passed over the phone Struan had lifted, too.

"Now what's it worth to not go tell that stupid cow who runs this place about his midnight flit?"

I curled my lip. "We had a deal."

"Do ye know how far we had to go to chase him down? He did almost as good as ye, lad." He cackled an ugly laugh.

Struan kept his head down.

My temper rose. Jenkins ran a croft on the island and also repaired boats. His family had been here for generations, and he thought himself the voice of the people.

He was also a fucking pervert.

When Burn had been delivered to the hostel, Jenkins had offered Keep money for a couple of days alone with him. He called him 'pretty lad', and his gaze followed him everywhere.

For reasons known only to herself, Keep refused it. Possibly because our jailor, the man who kept us here, wouldn't want damaged goods, as Jenkins undoubtedly would leave our youngest resident.

Now, I had no choice but to work with the corrupted, filthy man.

One day, just like with our keeper and our jailor, I'd kill him. And I'd enjoy it.

"Three days of labour," I gritted out.

"There are other ways to pay," he drawled.

"No, there aren't," I repeated, tightening my muscles. "A week. Or I'm knocking on that front door now."

"Fine."

Jenkins shoved Struan at me, and I pushed him behind me, into the hostel.

"Any lasses showed up to join your crew of misfits? I ain't picky." Jenkins sniffed.

I shut the door in his face.

Inside, Struan backed to the storeroom door. "Why are ye calling the shots? Why ye and not the keeper?"

I scanned him for injuries, noting only a bruised temple. Fucking little idiot. "What happened last time ye ran and she was the one to bring ye in?"

His gaze slid to the hallway corner, to where the isolation room waited.

"Exactly," I continued. "If Keep knew you'd gone—"

"Why not tell her? What the fuck is in it for ye? Why not just let me go?"

A door swung open with a creak, somewhere within the building.

"Kitchen, quick," I said, hushed.

Struan and I moved down the hall, through the inner door that was locked at night, and entered the kitchen.

I snatched up a knife from the counter and dove at him.

A fast and accurate slice cut away his zip ties, and I pocketed them, placing the knife back on the work surface. Struan sucked in a breath, still glowering at me.

I sensed Keep appear at the door without her even saying a word.

Her beady gaze rested on the broad back of the newest of us. Suspicion played out over her features, and I held my breath. Struan's new bruise and dirty clothes didn't mean shite around here, but the man was a loose cannon. Unpredictable.

He didn't turn.

She missed the signs. "When will that one be out to work?"

"When I'm sure he willnae run," I replied.

She grunted. "What a waste. It's been over a month. He could be out there and earning like the rest of ye. Think this place runs on air?"

"I'll trial him this week."

She clucked her tongue and left us.

With anger holding my muscles tight, I opened the cupboard and grabbed tins of lentils and beans plus bags of vegetables, and slammed them onto the counter in front of our runaway. We couldn't talk now. Keep was lazy as fuck but I'd bet listened in more than we knew.

"Make a stew. We'll be home at dusk," I ordered, adding as low as possible, "We'll talk later."

Then I got my stressed-out self back to work.

12

Struan

Evening came, and the other residents returned. They ate the meal I'd cooked and, from the curious looks, all knew about my trip. That I'd stolen their phone and nearly reached freedom.

No one asked.

After Sin's hissed threat, I knew something was coming. Energy infected me, the danger real. There was not one thing I could do about it.

Late into the night, Sin finally stood from his bunk. Lights had been off for hours, but no one slept. I could hear it in their breathing.

Like ghosts, the other two rose with him. I found my feet, stepping into my still-damp boots. My wrists stung from where the plastic ties had bit in, and my head ached.

As a group, we exited the bedroom and moved down the hall to the locked inner door.

Sin produced a key and silently opened it.

Fucking hell.

I glared at him. For all I knew, this guy was the ringleader.

At the back door, he did the same, then we were outside in the blustering evening. Wind whipped me, but I didn't hesitate to follow them out onto the moor. At a nudge on my arm, I peered back. Scar handed me a hoodie.

"Thanks," I muttered and pulled it on.

A few minutes on, we hit the beach.

Black night met the wide ocean, no line between the two. I kept walking, half expecting to be smacked over the head and tossed into the water.

At a rise of ground, Sin halted and stepped into a hollow. Protected by a small hill, it made a seating area, sheltered from the weather. A kind of bench had been carved out of the sand and rock, and we sat, Burn huddling close to Sin, me and Scar on the ends.

As we'd walked, the others had collected sticks and branches from the ground. They tossed them into a pit at our feet, then Burn leaned forward, squirted something from a bottle, and sparked the fire to life.

In all the time I'd seen him messing around with that lighter, it had never once produced a flame. It did now.

The instant glow drove shadows over the men's faces. I gripped the edge of the rocky shelf, ready to take a punch. Whatever punishment they wanted to give.

Burn was the first to speak. He settled his gaze on me, his expression determined. "I ran three times. The first, I got a broken nose, the last, a worse beating for Sin than he ever had before. That stopped me in my tracks."

"I never ran." Scar took his turn. "What was the point? I had nowhere to go. At least here I was fed."

Then Sin spoke. His voice, already gravelly and deep,

was only just audible over the whine of the wind. "I was the first here. I ran six times."

"Got down to England on his last go," Burn supplied.

I stared. "How were ye found?"

All three laughed.

Burn swung his leg over the fire, the flames rushing to meet his jeans. "Did ye think these were jewellery?" He flashed his ankle tracker.

I growled. "They track us, I know. But why bother? Why go to all the trouble of keeping us here and bringing us back? How...?"

I stalled, about to ask for the details I'd sworn I didn't want. But the picture they were painting suggested I couldn't escape this place, or its inhabitants.

"How long?" I finished.

"Almost a year for me," Sin replied. "Eight months for Scar. Six for Burn."

"And one for ye," Burn added. "If you'd been caught by Keep today, our freedom would've been cut again, so wise up and listen to us. We've all done it. We all fought in one way or another. It does nae good. They always catch us, and it makes everything harder."

"If you're expecting an apology," I snarled, "ye can suck my dick."

He rolled his eyes, flicking the wheel of the Zippo in his fingers. The flame flared and died.

I switched my attention to Sin. "How is it you're all-powerful? Why did the men jump to your command today? And what is the week ye bargained with for not telling Keep?"

Simultaneously, Scar and Burn groaned.

"A whole week?" the latter complained.

Sin's dark eyebrows dug together, and his focus fell on me like a lead weight. "If we can't leave this place, I decided to make it work for us. Not long before ye arrived, I offered our labour to a couple of the men who own crofts on the island."

"What the fuck is a croft?" I asked.

"Farmland, rented from the island's owner. Sheep, polytunnels, that kind of shite. We break our backs, they pay a pittance, half of which I give to Keep for her silence, and the rest we split between us and use for essentials."

That explained where they went every day.

And also that the keeper could be bribed.

"How do ye spend the money?" I asked.

"We go off island. The car you stole is Keep's," Scar answered. "Sin has used it a couple of times to get supplies, otherwise we have a contact on the island who helps us. Cheaper not to have to bribe someone to let us on a boat or to disable Keep's tracking system for too long, like we had to do for ye last night. She only checks it if she knows one of us has run, otherwise it's ignored."

That answered another question I had.

It also sketched an image of their life beyond what I knew.

Scar continued on. "We have our phone, too, as ye know—thanks for not breaking that by the way, but there's no Wi-Fi here, and we don't have any credit left. That's our next big buy. Ye cannae believe the relief when you hook up to the internet after so long."

The warmth of the fire didn't burn away my guilt. I'd stolen the phone from these men. On Skye, it had worked fine, which meant I'd used up the last of their credit.

I hunched in and busied myself poking a stick into the

fire. Despite it being autumn, the hostel had no heating. The nights and mornings were already icy. If that continued in to winter, it would be fucking freezing.

Dread trickled down my spine.

I'd be here over winter. Sin had been captured a year ago, if I could trust him enough to believe him. I'd been treated the same as him. I'd been thrown into this and, from what they'd told me, I wasn't going to get out easy.

No matter how far I ran, I'd be returned.

"Why are we here?" I finally asked.

All three shifted subtly, glances exchanged like they needed to decide between them how much to share.

Scar entwined his fingers and rested his forearms on his knees, his focus jumping from the flames to me. "What do the four of us have in common?"

I raised a shoulder.

"We're all male, Scottish, and close in age. Burn's seventeen, I'm eighteen, ye and Sin are pushing twenty. I assume ye didn't grow up in the lap of luxury?"

I choked. "Naw."

"None of us did either, 'cept I had a couple of years with my grandparents that weren't too bad." He swallowed but continued. "What about criminal activities? Any of those on your record?"

Fuck giving them my life story. "One or two."

Sin gave up a dark laugh. "Let me guess. Fighting?"

I held his stare, annoyed that he'd so easily labelled me. And correctly.

Scar raised a hand. "Knife crime. But accidental."

Burn waved his lighter. Arson, I figured.

Great, so I lived with a pyro.

I swung my attention back to the big man. "What

about ye? What's your sin?"

The fire flared, a blaze of sparks rising in front of his black eyes. "Murder."

"Bullshit," I coughed into my fist.

Scar shook his head, amusement plain. "Point is, none of us are angels, and we've been taken out of a shite existence to be left here. And what is this? A prison, or a place we've been sent to forget us? We're under the charge of a single woman who manages us by threat of violence and the occasional act of torture, but also the whole islands *knows*. Every last one of them. Both Sin and Burn asked for help from the villagers, explaining what was going on here, but they refused point blank. From all we can tell, we're in the centre of a conspiracy."

My stomach tightened. "Conspiracy theories are just a way for idiots to feel special." But colour me stupid, I was starting to believe it. "The keeper must know the reason."

Burn sneered. "I've asked."

"How? Politely? What if we made her?"

"I punched her in her ugly face once when I made a run for it. She shocked me with her Taser. Bitch can defend herself."

At his story, Sin palmed his face, his expression pained. I didn't want to believe him capable of caring.

"There's four of us," I said. "We can overpower her. Get into her office."

Scar's lip curved, the line down the side of his face crinkling. "Don't need to battle her to do that. I've been in her office several times, but all I've found on us is a basic file each."

"What does it contain?"

"Name, age, previous address. A photo. Then she adds

the tracker ID. Nothing more."

Which meant that she hadn't been given shite. Someone else held our fates.

I watched the base of the fire, where blue-green flames danced over the fuel. A weight held on me—the three inmates staring.

Sin's voice had me focusing on his dark eyes.

"Will anyone miss you?" he asked, low.

My insides tightened, and I gave a mocking laugh. "Just because you're a psychopath only a mother could love doesnae mean I'm the same."

His knowing glower pissed me off.

"All right. No," I snapped. "No fucker is out there wondering what happened to me."

"Same for all of us. Gotta wonder why that is," Scar said.

But that was a subject I wasn't letting any of these arseholes near. I lifted my chin. "So we can't escape. Keep is just a puppet with a hobby of violence. Ye all decided to settle down and get to work. Very fucking nice for ye. Have a great life."

"We're naw settled down," Scar cut in. He shot a glance at Sin.

The big man's attention fixed on me, black waves churning farther down the beach. "We're building our strength and gathering intelligence."

"What does that mean?"

"It means that I've naw been sitting around idly letting unknown people fuck me over. A year, I've been here. Each additional lad delivered is a new piece of the puzzle of what this is all about. Every visit from the jailor gives me more information."

"The jailor," I repeated. I'd half wondered if he was a paying customer with a violence kink, like Scar had suggested, but from the way all three sat up taller, I knew I was wrong.

"Aye," Scar took over. "Ye heard what he says to Sin. The abusive, manipulative shite he spouts and makes Sin repeat. *Worthless, useless, nothing.* What the hell is that about? Why hide us here and try to break us? Why let Sin take all the beatings and the pain—?"

Sin leapt up and paced to the edge of the pool of firelight and out across the beach.

Scar stalled in his sentence, his gaze on his leader as he walked away. He swallowed, concluding, "He's the one who has the answers."

Silence descended over us. I chewed over the details, lost in my head.

After a few minutes, Sin returned, his expression even more troubled than before. "There's someone on the beach. We need to leave."

As one, the rest of us stood, and we hit the track that led back to the hostel. Halfway there, Sin spoke into the night air.

"He's mine," he said, not looking around. "The abusive arsehole, I mean. When we get to the end of this, when they come for us and the purpose is revealed, murder, prison, whatever, I'm taking him down. I dinna care what ye think, Struan, or how much ye refuse to be one of us, this is non-negotiable, and ye will listen."

He turned, and his expression could've sliced me in two.

"That fucker's death will be mine."

13

Unknown

The pulse of a call hitting my phone woke me from a doze. Beside me, the blonde stretched in her sleep, her backside grazing my groin.

Sliding my thumb on the screen, I answered. "What is it?"

"A problem."

"Tell me."

"Theadora Stewart," the voice intoned.

My blood rushed south, and I ground against the nicely padded rear.

"What about her?"

Reaching under the sheets, I wrenched down my shorts then grasped the woman at the apex of her bare legs. Wet pussy coated my fingers.

She gasped, waking, and I clamped my palm over her mouth, silencing her with fingers covered in her juices.

"Befriend her. Isolate her. Make her yours," my caller demanded.

The blonde twisted and kissed my neck, and I pushe

her down my body to where I needed attention. I'd too easily picked up this nameless slut at a bar in the city. She hadn't objected to my rough treatment. I didn't give a fuck if she wanted round two now or not.

"Why?" I asked, steeling myself.

Stupid question. The caller went silent, empty air hanging. Blondie licked me. Pressure built in my brain.

"Sorry," I added fast.

"Just do it." They hung up.

Irritation flashed over me, and I tossed my phone then clamped a hand on the woman's head before rolling to my back and forcing her harder against me. Then I let her tongue and suction direct my fury until I came with a loud cry.

It did nothing to clear my mind.

"Get out," I told her.

The woman cursed me and grabbed her dress from the floor.

I didn't give a crap.

I had a plan to play out. And its name was Theadora.

14

Thea

Today, midway through December, marked the third month since I'd last spoken with my dad. Repeatedly, I'd tried his phone.

No answer, not even a text.

I sighed and stared out of the window at the shiny wet Edinburgh rooftops.

My days had been busy, my workload backbreaking. In a week, it would be the winter holidays, and everyone would be leaving for their family homes for Christmas.

My family home had been sold off after my parents' divorce, while I was away at boarding school. The house had been lovely, but whenever my parents were in the same room, they argued with bitter words and sarcastic comments. I'd played peacekeeper as far back as I could remember, doing everything I could to mollify them. Keep them to separate rooms. Amuse and distract them.

No amount of fancy furniture, handprinted wallpaper, and high-end design could make a happy home when the residents weren't willing.

Dad rented a flat in central London now, not far from Hyde Park. I'd called his neighbour to ask if they could look in on him for me, and the woman had said she could hear Dad inside, but he hadn't answered.

Which probably meant he was holed up with a person. Maybe a new girlfriend he hadn't wanted to tell me about. Well, that would make a fun introduction if I appeared next week.

He didn't need me. Likewise, Granny was settled in with her carers and doing good.

Maybe it would be better if I stayed here in my Edinburgh digs.

The thought crossed my mind that I could ask Mum if I could spend Christmas with her, but I disregarded it immediately. She celebrated Thanksgiving now. I hadn't been invited.

I took a shuddering breath, a truth about myself becoming apparent. I just wanted to be wanted. For one person to seek me out, to spend time with me because they liked me.

Struan had. Kind of. He'd befriended me from an empty, silent account.

I checked it daily.

My abandoned knitting project sat on my dresser, and I simultaneously wanted to finish the damn thing and shred it. A scarf would be perfect right now, the weather cold, but I'd barely had time to think so hadn't finished the final rows of knitting.

A knock came at my bedroom door. "Thea?" Jenna, my flatmate, called. "There's someone here to see you."

The door swung open before I'd even turned, and Esme stood in the frame.

After the horrible evening over a month ago with her father and brother, and the perverted McInver, I'd tried to speak to her then gave up. Henry had sent me multiple messages, but it had been easy to ignore him amid the piles of study.

Esme flicked her weight of bouncy yellow curls over one shoulder and set her hands on her hips. "What on earth is the matter with you?"

I fluttered my fingers at the neckline of my plain t-shirt. "Nothing. What do you mean?"

"Henry says you're blanking him. For heaven's sake, Thea. One old man says boo to you, and you curl up in a ball, crying."

I winced. Either her dad or her brother had told her the story, then. But obviously not all of it. "It wasn't like that. You would know if you'd come to that dinner. He grabbed me, and the things he said…"

She tutted and moved into the room, closing the door behind her. With a quick glance around, lingering on my knitting, she curled her lip in a pretty grimace. "I thought you were tougher than that. You won't get anywhere in life if some grimy old man calling you a cunt upsets you. Honey, get used to it."

"It was so much worse than that."

"Hush. This is just what they're like. All the same. To them, we are nothing but decorative items they want to fuck. Cum receptacles, if you will. Daddy would never have let him hurt you."

I dropped my gaze downwards, because her father had done nothing to help me, only holding me in place.

"Maybe you got scared. He said your heel caught on the floor so you were stuck." Esme lightly touched my upper arms, her concerned gaze seeking mine. "You see? He was only trying to help. I know it must've felt very alarming, but really, it's better you know what to expect from men so you can practice the words needed to charm your way out of it next time."

She shook me gently then perched on my bed, crossing one knee over the other, her close-fitting plaid skirt exposing perfect legs.

I worked through my memories of the night. Weeks had passed, but I hadn't been mistaken. No matter how flustered, I'd have noticed my heel.

"Which brings me onto my next question," Esme continued. "We want you to join us for Christmas in Inverness. Henry's mother will cook. There will be games. Mulled wine. We'll probably get carol singers—they always show up. It'll be fabulous."

My heart thumped. A family Christmas had long been a dream of mine. Yet I couldn't forgive Mr Charterman. Nor did I want to talk to Henry right now.

"Please say yes," she added. "It will be terribly dull without you there."

"I don't think so," I denied, warring between fear and the desire to go simply because she'd asked. "I'd like to spend some time alone with Dad."

Esme flapped a manicured hand. "Your father is too busy fucking Delia Aspen. Quite the scandal they are making in their social circle, as she's still married and her husband is a hot-shot lawyer. Have you met her?"

A piece of me withered and died. Dad was having an affair, which I'd suspected, but I had to hear about it secondhand. I wasn't even important enough for him to clue in himself.

I gave up an exhausted sigh and dropped down beside Esme on the bed. "No, I haven't. I don't want to either."

"Exactly. Christmas with us will be far more fun."

My phone buzzed in my hand, and I checked the screen, unrealistically hoping it was my father.

But it was a message from Lottie.

Esme peered over my shoulder. "Who's that?"

"My friend from Torlum."

"Oh, an islander. Probably about her plans to marry a farmer cousin and knit jumpers to keep the sheep warm." Esme took my phone and tossed the device into my pillows. "Tell you what, let me cheer you up. We'll go for drinks together, just you and me. I'll invite a couple of others along to entertain us. Aren't I good to you?"

She stood and swung open my wardrobe door. "Oh, Thea. This is hopeless. I'll take you shopping as well. But that's a problem for another day."

At any other time, I would've basked under the glow of Esme's attention. I'd always wanted this, her as a close friend. Not just the short chats we had when there was nothing else to do at family functions.

But that urge was missing now. Calmly, I turned her down, earning minutes of pleading and a final pout before she left. My roommates were having a pizza, wine, and movie night, so I stuck myself to the couch and tried to rid myself of the clinging, horrible memories.

Mid evening, I went to bed. One glass of wine had become several, and I'd let myself get a little drunk.

In the rush to distract myself earlier, I hadn't retrieved my phone, and I clumsily fished it out from under my pillow, putting together in my mind a long overdue reply to Lottie.

Except the notification had been replaced by a newer one.

A picture message waited on screen.

My breath caught in my lungs. The sender was the @ islandboy account.

I hurried to open the picture, then goggled at my screen. Struan's savagely handsome face stared back at me.

My pulse skittered.

It was him.

He'd actually made contact.

Instant heat spread from the centre of my chest, and my nipples tingled inside my lacy bra. Maybe it was the alcohol, or the simple effect this man had on me, but that same flare of sexuality I'd had with him in the cave returned tenfold.

I'd thought I'd lost it, this heady, sensual rush.

I giggled and ghosted a hand down my chest, my fingertips grazing the swell of one of my boobs, and the heel of my palm plumping the other.

"Why you?" I chatted to the picture. "Why is it only you who does this to me?"

Lying back on my bed, I held the phone above me, its light my only illumination. Then I let my hand drift lower, finding the hem of my dress. The image of Struan watched me, and I let my gaze take its fill of him.

He was healthier now. No blood or bruises. The background a beautiful and isolated beach.

His now-shorter black hair could've been artfully arranged into the tangle of strands over his forehead, but I instinctively knew he'd never spend time on his appearance. The breeze had been his stylist.

The slight lift of his chin and his concave cheeks

under prominent cheekbones gave him a confident, cocky look.

Sexy as anything.

But it was his blue eyes. His mouth. Those fascinated me.

I inched up my dress, braver for being drunk and the fact this dangerous man had sought me out. My fingertips glanced over my mound, and I uttered a hushed moan. Never in the past had I been bothered by these kinds of needs. The sort which my housemates talked about, and bought toys for, or had boyfriends or booty calls to handle. I'd never owned a vibrator, and even the idea of using one was far outside my comfort zone.

Right now, this picture was the most erotic thing I'd ever possessed.

Chasing the good feelings, I rubbed over the top of my underwear, touching myself where no one else had ever done so.

But the damp material was in my way. Emboldened by my heady state, I pushed it aside, finding my wet, slippery centre, that most private of spaces.

When I was sixteen, I'd started birth control. Though my periods were light, I'd wanted to be able to manage my cycle. I'd never actually needed the implant to stop pregnancy.

The weirdest sense came over me. The absolute knowledge that if Struan walked into this room now, I'd spread my legs for him. I'd want him inside me.

Breathing fast, I felt over myself, where I was already swollen. Plump. At a single touch of my clit, I hissed in pleasure. But that felt too much. Like I'd hurt myself or explode if I continued.

"What would you do to me?" I asked the photo. "I bet you wouldn't hesitate. You'd want to fuck me, but you'd make me come first."

Such dirty words, but like Esme said, if I didn't own them, they'd own me.

Before I could chicken out, I glided a finger straight down the centre of me.

Inside my cunt. I forced myself to mentally use the word.

This wasn't the first time I'd explored myself, but the only time I'd ever had a wealth of feelings to go with it. I drove my finger in and out, then round in a circle, pleasure radiating from the intrusion.

I panted, repeating the action, my gaze fixed on Struan.

His actions would be better than mine. He'd know exactly what would feel good.

Then I closed my eyes and inserted a second digit, my fingers becoming his thicker ones, my movements greater.

The answering throb of my body belonged to him.

"Thea?" Jenna called from outside my room. "Did you want any of the leftover pizza? Shame to waste it."

"Nope," I yelped, withdrawing my hands. In a fluster, I righted my clothes, my giggle playing out in my voice. "I'm, um, busy."

She gave a short laugh but thankfully didn't enter.

I groaned and turned my face into the pillow.

For a long moment, I just lay there, allowing my blood to cool. What had I even been doing? All that...heat over one picture. Not even a sexy shot, like the porn that too often got circulated in student chat groups.

I blew out a breath, then activated my phone's camera,

leaning to switch on my bedside lamp.

I was flushed, my cheeks pink from the activity.

Without thinking too much on it, I snapped a photo and sent it to @islandboy.

No reply came, the message delivered but not seen. But my mood had improved beyond anything. I slept better than I had in a long time.

Early the next morning, I suddenly remembered Lottie's message. But when I went into the app, it had gone.

Maybe it had been sent in error, and she'd send an update correcting it.

But by the time Friday came, I'd heard nothing more. It was the end of term now, and all my housemates were packing to leave.

Thea: Did I imagine a message from you?

Her reply was instant.

Lottie: You deleted it. I figured you didn't want to know.

I stared, then my fingers flew over the keys.

Thea: I didn't! I thought you had. What did you say?

Lottie: Your grandmother's carer left and I wondered if you'd been told.

Last time I'd called Granny's house had been a couple of weeks ago. The carer had said all was fine. If an update had gone to Dad since then, he was off having his affair, and everyone else had been forgotten.

Thea: She left? Dad's been busy so he didn't tell me, and the carer never told me. Do you know who's looking after Granny now?

Lottie: My da's cousin stepped in. She said the place was grimy.

My skin crawled.

I hadn't packed my bags like every other student in

Edinburgh, or booked a ticket to London, definitely not wanting to walk into the love-in my father was having. Nor had I given in to Esme and agreed to spend the holidays with the Chartermans, though she asked several times. Even demanded.

I couldn't let my grandmother suffer, which meant going north instead.

Thea: Can you do me a favour? Go over there and check in on her? I've finished my term and can come up to help.

Lottie: And be here for Christmas? You were once, when we were eight and nine. It was the best.

Today was the twentieth, so if I did go, I'd make a proper visit out of it and look after Granny.

I still had her key, hidden away in the pocket of my travel bag on a length of blue wool.

Thea: That's a possibility.

Lottie: Hell yes! I have something I need to talk to you about, but we can do that when you're here. I'm on my way over to your gran's now. Hold, please.

I pottered around my room, taking a cashmere V-neck sweater from my chest of drawers then added another to it. If I was going for a few days, I might need more than one change of clothes.

I snatched up my makeup bag and added it to the pile on my quilt. My knitting, too. I'd need something to do on the boat.

Then, as I had done multiple times all week, I opened the app where Struan had messaged me. My photo showed as delivered, but no reply had come back.

I didn't need to be so shy and wait for him each time. Before I could second-guess myself, I tapped out a message saying I'd be on Torlum by morning.

Lottie's reply made me jump.

Lottie: I'm here. It's not good. The place is pretty dank, and my relative says she can't handle it on her own. She tried to speak to your dad but never got a reply. Come soon.

Thea: I'll book the ferry now.

I leapt to the task, excitement rising in me amid the concern for my grandmother. Along with everything else, I might get to see Struan.

If we came face to face again, I'd tell him exactly what he did to me.

15

Struan

"What do ye miss the most about normal life?" Burn asked from his bunk.

A faint glow around the boarded-up window provided the only light in the bedroom. Soon, we'd have to get up for work, but no one was budging yet.

"Snacks," Scar answered after a moment's pause. "Junk food. Sugar."

"God," Burn drawled. "Same. I'd kill for popcorn. Chocolate-coated."

I ran a finger under Thea's hairband around my wrist—a habit since I'd relocated it from my ankle.

"The fuck?" came Sin's deeper tones. "Who puts chocolate on popcorn?"

"In one foster home I was in, the da used to have a film night every Friday. He'd make it for that. Just a drizzle of chocolate over the bowl, but it was the nicest thing ever."

Sin gave a tetchy huff, like the combination was somehow offensive.

"All right, what's yours?" Burn asked him.

"Sex," the big man answered. "All the fucking time. A sweet lass, nice tits, round, padded hips to hold onto."

"Can't relate," Burn replied, amusement in his tone.

Scar laughed with him. "Same. I'll die a virgin from being in this place."

Burn continued, "What about you, new boy?"

"Meat." I yawned. "And sex, too. Fucking, then grabbing a burger. In that order."

Sin rumbled a laugh, and I grinned in the dark. I didn't love having things in common with him, but it wasn't the worst either.

After my last escape attempt, and the conversation on the beach, I'd stopped trying to run. For now, anyway. The points the others had made, about having nowhere else to go, and it not being so bad here, were true. The question over *why* we were here had to be answered, but until then, we had food, some small degree of freedom, and were mostly left alone. The abusive arsehole hadn't returned, so we'd fallen into something of a routine.

Working, working out, bulking up.

One evening, they'd taken me surfing. Burn talked non-stop about riding waves, and the moment the weather was right, we set out onto the beach in the dark. Lit a fire. Pulled on decades-old wetsuits and took to the water.

After a couple of goes, I'd turned addict.

We hadn't got to the best buds stage, but I trusted them a little more. Eased up on my hostility. They'd even let me use the phone which had led to my act of stupidity.

I'd sent Theadora a picture of myself.

It had been a spur-of-the-moment action I now regretted. The urge to connect with her was only because I wanted to fuck that sweet innocence out of her. It would fade.

Since then, phone signal had been out.

Probably for the best. Today was my birthday, not that I'd tell these arseholes that, and I needed not to do anything stupid just because I was doubly miserable.

A thud of feet told me Burn had hopped down from his bunk—he was the only one on the top row. "So, snacks, sex, and meat. Bring it, universe. In the meantime, up, all of ye. We have work to do."

He flipped on the stark yellow light, and the rest of us groaned.

"What are ye doing?" he said.

"Swiped a pen from Keep," Scar replied.

"Is that a surfer?" Burn's tone turned interested. "Holy shite, that's amazing. Forgot ye could draw."

"Not like I get much chance."

I leaned to see what the fuss was about. In his *Boys Get Blue Too* shirt, Scar eased out of his bunk, an ink drawing on his forearm like a tattoo. In it, a surfer carved choppy waves in front of an island. With his stolen pen, he added a circle around it, and in a heartbeat, I needed it on my skin, too.

It was us. But free.

Burn gazed at it. "Can ye draw it on me?"

Scar obliged, his lines clean and the ink work identical. Without a word, Sin sat on the floor by his bunk and pulled up his t-shirt sleeve, offering Scar his bulky biceps to scrawl on.

When his was done, all three of them looked to me.

"Fuck it, not like my ink is going to be finished anytime soon," I mumbled and knelt the other side of Scar so he could brand me, nestling the motif in amongst my partial sleeve.

None of us said another word, but something settled over my skin greater than just the temporary tattoo.

Aye, universe. Whatever ye had on offer today, I wanted in.

*E*ight hours later, dark clouds rose overhead, the solid grey a backdrop to the white-sand beach.

We didn't need the rain. The rocks underfoot were already slippery as fuck. The sand sodden. The heavy skies just seemed to build and tower, menacing us as we worked.

Just like the man who stood watching us.

I straightened. "Burn," I said, low.

The younger man chucked his armful of rubbery seaweed into the large nylon bag and followed my gaze. Then scowled.

All day, we'd gathered the stinking sea trash from the beach and taken it to a croft where it would rot all winter ready to be used in the spring.

I wanted to bury the crofter underneath all this seaweed.

Let their corpse rot down along with it.

Everyone who lived here and enabled our abuse needed to die a slow and painful death.

I wanted to do the same with the man watching us, or more precisely, staring at Burn.

"Jenkins, perving again." Burn grimaced.

Jenkins, the islander who took delight in bringing me back. Fuck this guy. "Give me a reason to go over there and smack him down."

"Nah, he isn't worth the hassle, but fuck standing here while he wanks himself through his pocket. We'll finish this last bag then we're done," Burn decided.

We filled the bag, took a handle each, and hefted it between us.

Jenkins moved towards us. His dirty gaze took us in. "You're at my place tomorrow."

I give a single shake of my head. "Not happening."

"I need a trench dug. Ye owe me."

I dropped the bag. "We worked a free week for ye. Nobody owes anything."

But he wasn't paying attention to me. Instead, his gaze slipped over Burn's body.

The younger man scowled. "Dinna look at me like that."

Jenkins flared his nostrils. "Want to make some extra money?"

I snarled and stepped in front of Burn. All the hard work and exercises Sin had us do had built my muscle back up. I was dying to use it on this guy.

The dirty bastard peered around me. "How old are ye? I won't hurt ye. Unless you want me to."

I went to speak, to tell this pervert exactly where he could go, but Burn's arm landed around my shoulder.

He leaned on me but lifted his chin to Jenkins. "Tell me what ye like."

The older man grinned, showing stained teeth. "What, ye want a list?"

At Burn's waiting, his smile died, and fever burned in

his eyes. "First, fight me. Get me going. Then, when you're facedown on the mattress, I'll tie ye up, arms to ankles, so ye cannae move. Can ye whimper? I like that."

Disgust drove bile up my throat. But Burn's grip on my shoulder told me he had this.

"Make the whimpering sound," he said to Jenkins. "So I know exactly how to do it."

Jenkins took a half step forward, his mouth open and his expression rapt. Then the fucking arsehole uttered a mewling sound like a hurt animal.

I gagged, but Burn's expression morphed from interest to hate. He advanced on Jenkins until they were toe to toe, and I moved, too, keeping right at his shoulder.

"What a pretty sound," Burn said, deathly calm. "It's the one I expect to hear when I burn your fucking house down with ye in your bed."

"Ye can't... How dare ye threaten me."

"Easily, ye twisted sack of shite. I've done it before and I'm happy to give ye a demonstration." He slipped his Zippo lighter from his pocket and flicked the wheel.

From my months of living here, I knew he only kept fuel in it when we went to the beach at night. Presumably to stop Keep from having a problem with it. Otherwise, he wielded it like a nervous habit.

Burn inched towards Jenkins, that *flick, flick, flick* continuing. The dirty bastard's gaze glued to his hand.

"Ask yourself why I'm here." Burn continued his intimidation tactic. "I'm just a kid. Harmless. Why would I burn anyone alive? Why would the police accuse me of hunting down dirty old men and scorching them until their flesh crumbled?"

Jenkins stumbled and fell on his arse. Picking himself

up, he formed an ugly slash with his mouth. "You've made a mistake. Ye cannae get away with threatening me. On this island, I have the power. I'll talk to your keeper. If ye think your life is hard, see how bad I can make it."

He stormed away.

Burn tilted his head and watched him leave. "Did I go too far? Actually, I don't give a shite. I hate the way he looks at me."

I raised one eyebrow. "Is any of what ye said true?"

"Why, are ye scared?"

He picked up the handle of the nylon sack again, and I took up the other side, and we set off across the moor.

"No," I told him after a moment's pause.

It was true. I might be stuck with these men, and forced to share my space with them, but my fear of being murdered by one of these arseholes had reduced to almost nothing.

"Good." Burn lifted his chin. "I'm wanted. Like, for real. If I go back to the mainland, I'll be thrown into jail."

I blinked at him, at this energetic seventeen-year-old who had been kinder to me than I deserved. "What for?"

"Arson, obviously. It's one of the reasons Sin hasn't made a plan to run." He shut his mouth with an audible snap. "Anyway, if Jenkins wants to try me, I'm ready to take him on. Fuck knows I've had the practice."

After the drop off, we set our tracks for home, but Burn had gone quiet.

It took a while for him to speak again. "Why do people go like that? Like Jenkins. At some point, they step over the line of being a normal human and think they have a right to hurt others."

I shrugged. "I've seen way too many evil dickheads in

my time to think it's not normal for some. The men who used to come to Ma—"

It was my turn to shut the fuck up. Horror filled me at the words I'd been about to share. I didn't want to think about that, but the images crowded in all the same. The fear of who was behind the door. What they'd do to my mother. It was in the past, because she'd changed how she'd worked after a time. When I was older, she'd leave me with her friends.

The fear shifted to whether she'd come back.

The sense of abandonment had never eased.

Burn let me lapse into silence while I tried to force away the darkness.

Back at the hostel, the rich scent of cooking filled the bunk room. Instantly, my mouth watered. I leapt on the distraction. "Is that meat?"

Scar straightened from where he hovered over my bunk. "Sin got lucky with his island contact. She smuggled in some goodies."

"She?" But my words dried up.

On my bed, an item waited.

"What's that?" I asked.

Sin appeared in the doorway, resting one bulky shoulder on the frame. Scar and Burn watched me, identical grins on their faces.

"It's your birthday. It's naw a happy one, but we wanted to mark it," Scar said. "We have burgers on the grill. The meat ye wanted. Vegetable fries we'll pretend are normal ones. Ketchup sachets, too."

"And a fucking gift," Sin concluded. "Pick it up. I need to get back to the food."

I broke through my dumbfounded state to grab the

wee packet. I couldn't look at the three of them. They knew the day. They'd planned this. Between us, we had so little. The clothes on our backs plus a few spares. Three books on the shelf. No TV. No games. No warm blankets or comforts of any kind. The phone we had to keep hidden which barely connected to the Internet half the time.

Even the money we earned only went on essentials. Razors. Soap we'd used to wash ourselves and our clothes.

I stared at the plastic LED light they'd bought me.

"It's not much, but you're one of us now," Scar said with a grin.

My mind was blown.

The few times we'd been out surfing, all of us in our ratty, holed wetsuits, cut to go over the trackers, I'd envied them their fucking flashing lights. Each a neon marker in the dark, used so they could see each other. Sin's was green, Scar's purple, Burn's orange. It made them a tribe. I'd been on the outside, and this gesture...

"Yours is blue," Sin informed me.

I clicked it on, and neon-blue light blinked.

A grin pulled at my lips, but I kept my focus on the LED. "Thanks," I told the three.

They murmured their replies, and the moment was over.

Except I still reeled.

Burn sidled up. "A notification came up for ye on the phone. A private message, I assume for ye. I didn't look."

He handed over the phone, and I opened the @island-boy account.

A picture of Theadora waited.

A second message showed as pending but wouldn't load.

But that was fine because this was everything.

Flushed pink cheeks, her mouth slightly open, a curl of dark hair resting on her cheek.

Fuck. My blood rushed to my dick, and I stifled a laugh. I had no way of seeing her, none at all, but Christ did I want her.

This was up there with the best birthday ever.

A clattering and raised voices came from the kitchen, then Sin emerged back into the bunk room. With his eyebrows forming two dark slashes, he swore under his breath and crossed the room to stand near the boarded-up window.

Keeper followed him in. Her beady-eyed gaze skipped over us all. At the first sound, I'd tossed the phone across my bed so it slid down the gap against the wall, dropping the LED after it.

"Contraband check. Don't any of you move a muscle," the woman said far too happily. In her hand, her Taser crackled.

Over the months, I'd got a clearer picture of Keep's role here. On the occasions any of the islanders came to the hostel, she answered the door and got rid of them fast. One day a fortnight, she'd lock us in our bedroom for the whole day, no food, while she went out. Presumably taking the boat off the island for shopping as our storeroom would be restocked soon after.

If Sin went to speak to her, it was in private. The rest of us, she ignored.

Never once had she searched our room.

"Bathroom," she commanded.

The four of us exchanged glances but filtered into the shower room. Keep took the door handle but, at the last second, snatched my upper arm in her grip.

"Stop right there."

I gritted my jaw. I could hurt her easily. She might jab at me with that Taser, but I'd be faster. One punch and she'd be on the floor.

I'd never hit a woman before, but in her case, I'd make the exception.

Keep squinted, peering into my eyes. "Don't think I don't know about your past. About what you did. I know it all."

She didn't know shite about me. I'd bet her files were mostly empty. But I didn't want her to take my things. The gifts were the start of a bond between me and the others here. I didn't want to lose them.

But the phone... In a heartbeat, I felt the pull to the single connection I had on the planet. To Theadora. Who still wanted to see me.

"Ruin," Keep breathed. "There, that's your name."

Sin stepped up and placed his hand on my chest, propelling me deeper into the room. Keep scowled at him but locked us in.

Noises came of her ransacking our room.

"Ruin," Scar muttered.

Ruin.

Fuck that name and her shite. I set my voice low. "Whatever she finds, I'll say is mine. That it's my birth—"

All three gave the same sharp exclamation; a slice of hands through the air and eyes wide, the message clear for me to shut up.

Scar got in my face, bringing my ear to his mouth so I could hear his barely there whisper. "This is my fault for the pen. Whatever ye do, don't tell her your date of birth.

She cannae know."

"Why?" I mouthed back. "She already does. It's on my paperwork. That's the reason she's in here searching, I bet."

But he shook his head, adamant, his expression growing fiercer. "No, age not date of birth. Trust me. She cannae know."

What the hell was this?

A warning played in my mind. I focused on one man then the next. All stared with the same intensity.

They all knew something. Shared a secret.

I was the one in the dark, and they were trying to keep me that way.

No amount of time or presents could change that.

"Whatever," I spat and kicked off the wall to stand the other side of the bathroom.

Half an hour later, my worst fears were confirmed. Our meal had been destroyed. Everything had gone. The phone, the books, the damn light.

Every last item.

16

Thea

Slamming the washing machine door, I pressed the power button, Granny's bedsheets changed, the kitchen cleared, and the house a lot cleaner. Lottie had worked beside me, her relative taking a much-needed break.

The paid carer had never returned.

My grandmother had slept solidly since my arrival this morning. I couldn't tell how she was, though her small frame appeared even more frail than before. I'd chatted to her, just so she heard my voice, relating stories from when I was little. How the islanders always said I looked a lot like her, whenever we came here. Same hair, eyes, and kind ways. I hoped I could live up to that claim. I'd pottered around her room as I spoke, trying to find a locked box of any kind, but found nothing.

If Granny had a secret for me, I couldn't work it out.

"What was it you wanted to tell me?" I asked Lottie.

In her message telling me to come, she'd hinted at news.

Lottie slid a glance to the open back door where her cousin, Annis, perched on the steps, a cup of tea in one hand while she talked on the phone.

"Upstairs," my friend whispered.

Together, we found our way to my bedroom, and I closed us in.

Lottie kept her voice low, though we had to be out of earshot. "I've met them."

"Who?"

"The boys from the hostel. The criminals." Red flooded her pale cheeks. "No one can know. Dad would disown me. But I like them. One of them anyway."

Irrational jealousy rose in a heated wave. I suppressed it and tried to rationalise my feelings. I hadn't been here. Struan wasn't mine. Two short conversations and a picture exchange meant nothing.

"Which one?" I said as casually as I could.

"Sinclair. I don't think he likes me, but he is so hot. Always grumpy. Short with his words. But once, he smiled at me." She dropped back onto the bed, clutching her chest. "That's my love language. The tiny scrap of affection amid total disregard. We are basically married now."

I giggled in relief and at her dramatics. "Does he know?"

Lottie's eyes rounded. "Hell no. That would be humiliating. You should see him, though. He's huge, with these thick arms I keep picturing holding me. He's always glowering in my imagination, too, but he's so hot. Like if Henry Cavill and Robert Pattison had a lovechild. He gives me the shivers."

I sat and nudged her with my shoulder. "What did you do to meet him? Rock up to the hostel and ask if they wanted to come out to play?"

"I happened to be walking along the beach one night when they went surfing. Sin was really cagey, but I swore I wouldn't tell anyone. I bet they wouldn't mind ye knowing. Anyway, I offered to help them get things if they needed supplies and I've done that a couple of times now."

I toyed with the edge of the knitted quilt. "Did you see Struan?"

"I have but never spoken to him. They are a really tight pack, ye know? Always looking out for each other, and I know this is going to sound weird, but they are so free."

I couldn't help spluttering a laugh. "They're prisoners."

"I know. But Sin goes to the mainland sometimes. He talked to me about it because he needed help with the boat. The ferry wouldn't let him on, so he borrows ours. But that's risky if he's caught, so more often than not, he waits to see me and I help him out."

Struan hadn't answered my message about coming to the island. But he had sent that picture, and I was trying to take what I wanted rather than wait for it to come to me.

I cleared my throat. "When will you see them next?"

Lottie hopped up and rubbed her hands together. "I knew it, ye want to come along. We'll go tonight. I have all the cover I need with ye being here, and it's meant to be a mild evening, so they'll be out."

Annis' voice hailed us, breaking our moment of privacy. But that was fine by me. I jogged back downstairs with new purpose. Tonight, one way or another, I'd see the man who haunted my dreams.

At midnight, Lottie and I snuck down the concrete

steps at the back of the house and fled into the dark. She was supposed to be sleeping over with me, and Annis had a bed downstairs so she could be there for my grandmother.

Both slept soundly—we'd checked before we dared go out.

Just like back in September, my late-night flit filled me with excitement. The two of us danced along the road then took a shortcut to keep from being spotted. It was no one else's business what I did, but Lottie would be in trouble if her father knew who she was hanging around with.

She'd stolen food for them, too, bringing with her a selection of snacks, stating that they never had anything like that so would be hyped up for it.

Happiness surged and crested within me. I didn't want to be the meek thing anymore. I didn't want to be safe and boring.

We neared the beach where Lottie had hung out with them, and trepidation built with each step. I was strung as tight as a violin string, every inch of me alive and alert for the moment.

We crested the rise to look out on the expanse of sand.

Figures moved in the water, slicing over the waves on white surfboards.

Neon lights flashed faintly on three of the men, piercing the night and marking their paths, but one was dark.

Lottie took in a fast breath, and my heart hammered.

She grabbed my fingers, and we ran down the sand dune. At the water's edge, we stopped.

"Hey," Lottie called. "We come bearing gifts."

All four men stalled, and their gazes fixed on us.

I shivered, huddling deep inside the fluffy hood of my

parka.

He could ignore me and continue surfing. I hadn't realised it, but too much rode on this moment. Somewhere in the deep recesses of my mind, Struan had become a symbol of the change I was trying to put in place. The punky attitude he wore like armour, the things he did to express himself, like fighting his jailors and throwing himself out of the window, I wanted to be like him.

I wanted him.

I'd always been such a mousy thing. Never once had I screamed at my parents to stop hurting each other, to love me and not use me as a pawn in their power struggles. And more recently, I'd just stood there while a perverted old man talked about me, grabbed me, and I did nothing but run away and cry.

In a heartbeat, I got what Lottie meant. These men were prisoners, but they were true to themselves. And in that was a kind of freedom, though I doubted they'd agree.

We got to within twenty feet, and the dry sand shifted to damp gravel under my boots. I was close enough to recognise Struan from the pack.

He was the one with no neon blinker, only moonlight over his distinctive features clueing me in.

"Lottie," one of the other men said, his deep voice carried by the waves.

But my attention was all for Struan. And his for me.

He peered into the darkness, paddling to keep his board steady. "Theadora?"

"Struan," I answered.

It was like a gun had fired, releasing him from his hold. He dropped chest down on the surfboard and churned the water, riding a swell to come directly to me.

Likewise, the other men made their way in until all four reached the shallows, the surfboards dragging on the gravel.

In a dark wetsuit too short for his frame, Struan tossed his board to the sand then loomed over me. I staggered half a step, totally overwhelmed.

Some kind of emotion played with his features. "Ye came back."

"Told you I would." Nerves rattled me.

He opened and closed his mouth, as if my act of returning meant something to him.

"I thought about you," I continued. "I talked to my professor to ask if there was any legit way that you could be kept here. There isn't, by the way. Then when you sent me your picture, I was so relieved that you were outside. I'd pictured you…"

"In a cage?"

"Perhaps."

I skimmed a fast look over him.

Despite this being the mildest December I could recall, he should be shivering. The wetsuit had been cut at the wrists and ankles to accommodate his size. The muscles that had only got bigger.

Then I spotted something that stalled my words.

Around his wrist was a leather bracelet.

My hairband, given to him in the cave.

His gaze tracked mine. "Is it a surprise to find me out here enjoying myself?"

"There aren't many options for fun on Torlum."

"How do ye know I dinna have a line of lasses waiting to entertain me?"

My laugh came as a surprise, driving away some of

my shock, and I arched an eyebrow. "There are ten people under the age of thirty on this island, and most of them are little kids. Lottie is the only datable woman, and she's my friend." I pushed it further, extending a trembling finger to press a featherlight touch to the band on his wrist. "Besides, you like me."

Despite the evidence, the token of mine he'd kept, my words were hollow. Pretending at what I wished I could be sure about. But my confidence had to be faked until it could be self-made.

Challenge flared in Struan's eyes.

I expected more questions, but he gripped my jacket at the lapels and held me still. My heart raced.

He stared for a long moment, his gaze flitting over my features, then he muttered a soft 'fuck' and crashed his lips on mine.

Holy heck.

Instantly, I kissed him back, driving my fingers into his wet hair.

I had zero experience, but the moment his lips touched mine, instinct drove me on.

Struan took hold of my face, his fingertips tightening on my jaw to the point it almost hurt. I didn't care. This was everything I'd hoped for. More than I'd dreamed about because it was real.

He moved with fierce possession, coaxing a flood of sensuality out of me. Then he licked at the seam of my mouth, and I opened for him. His tongue stroked over mine, entering my body like he owned it.

He tasted of something dark and delicious. Chemicals and carnal man. Seawater and shock. Utter lust took over me, and I was so far in over my head, I should be drowning.

The snicker of a laugh played out in the background, but I could do nothing but hold on for dear life.

There was an edge to the kiss, a hint of something dangerous, savage. His grip, his teeth, his complete ownership of the moment.

It only made me want him more.

Then Struan broke our lips apart and rested his forehead on mine, saltwater droplets kissing my skin. "I've wanted to do that ever since the cave. No, before. The ferry. From now on, I willnae hesitate, so don't expect an apology."

A thrill ran over me. "I don't need an apology. I want you to do it again."

His gaze bored into mine.

"Hey, Ruin, we have food," one of the men called.

"Ruin?" I repeated.

"My name now. Because I ruin good things. Ye should take note."

He could break me. The intensity of his focus alone weighed me down. I didn't doubt his words. But I was only drawn in closer. The ache in my body could only be eased by him.

"I'm not going anywhere," I vowed. "I'm here alone, staying at my grandmother's. My dad's gone AWOL, so I'll be here for Christmas."

"Fuck Christmas." He released his fierce grip on me, and the ghost of a smile flirted with his lips.

A cold breeze swept down on the beach, and I shivered more for the dampness on me and the loss of his close heat. Lottie and the three men had made their way up the beach. A fire glowed in a hidden nook.

"You should get dressed and sit by that fire so you don't freeze," I told Struan.

He stared for a moment, that little smirk dying. "Always so caring." Then he turned on his bare heel, snatched up the surfboard, and strode over to the group. I scurried to keep up.

In the light of the fire, the other men had already stripped their wetsuits and were mostly dressed, stuffing their faces with the snacks Lottie had brought.

None of them called us out on our public display, but plenty of amused glances came my way. I dropped onto a rocky seat next to Lottie, strung out, no doubt red-faced, and still magnetically focused on Struan. Even when he moved a few feet away to undress, baring his whole body before he pulled his clothes on, I didn't look away.

It was fleeting, my glimpse at his long limbs, dusted with dark hair, his tight backside, then up to his muscular back and half-tattooed arms. But the sight only reinforced my decisions.

I didn't want to be the good girl anymore.

One taste of the bad boy and there was no going back.

17

Struan

Across the fire, I watched Thea, as her friend called her, dark thoughts swarming inside me. The others talked about surfing, Burn going on about breaks and peaks. The second lass had brought food, filling in a gap in my mind about who on the island was helping Sin. But my attention remained fixed on Thea.

She'd come back.

She wanted me.

A decision slammed into my mind, irrevocable and solid.

Mine.

It made no sense, I barely knew her, but those small kindnesses she'd shown on the boat, in the cave, then tonight, coming here and telling me she'd been thinking about me...

It was a lonely life here, cut off from a place I'd barely fit into before. I had no family left, no friends, and Thea's appearance was a gift. Water in a desert for a dying man.

Aye, mine.

The conversation had moved on to the flashing lights the others carried.

Thea peered at me in my position at the edge of the group, still standing and unable to settle. "Why don't you have one?"

"He did," Burn announced. "It was his birthday present, for about ten seconds. Our keeper found it and confiscated it into her office. The rest were hidden with our surfboards, so it was the worst timing."

"Along with every other good thing we had. Food, books, our phone," Scar complained. "My fault. I riled her."

Thea's gaze skipped between them then came back to me. "Your birthday gift? When was that?"

"Yesterday," I muttered.

Her bright gaze held mine. "We should get it back."

I huffed a laugh. "Up for some breaking and entering?"

Her eyes flared in challenge. "It isn't right that she has your property. It isn't right that you're here at all, but taking the things that make it bearable is a new level of wrong."

Scar and Burn leaned in, coming alive at the suggestion.

"Ye could create a distraction while we sneak in," Scar suggested.

"Yeah, chat with her. Delay her at the door," Burn added.

Sin gave a single shake of his head that stopped the chatter. "We've worked hard to keep things even with her. What do ye think she'll do if she discovers we've done that? It'll mean some new punishment."

Fuck him. I was still pissed off that he continued to

leave me out of his secrets. I'd spent far less time with Theadora but trusted that she told me the truth. "Nah. We're doing this thing. We need that phone back. I want my damn light. Keep might not even notice."

Besides that, I'd wanted to get into her office for a while now. Who knew what secrets she hid in there. What contacts she had. Knowledge like who had sold us into this.

Who'd paid off the people around us.

Who owned this fucking island.

Sin might have his plan to wait it out, but my rising energy demanded action.

"Tomorrow morning," I decided. "We'll do exactly what ye just described. Distract her, burgle our property back, and not lie down and let her walk all over us. If she wants to make a second grab at it all, she can try."

We whooped it up and agreed on the plan, though Sin only sat back and glowered.

The fire had burned to embers, and Theadora wrapped her arms around herself, shivering.

"Get up," I ordered her.

She blinked but stood obediently and came to me.

I made an *up* motion to everyone else. "The lasses are cold. We should walk them home."

Mumbles of agreement followed, and we kicked out the fire with sand then left the beach.

Theadora stuck close to my side, leading the way. We walked in silence, taking a path through the moor to avoid the village, the rest of the group following and talking about the plan for the morning.

Finally, we reached the garden wall of a large house. I hadn't known which place was her grandmother's, but it made sense that it was the fanciest house on the island. Everything about the lass screamed money. Her clothes, her voice, the easy way she accepted or challenged facts. Like the world and all the arseholes in it could be reasoned with.

At the kitchen steps, her friend uttered a quiet good-night and slipped into the building, sparing a lingering look at Sin.

The others retreated, leaving us alone.

"You know where I'm staying now," Thea said, hushed. "I'll be here for a few days. We'll see each other tomorrow."

That wasn't enough. Like I'd done before, I took a handful of her jacket and pulled her against me, smirking at her sharp exhale.

Then I took her pretty mouth in a hard kiss.

She melted onto me, opening her lips.

A rush of raging lust broke over me, and I backed her to the wall. Thea gave up control, instantly compliant, moving with me.

This, *fuck,* I needed it.

Our kiss turned dirty, and I pushed my thigh between her legs, fucking her mouth with my tongue. She fisted my shirt, following my lead.

I ground my hard dick against her, the ridges of our clothes creating friction.

It wasn't enough. I wanted to peel off her layers and expose her body to me, take handfuls of her tits and suck her nipples until she begged for more. Then I'd lick her pussy until I knew nothing but her taste.

I'd fuck her until we both hurt, but neither wanted to stop.

A warning played out in my mind, stalling me.

I was accelerating from nothing to everything, and trusting Thea could end me. I shouldn't. I shouldn't trust anyone.

I broke the kiss and stared down at her. "Why are ye here? I mean, why come looking for me? Why think about me?"

She gazed back and swallowed. "I haven't been able to stop thinking about you. I don't just mean the fact you were kidnapped and brought here, I mean for you. I don't understand it."

I didn't either, but it was exactly what I'd experienced.

She continued, still gripping on to me like her life depended on it. "The first time I saw you was shocking, with the blood and handcuffs, like you were a wild animal. Then in the cave—"

"I behaved like one." I'd reared over her and made demands.

Thea smiled, and it was like the fucking sun had come out in the middle of the night. "I liked it."

My whole body warmed.

"I liked helping you," she added. "But I'd be lying if I said that was all. There was this draw, too."

"Is it still there?"

She ducked her head, and if we had light, I knew her cheeks would be red.

"Yes. Worse."

"Ye want me." I forced her chin up so I could see her eyes once more. "I turn ye on. Don't sweat about it, ye do exactly the same to me, sweetheart. Every time I'm near ye."

I grabbed her hand and drew it down our bodies

to my dick. Her hand froze then, after a beat, her fingers curled around the bulge in my jeans.

"I haven't done this before," she confided, stroking me. "Our kiss was my first, too."

I groaned and notched my head against her shoulder. Then I snatched both her hands and pinned them behind her back so she couldn't torture me more. My pulse raced.

"Never known anything like this," I gritted out. "So listen up. I don't know what it is either, or why it's so strong, but I need ye to promise me something."

"Anything."

"That you're real. Everything you've told me. No lies."

Thea jutted out her chin. "I'm not a liar. All the details I told you about my life are true. I'm nineteen, a student, my mum left me for the States, and now my dad has abandoned me, too. I need to look after my grandmother, but I was more excited to come here because of you. I never had any real attraction to a boy, but..."

"Ye lie awake picturing me. Ye think about my body when you're alone. Ye dream about fucking me, losing that virginity of yours on my dick."

"Yes," she whispered.

With every word, I was rapidly becoming obsessed. I'd known nothing but this place for months, and Thea was my lifeline. A bridge to the other world.

"I wanted to call ye last time I ran," I confessed, my damn heart not slowing. "I had nowhere to go, and I made that account instead of just fucking speaking to ye. I didn't know what you'd say to me."

"You ran? How?"

Then she hadn't even been told about the boat I stole. It had been in the back of my mind that I could be charged with theft, but nothing had come of it.

I kissed her neck. "Doesn't matter. I got caught and brought back."

Thea hugged me. Goddamned put her arms around me and held me to her. I hadn't been hugged in forever.

"I would've taken you in. Hidden you. Struan, come inside the house with me."

Christ. The only thing that mattered now was the single word I had to say next.

The fact she needed to get used to.

"Mine," I said against her cheek, baring my teeth and running them down the column of her neck.

I bit her softly and took a deep inhale, fucking loving her shudder of need.

Then I pushed off the wall and walked away before I entirely lost control.

The others had made it to the back door of the hostel when I caught up with them. Sin turned to spot me and grunted his disapproval.

"How do ye know that lass?"

"From around."

Scar coughed out a laugh into his fist. "Looked more than that to me."

Our self-appointed leader dug his eyebrows deeper. "All right, then how well do ye know her?"

"Well enough."

If that only pissed him off more, I didn't care. My business, not his.

And I was still off my head on the fucking hug Thea delivered. Her offer.

I shot a glance at him. "Seems to me ye have something going on with her friend, so if ye have a problem with it, check closer to home first."

Sin gave an exasperated sigh, keeping his voice low. "If ye think I'm fucking the lass, guess again. I've done my homework. I know exactly who she is."

"And who's that?"

"She calls herself Lottie, but she's Violet Hunter, only daughter of Forbes Hunter, one of the men who brought me kicking and screaming to this place. What do ye think will happen if I mess with her? And what is her motivation, revenge against her old man for something? Don't act stupid, Struan. What lass would look at us and see anything other than bad-boy dick, good enough for one night only? Answer me why the girl from the wealthiest family here is set on ye?"

I ground my teeth together. "Ye have no idea. That house is her grandmother's. She only comes to visit. She isn't part of this world."

"Or she's trying to get close to you for some other reason."

"Thea's not a spy. She's mine." Done with him, I pushed past into the hostel, silently throwing myself in my bunk.

Sin and the others entered the room a minute after, and I felt his gaze on me, judging and disapproving.

I turned to the wall and focused on my one salvation—Thea's perfect kiss. Her first.

Sin's warning was based on his own messed-up situation.

I'd asked Thea and believed her answer, so why the hell had I walked away from her? For her sake, or mine?

It had been a big mistake. One that needed fixing.

18

Thea

In the dark room, I lay awake, my body alive with feeling. One kiss, and everything had changed. A second and I'd been feeling things that I'd only read about in romance books. I drifted my hands under the thick duvet, wriggling down on the bed. Lottie slept in the room next door, so I had to be quiet. No problem when I barely knew what I was doing.

I inched my fingers under my thin cami top then grazed over the swell of my breasts, caressing my already hard nipples. Pleasure zapped through me, echoing at the juncture of my thighs. A short gasp left me, and I pressed my lips together, forcing myself to be silent. Maybe I just had to be quicker about this so I could ease the ache.

Before, when I'd tried this, I'd imagined Struan's touch. I did the same now, picturing his hot mouth sucking on me. Kissing my belly, moving lower.

I traced a path down my middle until I found the waistband of my sleep shorts. Then I dipped under, straight into the centre of my soaking wet core. Closing my eyes, I caressed myself, my mouth open as my breathing came harder.

If only Struan was here, he'd take over and make me feel good. He'd know exactly what to do. He'd own my body, and I'd love it.

A tap sounded at my window.

I froze, alert and listening. Another tap sounded, something hitting the glass. Leaping up from my bed, I crossed to the window and peered out into the dark. A figure waited below. In the faintest starlight, I made out Struan's features.

He'd come back. Oh God.

Without hesitation, I left my room and silently padded downstairs to open the back door. There, I came face to face with the man I'd seconds ago been fantasising about. Just like I'd summoned him.

For a beat, both of us watched the other. Then his gaze sank, and he took slow perusal of my body. I shivered in the chilly night air but didn't move to cover myself. In my tiny shorts and cami, nothing of my form was left to the imagination. My nipples poked through the material, every swell and curve on display for him.

Struan's lips twisted into a smirk. He climbed the step and drove me into the house, crowding my body with his. His lips landed on mine, and he backed me to the wall, swinging the door closed behind us.

In the dark hallway, he kissed me in a desperate move, and I opened to taste him, entirely gone for this moment. He'd come back for me. Just like he'd said on the beach that I came back to him.

Without letting up at my lips, Struan gripped my shoulders then ran his hands down to my elbows and onto my wrists. He forced them behind my back, securing them in one hand so I was restrained, my breasts pushed forward.

His breathing came hard, and he inched back to peer into my eyes. "There's other people here, aye?"

I nodded fast.

"Tell me where we can go."

I gestured to the stairs with my head, and Struan drew me in front of him. We started climbing, my hands still pinned behind me as if I was his prisoner.

No sound had come from downstairs, where Granny and her carer slept, and faint breathing came from Lottie's room. I needed them all to stay asleep.

In my bedroom, he closed the door and positioned me in front of it, leaving me there. Then he crossed to sit on my bed, his legs wide. Holding my gaze, he stripped his boots then his hoodie, tossing it to the floor.

I stared, my chest rising and falling. My dreams were a poor comparison to the electricity in the air, the anticipation of this. How badly I wanted him. If I'd been turned on before, now, I burned.

Bathed in moonlight, Struan rested back on his arms, his gaze never leaving me. "Take off your shirt."

I shuddered and grabbed the hem of my cami, pulling it over my head then casting it aside. The cool air licked my skin, pebbling my nipples even harder, and I closed my eyes against the onslaught of feeling. How exposed I was. No man had ever seen me like this.

Struan's pure focus on me lit me up.

"Theadora, eyes on me." His ghost of a smile reappeared the moment my gaze was back on him. "Ye want this, aye?"

My breathing sped up. "Yes. I need you to tell me what to do," I stuttered.

"On your knees," he replied, low.

Instantly, I obeyed, kneeling on the wooden floor-boards, clasping my hands once more at the small of my back.

"Crawl to me."

My brain fritzed out. On all fours, I crawled to the rug, my breasts swinging. I'd always been an obedient girl, but I had no idea how that would work for me in the bedroom. That every simple command would send a fresh wave of lust through me. Somehow, Struan knew it. Used it with me. Maybe he needed this, too, the feeling of being in control, or maybe he just read me like a book. I didn't care. I only wanted to obey him.

I reached him and rose to place both hands on his jean-clad thighs.

"Good girl," he said, his voice strained.

That praise...

An onslaught of desire rushed in my blood.

"Say that again," I demanded.

On a fast inhale, Struan bracketed my ribs with his fingers and picked me up as if I weighed nothing. He turned me and deposited me on his lap so my back was to his front, his body hot, his dick hard under me. Then he splayed a hand on the centre of my chest, holding me to him.

"Good. Girl."

Across the room, a heavy Victorian mirror angled towards us, reflecting our silvered image. I gaped at it, not recognising myself. With my dark curls loose and spilling over one shoulder, and only a tiny pair of shorts covering me, I looked like a goddess.

Behind me, Struan's larger body framed mine. I arched my spine and ground on him, pure instinct driving me.

A porno played out in the mirror, and I couldn't tear my attention away.

Struan pressed a kiss to my bare shoulder, his gaze locked on where mine was. He caressed my waist then took two handfuls of my breasts, squeezing and shaping me. I moaned softly, sweat breaking out on my brow. With his fingers and thumbs, Struan rolled my nipples, coaxing another almost silent gasp out of me. His lips wandered up my neck, and he bit on my earlobe.

I dropped my head back on his shoulder, my eyes shuttering closed.

He could do anything to me right now and I'd allow it. Encourage it. Demand it.

But his movements ceased. "Keep watching."

I gazed at him, and Struan grabbed my chin and forced my face forwards again.

A nervous laugh left me, and he tutted in my ear.

"Look away, and I'll stop. I need ye to see everything I do to ye."

Under me, his powerful thigh muscles tightened. On the beach, I'd seen him naked, but somehow this, with me mostly naked and him fully clothed, was infinitely more erotic.

His grip left my face and travelled to my closed legs, then Struan reached to take hold of my knee. He tapped twice with his forefinger. "Open. I want to see how wet ye are for me."

Forcing myself to stare, I opened my legs, baring my

white shorts. A wet mark stained where they covered my core.

Struan breathed harder, and his fingers trailed up the inside of my thigh, lighting a fire in their path. "Tell me what ye need, Theadora."

"All of this. Anything you want to do." My words came out breathy. Desperate.

"Ye want me to make ye come with my hands while ye watch, or fuck ye?" At my hesitation, he pressed his teeth to my neck. "Don't tempt me. I'm a desperate man. I'll take your virginity here and now. I willnae be gentle."

Still, I couldn't answer him. I needed his touch, and to push this as far as it could go, but it was my first time doing anything. I had no knowledge beyond what I'd read. It scared me. He did, too, if I was honest with myself.

Struan growled and gripped the hem of my tiny shorts with both hands. Then he wrenched the material, tearing them in half and exposing me completely.

The shredded shorts fell away, and he palmed my centre, the heel of his hand directly over my clit and his fingertips sinking into my wet heat. His other hand grasped my thigh hard.

Trembling, I pressed my lips together to stop from crying out. If I looked away, he'd end this, so I glued my focus to where he touched me. To where his fingers shone with my moisture.

Struan moved his hand, driving spikes of pleasure through me.

"So wet for me. So fucking sweet. Tell me ye need this," he demanded.

"I...I..." I stammered.

Words failed me, so I rocked my hips instead, impaling myself more on his fingertips. He brought one arm around me and held my throat, pinning me to him.

Then, with his other hand, he forced a finger deep inside me. I gave up a squeak and twisted to find his lips. Struan allowed it, kissing me for a second as he added a second finger, then pushing my face with his so we both could watch his actions. Gliding his fingers in and out of me, he ground the heel of his hand against my clit in circles, his rhythm faultless.

I lost myself in the sensation. This was beyond what I'd done to myself, igniting a fire I didn't know possible. From the first sight of him, he'd drawn out feelings in me, now he was dealing them out on my flesh.

Faster he worked me, his hips bucking under me. I pressed back into him, spikes of pleasure emanating to every inch of my flesh.

A coil of tight heat wound, starting at a point inside me and boosted by each grind on my clit. I hitched a breath, and Struan doubled down on the action, hitting the same spot, learning me in a way I never had. Clamped to him, I could only watch and feel.

His mastery of my pleasure. His fingers and touch too perfect.

What would it be like to have him at my mercy like this? He'd need to tell me what to do, but I wanted to make it good for him, too. For him to feel everything I was feeling.

Gliding harder into me, Struan upped the pressure at exactly the right second.

Fire shot through me.

Around his fingers, I pulsed, pleasure exploding. It shocked me, and I cried out, forgetting myself. Struan dropped his grip on my throat to palm my cheek, swallowing my sounds with his kiss. He didn't stop, keeping my orgasm going. Every inch of me tingled. Every nerve ending sang with good feeling.

God, I'd never known anything like it.

Then we were moving. Standing, Struan spun around and dropped me onto my bed. His hands went to his jeans button, and he yanked them open, freeing his hard dick.

I stared, pushing up on my elbows.

Alarm shot through me. In equal parts I wanted him to force his way inside me, and the very same act scared the life out of me.

He was so big. I didn't want to be hurt. Not after such an incredible experience.

Grabbing my knee, he forced my legs wide again and reared over me. Above my body, he loomed, one muscled arm braced next to my head, just like in the cave. His dick was inches from my core, and I shook, suddenly terrified. Anticipating pain. Waiting for him to fill me in a punishing, hard thrust.

He fucked his fist, his expression contorted. White-knuckled, he moved faster, an almost silent growl coming from deep in his throat, his breath fast. Then soundlessly, he jerked. Strings of white liquid decorated my belly and breasts. Struan groaned, his eyes closed and his features twisted.

He *came,* oh God, that was so hot. His tiny sounds branded themselves in my mind.

Dazed, I pressed a kiss to his hair.

He sprang back like I'd stung him. Stumbling back, he tucked himself away then snatched up his hoodie.

"You don't have to—" I started.

But he was already out the door. Leaving me to catch my breath after the most incredible experience of my life.

19

Struan

A knocking rattled through the hostel, earlier than expected, but we were prepared. Overtones of bright chatter grew louder as Scar and I crept along the corridor.

He'd wanted to go in alone, as he had done a couple of times in the past. But I wasn't missing out.

Through the glass in the door, we spied Keep at the front door, talking to Thea. My lass waved her arms around, a huge smile on her face despite our miserable keeper's forbidding stance.

On cue, Lottie jogged over, spluttering loudly.

The idea was she'd chastise Keep for talking about the place to a non-Islander, getting into a row and giving us just enough time to carry out our search. The backup was Burn, who'd cause a fuss if we weren't out in time.

Keep let the door close behind her, and this was our chance.

Ducking down, we silently opened the inner door then darted across the reception, behind Keep's back.

Then we were in her open office. Her suite of rooms lay the other side, but if our things were in there, we were fucked.

Without pause, we opened drawers and rifled through cupboards.

All the while, I kept an ear on the sounds from outside. I could just see Thea beyond the window, not Keep, but I had to trust in the plan.

Trust in *her*. After everything we did last night, I'd crossed that line and didn't want to go back.

The seconds ticked by as we searched. An unlocked cupboard held a single unused tracking cuff. A wee fridge buzzed in the corner.

A chest-height filing cabinet was next.

Inside, five files waited.

I flicked through them. Sinclair, Camden, Jamieson, Struan, then one final empty one.

I hesitated over the one with my name on it, but Scar pushed the drawer closed, scowling to hurry me up.

He was right. I had to focus.

Next, I checked the desk, almost yelping when, in the centre of the drawer, our phone sat.

Scar punched the air and slid it into his pocket, grabbing a pen right after. He turned to go, but I shook my head.

"What?" he mouthed.

"My surf light," I replied silently.

I wasn't going without it. Scar's gaze darkened in a warning, but he sighed and got back to work, searching the rest of the items in the drawer but coming up empty. I moved on to the shelves by the window.

In the corner of my vision, Thea's hand slashed down by her side.

I jerked my head up and waved at Scar.

But it was too late.

With a mutter about interfering busybodies, our keeper locked the front door of the hostel, ignoring the women's questions and protests.

In here, we were trapped.

The only way out was to run past her, which would no doubt mean the permanent loss of the phone. Or we could go into her private rooms.

There was no choice. Yanking Scar by the arm, I opened the door and pushed him inside, following fast.

Closed in, we both breathed fast. He shook his head at me, and my heart dropped at the panic in his eyes. If she found us here, I had no idea what she'd do. Maybe call the jailor to come and teach one of us a lesson. A pang of regret hit me at my lack of foresight.

Sin always took the beatings.

We had to get out unseen.

Silent footed down the carpet, I held my breath against the damp, sweaty smell, and peered into the first room. Her kitchen, half the size of ours, but far better kitted out. She had a coffee machine, toaster, a microwave, for fuck's sake.

Plus a large window.

But this room was right next door to the office, and if we jumped from here, she'd probably see.

I jabbed a finger down the corridor, and Scar kept moving. At the end, a wide bedroom with a comfortable sofa waited.

"She has a TV." Scar clapped his hand over his mouth then pointed wildly beside it, his excitement growing. "A router. Wi-Fi."

He sank to his knees and took a fast picture of the back of the router with the phone.

My attention had locked elsewhere.

On the hook above a picture, my light dangled, the top one of a selection of keyrings, one saying 'I love Scotland', another a flat rubber Loch Ness monster.

I snatched mine down and pocketed it, my gaze lingering on the picture itself. It was a large map of Torlum, yellowed and crinkled.

I read the note in the corner.

Landowners and holders of all crofter rights: The Stewarts.

Stewart. That was Thea's surname. Presumably her grandmother's, too.

Island owners?

A noise came from up the corridor, the office door opening. Snapping my attention back to the present, I darted to the window, examining the opening. Outside, Thea and her friend appeared a hundred metres back from the hostel. Thea spotted me and grabbed at her friend. Both gestured like crazy for us to come out.

We didn't hesitate.

I swung open the window and dove out, landing with a roll on the grass. Scar dropped to the ground straight after, reaching up to push the window in. There was nothing we could do about engaging handles on the inside, but we'd done it.

Except I'd got more than I bargained for. We sprinted away, meeting the two women out of sight of the hostel.

Thea beamed at me, but I didn't return it.

Sin wasn't right. He couldn't be. She wasn't part of the conspiracy. I wouldn't believe it.

Her smile faltered. "Did you get it?"

Scar chuckled and held up the phone. "Mission successful. And the light, too. We did good. But we have to get
back inside. Keep will expect us to go to work soon."

I couldn't summon any words. Instead, I ducked my
forehead to hers and stared into her eyes as if I could find
the whole story there. She gazed back at me, her expression open. Honest.

Scar tugged my arm and pointed at the back door. Sin
waited. We had to go.

"The beach. Tonight," I demanded, and yet again I
had to walk away.

That evening, Scar got the phone hooked
up to the Wi-Fi. It worked. He chatted on about how we'd
have to hide it from the keeper, as if she couldn't find it, she
couldn't take it again, no matter how angry she got, but I
wasn't interested.

I had to seek out the facts so I knew how to feel.

At his bunk, I glanced around to check we were alone.
Sin and Burn were clearing up the kitchen.

"How can I find out who owns this island?" I asked
him.

He was the smartest of us, I'd been told more than
once.

Scar cocked his head. "The crofts we work on are rented. There's some kind of island rights and a formal agree-

ment between the crofters and the landowner. That will be documented somewhere."

Good enough. The rest, I could find out for myself.

"I need to use the phone," I told him.

He handed it over, and I leaned on the wall, clicking my way deeper down the rabbit hole.

Too easily, I found what I was looking for.

And it tore my tiny green shoot of hope into pieces.

20

Thea

In the hall, the landline trilled. My grandmother slept, so I jogged up and answered the old-fashioned handset.

"Hello?"

"Theadora, just the person I was looking for," Mr Charterman almost purred.

Ugh, this guy.

An eerie feeling slunk down my spine, and I gritted my teeth. "I was just going to sit with my grandmother, I can't talk—"

"Then you're on Torlum. Esme will be disappointed that you've jilted her. Before you run away, we need to discuss matters regarding your father's estate."

I sighed and propped a hand on my hip. "If you mean Granny's, she's still well and truly alive."

"No, Thea. Your father. He's been missing now for over three months. Matters are stacking up. Decisions need to be made."

My mouth dropped open. "Dad isn't missing."

Silence met my declaration.

My sense of discomfort ramped up. Where the heck was my father? My only updates were that his neighbour heard noises in his house and what Esme told me about his affair.

"Esme filled me in on what he's been up to," I spluttered. "The woman he's involved with."

"There is no woman. My daughter is mistaken. Nobody has seen your father in months. He hasn't been into his office, nor has he contacted his secretary to explain why. You were the last person to see him alive."

I placed my palm on the dark-green wall tiles, my heart rate picking up. "I don't understand."

"It's very simple. Your dad has gone, and you are now responsible for his effects."

"Why? He isn't dead. He's just..."

"Just what? Hiding from the world? Drunk? Since September? Give up your childish ideas. He's gone, and you will need to file a missing person's report then think about the decisions that will need to be made. Augustus has left many legal actions unresolved. I have—"

I chucked the phone back onto its cradle and clasped my hand over my mouth. No. He was wrong. All of this was wrong.

I marched to Granny's room and stepped inside. "Annis?"

On an armchair next to the bed, the carer looked up from her book. "Is everything okay?"

"Have you spoken to my dad recently?" I asked. Too fast. The world not making sense.

"No. As far as I know, he hasn't been on the island. Why?"

"He's missing," I spluttered.

On the bed, my grandmother shifted.

She had barely been awake since I'd arrived, and I closed my eyes at my thoughtlessness.

"He's fine," I added more gently, moving to her side. "What I meant was—"

"Oh, the evil," Granny croaked out. She blinked her reddened eyes then twisted more, seeking me out. "Augustus was such a good boy. Money is the devil that eats men's hearts."

She wept, her voice high like a child's.

"No, Dad's fine. I'm sure of it." I rubbed her arm, annoyance at myself flashing over the panic.

Granny grabbed at my hand. "Stella, listen to me. It's a plot. They'll come for me next. Then ye. Ye have to run!"

"There now, Rhona. We cannae have this. Nothing's wrong now. Let's calm ye down," Annis soothed. To me, she raised her eyebrows then tipped her head at the door.

I got the meaning. Leave Granny alone now I'd upset her.

Miserable, I fled and perched on the bottom step of the staircase.

What did I know as fact?

Dad hadn't replied to any of my calls or messages, though that wasn't unusual in the short-term. He was naturally elusive.

No one had seen him.

According to his lawyer, he hadn't been at work.

Okay. That was a place to start.

I took out my phone and dialled Dad's office. He had a pool of PAs who managed his diary, but none I knew personally.

A man answered the call and in cheerful tones, advised me that Dad wasn't available and no, he had no information on when he would be back. I asked if he could pass a message around to see if anyone knew anything, but when I hung up, I had little hope. It was right before Christmas, and the place would shut down for two weeks. Dad didn't have a manager as such, as he contracted in and was paid based on his results in party fundraising, so there was no single person in charge of him.

He had no personal social media, no close friends I knew well enough to contact.

The name Esme had given rose in my mind. *Delia Aspen,* the woman he was supposedly having a scandalous affair with. I hadn't dared look her up, not wanting the sordid details, but I did now, my fingers flying over my phone screen.

Pictures loaded of her with her famous husband. I scanned the articles. No scandal. No hint of adultery. Nothing of what Esme had claimed.

I sat back and stared into space, my mind working overtime.

After a few minutes, Annis joined me. "Rhona's sleeping again now."

"Sorry I upset her. I'm such a fool. I should never have spoken about Dad like that around her."

She rubbed my arm. "Don't trouble yourself. She has moments like that often, crying about someone trying to hurt her, or stealing her money. What happened with your dad?"

I told her the short version of the story. She sympathised but had no information.

Then her expression changed to one of a more interested curiosity. "Without wishing your grandmother's life away, soon, this will all be yours."

I blinked at her.

"We always assumed your father would move here when the time came." She gave a nervous laugh. "Some of the Torlum folk worried that he might change things. Ye wouldnae want to live here, I'm sure. So far from your university friends and busy city life. I imagine not much would change with ye in charge."

I shook my head. "In charge of what?"

"The island, of course. It's always been your family's, and you're the heiress now. All of this is about to become yours."

Realisation staggered me. Dad had always called Torlum *our island,* but never once had I asked what he meant. I assumed because it was his childhood home, but he'd worked hard to neutralise his accent and raised me far away.

He hated Torlum.

He'd been in line to inherit it.

"Is this a joke?" I asked, instantly feeling stupid.

Annis' eyes widened. "Did ye not know?"

God, how was this possible? If my family owned this island... That meant all of it.

The beaches, the harbour, the lighthouse.

The prison where Struan and his friends were being held.

We were in on the conspiracy.

There was no chance this could all have happened without consent from the island owner. Lottie told me her family had been paid off. Granny couldn't give that permission, and Dad had set himself up to act in her stead.

I'd cosigned those papers back in September. What if that had been to do with this and not just the rights to care for my grandmother? It had to be.

Dread, boosted by the question of Dad's whereabouts alone, churned my gut and soured my tongue.

Struan had asked me a question. A specific demand to be sure I wasn't part of this before he could trust me.

I hadn't known the truth to make it a lie, but it had been all the same.

21

Struan

Midnight came, and our fire burned high on the beach, fuelled by strong winds. The coming of a storm. Thea's friend had stolen a bottle of whisky for us but arrived alone.

I was halfway to drunk and dangerously angry.

"There she is," the lass uttered happily.

Sin watched her, alone at his position by the fire.

Thea crossed the sands, a slight figure with the dark waves towering and crashing behind her.

Fucking treacherous.

I stepped from the shadows into the firelight and seized the bottle from Burn. Drinking deep, I allowed the alcohol to take over everything I didn't want to feel.

As she neared, Thea fixed her attention on me, stopping ten feet away. "Can I talk to you?"

I took another deep drink of the whisky. "Talk or lie?"

Silence fell over the group.

Thea's eyes crinkled at the corners, her mouth pulling down. Regret. If for a moment I thought she might be in the dark over this, her reaction burned away that hope.

This was her soft heart showing. Her guilt.

I'd trusted her.

I should be fucking shot.

She watched me, her gaze flitting to the bottle in my hand. "There's something I need to tell you, but I'd rather it was in private."

I shrugged and didn't move.

"I found it out today. About my family and this place." She shuffled closer. "I didn't know. No one ever told me, but my family owns Torlum."

In the corner of my vision, Sin sat forward. All day, he'd been shooting me glances. He was going to love this. How right he'd been.

Scar's shocked voice met her words. "Ye own this island?"

Thea palmed the back of her neck. "Apparently. I never heard anyone talk about it before. Or I never put two and two together."

"Bull," I bit out.

Her unhappy gaze found me again. "I knew this might upset you. Considering—"

"Considering what?" I half yelled. "The fact that the owners of this place are as much our jailors as the man who comes to issue beatings, or the woman who electro-cutes us? Or the fact that ye lied and are still lying now?"

"I'm speaking the truth," she mumbled, then she shut her mouth, her eyes welling.

It only annoyed me more.

My already out-of-control temper rose in an inferno.

"Do ye want to know how I found out?" I swigged the whisky, draining the bottle. "I saw a map of the place with your family's name listed as the landowner. But it was old, and I didn't want to jump to conclusions. So I did my research. Each one of these fucking arseholes who keep us here, who chase us down if we run, who use our labour and offer money to fuck us all answer to one person. The landowner."

I thought life had broken me, all the losses I'd suffered, all the pain and fear and desperation, but I'd been wrong.

I'd let myself hope and I'd never be so fucking stupid again.

Raising my hand, I pulled the band from my wrist and tossed it into the fire. Then I delivered my final blow. "It's your name listed, sweetheart. Theadora Stewart. The change in ownership recorded on the day I was imprisoned here. Your signature on the paperwork. It's all on file and viewable to everyone. So don't tell me ye never knew. Ye saw what happened to me and then signed the papers legitimising it. Fuck ye. Ye were never anything but a place to stick my dick anyway."

Thea staggered a few steps away, her expression crumpling. I couldn't watch. Didn't care.

Pain speared through me, and that needed to die. I turned to her friend who stood nearby, her fingers clamped to her mouth in horror.

Before I could think twice, I dragged the lass's hands out of the way and, fighting every instinct, forced my lips on hers.

When I next looked, Thea had fled.

22

Thea

At the lobby entrance to the Hyde Park home Dad rented, I let myself in with a key and climbed the stairs. The place was a converted mansion, and his flat was right at the top of the stylish Georgian space.

I approached his door, out of breath more from fear than action, and rapped with my knuckles.

"Dad," I called.

Nothing.

This should be shaking me up, but other than apprehension I felt...nothing.

Today was Christmas Eve. Since I'd left Torlum, I hadn't been able to shake my dark mood. Struan's revelations and his anger haunted me. It was true, everything he'd said. I'd fled the island, returned to my university flat, and licked my wounds.

Then I'd researched. Sure enough, a website dedicated to the crofts listed me as the owner of Torlum.

The only explanation was the papers I'd signed in the

autumn. I'd suspected something and now knew for sure. Yet my father hadn't said a word. The more I thought about it, the stranger it got. I'd believed him to be giving himself rights over my grandmother, but instead he'd arranged for legal ownership of the island to come to me.

In all our years of going to Torlum, he'd never mentioned anything about our family's role there. He'd mostly erased the Scottishness from his life, and from mine. It had been in our blood and far more deeply tied.

The implications ran riot.

When I'd signed that document, with one flick of my wrist, I'd made myself the jailor of the men there. And I hadn't even known.

Needing answers from my father, I'd got straight on the train for here. I'd already called his lawyer's office to look into my rights—if I owned the place, that jail would close—

but there were complications they said would take time to handle, specifically with my grandmother still being alive. Nothing was straightforward. Everything was awful.

I thumped harder on Dad's door. "I'm coming in."

Fitting the key to the lock, I entered his private space. As a teenager, I'd stayed here in the school holidays, but it never felt like home. Heavy, dark wood furniture squatted here and there, the brown leather sofas horrible for sleeping on.

The air tasted of dust.

"Dad?" I called more softly and crept into the lounge, but my expectations had hit rock bottom.

A stillness held over the place. No movement. No signs of life at all. The open door gave me a glimpse into his kitchen. Fruit rotted in a bowl on the counter, furry-coated and grey, and Dad's car keys sat next to the bowl.

I *knew.*

Dad hadn't been here in months.

Either that, or worse. My heart sped, and goosebumps rose on my skin.

What if...?

If he'd died here, would anyone know?

One foot in front of the other, I forced myself to move down the hall. At his bedroom, I cringed and reached for his door handle.

This was a nightmare. Horrible. My fingers shook.

The door creaked, swinging wide. I stared at his bed.

Made. Tidy.

Dull light fell over it from the open blinds, filtering into the bathroom where I had clear sight of the empty space.

God, but I'd expected a dead body. I whimpered in relief.

Someone cleared their throat behind me, carving up the quiet.

I jumped and whipped around.

Dad's landlady stood at the other end of the hall, in the entranceway. "Theadora? I thought I heard sounds. I hoped it was your father."

"No, just me." I closed my eyes for a second to regain control. "Have you seen him?"

She folded her arms. "No, I told you on the phone he hasn't been here. He's three months late with the rent."

Three months? God. "I'm sorry. I'm going to take a look around to see if there's any clues to where he is."

"No, I'm the sorry one. Particularly as we're right on

Christmas. Honey, I need this place back. I have a mortgage to pay. I was going to call and tell you, but I've booked a storage company to come pack everything away."

My mouth dropped open. "But this is his home."

"He hasn't been here in a long time. It's in the terms of his lease. I was going to give you the storage code. It'll all be there waiting if…"

She stopped her sentence.

If he reappeared? My hopes for that were gone.

"Besides," she sniffed. "It will stop those men from showing up here, poking around. I've had enough of them asking questions and menacing my tenants."

"What men?"

"Debt collectors, if you ask me."

I cringed, and she shuffled away, leaving me to poke around the rooms.

Most of Dad's personal possessions were here. His watch, his passport, his clothes. The only things I couldn't find were his wallet and phone.

Packing the most important items into a sports bag, and his documents and letters into a box, I gave the place one last look.

My investigations here were over. It was like Dad had vanished off the face of the planet. I could no longer hide from the truth.

Returning my key to his landlady, I found Dad's Jaguar parked outside and drove it the long way home to Edinburgh.

My lows just kept getting lower.

On Christmas Day, all alone, I called my mother. I'd texted her occasional updates, but any talk of Dad annoyed her, so she hadn't had the latest.

She tutted. "How like my ex-husband to cause problems for everyone else. What the hell is he thinking. I can't be dealing with this right now."

"Was he ever in trouble during your marriage?" I pushed on, knowing I was in for an earful.

"Oh, Thea, why would you ask me about him? Isn't it enough that I suffer the memories of being stuck with him for so long? I did it all for you, so the least you can do is let it be."

I heaved a sigh, so over my family. "I just need to know. Did he ever have a problem with debt, for example?"

"He was a gambling addict, or on the way. And he flashed the cash for other women. That never surprised me. I was only ever a rebound for him, then trapped by pregnancy. The woman before me broke his heart, or so he claimed. If you ask me, there was no heart there in the first place to be broken."

My questions and need for sympathy were drowned out by Mum's complaints about how my father had done her wrong. I'd heard most of it already, but to know he had a gambling problem destroyed any final hope that I could redeem him.

I sank into a pity party for one.

The paperwork from Dad's flat, mostly only bills and work documents, yielded no more answers. There were no clues, nowhere else for me to search. I'd hit a dead end.

A few days on, I filed a missing person's report with the police.

When classes started back up, I had no choice but to resume life as normal. Except it wasn't. Nothing was normal, and I just had to live it.

*F*inally through the worst of the traffic, I eased the big Jaguar into a parking space two streets away from home, then trudged through the freezing February day to my flat.

Two of the women I shared with had changed accommodation this term, and only Jenna remained. It didn't matter.

She looked up from the sofas, her lips flat in annoyance. "Hey, check your mail. I had this letter about rent increases, and I can't even. Seriously, I'm going to need to find a cheaper place to live. How can they do this to me?"

"God, that sucks. I'm so sorry."

"Save your pity. You'll have one, too." She whomped back down and stabbed at her phone.

I trailed into my bedroom and flipped through the pile of letters, but that same warning hadn't come my way yet.

Great, something new to look forward to.

I laid out on my bed and unlocked my phone. Lottie had messaged me many times. After Struan kissed her, she'd pursued me home.

Told me the kiss wasn't real.

He'd clamped his hand over her mouth. Faked it.

It barely mattered. He'd been awful to both of us, and it had hurt far more than it should've. I'd told her we'd talk in the morning but left as soon as I could get on the boat.

Embarrassment had been a big part of it.

I'd been so ignorant. Probably my whole life. From our short text exchanges since, Lottie had assumed I'd known the island belonged to my grandmother. Everybody there knew.

Before that, she'd called me out for not knowing about the youth rehab scheme. Likewise, Henry had been shocked at how I'd missed our dads arguing.

I'd walked around blindly, or so it seemed.

But I didn't feel like the same person now. My happiness had been suspended, or caged.

I found the thread of conversation with Struan and hovered my finger over the delete button. I didn't want to see his face. Or remember his lust, or his anger.

A call hit the screen, my grandmother's carer.

I answered immediately. "Annis, is everything okay?"

"Theadora, I'm so sorry, but she's worse. The doctor was here this afternoon, and she suggested it might be good for you to return."

I clutched the phone tighter. "What does that mean? Did she ask for me?"

Annis sighed heavily. "No, dear. I believe she... There's no easy way to say this, I think she might be nearing her end."

I closed my eyes, dread dropping through me. Not Granny, too.

The carer continued on with the doctor's advice, but my head spun.

"I'll be there as soon as I can," I managed then killed the call.

I'd been wrong. My lows still had new depths to reach.

Two days later, early on Saturday morning, I drove Dad's Jaguar up country and out to the far northern coast of the Isle of Skye. The ferry took me from there back to Torlum, and a pulse of emotion threatened my frozen heart.

I'd asked Annis not to tell anyone else that I was coming, yet I still stepped onto the dock with fear threatening me.

I let my anger burn it away.

To hell with Struan. The only thing I was guilty of was ignorance. That would never happen again. I'd pretended to be strong when I'd last returned to the island. Pretended to have shed my weak outer shell. But it had all been centred around Struan. None of it had been about myself.

Everything was different now. I was only here for Granny.

At the looming Victorian home, Annis met me at the door, her eyes red and her fingers pressed to her lips.

I stopped dead on the path. "Don't tell me..."

"I'm sorry. It happened an hour ago. She went so peacefully."

I rushed inside and to my grandmother's room. But at the door I halted. I couldn't approach her lifeless body. The unmoving shape of her under her sheets.

She'd been so wonderful when I'd been a child. Her hugs, her soft lilting brogue. I couldn't reconcile that with her in her sickbed, and I wouldn't accept that she'd gone.

She'd left me, too.

I gasped and clutched the doorframe.

Awful emotion rushed, and for a long minute, I couldn't move. Yet I forced my muscles to unlock. She deserved better.

Steeling myself, I crossed the room and perched on the chair next to her bed.

Grief broke over me. I took her hand and brushed a thumb over her age-marked, paper-thin skin. "I'm so sorry I wasn't here. I love you so much, and I'm going to miss you forever. I know you'll be reunited with my grandfather and the others of our family who've gone before you, but I wish you could've stayed for longer."

The next day, I arranged the funeral.

Two days later, I buried her at the island graveyard with a crowd of locals attending.

Lottie joined me and held my hand. Cried with me. We didn't talk about what happened in the winter. I saw no sign of the prisoners, nor did I go looking.

One fact was undeniable.

Now, I was truly the owner of this place.

The lawyers had taken too long to make any headway, but everything had changed. Their concerns over the legalities and transfer of rights had to have lifted the second Granny passed away.

I didn't need their say-so to end the use of the island as a prison. Not if it was in my power. I had to fix it today. After that, I wouldn't think of them again.

At the wake, in the tiny village hall, the islanders talked in a mixture of English and Gaelic, the familiar tones springing tears into my eyes over and again.

A man sidled up to me. "Little Theadora. How are ye holding up?"

I dried my tears. He'd already given me his regrets over Granny's death multiple times, but I couldn't remember his name. "I'm good. Thank you, Mr..."

"Jenkins." His small eyes focused on me. "What a burden, all of this on your slender shoulders."

I suppressed a shudder. "I'm handling it as best I can."

"But from so far away. Ye need a local man to look after your concerns. I'll help."

I tilted my head, appraising him. "What concerns?"

He rocked on his feet, his thumbs tucked in his waistband. "Ye are in need of a land manager. Collecting the rent. Doing the inspections. Making sure everyone stays in line. Ye don't have to use the same man your father employed. I'll step in."

"Who did my father use?"

"Some pompous official named Jones. Comes here from time to time, poking his nose in." Jenkins gave a disapproving sigh. "Ye should put an islander in that position. It's what we're due."

My heart shrivelled all the more.

I gave a pretence of a smile. "I'll consider it."

Half turning to dismiss him, I stalled and twisted back. "Who do I speak to about the old youth hostel?"

Jenkins' smile dropped. "What's your interest in that place?"

"If I own this island, my interest is in every part of it."

His gaze flicked between my eyes, as if he was searching for a clue to my heart. "It's wrong what they're doing there," he uttered. "I know your grandmother wouldn't have liked it, God rest her. I don't know if ye recall, but she had a great interest in the more unfortunate among us. Battered women. Homeless kids. Anyone down on their luck, she'd want to help. I know, because we often talked on it. If she'd been in her right mind, that place would never have existed. A prison, here? Not on her watch. It shouldnae be on yours either."

Surprise danced through me. Maybe not everyone here had been paid off.

"I want it closed down," I said before I could stop myself.

Jenkins glanced around and pulled me aside. Curious

gazes followed us, including from Lottie's dad. From what she'd told me, he was deep in the secret.

"It should be," Jenkins whispered. "Leave it with me. I can do it for ye. I'll go there and make sure the residents are moved somewhere better. It can happen fast and be kept a secret. Folks won't like the change, but we have to do what's right."

I couldn't do this alone. Lottie might agree with my plan to shut it down, but her dad had been complicit in the start-up. She'd be conflicted, and I didn't want to put my friend in that position. I had no one else to ask.

Vaguely, I remembered Jenkins from when I was little. Perhaps Granny had trusted him. I couldn't, but I'd take the help.

"Okay, fine." I held the man's gaze. "Dismiss the keeper and give the men their freedom. If anyone has a problem with it, they can see me."

I left Torlum an hour later, the ferry churning up the icy sea.

Holding the deck rail, I stared out, a tiny sliver of emotion breaking free.

In the water, four dark shapes bobbed. Tiny neon lights flashed, marking their position. Three carved up the surf, but the fourth, with a blue light, remained still in the black waves.

Struan.

Making sure I didn't stay.

23

Lottie

Across the dinner table, Da berated my mother, his displeasure with everything somehow her fault. I pushed my dinner around my plate—a roast I'd spent hours over. But my appetite was absent. I needed off this island. There was nothing for me here. All my studies were online, and on days like today, where the dark March weather stole the light and late winter storms pinned us down, I couldn't even leave the house.

I was slowly going out of my mind.

Yet I could never go.

For the first reason, Da would hunt me down. The second was the child in Ma's belly. My mother had to agree to go, too, and hide with me somewhere. Have the baby away from my father's abuse and control.

She wouldn't even discuss it.

My phone buzzed against my leg. I slid it from my jeans pocket and peered at the screen.

My pulse spiked.

"Who is it?" Da demanded. "Didn't I tell ye no phones

at the dinner table? Ye have the manners of your ma."

Resisting a smart reply that would earn me a slap to the head, I held it up to show him. "Just Theadora. I'm not hungry. If ye don't mind, I'm going to chat with her. Ye know how sad she's been since her grandmother passed. Back in a minute to clear up my plate."

He let me go, and I dashed away upstairs. In my room, I locked the door then answered the call.

"Hello?" I breathed.

A long pause followed. "Hello, Violet."

I closed my eyes against a rush of feeling.

My phone screen might have read *Theadora,* but that was a fake name I added in case anyone saw our conversations. A full stop added to the end of her name created a separate record.

For Sin's number.

He'd never called me. I'd had a handful of texts only.

"Do ye need something?" I whispered.

He hadn't messaged me since the night Struan and Theadora had imploded.

Since Struan had pretended to kiss me, his fingers to my lips, and I'd punched him for the act. Sin had leapt up to face-off with him, but I'd walked away before witnessing it become a fight.

Since then, I'd...missed him. I barely knew him, but Sin was the only interesting thing here. He'd never look twice at me, but pretty quickly, he'd become my secret obsession.

"A favour," he said in his slow, deep voice. "I have nothing to pay you with—"

"I don't care. Just tell me. I'll help."

Another pause came while he considered his words.

"I want to help Struan. I know he isn't your favourite person, but there's only four of us here, and I can't ignore him."

I rolled my eyes, not that he could see. "I don't hate him for my sake. He behaved like an idiot, but the fake kiss was just that. I only dislike him now because he upset my friend."

"Fake?"

"Couldn't ye tell?"

A short groan followed. "Fuck. No. I nearly broke his jaw for that."

Now it was my turn for a moment of quiet. "Seriously?"

No answer came, but a flush of heat spread through me. He'd defended me. Oh boy.

"So," I continued, trying to be breezy. "What's the problem?"

"He isn't talking to any of us, eating with us, or even sleeping in his bunk."

"Since Thea left?"

She'd hardly replied to my messages. Then again, she'd lost her grandmother and her dad was missing. It was hardly surprising she'd shut down.

Sin sucked in a breath. "Aye. Can ye get her to come back?"

"No, not for him. Why should I set my friend up just for him to be an arsehole to her?"

"How is she?" Sin challenged. "Isn't she hurting from this, too? I don't know what their deal was, but we all know what blew them up."

"The deal was she found out something she didn't know right at the same point he did. How is that her fault?"

He considered that. "Do ye trust her?"

"I've known her since I was tiny. We played together every summer. Of course I trust her."

"If that lass was in the dark about her family and Torlum then she'll be suffering."

I chewed my lip. I wanted my friend back. If correcting the misunderstanding between her and the guy she liked made a difference, then that was a good thing. But it would be for her sake only.

"Struan is full of anger, and that night, it was directed at the wrong person," Sin continued. "If we get them back together, both would be better for it."

"Is he sorry?"

"That's for him to say. I cannae answer. I just want to fix the wrong."

"I do, too."

"Then think about what I asked," he ordered.

"You're a good man, Sin," I added quietly.

A pause followed.

"Call me Sinclair." Without waiting for an answer, he hung up.

I held the phone to my chest, my breathing too rapid. I'd been more than a little deep in lust with the tall, brooding man. Now I knew he had a heart, cared enough to try to reconcile two hurt people, I was well and truly a goner.

24

Sin

Gripping the phone too hard, I delivered it back to Scar to be hidden. A movable floorboard under the bunks had protected our stash before, but not well enough. Now, Scar kept the phone on him, and we all carried our lights, the last of our personal effects.

Keep could ransack the room all she liked, but she wouldn't get the goods back.

I'd taken a shock to the arm when she'd come in here raging about our burglary, as she called it, but it barely harmed me.

She'd aimed for Burn. Could've killed him. One day, her death would be at my hands.

Fire flickered in my blood.

Some kind of change was coming, I could feel it. Pressure in the air. The winter months had been hard living. Long, dark days and frozen nights. But we'd survived it. Spring would be here soon.

Maybe that's what I was feeling. The need to explore, build things. To fuck.

My mind drifted back to Violet.

The lass was too kind. Too fucking forgiving.

On the call, I'd lied to her, and she'd believed every word. We needed Theadora back, but for another reason entirely.

And every time Violet spoke, I pictured her under me. Obeying me.

My cock pulsed at the thought.

"Need a shower," I muttered to Scar then strode into the bathroom.

With a flick of my wrist, I locked the door.

The shower steamed, and I stripped then stepped under the spray, getting harder by the second.

I knew my limits, knew my need for control. I'd set a boundary with Violet and I wouldn't breach that. Which meant only one option for handling my ever-present need to fuck her.

With one hand braced against the cold wall tiles, I gripped my shaft and stroked myself. Closing my eyes, I stifled my groan at the instant pleasure.

Braided blonde hair.

Pretty, inquisitive eyes.

Her happy agreement to do whatever I asked.

I let myself consider it all. Let myself mentally peel off her clothes to expose her curvy, naked body to me. I'd worship her. Leave no part of her untouched.

My cock hardened more, and I fucked my fist, imagining it was her mouth. She'd look so sweet on her knees for me. Opening her lips to suck me down. My thumb sweeping through my precum was her tongue. My rigid hold was her hand. She'd be such a good girl. Trying anything I asked to please me.

I jacked my fist, moving faster.

I'd return the favour, eating her out until she screamed. Getting quickly addicted to her taste. To the feel of her soft tits in my hand and mouth. Then I'd pin her down and thrust deep inside her.

My cock jerked, so hard now I was losing my mind.

"Violet," I said soundlessly into the damp air.

"Sinclair," I imagined her whispering in return.

I came in a fucking flood. Cum spilled in rivulets onto the wall. My head swam with pleasure, and my balls emptied their contents down the drain.

Such a fucking waste. I wanted Violet to take everything I had. Every last drop.

But that could never be.

Even if she wanted me, for real, and not just to make eyes at or to piss her father off, it was never going to happen.

"Fuck," I bit out, frustration replacing my lust and destroying my temporary high.

At least that ache had been tamed for a while.

I cleaned up then scrubbed down the wall and floor, dressed again, and left the bathroom.

Struan's bunk was missing its mattress. It had been ever since he'd moved to the isolation cell. I was sick of his shite, even if I didn't blame him for any emotional response to being in this place.

And had almost forgiven him for touching Violet without her permission. Only because she didn't seem to care.

At his open door, I glowered down at him, reclined on the thin mattress on the floor. He stared into space, the only sign he was still part of our world the redrawn surf tattoo on his arm. Scar must've gone over it for him, like he'd done for the rest of us.

The fact he'd allowed it gave me hope.

"How long are ye planning to sulk for?"

Struan brought a slow look to me. "Fuck off."

"There's shite I want to talk to ye about." Things I'd shared with Scar and Burn, but not with him yet.

"Too late. I dinna care."

"What will make ye?"

He only watched me. Christ, but this lad knew how to hold a grudge.

Then a smirk broke through his miserable expression. "Another kiss from Violet."

If he'd said that at any point in the last two months, I would have hit him again and finished the job of breaking his face. Now, I only sneered. "Ye owe her an apology. Other than that, get over yourself."

"What if I don't want to? I live here, and I'm going to fucking die here."

Burn appeared behind me, his eyes wide in alarm and a cloth over his shoulder from where he was cooking dinner. He pointed down the corridor. "Jenkins is at the front door, talking to Keep. I heard my name."

Seriously, fuck that guy. He'd been here a couple of times in the past month, and we didn't know why, or what he was talking about with our keeper. Now he was back, my hackles rose.

"Wait here." I strode past Burn.

At the glass door to the reception area, I twisted the handle. Locked.

Keeper stood at the main entrance, her back to me. Voices made it through the glass.

"...mine. Ye can't stop me," Jenkins snarled at her.

"Ye want him, then make me a better offer," she snapped. "I have my orders, and it needs to be worth my while."

"I'm naw paying for something that's rightfully mine."

"Prove it."

They stared each other down. In her left hand, Keeper's Taser sparked.

After a beat, Jenkins swore. "I own them. I'll be back to collect my due." He smacked the doorframe then wheeled away.

Our keeper locked up and turned, her gaze resting on me. Her lips tilted up in an evil grin.

I didn't like that smile. Didn't like anything about her, but definitely not the pretence of protecting us. Whatever payday she was expecting, it would be at the cost of one of us.

Over my dead body would I let that happen.

25

Thea

Sender: Lionel Charterman.

Message: Theadora, as per my repeated messages, you will attend a meeting at the below address to discuss the terms of your inheritance. I am the executor of the estate, therefore, you cannot ignore this message. I will expect confirmation via my secretary directly.

In the car park outside the lecture hall, I sat in the Jaguar and glared at the email, my eyes bleary.

Today had been tough, and I still had a final term left of my second year. I was struggling to stay interested. I'd chosen this degree to make my dad happy. I didn't love it. I didn't feel anything for it.

Or much else.

The message from Charterman was the last straw. The lawyer had left multiple messages stating that I had to speak to him. The address on the email was his home.

I'd sent a single response stating that I would talk to anyone else in his business apart from him, and this was his reply.

I hated the bastard with a passion.

"Miss Stewart?" a voice hailed me.

I twisted to see my tutor approaching my open car door. "Mr Hudson. Is everything okay?"

"I was hoping to catch you. This is a bit delicate. Would you please follow me to my office?"

I squinted at him but fell into step. Inside the admin building, Mr Hudson led me to his room and closed the door, gesturing for me to sit.

He moved behind his desk and steepled his fingers. "I'm afraid there has been an issue with the fees for your final term. We have been in contact with your father—"

I jerked forward. "You spoke to Dad?"

Mr Hudson put both hands out in a placatory gesture. "What I mean to say is we emailed your father but have received no response."

My shoulders shrank. "Oh."

"The issue extends to your housing as well. We allowed leeway of a couple of weeks, but that time has passed."

I shook my head, trying to understand. Jenna had mentioned rent rises, but mine was flat out unpaid? "What does this mean? Are you kicking me out?"

"We would seek to avoid that, of course. This is an unusual situation. We typically insist on all fees at the beginning of the year, but made the exception to allow instalments because of your father circumstances."

Circumstances of his being in debt, I guessed. I should've seen this coming. "I'm sorry."

My tutor winced. "I am, too. We have received two of the three payments, but not the last. This final term is essential, I needn't add. You have exams to take."

I passed my hand over my face. "My father's a missing person. I had to declare him that because he hasn't been in contact since last September. That's nearly seven months now, so maybe they put a hold on his bank account, or it just ran out of money."

I had a small amount saved but otherwise relied on Dad for my course fees and the rent on my room in the shared flat.

Without his support, I'd be homeless.

I might be on my own in every way, but I wasn't without resources.

Lifting my chin, I interrupted Mr Hudson's expression of sorrow at my loss, apologies at the situation I found myself in, and platitudes that the university would do everything to help.

"I'll try to get the money. How much and when do you need it by?"

He gave me a figure and a deadline. Dumbfounded, I slipped away back to my car.

Inside the Jaguar's plush interior, in the leather seats that still carried the faint smell of my father, slivers of my emotion broke free.

Stuck in grief and denial, I hadn't wanted to think about my losses. Lottie had been trying to reach me, but I hadn't had the heart to respond. I'd barely been living, just existing and trying not to feel.

But if I didn't do anything now, I'd be out of my flat. My degree wasted. Whether I cared about the latter or not, I still had to have somewhere to go.

I pulled at the fine gold chain around my neck, Granny's key on the end. I never got the chance to ask her what it unlocked, but maybe now, assuming I was her heir and therefore the owner of her house, I could find out.

It beat speaking with Charterman, which was my only other option.

With a sigh, I called Lottie. We were long overdue a chat, and I felt bad about it.

She answered immediately. "Hey, how are ye?"

"I think I need to come back to the island. Can you tell me if Struan and the others have gone yet?"

"They're still here. Where would they go?"

My mouth dropped open. "The first thing I did when my grandmother died was to close the hostel down. I tried before, but the lawyers couldn't give me a straight answer about if I had the rights."

"Close it down how?"

"One of the islanders wanted the job of land manager. I wasn't about to give him that, but I asked him to shut the place down. This was back in February, right after the funeral."

Lottie sucked in a breath. "That never happened. Nothing has changed."

"Really?" Dismay hit me. "Shit. I should've gone there myself, but after all that happened, I just wanted it handled. I've been a coward."

My friend protested, then hesitated over something else she had to say. "Sin called me a couple of weeks ago because he was worried about Struan. That's one of the things I wanted to talk to ye about."

Try as I might, I couldn't resist my next question. "Why is he worried?"

"Some bull about how Struan's withdrawn, just like ye are, though I doubt he has the same good reasons. Sin seems to think that the two of ye have a bond, and if ye get together to talk, you'll both be okay. Wishful thinking, right? The way that guy behaved was horrible."

"As much to you as to me."

"I told ye that kiss was a fake, designed to hurt ye. Like a spiteful boy in a playground. So no, it's nothing like the same. I didn't care about him. Ye did."

I still did. I cared, hated, and thought about him endlessly. One tiny series of interactions with the man, and I couldn't get him out of my head.

All this time, he'd still been imprisoned while I believed I'd set him free.

I fished the car keys from my bag and started the engine. "Since my dad left, and Granny died, I've just been waiting for the next disaster. And you know what? It just keeps getting worse. The university might kick me off my course and out of my home. The only chance I have of sorting out my financial mess is talking to a man who tried to help someone sexually assault me." I hadn't meant to share the last point in a rant, but it was out.

Accelerating out of the university grounds, I was on a mission to return to my flat and pack a bag. "Expect me there tomorrow. I'm going to need a hug."

"You've got it. I can wait to have ye back."

*O*n the Isle of Skye, I stopped in a village and raided their stores, filling a basket with food. Regardless of what I thought about Struan, his friends would welcome this. Back in December, one of them had told a story of how their keeper had destroyed a meal of burgers, so I bought up three boxes, plus fresh buns, and ketchup.

At the ferry dock, stormy seas raged. The ferry master shook his head and cancelled the trip, at least for the next few hours.

I sat in my car and brooded.

Previously, when I'd made this crossing, I'd been so nervous. Now, the innocence behind that emotion had left me. To a degree. I still trembled inwardly at the thought of seeing Struan again, but too much else had happened to me that I was no longer the same girl from last year.

Fact was, I still wanted him.

I wanted him to praise me, to come to me in the dark. I still dreamed it, but more. Darker images swarmed my mind. Him inside me, making me do whatever he wanted.

My breathing quickened, then the blast of the horn shocked me out of my stupor. At the ferry, the harbour-master lowered the ramp, the cue that the trip was back on. I grabbed the shopping and my overnight bag and boarded the boat.

We powered through rough seas, waves smashing the bow. Hunkered down in my seat, I curled in on myself, trying to picture what would happen if I drowned. Who would grieve me? Maybe only Lottie. I'd made such a small dent on the world.

We finally made it into Torlum's tiny harbour, and I fled the boat and hurried past the village, up the road to my grandmother's home.

I entered the Victorian, automatically smiling. I let it die on my lips. Granny wasn't here to see. Instead, I stared at the so-familiar green tiles and let the grief wash over me again.

This place was mine now. Nobody lived here anymore.

From the corridor, I passed into the kitchen. The clock that ticked high on the wall was the only sign that anyone had lived here recently. I knew from messages from Annis that she'd given the place a final deep clean before she left.

Otherwise, it had the same deserted feel of Dad's flat.

Across the other side of the kitchen was the office my father had sometimes used. In the back of my mind, this had been my target. A place where I might find information. If I had an inheritance beyond this building and the island, surely papers would be stored here as well as in Charterman's possession. Even if not, I needed evidence if I was to sell any part of it and keep my room and get to do my exams.

I put the shopping bags into the fridge then entered the quiet room.

If I'd thought the house forbidding, this space within it had an even creepier feel.

I traced a finger over the desk. Then I stopped and angled my head. Above the drawer, on the otherwise empty surface, a handprint disturbed the dust. It was only visible from one angle. If I'd gone directly for the drawer, I would've erased it without noticing.

Moving around the desk, I put my hand over the print. Larger than mine. The fingers longer and the outline thicker. A man's, perhaps.

Today was the first of April, and my grandmother had died in February. So at some point in the last six weeks, someone else had been in here and poked around. I knew for a fact that Annis had cleaned in here, because she'd checked to make sure I was happy with her entering the room.

With a frown, I opened the desk drawer. It was filled with junk, pens and odd pieces of paper in the shallow tray. Nothing of interest.

A few minutes of searching the books on the shelves and a cabinet gave up the same. My grandfather had stacks of military books and pamphlets, and someone had kept old newspapers. I had no clue what I'd do with those, if I ever had to make a decision on the house. With relief and disappointment mixing, I left the room. The kitchen had darkened, evening setting in. Finding my phone, I texted Lottie that I'd arrived.

Lottie: Da is in a rage. He won't let me leave. I'll come over tomorrow as soon as he's gone to work.

Thea: Do you need help?

Lottie: It's not me he's angry at. I'll be okay. Sorry you have to spend the evening alone.

Another message quickly followed.

Lottie: Oh, the men will be at the beach later. They always are when there's a big swell for surfing. Ignore Struan and talk to the younger ones. They're fun.

I blew out a breath then pocketed my phone, worrying about her now, too.

Two hours later, I'd carried out a thorough search of the house and collected together masses of family history, pictures, and yellowed, fragile birth certificates, but no documents on the island itself. Nothing on ownership. No last will and testament style letters.

Back in the kitchen, hunger gnawed at me. I took a pack of burgers from the fridge, then without thinking it through, grabbed the other two and put them all on the grill, lighting the gas with a match.

Once cooked, I made up double cheeseburgers, eating one as I went, piled them into some of Granny's many Tupperware containers, and slipped my coat on. Then I stepped out into the night, head down against the wind, and made my way to the beach.

This time, the four men were at their fire, and all raised their gazes to me. Pulse skipping, I marched straight up and handed the bag to one of the younger men. Burn, I'd heard him called.

But my gaze remained on Struan. And his on me.

"Holy fuck. Food," Burn exclaimed.

The other two dove in, greetings coming my way alongside the happy sounds of men devouring the meal I'd made.

I took a step backwards. Another.

Then I turned on my heel and marched away.

Not once in the fast walk back to the house did I peer around. Yet I sensed I was being followed all the same.

Electricity trickled down my spine.

The urge to run rose.

But I kept my pace steady.

At the back door of Granny's house, I let myself in then finally peered out into the black. Nothing moved in the garden. No moon lit the landscape tonight. I waited for a minute, scanning the surroundings for any sign of life.

No one appeared.

Disappointment engulfed me. I'd imagined it. I slammed the door, locking it for good measure.

Stupid. Did I really think that he'd follow me? Why, when he so clearly still hated me? I didn't need him, I didn't want him—

A creak came from the floorboards upstairs.

My heart skipped a beat. "Hello?" I called out then flipped the light switch.

Nothing happened. I flipped it again, but the place remained in darkness. No electricity. Maybe it had been the storm.

Or perhaps the power had been out the whole time I'd been here. I hadn't noticed whether the fridge was cold, and the grill used gas.

Damn. I was in for a chilly night.

Using my phone as a torch, I retrieved my overnight bag from the kitchen counter, willing my nerves to calm. The house creaked all the time. Nobody knew I was here aside from Lottie and the men on the beach.

Yet there had possibly been an intruder before. The fingerprints on the desk suggested so.

In the hall, I paused at the bottom of the main staircase and shone the torch around. Shadows loomed and fled. Alarm built inside me until my hand shook.

Another creak echoed, but behind me now. I jumped and spun around, shining the light at the front door.

Nobody there.

God, this was freaky as hell. If ever there was a candidate for a haunted house, this old, echoing Victorian was it.

Breathing through my nose, I forced down my feelings of helplessness and jogged up the staircase. If I could lock myself in my room for the night, I'd feel a lot safer. A chair behind the door. No other entrances and exits aside from the window.

On the upstairs landing, I marched past open rooms

until I reached the one at the end. My room. But as I swung open the door, my phone light extinguished.

"You have to be kidding me," I muttered.

I tapped the screen. Shook it. It didn't light up. I hit the on button, and nothing happened still. It had run out of power. Frustration rushed in me, fuelling my already high emotions. The whole time I'd been sitting in the car, I could have been charging it. I hadn't bothered because I knew I could plug it in as soon as I got here.

Had the power been on.

Instead, I'd conducted my search. Chatted with Lottie. Picked up the knitting I'd discarded long months ago. The blue Merino wool scarf that was so near completion, and which now perched at the top of my overnight bag.

Helplessness washed over me, and I forced it away. Being alone and in the dark wasn't going to kill me. I was being ridiculous.

Fine. All I needed was to barricade myself in, go to bed, and sleep until daylight persuaded the monsters away.

Slipping around the bedroom door, I closed and locked it, then leaned back against the wood. I knew this room well, so I walked forward until my shoes touched the edge of the rug.

Three feet ahead of me, the bed springs creaked.

Fear hit me, and I sprang back, instant panic ripping away my sense of sanctuary.

Somebody was here, locked in the room with me.

I gasped and turned, almost falling over my own feet. Darting blindly forward, I crashed into the wall, bouncing back.

Fingers grasped my shoulder.

An ungodly shriek fell from my lips, and I flailed out,

hitting flesh. "Get off me. Get out!"

But the grip intensified, and my unknown assailant grabbed my free hand and yanked both behind my back. Then they spun me around and pushed my cheek to the wall. I wrenched at their hold but couldn't budge them.

My panic peaked. I was going to be murdered. I hadn't checked the house, or grabbed a weapon, and this was my fault. This was how I was going to die.

The person bracketed my body with theirs until they lowered their face to my ear.

I winced, slamming closed my eyes as if that could save me.

Then a scent prickled my nose. Sea salt. Another, more familiar, followed it.

Struan.

In a beat, every tiny identifying factor hit me. The sound of his breathing. The way he was touching me. I could've wept.

"Asshole," I whispered.

"Liar," he replied.

All my muscles gave out, and I fell back, my head landing on his shoulder.

How dare he? Why scare me like that?

I hated him, hated this, yet I couldn't bring myself to voice it. Brand-new emotions stole over the place of my fear.

The intruder barely shifted under my weight, and instead ran a large hand around me to grip the base of my throat, holding me up.

Hot lips landed below my ear. But there was anger in the move. This was no happy kiss. A thrill hit my pleasure centres all the same.

My moan came unbidden.

He unfastened my coat and dragged it from my shoulders. My jumper went the same way, torn from me and discarded. My bra followed, yanked at before being unclasped, as if my attacker couldn't wait. Then he was touching me, his palms over my breasts, his fingers digging in. Moulding me. Shaping me. Getting off on the feel of me.

I never thought I'd be into pain, but the rough treatment only had me more excited. No matter how much he despised me, I'd clung to the foolish idea that Struan would never truly hurt me. That if I told him no, he'd stop.

I didn't want that.

With his hands still cupping me, I slipped my thumbs into my leggings waistband and stripped the last of my clothes, until I stood entirely naked in the dark, only the gold key hanging on its chain around my neck.

Struan paused, and a hand ghosted down over my belly and to my thigh, feeling what I'd done. How I'd finished the job he'd started. He made a masculine sound, half growl, half groan, then turned me so my back hit the wall.

Then he dropped to his knees, hauled my thigh over his shoulder, and buried his face between my legs.

I squealed and drove my fingers into his hair. This time around, the noises I made didn't matter. No one was going to come running. He could do anything to me, and I had no escape.

All I needed was to feel.

Struan speared his tongue straight through my wet, needy centre, then inside me. With one hand, he gripped my thigh, holding me up, and used the other to open me for him.

With hunger, he feasted on me.

Pleasure spilled through me, building as he gave me no pause. When he sucked on my clit, I yelled again, arching against the wall to allow him better access.

He'd given me an orgasm in this room before, but everything about this was different. Then, I'd invited him in, trembling at my fear of the unknown. Now, he'd brought the fear, using it as a weapon.

I wouldn't let myself be a victim.

All the panic, the adrenaline and dread, those needed to be my tools. My heightened senses made this better. My mind jumped from afraid to on fire.

I palmed my breasts, copying how he'd touched me. There was safety in the darkness of the room. The sensory deprivation. It concentrated all on touch. On how he moved on me.

Struan gripped my thigh so hard I'd bruise.

At another moan from me, he slid two fingers inside me, crooking them while he locked on to my clit with his mouth. He rolled me with his tongue then sucked, repeating the action again.

God. I flattened my hands to the cold wall, that incredible feeling he'd coaxed from me before returning tenfold. With every coordinated move, the heat coiled tighter. A slow winding within me, infecting my cells and dominating every thought.

All of a sudden, it was too much. Fever shook me, and I barrelled towards a crash, a splintering I couldn't control. Still, I couldn't speak to demand he ease up. I whimpered, and he upped his pace even more.

He was mean. Cruel. Evil—

An explosion detonated inside me.

"Struan," I gasped and half fell over him, boneless and shaking.

Bliss spread through each vein, and I smiled despite myself.

In a punch of energy, he stood and crowded me to the wall. Clothing rustled and ripped past my face. His hoodie? I reached out blindly, touching his bare chest.

But I wasn't in charge here. He growled out something I couldn't hear, then strong arms banded around me. He lifted me, pinning me to the wall while I automatically wound my legs around his waist.

Suddenly, I felt it. His dick right against my core. The blunt end pressing to my flesh.

And I froze up. The hoodie and t-shirt hadn't been all he'd handled—he'd opened his jeans, too. Got me into position.

"I'm not done with ye yet," he gritted out.

In the dim recesses of my mind, I pictured how I'd expected this to go down. I'd lose my virginity in a soft bed to a sweet boy. Someone who loved me.

Not pinned to the wall by a man who'd struck fear into my heart. Who hated me and probably meant this as a punishment.

Except Struan wasn't moving.

He was...waiting.

I kept my damn mouth closed. Another truth dominated. My body needed this. To be joined with his. To own his pleasure, too.

Even if it was just this once and I never saw him again.

He adjusted his hold on me then, with a rush of breath, drove his hard dick inside me.

I cried out, not in pain, but at the strangeness of it. He filled me, his forehead pressed to my neck.

Easing out, he slammed home. Again. This was so different to how his hands and tongue had felt. That had been pure fire. This... I wasn't so sure. He was in me.

I ducked my head and held on to his shoulders, the solid muscles shifting under his skin. I'd never touched a man's naked body before. Never had the chance to let my fingers roam over him.

I didn't now. It was all I could do to receive. Let him do this to me.

Another thrust and he stalled, his hand dropping down. He wrestled with his jeans, then something clicked.

Blue light flashed.

He clicked it again, and the light stayed steady. His surfing beacon. Now I could see him. See...everything.

The neon blue drove deep shadows across the room, scaring the dark away. Struan dropped it directly beneath us and put space between our bodies.

I stared in fascination at the solid length of his dick still connected to me. Then he jacked his hips and buried himself in my heat once more.

Feeling it had been one thing, but the sight was something else. All those inches disappearing into me. His claiming of my first time. My ownership of this new and erotic experience.

Fresh pleasure burst over me. I let out a moan.

Struan made a strangled sound and ducked to lick the pulse point at my throat. He drifted lower, sucking hard and drawing his teeth down my chest. At this angle, I was only riding the tip of him, the angle stretching my entrance and spiking winding pleasure.

Then he hiked me higher to reach my nipple and bit down.

"God," I gasped.

A low laugh was my answer. His mouth tipped up in that infuriating smirk. He grazed his teeth over me, and still I watched, angling my head.

Struan drew back and held my gaze. "If I killed ye now, no one owns this island. No one owns me. Are ye afraid?"

"No," I lied.

"Good girl."

Deliberately, and slowly, he sucked the swell of my breast. He nudged the key on its chain aside to do it again, purposeful in the move, tiny prickles of pain following.

It took me a second to work out what he was doing.

Marking me.

Leaving love bites on my skin.

He grazed higher and did the same to my throat, and annoyance flashed through me. Once, he'd called me his. But I wasn't anymore. He didn't have the right to leave marks.

I fisted his hair and drew his face back, our gazes linking.

His eyes glittered, and I stifled a surge of fear.

Despite all the time that had passed, I still barely knew this man. I didn't know what he was capable of. He'd torn my clothes and yelled at me. Lashed out to hurt me. Yet so easily I'd let him into my body. I was an idiot.

Holding my gaze, he thrust deep inside me once more, watching my every reaction.

Struan started a rhythm, picking up speed.

My breathing sped, and I gripped his hair harder, never looking away from those midnight blue eyes of his.

Spiralling heat picked up deep in my belly. Our damp, sweaty skin slapped together. Then Struan gave a guttural moan. Desire swept over me. That sound. I'd never forget it.

Losing eye contact, he buried his face in my throat and drove into me over and again. I held on for the ride, fireworks detonating in my flesh, building up to something bigger.

This was all too irresistible, too compelling. Nothing could steal my focus. I needed this with him.

"Going to come," he suddenly warned through gritted teeth.

I moaned in surprise. He hadn't asked, but I had us covered with my implant.

Even if I hadn't, in the moment, I didn't care. I loved this.

Charged up, I dropped my head to his shoulder and absorbed every hit. I forced a hand between our bodies and stroked my clit, once, twice. The fire he'd been stoking ignited into flames in my body. My second orgasm smacked me down, blinding pleasure sparking through every limb.

At the same moment, Struan gave a broken cry and stilled, his dick throbbing inside me.

I lost all sense, nothing in my head but sheer joy of the moment.

Clinging on to Struan, I gasped open-mouthed, pulsing around him while he came into me. Mindless. Complete.

For a long moment, he held on, breathing just as hard. Then he straightened and dislodged my arms, withdrawing to set me on my feet. I slumped against the wall, watching as he snatched up his clothes, dressing fast.

Between my legs, wet seeped out. I wondered if I was bleeding. A dull ache spread. Cold crept in where it had been kept at bay by our combined heat.

Then Struan stepped in closer, and for a second, I thought he was going to kiss me. Our mouths hadn't met for the whole time we'd been together tonight.

Instead, he curled his lip. "There's nothing for ye here. Ye shouldn't have come back."

I raised a shoulder, still naked and doing nothing to hide it. "If I own this place, I have every right to be here. You can leave, but first, I have something to say."

He tilted his head, his brow furrowed.

"I ordered the hostel closed down," I added. "Last time I was here, I instructed one of the islanders to make sure it was done. Go. No one's going to stop you this time."

"What islander?" he asked, a deadly tone to his words.

"Jenkins."

Struan laughed, but it wasn't a happy sound. Without another word, he left.

26

Thea

A hammering at the door woke me with a start. Daylight flooded my room, and I sat up and rubbed my eyes. *Right.* I was on Torlum.

"Thea," Lottie's voice called.

I jumped from the bed and dragged on my leggings, shrugging on a long jumper as I padded out of my room and downstairs. My feet slapped against the icy floor tiles, and I reached the door and swung it wide.

Lottie launched at me for a hug, then pulled back, eyes wide. "What is that on your neck?"

I pressed my fingertips to my throat. "What do you mean?"

My friend uttered a laugh and guided me to the hall mirror. Dark bruises decorated my neck and chest, and I gaped.

"Um..."

Lottie danced back to close the door, then waggled her eyebrows at me and drew me into the kitchen. "Ye went to the beach last night?"

I perched on a stool, all kinds of strange yet delicious aches registering in my body. "I went. Struan followed me home."

Lottie sat next to me and picked up her blonde braid, toying with the end in a familiar habit. "Uh-huh. And clearly stuff happened."

"Everything happened."

Her eyes widened. "That was your first time, right? What was it like?"

"I want to say magical and beautiful, but that would be a lie. It was dirty and exciting. It was pitch-black from the power cut, and that somehow made it easier."

She gave me a quizzical look. "What power cut?"

I rolled my eyes. That had been him, then. Another trick to mess with me. "Never mind. It doesn't matter what happened with him. It was a one-off. He still hates me. I hate him."

Lottie yanked my jumper aside, admiring the bruises. "Oh yeah, all these hate bites say that loud and clear."

I batted her hand away and reached to turn on the kettle. The button lit, and the kettle rumbled instantly, and I grouched under my breath. Last night, I'd washed in icy cold water, in the dark, before bundling myself up in bed. I hadn't even bothered trying a light switch, but I bet it would've worked.

"I'm going to make tea. I have so much to tell you about. I'm sorry I went quiet."

"Don't be daft. Ye had everything to deal with." Her eyes darkened. "Including some guy who let ye almost be assaulted. What the hell was all that about?"

I'd forgotten I'd told her about Charterman on the phone. While I brewed the tea, I filled Lottie in on my father, Charterman being the executor of my grandmother's will, and my problems with university. When I came to the part about McInver grabbing me, I forced myself to relive the scene.

The vast mansion, empty of life. The riches left on display. The way Charterman spoke to him, and the way he spoke to me like women were only useful for one thing.

How had Esme phrased it? Cum receptacles?

"The dirty old bastard," Lottie said. "I hope his shrivelled old cock and balls fall off. Did you report him to the police?"

"No. I should've, but Henry's sister, Esme, told me that our fathers were working with McInver. Or interested in him in some way. I didn't want to ruin that for them. Until now, I blocked out my memories of that night, but what if it's something to do with Dad's disappearance?"

"What do ye mean? Like the old man did something to him?"

I shook my head softly, the hot tea steaming in front of me. "I don't know. He's too frail to be a suspect himself. How can a person disappear completely? I've been expecting him to reappear, but it hasn't happened. This is my only clue."

Lottie winced. "Actually, that lawyer is the person to talk to. If you went to him, at his office, and with backup, he couldn't hurt ye."

True. As much I disliked Charterman, I couldn't ignore him much longer.

"You're right. Will you come with me?"

Lottie's expression turned bleak. "I want to, but I don't know. My dad... Why don't you get Charterman to come here? We can meet him in this house."

The distant memory registered about Lottie's father getting angry. I couldn't remember spending any time with her parents— we always met on the beach, or she came here—but I'd always suspected her home life was unhappy.

I took her fingers in mine. "Is there a problem with your dad?"

She wrinkled her nose and squeezed my hand. "Isn't there with everyone's dad? Yours is missing, mine is...what he is." Lottie hopped from the stool. "I tell you what's been driving me crazy, that key your grandmother gave ye."

I took the chain in my fingers and pulled it from my jumper. At my grandmother's funeral, I'd told Lottie about it.

She was distracting me from questions about her father, I knew that. But I allowed it. When she was ready, she'd confide in me. God knew I had enough secrets myself.

"I've hunted all over the house. There's no safe, no locked drawers, no secret rooms."

"But it was important enough for her to keep hold of and gift to ye. Even in the worst of her dementia, she remembered."

I puzzled over that. "That means it was something familiar, and that had been here a really long time, predating her illness. But then that could be anything in this house. Nothing has changed in decades."

"Want help looking?"

I nodded and set about yet another search of the house. We examined every cupboard, picture frame, and poked around under beds and even tapped floorboards. After a couple of hours, I had a great idea of the contents of my grandmother's house but no insight into her hidden mysteries.

We drifted along the hall, and I paused at the tall, framed picture of my grandparents' wedding. In a full lace gown, my grandmother smiled, her features clear.

"What did you want to tell me, Granny?"

Lottie peeked back and giggled. "Maybe she just really liked treasure hunts. Hey, you're so similar to her."

"Everyone always said that. Maybe that's why I felt a strong connection to her, despite Dad not liking coming here. Both Granny and I loved knitting and mystery stories. She bought me so many books."

Back in the kitchen, Lottie gazed at the key. "On that mystery story theme, how would a detective go about this?"

"They'd probably say the most obvious answer is generally the truth."

"Then what's that? A jewellery box?"

After the funeral, I'd taken Granny's small amount of jewellery back to Edinburgh. Her engagement and wedding rings plus a couple of other items.

"She didn't have one. The most obvious place to me is my grandfather's old desk in the office."

"But ye checked in there."

I had, but even so, I stepped over to the room once more.

Lottie followed, tucking her fingers into her armpits. "Why does it feel so wrong being in this room? Like going into the headmaster's office."

"It's eerie in here. It was in this room that I unknowingly signed the paperwork that gifted me the island. Everything about it feels wrong. Haunted."

A thought flitted across my mind, tantalising but fleeting. I'd asked to be given the rights to direct Granny's care. Charterman had looked at me strangely. After, Henry said he and my father had argued, but then I'd signed papers both must have known the contents of.

Ones which took my father out of the line of inheritance.

Did that mean anything? The more I heard about his debt issues, it felt important—the island presumably was valuable, but I had no real idea why he'd want that. To not have that asset.

Yet another mystery.

At the desk, I slid out the big central drawer and wrangled it to the desktop. Then I ducked and peeked in the gap. A thin, wooden frame formed the shelf. Not deep enough to contain a compartment. Ducking under, I tapped the corners and the legs. Nothing sounded hollow.

Lottie poked around the contents of the drawer. "So much old stuff."

She tidied a stack of papers in her hands.

In the corner of the drawer's base, a tiny mark caught my attention.

"What's that?" I leaned in and touched my finger to the mark.

It was a hole, metal-lined. My interest spiked, and I scrabbled to extract the other papers and mess, depositing it all on the chair. Lottie helped and, when it was empty, I took the key from my neck and fitted it to the hole.

It turned.

The entire base dislodged from the drawer's false bottom, and using the quarter-turned key, I pulled it out.

"Holy fuck balls." Lottie clapped her fingers to her

mouth. "Money."

I stared down at the stacks and stacks of notes, neat rows each an inch thick.

My friend giggled and picked up a tower of twenties, thumbing through them. "It really was a treasure hunt. Your grandmother was hoarding cash. I've heard about this, how elderly people keep money under their beds because they don't trust banks. How much do ye think is even here?"

A soft breath left me. "I don't know. Thousands?"

"Oh my God. It's got to be enough for you to finish out at uni. This is at least a grand here and there's, what, three rows of five. Some of it looks like outdated currency, but most isn't. It's a gift from beyond the grave."

She took up another stack then furrowed her brow. "What's that underneath?"

I pushed the money aside, extracting an old photo from the drawer.

A man, maybe in his twenties, peered out of the brownish print.

"Not your grandfather," Lottie said.

"No. But he's familiar somehow."

I held the picture up, and we both squinted at it.

I was going mad. "This is going to sound crazy, but don't you think he looks like Struan?"

My friend's eyebrows rose. "Weirdly, I was just about to say something like that. Aye, there's a resemblance. Seems your taste in men runs in the family. Both of ye liked the glowering, dark-haired ones."

I pondered it. "You think he's an old flame? She was devoted to my grandfather. At least I always believed so. Dad once said she'd had other offers of marriage before and after his death."

"Why keep a photo in her secret hiding place otherwise?" Lottie shrugged, then her phone buzzed in her pocket. She handed me the notes then stared at her screen. "It's from Sinclair. I mean Sin. He wants to meet tonight."

A mix of emotions churned inside me. The money should be a relief, but I was somehow disappointed. For so long, I'd carried this mystery around with me. Some final message from my grandmother. And while the money was great and solved the problem of me continuing my life, it left me empty.

My old life had been slowly eroded away. Mum left, Dad vanished, Granny died. I could finish out university, but then what? Where would I go? I couldn't live here. Even if my best friend was on the island, at some point she'd leave. Struan and his friends would go, too.

That brought me back to the present.

I gestured at Lottie's phone. "Tell him that Struan has a message from me to give to them. And if Struan wants to see me, he has to come here this afternoon. Otherwise I'll leave on the ferry this evening. I have exams next week. I have to get back."

She tapped at the screen, her mouth turning down. "I wish ye could stay, but that money is a gift. Ye should honour your grandmother and use it wisely."

"You're right. I'll continue with the last term and get through exams. I'll call Charterman, too, though that's less urgent now. Enough to keep me busy, right?"

No matter how wrong leaving felt, I couldn't trust that feeling. The tug to stay here and pretend I was safe.

I spent the last couple of hours alone, Lottie needing to get back ahead of her father returning. Then, with the money hidden in my overnight bag, I locked up and walked down to the dock.

The strangest thing about going? My knitting had vanished, the needles where I'd put them, the almost-finished, abandoned-for-a-year soft, blue scarf gone.

Struan didn't show. And I wasn't surprised.

27

Unknown

I paced the room, anger licking me like fire. Why hadn't she broken? Everything was in play. Theadora was all alone. Penniless. Her other options removed or dismissed.

There was only one path for her now.

She was a woman, useful to me at last.

She wasn't supposed to have grown a backbone, too.

I hadn't spent years building up to this to have that little bitch risk it all. I would have my revenge on them all. Money to burn. My life back again.

If only we'd gone through with the initial plan and slit the boys' throats in their beds. We'd be murderers, several times over, but it would be worth it. I'd been the one to find them, to follow my nose, track down their trails.

One of the men, I'd been all too aware of ever since his birth.

It should've been my decision to make.

But as much as I wanted it, McInver was better off being persuaded, not backed into a corner. The legal situation would be simpler with his signature. No one would look too closely.

Which brought me back to my problem child.

If Theadora wasn't going to come to us, the fight would go to her.

When the moment was right, she'd be brought in.

28

Struan

A day of being locked down had me going out of my mind. Earlier this evening, Thea left. *Again.* I fucking despised the feeling of helplessness.

Stuck in the bunk room, I could have called her. But there was too great a risk of us losing our phone. Our keeper had us in here for a reason, ordered us to charge our trackers.

Something was happening.

Nervous energy bounced around me. From the behaviour of the other three men, we all felt it.

"What if it's a new person?" Burn said quietly from his bunk. "Maybe we'll finally get to meet number five."

I shot my head up. "Who's number five?"

He peeked at Sin and swallowed.

Sin stared back for a beat then jerked his head at the bathroom. They filed in and hugged the wall while Sin hit the button for the shower. Instantly, I understood the purpose. The sound of running water would block out our voices in case Keep was listening in.

I joined them, and Burn flicked his gaze between us, landing on me.

"Scar said that in Keep's office, there are five files in her cabinet. Number four was empty until ye arrived. There are five trackers, too. Four on us, one waiting to be added to the system. Why only five unless there was only ever going to be that number of us here?"

I'd seen the five files but hadn't thought much on it since. "And none of ye thought to mention this?"

Sin leaned towards me. "Are ye joking? Repeatedly, we've tried to talk with ye, and you've pushed back at every opportunity."

I set my features to a neutral mask and folded my arms, not intimidated by the giant man. "Are ye seriously expecting me to trust ye? Ye, who offers fake friendship while hiding the real truths?"

"If I wasnae up front with ye, it was because I couldn't be sure about what you'd do. But ye can trust me. We're all in this together. None of us are to blame. We have to live together. And now Theadora has left, we've lost our chance to talk to her about this place."

"She already did. She sold us out."

He stared at me. "Who to?"

"Jenkins. She gave him the job to shut this place down. Basically handed our arses to him." It was unfair of me, but I only spoke the truth. Whatever her intentions, she'd put us into a far worse scenario than before.

Sin palmed his neck and wheeled around. "That's why he's been haunting the fucking doorstep. Did ye tell her to call him off?"

I jutted out my chin. "No. I don't want anything from her. Ye shouldn't either. We can handle this ourselves.

So tell me your grand theory. All this intelligence you've been gathering, all the beatings you've taken, what have ye summed up?"

Sin exchanged a glance with the other two, then brought his gaze back to me. My heart sped, and I tried not to show the effects.

"We're related," he said.

Surprise caught me. I went to deny his claim, but too fast, things started adding up. The way Burn cosied up to him like a brother. The similarities between us. All of us had black hair, Scar and Burn were of a similar build, just as I was with Sin. Though he was taller by several inches, we'd added muscle in the same way, even moved the same fucking way sometimes.

"Related how?"

"Burn and I are half-brothers. When he arrived here, we compared stories. We're from the same area, Aberdeen boys. But the connections got deeper and stranger. I'd heard my mother mention his mother's name. She hated her for stealing some rich arsehole she was seeing. It happened when I was small, but she kept the grudge her whole life, and even pointed out the woman to me once, accusing her of stealing our meal ticket. At the time, this other woman had a wee boy at her side. Burn, I'm almost sure. And I'm reasonably certain that man she hated so much was my da, and Burn's, too. I'm less sure about ye and Scar. What can ye tell me about your background?"

In turn, I stared at each of them, hair texture, eye shape, all of it taking on a different meaning now. If I'd have been open with them from the start, this might've come out sooner. I might have felt... What? Connected?

Up until this point, I hadn't wanted that.

I was starting to forget why that was. Now, I understood why Sin hadn't just left. It wasn't a prisoner bond but a family one.

"I never knew my father," I answered. "Ma would never tell me his name. She…"

"No judgement here," Burn said. "My mother slept with rich men for money. She was so pretty but a hooker, aye? She died when I was ten."

I hung my head, not wanting to get into this conversation, but equally knowing I couldn't keep avoiding it. On the night I'd been captured, Ma had told me she was going to jail. I'd left in anger, never to see her again. What a fuck-up. "Same. Ma was beautiful. I mean is, she is naw dead. She called it high-class escort work. She'd disappear for days sometimes, staying with whatever guy had bought her time."

"Where is she now?" Sin asked quietly.

"Prison. A real one. Eight years for fraud."

"You're the only one with the mother still alive, then," he added. "Mine died of a drug overdose, though I never saw her at the end. Scar was orphaned when he was wee, and his grandparents took him in until they were too old to care for him."

"They didn't know who my da was," Scar said. "But it doesn't take a genius to guess."

I blinked, too many thoughts crowding in. I stumbled over my words. "Ye think we're all brothers." A statement, not a question.

He nodded, then the other two agreed with a quiet aye.

The implications rippled over my mind. "Then if that's true, the man who fucked our mothers is the one kidnapping and keeping us here."

Noises came from the entrance to the hostel, echoing down the corridor even over the sound of the running water. I stiffened, and the others stood tall.

"We don't know that," Sin said, fast. "I've no clue on the motivation, only the background. Scar once said this was a place where we'd been sent to forget about us. What if it's to hide us? And if so, from what? If this is another dark-haired lad, it's a good bet we're right. Even more if they're young."

"Why?"

"Because apart from ye, the rest of us were brought here in age order. Prioritised."

I stared at him. "Ma and I moved around a lot."

His scrutiny was cutting. "It took them longer to find ye, then. Or you'd have been here first."

First? Heat rushed through me, thoughts colliding. "Why did ye make such a big deal over my age?" I blurted. "What does it matter?"

"The oldest cops the beatings," Scar supplied for him. "On day one of ye getting here, I faked your records to make ye younger that Sin. He asked that so ye wouldnae be hurt. But your birthday is a week before his."

I was the oldest? He'd...protected me? My own mother had barely done that. I tilted my head at him, seeing him in a whole new light. "Why?"

Sin stared back then cursed and broke my gaze. "I could handle it. It was also a test. Whether the jailor knew that detail. He didn't. Another piece of intelligence gained."

I sucked in a breath. "Then someone else is involved."

Sharp interest gleamed in Sin's eyes, and he nodded.

"Exactly."

Footsteps sounded in the corridor, more than one set. Burn killed the shower, and we all emerged back into the bedroom, muscles tensed. My emotions rocked around like waves in a storm.

From outside, Keep muttered something, then the lock disengaged and the door opened.

A wee scrap of a child fell through the opening, their expression terrified and clothes filthy.

Black hair. Blue eyes. An ankle tracker fitted to a skinny leg.

And in one key way different from us.

Our newcomer was a girl.

*T*he door slammed, the key twisting in the lock. All four of us stared at the wee lass.

Our sister, if the theory was correct.

She stared back at us with huge blue eyes, her face tear-streaked. A locked jaw and proud look couldn't hide obvious fear.

Burn was the first to move, sitting cross-legged in front of her. "Hey, I'm Burn. Can ye tell me your name?"

Her scared gaze flitted over all of us then settled on him. "Cassie. It's Cassiopeia, but I hate that."

"It's nice to meet ye, Cassie. How old are ye?"

"Six and a half."

He pointed back. "That's Sin, there. Then Scar and

Ruin. No one here is going to hurt ye."

Her little shoulders came down a fraction. "That woman twisted my arm and pulled me by my hair."

"None of us will do that. We willnae let her touch ye again either. I imagine today was scary, but it's over now. We'll protect ye."

Burn took control, pointing out the beds and the bathroom to her, chattering calmly and making sounds of reassurance.

I glowered at the door. "This isnae right."

Sin snorted. "Now he's catching on. None of this has ever been right."

I lowered my gaze at him, too mixed up over what had to be the last of their secrets. "What I mean is that they're giving up the pretence of what this place is. How could they bring a child here? She needs her ma. More people will be looking for her than they did for the rest of us."

"I don't have a ma," a little voice answered. "Or a da. Am I in prison?"

I peered at the lass, seeing only familiarity in every one of her features. Burn's angelic appearance that hid a dangerous psycho side. Scar's careful regard. Sin's stern brow.

"No, ye havenae done anything wrong. This is a mistake. Where did ye come from?" I asked, trying to soften my tone though it was far from natural for me.

Cassie clutched her arms tightly around herself and didn't reply.

Burn tried a few more questions, but she'd gone silent.

The implication was plain. Like the rest of us, she was probably cut off from anyone who cared. Alone, stolen, and hidden.

"What do we do now?" Burn asked the rest of us. "She doesnae have a bag, and we don't have any of the things a lass might need."

Theadora would probably help, if I asked. I shook off the idea. "Sin, ye need to call Lottie. She's bound to have clothes, aye?"

He grunted acknowledgement, but his focus was elsewhere.

The room fell silent. I swung a look around to find Burn and Scar both watching the big guy.

I rounded on him. "What is it?"

Scar spoke first. "The jailor. He'll come back now, won't he?"

In all the time I'd been here, the man who'd beaten and abused Sin had only visited once. Directly after my arrival.

"That's when he comes." I caught up. "After each new one of us is captured, he comes here to make sure the oldest hears his message and passes it on. That is fucked up."

Burn hissed at me. "Language." At my raised eyebrow, he tutted. "I had a foster sister in the last place I was in. Ye cannae talk like that around kids."

That was news to me. The company my mother kept never watched their tongues for my sake.

Slowly, I let it sink in. "Sorry," I muttered. "Whatever. When he comes, this time, it'll be my turn."

"No," Sin denied. "We're sticking with how things are."

I flattened my lips. "Fighting is what I do. I'm good at it. We don't need to test anything with him anymore."

Sin's scowl held brimming anger. "I'm good with my

fists, too, but I'd bet my control is better than yours. Save your strength. This is my battle. I chose it. I dinna give a damn about anything else. You'll let me."

We both glared until I rolled my shoulders and accepted his request.

Burn turned back to Cassie. "Go ahead and get washed up. No one will disturb ye."

He ushered her into the bathroom, closed her in, then marched back over to us. "If ye two have stopped measuring your dicks, we need to talk about this situation. What kind of monster puts a small girl in a room with four adult males? It isnae right that she's here. Any of us could be perverts like Jenkins."

Hot emotion rushed in me. After everything my mother had been through, all the dirty bastards she suffered to keep us fed, I resented being tarred with that brush. "I'm no fucking pervert."

"Fuck that," Sin agreed.

"Never," Scar added.

Burn shook his head. "I wasn't saying that. Even if they're thinking she's our sister, we're not supposed to know that. I dinna care that they've left us here to rot, but a wee lass? It's just wrong."

Our sister.

I had a sister and brothers. Yet again, my world shifted on its axis, and I was out of control.

"Aye, and the final piece to the puzzle." Sin brushed his hand over his jaw, his gaze troubled. "I always assumed when the fifth of us turned up, things would become clearer. Come to a head. Bring the battle. Even if I'm right, and we are all brothers and sister, I'm still no clearer as to why we're here. But I'll tell ye all one thing. This time, when the jailor comes, his visit will be his last."

29

Struan

Across the beach, Lottie approached, her eyes wide and her fingertips at her lips. In her other hand, she carried a bulging bag, a coat slung across the top. For two days, Keep had kept us locked down. Every evening, we'd expected the jailor, but he never came.

Each night, Cassie cried in her sleep. Burn had styled himself as her number one protector, but even he couldn't settle her fears.

We were all strangers to her, and the place we lived was nasty. Cold.

Then this morning, as the first light of dawn crept around our boarded-up window, I'd woken to see the wee lass curled up at the bottom of Sin's bed, her own blanket wrapped tightly around her, and her expression finally peaceful.

I guessed there was no accounting for taste. Even if I had grudging respect for him now.

"Holy shite," Lottie uttered when we were close

enough in the cool evening air. "I know what I heard, but my eyes are having a hard job believing it." She peeked down at Cassie. "Hey there, sweetie. Aren't ye a pretty thing? I'm Lottie. I've brought ye some of my old clothes and a jacket."

She raised her attention to Burn who hovered over our newest and littlest resident. "I won't stay long. I can't be seen talking to ye. There's a couple of things I couldn't get, but all the essentials are there. A hairbrush being the main one I think she needs."

She wasn't wrong. Cassie's hair was in danger of becoming a rat's nest of black curls.

"I don't have any of my toys or clothes," Cassie uttered. "And the boys don't have anything for girls."

Fuck. Toys. I hadn't even thought of that.

Lottie reached out and stroked back a curl. "Of course they don't. They're a bunch of Neanderthals. Want me to braid this for ye? Next time, I'll try to bring a detangling spray, but we'll see what we can do quickly now."

Cassie gave a nod, curiosity in her gaze at Thea's friend.

Burn tipped his head at the rest of us, gesturing that he wanted to talk. While Lottie threaded the coat onto Cassie's skinny arms then found her hairbrush, he ushered us aside until we were out of earshot.

"We need new rules," he said. "We cannae continue on the way we have now Cassie's here. First, no jerking off in the shower. I mean ye two more than anyone." He pointed at me and Sin. "Don't deny it. Sound travels. I've heard far more moaning of Thea's and Lottie's names than I ever wanted to."

"Fuck off," I spat at the same time Sin snapped, "Shut

your damn mouth."

Across the sands, Lottie was teasing the worst of the knots from Cassie's hair, but her gaze flitted to us.

Burn's mouth fell open in delight, and he exchanged an amused look with Scar before continuing. "Secondly, she needs more privacy."

I shook my head. "Where the fuck are we supposed to go? I agree, but there's only so much we can do."

"And that's a third thing," Burn argued. "Ye swear all the time. Cut it out."

"No, I fucking don't." I blinked at my own words, earning a laugh from both Burn and Scar.

Sin lifted his chin. "We can string up a sheet around her bunk so she feels more like she has her own space. Kind of like when Struan decided to live in the cupboard for a month. That's probably the best we can do."

I glowered at him, but there was no malice in it. Cassie's arrival had mellowed me. Maybe the knowledge that we were related, too. The feeling of being disconnected and lost had gone.

"Guys?" Lottie called.

We made our way back over to where she was twisting the final lengths of Cassie's hair into a plait.

"I have to go," she said. "I can't go to the mainland at the moment, so it might take a while to get the things she needs. I'll let ye know when I can meet up again."

Sin took a half step forward so he was towering over her. "Why aren't ye able to go off the island?"

Her cheeks pinkened. "I just can't." Her gaze slid to me. "Before I leave... This is going to sound like a really stupid question, but Thea asked it of me, and I have no idea. Why are ye still here? She said that as owner of the island, she'd closed down the hostel."

At Theadora's name, my mood dropped straight back to miserable.

Burn leaned in and took the bag of clothes from Lottie, then he and Scar led Cassie away.

Sin shook his head once. "It's more complicated than that. We're still being tracked. The islanders willnae let us get away. Including your da, Violet. We're naw free."

My frustration rose again, never-ending when it came to Theadora. "Tell her we're sorry she can't play magician and vanish all our troubles away."

Lottie's nostrils flared, and she focused on me. "She only wants to help."

"Oh really? Is that why she gave Jenkins control over us?"

From her jolt of awareness, I could tell this was news to her, and that she knew exactly what kind of person Jenkins was.

Which only drove home how bad an idea it had been.

I curled my lip in a sneer. "She might as well have just thrown us to the wolves for all the help she gave."

Lottie's eyes flashed with emotion. "Jenkins is a terrible choice, but I didn't know she made it, and I bet she doesn't know anything about him. I do know that she's a good person who doesn't deserve to be talked about like this."

I gave a short laugh, but Lottie wasn't done.

"If you only knew what she'd been through—"

"What she's been through? Aye, poor little rich girl up there in her ivory tower."

Lottie squared up to me, outrage in the set of her jaw. She jabbed a finger in my direction. "Her dad disappearing. Her grandmother dying. The arsehole holding her inheritance hostage. An inheritance she never asked for and doesnae want because of all the shite it brings with it. Then she was hurt. How do ye think she feels when she comes here? If you'd done anything more than treat her like a booty call, you'd know. So don't be a dick about her. Don't come at my best friend with that shitty attitude. She's a good person and she's trying hard. Ye, on the other hand, are just a jerk."

Shock stole my response. "Who hurt her?"

Briefly, Lottie closed her eyes. "Forget I said anything. If ye don't like her, I don't want to hear it. Just stay away from her. And stay away from me, too."

She stormed off, leaving footprints in her wake.

Sin grumbled something, but I didn't want to hear. All that was present in my mind was the thought of someone hurting her. Maybe laying his bastard hands on her while she said no. Fuck, I'd faked doing the same with her friend. Hot flashed over me followed by an icy chill.

"I'm fucking sorry," I bellowed after Lottie.

But the lass was long gone.

*T*wo weeks on, and nothing had changed. We'd had no sign of the jailor. Lottie had left a bag of things for Cassie at our beach hideaway, which we then kept carefully hidden from Keep. With the stuff she wore, we had to hope our keeper was ignorant enough not to notice. So far, so good. Likewise, Cassie was under strict instruction never to mention Lottie, but otherwise we hadn't seen the lass.

Thea didn't return to the island.

I was sick of waiting. Sick of feeling like an animal in a cage about to be destroyed or left to rot.

In the hostel's kitchen, I scrubbed at the big pot I'd made porridge in this morning, taking out my anger on the dull scratched-up metal.

Burn entered the kitchen and banged around, opening all the cupboard doors, searching for something. "Cassie has a fever."

During the past couple of weeks, the newest member of our crew had quickly become part of our routine. She was sweet. Quieter than the rest of us, probably smarter, too, and slowly she had come out of her shell. The wee lass had a sense of humour. She found us funny. Burn adored her, and I had a sneaky suspicion that Sin did, too. During a spring storm, I'd again found her curled up at the end of his bed, flinching in her sleep at the thunder but calming when he set a hand on her head.

I lifted my head from the scrubbing. "A fever? Since when?"

"I think overnight. She complained of a headache when she went to sleep."

"What do we do with that?"

"I don't fucking know. She's just really hot. That can't be good, right? Have ye seen any painkillers here?"

"No, but ye can't give adult stuff to kids, can ye?"

He glanced at me, and I registered the mild panic in his eyes.

I finished with the pan and turned to him. "Okay,

calm down. Look online to see what to do."

In the bunk room, Sin sprawled on the floor adjacent to Cassie's bunk with his back to the wall and his focus on her. On the lass's first night here, Scar had taken the bunk above mine so she could have a lower one.

Huddled on her mattress, the little girl curled in a ball, her face red and her breathing fast.

I set the backs of my fingers to her forehead. Burning skin met my touch.

Scar was already searching on our phone. "Okay, it says fevers are normal but they can be dangerous if they get too high or last too long. We need to bring the temperature down with Calpol or something like that with paracetamol. Low-dose stuff meant for kids. I'm going to text Lottie."

Automatically, he raised his gaze to Sin.

The big man gave a nod of agreement. "Faster to call her."

Scar held out the phone, but Sin hesitated.

I grabbed it instead and hit her name. It rang a few times then she picked up, her voice low and breathy like she'd ran somewhere private. "Hello?"

"It's Struan. Don't hang up. We need your help."

"What's wrong?"

"Cassie is sick. We need medicine to bring down a fever. Can ye help?"

Shouting came from her end of the call.

Lottie uttered a fake laugh. "God, exams sound like a real drag, Thea. I'll be so glad when you're done and ye can come here."

My damn heart thumped. "When is she coming?" I asked before I could stop myself.

The shouting came again and louder, her da, no doubt. I picked up a few words. *Stupid bitch. Just like your mother. Where are ye?*

Abruptly the call ended. I pulled the phone from my ear and swore.

"What happened?" Scar asked.

"Her da's in a rage. I don't know if we can rely on her help."

"What the fuck did he do?" Sin sat forward.

From the bed, Cassie uttered a sob. Sin's expression dropped, and he knelt at her bedside. "Sorry I shouted. We'll make ye better, aye? Just rest up."

He rose to his feet and pointed at me and Scar, then at the door. Without a word, we fell in, and the three of us left the bunk room.

"If Lottie can't help us, we need to fix this ourselves," he said.

"What are you thinking?" Scar asked.

"One of us will have to go off island and to a chemist." Sin's gaze set on me.

Adrenaline hit me in a rush. For months, I'd pictured stealing a boat then taking Keep's car on a joyride. In more recent times, it had become harder to imagine leaving the others behind. I still had nowhere to go, and all the questions to be answered about this place.

Like it or not, I wasn't done with Torlum.

More, I dreamed of finding Theadora. Driving to her home, wherever that was. Waiting for her to find me in her bed. Having her again.

But those thoughts came at a cost. My emotions were wrapped up in it, too. I fucking yearned for her, like some lovesick idiot.

It was better to push her away than ever have her close again.

"I'll pull the big brother card. I'm going. I'll need cash, but I should be okay for a boat. Scar, can ye disable the tracking system?"

"Aye. But if Keep realises something is up—"

"It won't matter," I interrupted. "We're sitting here waiting for her to do shite, so if she works it out, let her call the jailor. Bring it. End this place."

My mind scrambled over a plan, but then I hit a snag. After the islanders had brought me back last time, surely somebody would have changed the code to Theadora's family's boat.

Which meant messaging her.

Scar and Sin talked fast about what we all needed to do, and I held out my hand, interrupting them.

"Give me the phone."

Scar handed it over, and I found my @islandboy account then logged on. Without letting myself think of anything other than helping Cassie, I messaged Theadora.

@islandboy: Has the code on the lock to your boat changed?

Emotion roiled inside me, spiking when the dots showed she was typing a response.

@theadorastewart: No.

No? That was it?

Whatever. I didn't have time for this. I tuned back in to the conversation, hearing the plan to distract Keep, steal her keys, and stop the alarm from sounding when I left. Action took over us all.

In an hour, I was ready to go.

In the bunk room, I snatched my stolen prized possession from where I'd wrapped it in my blankets, then carried it to Cassie's bed. I folded the soft blue knitted scarf into a pillow, the trailing thread tucked in from where it hadn't been finished, and placed it under the little lass's head.

Next thing I knew, I was out at sea, in broad daylight this time, and using up all my luck.

By the time the Isle of Skye came into view, the route far easier now I'd done it twice, I had a race on my hands to get to the chemist before closing. And I was ready to mow down anyone who got in my way.

*A*t Portree, the only town I knew, I sped to the shop, brakes squealing as I stepped on them. Keep's car had worked, though it shuddered like it was about to collapse into pieces.

Inside the chemist, I scanned the shelves and snatched up the purple box, a picture of a happy kid on the front. The woman behind the counter glared at me but took my cash.

On my way out, a noticeboard by the door caught my attention. On it was a flyer for a mechanic outreach programme.

A lifetime ago, I'd run into one of their people. Max. The redheaded guy who'd fixed my car after I'd tried to race him over the bridge to the mainland. I'd lost his number when the islanders had caught me, though I remembered the last three digits. And I'd never forgotten his arsehole request that I call myself *joyrider* when I messaged him.

His number was listed on the flyer.

He'd been a good person. Maybe someone I could call on if I needed to, say, if one day we escaped but the car wouldn't start. With Cassie in our group now, we'd need more help.

I snatched the leaflet, sending other happy-community shite flying.

"Hey," the woman at the counter called after me.

But I was gone, returned to the car, mission half successful. Now to get back to Cassie.

30

Thea

Ahead of me, from outside the rank of shops in Portree, an old grey Ford shot into the road, narrowly missing my car. I slammed on my brakes and glared at the driver. Dad's car had been playing up, not starting a couple of times. I had places to be, I didn't need this.

The man in the other car hauled on the wheel, ignoring the fact he'd almost caused a crash.

Shock and recognition rushed in. Dark hair, cut jaw, and his trademark glower. Struan was at the controls.

How on earth…?

I didn't wait for my brain to supply an answer. I'd dreamed about the next time I'd see him. My exams were finished now, and though I still had sessions to attend at uni, in only a few weeks, the year would be done. I'd have the long summer months alone.

Though it had made me sick to do it, I'd called Charterman's office and agreed to a meeting. His secretary hadn't given me instructions on anything I'd need, but it was better to go prepared. One item meant my quick return back to Torlum. Granny's birth certificate had been part of the stack I'd found in the house. I'd grab that then go.

I still had time to work out what to do with the place. Live there, sell it, sell the whole island. I didn't have a fixed idea, not while Dad was still absent, but I was certain that I didn't want Charterman to be hanging over me like a spectre.

Gunning the engine, I took off after Struan.

The trip from Portree to the harbour at Uig took only twenty minutes, but at no point did Struan slow. Halfway along, we skirted a loch, and I put my foot down and burned past him in the faster Jaguar.

Then I pulled the car across both lanes and blocked him in. Struan braked hard and leapt from his car, muscles bunched and rage pouring off him. I stepped from mine and cocked my hip.

Slowly, his gaze travelled over me, the shock I'd felt reflected back in his every move. He sucked in a breath and shook his head, utter disbelief scrawled all over him.

The last time I'd seen him, it had been icy cold, and the warmth that spring had brought to Northern Scotland did nothing to soften his harsh edges.

I had no clue what to say. Only the need that shot over me, infecting every cell. Instantly, I burned for him.

But over and over, Struan had scalded me.

Without a word, I raised an eyebrow then got back in my seat, shut myself in, and took off again. Without pause, Struan snarled his engine and followed.

I should be wondering all kinds of things. What the hell he was doing off the island. Whose car that was.

Where he'd been. But all I knew was a singular sense of being in his presence again.

By the time we reached the harbour, I parked, and he drew his car right alongside mine. I climbed out, and he was already there at my door.

His eyes glittered. I grabbed my bag and stepped out, forcing him to move out of my way. Then I locked up the car, nervous and excited and more alive than I'd felt in months.

The whole time, Struan didn't take his heavy attention off me.

At the end of the dock, the ferry bobbed in the water, a few minutes away from leaving. Yet Struan couldn't have come here by those means. This was why he'd checked the boat code. *Right.*

He walked backwards, and I followed, then at the rear of the cars, he rounded on me.

I expected him to speak. But like me, his words wouldn't come. Instead, he lifted his hand and brushed my hair over my shoulder and took grip of the back of my neck.

Propelling me with him, he walked me out of the car park, down the road, and to the slipway for smaller boats.

My breathing came hard. There wasn't a single other person in the world I'd let do this. Dominate me like this. Not after the experiences I'd had. But with him, it worked differently.

I didn't feel restrained. He made me feel safer. Turned on.

At the end of the concrete slope, I boarded my family's boat and finally registered what Struan was carrying. A box of medicine for a child.

"Whose child?" I asked.

Struan pushed the boat free and jumped in, getting us moving into the sea. He kept his gaze on the horizon, and his jaw locked. "You'll see," was his only concession.

Throughout the trip, a sense of urgency surrounded him. It filled me, too, until my nerves jangled.

We reached Torlum and docked the boat. I trod the walkway as if I was here alone, while Struan skirted the edge of the tiny harbour. There was no one else around, but he stayed out of sight until we were deep into the interior of the island.

At the hostel, Struan towed me around the back and to a side door. He entered, and with one tug on my hand, I was inside, too. For a moment, in the dark hallway, we faced each other, his chest rising and falling as hard as mine.

"One minute," he said.

But at my short nod, he didn't leave me alone, instead, taking me with him into the place I'd only ever explored as a youngster. In a bunk room lit only by a yellow light bulb, the others waited.

Burn jumped up and grabbed the box Struan had bought in Portree, surprise registering in his gaze as he noticed me. He didn't slow his moves, extracting the bottle of medicine before turning to a bunk.

A little girl curled up in the sheets. Cheeks pink and breathing too fast. Blue wool peeked from under her head, and with a start, I recognised my scarf.

Struan must have taken it, then used it as her pillow.

Extracting the medicine into the syringe, Burn spoke to us. "Her fever hasn't let up, and she was sick after ye left. We got her to drink a little water, but that was it."

With a careful touch, he lifted her head and set the syringe to her lips. The little girl stirred and drank the medicine.

"Good lass. One more dose and you'll feel better, I promise."

All of the men watched on in rapt interest as he delivered the rest of the medicine. As if this child's illness affected them all.

"Who is she?" I whispered to Struan.

Surely not a daughter to any of them, though in looks, there were many similarities.

The girl sank back into sleep, and the four men breathed a collective sigh of relief.

"One of us," Struan muttered.

He straightened and grabbed my hand in his once more. Beyond the room, we kept going. Outdoors, across the moor until we were nearing my grandmother's home.

Once, I'd run this way, and he'd pursued me. We'd ended up having sex. My first and only time. As if remembering, my body prickled with awareness. My heart beat faster, and my fingers shook as I reached to unlock the front door.

The late afternoon light spilled through to the floor, and I followed, Struan hot on my heels.

He slammed the door behind me.

All my questions fled. It was better if I didn't ask any. Perhaps there was only one thing we were good for with each other. Turning, I stepped into his space.

I gazed into his dark-blue eyes, witnessing his torment.

Then I pressed up on my toes and kissed him.

Last time, he'd denied me this. Or perhaps I simply

hadn't taken it.

People didn't change overnight. I hadn't. Every time I thought I was living in some way, I'd been knocked back, reverted to form. The scared little girl I'd always been. But I wasn't scared now.

If my legs shook and my fingers trembled, it was with anticipation.

Struan backed me to the green-tiled wall. With his mouth never leaving mine, he knocked my hand aside and cupped both my cheeks, a little too rough, but then again, he always was. And I welcomed his way of doing things.

His lips dominated mine, the kiss hard and branding.

I smiled into it.

I placed both hands on his chest, grazing with my nails down to his waistband. Struan pulled back as if I'd surprised him. My grin only grew, and I ran my teeth over my lower lip, trying to hide it.

Calculation registered in his expression. Abruptly, he snatched my wrists and restrained them above my head, then lowered to sink his teeth around my nipple, standing proud through my thin bra and t-shirt. I gasped and closed my eyes, hot pleasure flashing through me. He repeated the move, drawing his bite over my pebbled flesh.

I arched into his mouth.

A creak came from upstairs, another directly after.

Struan lifted his head. "What was that?"

I opened my eyes, mind scrambled. "Last time, it was you."

We both held still, our breathing the only sound.

Another creak came.

A frisson of fear replaced my good mood, but then indignation came swift on its heels. No. This was my home.

Pushing Struan aside, I marched for the stairs and started climbing.

"If someone's here, you need to leave," I called.

Footsteps drummed behind me, then he thrust himself ahead, grasping my arm to keep me close.

On the landing, Struan strode straight to my bedroom. I peered inside, watching on as Struan checked the wardrobe and under the bed. He gave a single shake of his head, so I turned around and moved onto my grandmother's old upstairs bedroom. She hadn't used it in years, and nothing had changed.

The two other bedrooms were equally empty, the bathroom the same. I even poked my head into the attic, but only empty space yawned back.

I hopped down from the ladder. "Must've been the floorboards, maybe from where we came in and disturbed the air."

"Who else has a key to this place?"

I tilted my head. "No one. Granny's carer did, but she posted it back through the letterbox."

My father was the only other person, and he was nowhere around to be using it.

Throughout the whole of the search, my need for Struan hadn't gone away. But the thought of someone else being here freaked me out.

Struan took a step so he was at the top of the stairs, his gaze still set on me. "If anyone's here," he bellowed. "Get the fuck out or get used to what you're about to hear."

I threw a wary look his way. We hadn't checked the other stairs that led down to the kitchen. Or anywhere else on the ground floor.

"I don't know..."

He prowled closer and I backed up until my ass hit the wall again. Wide-eyed, I watched him shift to press his lips to my throat. He kissed up in a line, trailing fire, and I gasped.

"Ye don't know?" he taunted, his lips at my ear. "Liar."

I glared at him. "Don't call me that."

"Why, what are ye going to do?"

In a fast move, he grabbed me and twisted me around, pinning me with his body. Binding my hair around his fist, he sank a hard kiss onto the back of my neck.

He sucked, and I writhed on him, feeling the unmistakable ridge of his dick against my ass.

"Why mark me?" I said on a breath. I didn't care. Wanted the bruises he gave.

"Because you're mine," he snarled, laying another hate-bite the other side.

With his knee, he shoved my legs wider, then reached to yank down my leggings. Before I'd taken a breath, he forced his hand between me and the wall, and into my underwear. He plunged a finger inside me.

A gasp left me, loud and unexpected.

"Struan," I begged, though without being entirely sure what I wanted.

If someone else was in the house, I couldn't be quiet. This already felt too good.

"What, sweetheart? Apparently ye need a reminder of who ye belong to."

Belong? I gave an exasperated groan. "I'm not yours."

A dark laugh was my answer. "Try telling that to your soaking wet pussy."

He withdrew his finger and stroked over my clit, using my wetness to tease me. Pleasure spiraled out and weakened my knees. He pressed harder, moving faster, and I let out a moan.

Struan growled, his breath hot on my neck.

"Are ye listening, intruder," he called behind us and down the stairs. "Can ye hear how much Theadora is loving this? Wait until I give her my dick."

He released my hair and yanked down the front of my top and bra. Then he felt up my breasts, one hand splayed across my chest, the other still working my core.

It all felt too good. Too all encompassing. At the same time, he tweaked my nipple and squeezed my clit. I moaned louder, entirely lost to his actions, only able to focus on the winding sensation deep in my belly.

He was so good at this, too good at knowing exactly how to play me. A few minutes and I was gasping, so close to climax.

Then abruptly, he withdrew his hands, leaving me hanging.

"What...?"

The lowering of his zipper brought me right back to the present.

Struan moved in on me once more, this time grinding his bare dick against my backside. I peered back to find his t-shirt had gone, his body exposed to me. I wanted to see him and half turned, but he smirked and pressed me harder to the wall.

"Want more of me? Tell me you're mine."

I set my lips in a stubborn frown, and he uttered that dark laugh again. With a wrench of material, he yanked my underwear so it fell away. That was the only warning I got before he withdrew his hips then plunged his dick inside me.

We both let out a yell. Eyes closed, I pressed my face to the wallpaper, gasping at the intrusion. Nothing had ever felt like this. Not so good, so vital.

My heart raced. My blood pumped hot.

Struan held my hip and ground into me like he couldn't get deep enough. I had no other comparison, but he felt so big, stretching my entrance and hitting places far inside.

I widened my stance, arching my back, and he used the space to bring his fingers back to my clit. God, this was almost too much. The first time we'd done this, the only other time, everything had been a shock. The feel of him, the weight inside me.

Now I knew what to expect, and I needed the race to the finish. For him to fall with me.

I fitted my fingers around his and moved with him, urging a quicker pace.

He grumbled, but even that sound was through a tight throat. I loved it, how turned on and into this he was. He wanted my pleasure, I demanded his.

Our fingers rubbed circles, his dick slid in and out. The pleasure of it built until I was teetering on the edge. So needy. So tense.

"Are ye scared?" he taunted. "If there's someone in the house, they could be coming at us now. This time, your intruder isnae me, sweetheart. I'm right here fucking your tight pussy. You're going to come and scream this place down."

Inside, I pulsed around his dick, the first sparks of my orgasm catching. My thighs burned, my whole body sang. Each jerk shoved him harder into me, driving us together faster and faster.

"Fuck," Struan growled out through gritted teeth. "Ye feel so good. So hot and tight. Come for me."

"Make me," I snapped back.

Heat swarmed me until I was right there, clinging to sanity and about to fly. Our bodies moved in sync. Struan rained open-mouthed kisses on my neck and shoulders, clutching me to him. Owning every part of me. A kiss turned into a bite, and my climax hit home.

I cried out, unashamed and out of control. My heart hammered, and I lost my mind, moaning again at the wave of pleasure. It crashed through me, unlike anything else I'd ever known. Beautiful and brilliant.

Struan fucked me with greater speed, powering through my orgasm, prolonging it. Then, with a desperate groan, he stilled and pulsed into me.

New desire rushed. We'd done this twice now with no condom. Presumably he didn't have access to any, and I didn't think to buy some, but I didn't care. Somehow, with him, anything went. He pushed and pulled at me, and I did the same with him.

I didn't want it any other way than with raw emotion and bare skin. With truth and honesty.

Struan released his tight hold on me and slid out. Each time we'd been intimate here, he'd left immediately after. Not today.

I twisted around, stooping to yank up my leggings. Struan retrieved his shirt, but before he could drag it on, I took it from his hands. Then I pointed at the open door to my bedroom.

"Wait on my bed."

He smirked, his gaze hazy. "No."

"Yes." I pressed a hand to his bare chest and walked

him backwards.

He let me, his expression shifting to wary. "Why?"

"I need a minute and I don't want you to leave."

I had to clean up. I also had things to say to him. Stuff I'd barely let myself think about but that bubbled under my surface, needing out.

More, I was scared out of my wits of the upcoming meeting with Charterman, and I wanted to share.

At the door, he stopped. "I need to know how Cassie's doing."

Who...? It clicked—the little girl. I gave a small nod. "What's wrong with her?"

"Fever."

"Any other symptoms?"

"I don't think so."

"The medicine will work. I suffered a lot from childhood illnesses. Every cold made me sicker than it should've. Probably because my parents stressed me out so much I was vulnerable. You got her what she needed. I only want thirty minutes of your time, then you can go."

A long pause had him staring at my eyes, his internal battle plain. I didn't want him to run. For once, we needed to sit together. Talk. Even if just for a short while.

Taking the decision from him, I propelled him inside, snatched the key from the door, then locked him in.

If he wanted me to play jailor, his wish was my command.

Struan

On Theadora's bed, I waited, bare-chested and...fucked. The lass had my shirt and some other pieces of me. She'd taken hold of the scrap of hope I thought long dead.

She'd returned to me. Again.

Years of trauma battered me.

I caught a glimpse of myself in Theadora's tall mirror and swore at my reflection. At the kid in a man's body, panicked over whether he'd see his mother again after she'd left. Memories carved me up, and I closed my eyes against the surge.

Late nights, waiting. Unable to sleep. Eat. *Breathe.* Staying quiet so I didn't piss off Ma's friend whose couch I had for the evening.

Sometimes it was a single night, usually several. Then she'd return, smelling of someone new, and happy. We'd have money for a week or two, and I both hated it and loved it. Wanted her in this good mood. Wanted her with me.

My breathing came too fast, all the bad rushing in.

It had broken me. My childhood had ruined every good part of who I could've been. It wasn't my mother's fault. She'd been dealt a shite hand, too. All the responsibility and no help from the bastard who'd fathered me. Who'd knocked up multiple women. It had all been one big disaster, and I couldn't get over it.

The lock clicked at Theadora's door, and she appeared, clothes changed and her phone in her hand. She tossed the key onto the rug.

"Lottie's at the hostel. She took a thermometer and said Cassie's temperature is normal. She thought you'd want to know. She also said you're good with your tracker for a little while." She moved closer, her smile dying. "Struan? Shit. Locking you in was a joke. You broke in here, so I knew you could climb out the window if you didn't want to wait."

Struggling out of my black hole, I scrubbed my hands over my face. "Distract me."

"From what?"

"Just do it."

Theadora's eyes rounded, but she stood between my legs and grazed her fingers up my arms, pausing at the scar she'd helped heal, then over my bare shoulders. I tipped my face up and let her kiss me.

Soft lips moved on mine.

This was nothing like the harsh pulls we'd taken of each other's mouths. I'd never received a kiss like it. Automatically, I held her hips, cupping her, tracing my thumbs over the edge where her leggings gave way to smooth skin.

We'd already had sex. I didn't have a need for this... whatever the fuck it was.

But I didn't stop it either.

It was working, stealing away all the negative thoughts and giving me something better in its place.

Theadora's quiet exploration continued, her fingers mapping my skin. Skimming my unfinished tattoos, tracing the one Scar had drawn, then my biceps. I flexed, and she smiled against my lips.

Inside my brain, the slow and careful kisses built into fresh need. I was hard again. Needing more. Everything.

The lass pressed at my chest to make me lie back, but I grabbed her and flipped us so she was flat on her back on the quilt and I was over her. I forced her legs apart and settled in the space between.

Theadora took in a rush of breath. "I wanted us to talk."

"So talk."

She gazed at me then pursed her lips. "I didn't know about Jenkins. Lottie texted me. I made a mistake thinking he'd help you. I got his number and called him earlier, then told him to stay away."

With a nod of approval, I rested more of my weight on her, my dick pinned between us, right at the juncture of her thighs. "Where did ye get a car from?"

"It's my dad's. I haven't seen him since the day you were brought here."

"He's missing," I stated.

She nodded, her pink lips slightly parted.

I needed to know more, fuck, I wanted to know everything. And do everything, too.

Reaching between us, I stripped her leggings in one easy tug, throwing them to the floor along with her socks. Then I did the same with her tiny white thong, admiring her as I dragged off my jeans. Thea removed her own top and bra.

I'd never done this before. Been completely naked with a girl in bed. My encounters had all taken place in dark corners of a club, or in alleys.

She pushed up on her elbows and gazed down at us, at my hard muscles and even harder dick, pink streaking her cheeks. Then she sucked in a breath and shivered.

The temperature in the room crept up.

It was almost too exposing, the daylight, the baring of everything.

Theadora dragged me onto her, fitting her mouth to mine again. With most of my weight on my side, I hugged her, letting our bodies fit together. Her tits on my chest. Our legs entwined.

Between us, my dick slid over the soft centre of her. Not inside, just against her slick heat.

She broke the kiss and reared back so she could see where we touched. My precum rubbing into her.

"You've never worried about getting me pregnant," she said. "Why?"

"I don't give a fuck," I admitted.

Her eyebrows dove together. "About me?"

"I give far too many fucks about ye."

"What if I cared about pregnancy?"

"I don't remember ye telling me to pull out."

She glowered, so fucking cute. "What about diseases?"

"You've only fucked me, and I've never fucked without a condom, before ye. I think we're good. Any more questions?"

With a jerk of my hips, I slid inside her.

Theadora gasped and pressed a balled-up fist to my

chest. "I have an implant. So I won't get pregnant."

Lazily, I fucked into her, in no rush to reach the finish. "Where?"

Taking my fingers, she placed them on her arm, over a tiny bump in her skin.

I grazed it with my nail. "This wee thing is all that's stopping ye from chaining yourself to me? What if I ripped it out?"

She shivered. "Is that what you want?"

My laugh came out dark. "No. I'd be a shite da. But I'm keeping ye whether ye like it or not."

"You don't own me."

"Aye, I do." I rolled us so she was on top now, and let my grin spread. Every other shite thought had faded. I stuck my hands behind my head and jacked my hips, too happy in watching how Theadora's tits bounced.

She moaned and flattened her palms to my chest, working out how to ride me.

"Ye are so fucking beautiful," I told her.

"Don't say things like that. I don't want to like you."

I laughed now and sat up, one arm propping me and the other hand tangling in her hair to bring her lips to mine.

Now she was back, we'd do this non-fucking-stop. Talk, fuck, be together.

Her friend had hinted that someone had hurt Theadora, and that lived somewhere deep inside me. I had to know. I'd kill them for it. Break them to pieces for daring to touch what was mine.

Perched on my lap, my lass arched her back, fully seated, stretched around my dick.

I kissed her throat, under her ear, and then her pretty

mouth.

A new feeling came over me, and I chased it, still moving slowly with her but obsessed with every part of this.

"Grind on my dick," I commanded.

She slid down me, using the angle.

"Good girl."

I rotated my hips, grinning at her hitch of breath and how she instantly grew wetter. "What is it about that which makes ye hot? I know ye want me in control. Is it obedience, or praise?"

"Praise, but shut up about it. I'm just figuring it out myself."

"No chance. I plan to exploit it."

Thea laughed, and a rush of vulnerability came over me. I didn't want this to end. Needed to make her smile more.

"I want to sleep with ye tonight." I confessed. "I'm naw sure if that's possible. If our keeper suddenly decides to spot-check us and finds me missing, she'll activate the trackers and hunt me down."

"I won't be here."

I ceased moving. "What?"

"I'm only on the island for a few hours."

Low-level panic shook me. "Tell me you're joking."

She shook her head, caution now in her eyes.

I rolled away and withdrew, depositing her on the bed. Then I backed up, my erection dying.

Theadora's brown-eyed gaze held mine. "I don't understand why you're surprised. I don't live here. My trips have only ever been short."

Everything she said was true, but I was five years old and being left again. What the fuck had I been thinking? I dropped my gaze to the floor, humiliation burning away all the happy emotions.

"I'll come back," she said softly. "I'm not sure when, but I will."

"Don't go."

"I have to. I have someone to meet."

"Spare me the details."

"Why, Struan? Talk to me."

I couldn't answer. I couldn't explain any of this.

Theadora sighed. "If you want me, if I'm more to you than just sex, tell me. Ask me for more. Do it now while we're finally talking. My head is full of life shit, decisions I have to make, but this thing?" She jumped from the bed and placed her fingers on my chest. "It's harder to make sense of than anything."

I shook my head once. "I won't beg."

"I didn't ask you to. I only want—"

"To leave. Aye. Got it."

She'd come and go as she pleased. She always had. And I'd done something so fucking stupid.

I'd got attached.

My chest hurt, and I backed away from her touch and rubbed my knuckles over the ache. This was all wrong. I couldn't do it again.

Snatching up my jeans, I shoved my legs into them. "Ye should go. In fact, I'll make it easier."

"What's the problem? Why is this so hard? You call me yours but freak out at the slightest thing."

I jammed my t-shirt over my head then grabbed my boots. I didn't trust myself to speak so worked in silence, just needing to get out.

Theadora gathered her quilt around herself and sat

on the edge of her bed, her pretty hair tumbling over one shoulder and pain in her eyes. Good. She should hurt.

"I won't do this again with you," she said so quietly I could barely hear. "I can take the push and pull, but this hurts. If you walk away, we're done."

"We never started, sweetheart."

Her boat left two hours later.

Astride my surfboard, I floated in the sea and watched her vanish. This was the last time. The end of our imprisonment here was coming to an end. I felt it in my blood.

And I'd never been so miserable in all of my life.

*T*he following day, Cassie was far more comfortable with no further spike in temperature. None of us had gone out to work, growing tension infecting all of us.

Entering the bunk room, Scar waved. "Lottie's approaching. I just saw her from the kitchen."

Sin slid the phone into his back pocket and strode to the door, and I tagged along, needing confirmation that she hated me. That her friend had confided in her what an arsehole I'd been, and that everything was back to normal.

The woman waited outside the back of the hostel. At the sight of us, she took a shuddering inhale and wiped at her eyes with her sleeve.

Sin swore. "What happened?"

"Nothing." She held out a carrier bag. "I promised this

for Cassie. It's a spray-on conditioner and some hair clips."

Thrusting it into Sin's hands, she turned to go.

But as Lottie moved, her fair hair shifted. Dark marks stained her throat.

Sin rounded her, stopping her in her tracks. "You're bruised. Who did that?"

She twisted away, her cheeks wet. "What does it matter?"

"It matters," Sin ground out.

"No, it doesn't. Everything is messed up. My family has imploded. Thea's gone to that awful man—"

"What man?" I snapped.

She shot her desperate gaze to me. "The lawyer. Charterman. She had no choice. I wanted to go with her, but my da won't let me leave, and he's taken my phone. Now she has to face him on her own. That man..." She took another shuddering inhale. "I didn't want to tell ye anything, but I don't know what else to do. I have such a bad feeling about this."

"Ye said that someone hurt her. Do ye mean him?" I couldn't help my tone, my rising panic.

"Yes. He held her still while some old guy assaulted her. And now she's going to him."

Sounds came from the front of the hostel, our keeper's voice carrying through the warm spring afternoon. Then I recognised a second voice. Jenkins.

Lottie backed away, fear in her eyes. "He can't see me here. He'll tell my dad."

"Where's Theadora meeting this lawyer?" I demanded.

"At his house this evening. A fact you'd know if ye didn't blow up at her."

"Give me an address."

She shook her head once, still moving backwards. "I don't know. Last thing she said to me was that she's meeting Henry, that's Charterman's son, first at a bar called the Clansman in Inverness. She said she'll catch up with me after. Are ye going to go?"

I nodded, already mentally halfway there.

Lottie gave me a look loaded down with distress. "Good. Don't let her get hurt."

She fled.

It would take a couple of hours to get over to the Isle of Skye, at least another two or three to drive to Inverness. For that, I needed Keep's car again.

I turned to Sin who glowered after the lass. "I've got to go. Fuck, what if I get there too late?"

He snatched up the phone and opened the browser. "What did she say his name is?"

"Charterman. Try lawyers in Inverness."

Search results loaded, pictures against some.

Sin froze.

"What?"

He clicked on a shot, then the next. A middle-aged man smiled back, all smart suit and neat hair.

"It's him," Sin uttered, deathly low. He didn't wait for me to ask, instead almost shaking with rage. "Our jailor. So that's his name. Lionel Charterman."

"Are ye sure? I thought he blindfolded ye?"

"He always did, except once, it slipped and I caught a glimpse as the door closed. I'd recognise him anywhere."

Hot fear stabbed into me. "And Theadora has gone to him."

The back door flew open, and Burn half fell out, Scar

behind him.

Blood poured from Burn's nose. "They've got her. They've taken Cassie."

As one, Sin and I bolted for the front of the building. At the entrance, in Keep's grip, Cassie struggled.

Jenkins stood six feet away. He spotted us and sneered at Keep. "They're all out. You're losing control."

She glowered at him. "I said to come back tomorrow morning. This would have been far easier."

He snatched for Cassie, dragging her tiny form against his body. "And I said I was done waiting. Ye denied me the boy, so this one's mine."

"The fuck she is," I bit out, advancing on them.

Cassie cringed in on herself, and Jenkins laughed.

"What do ye think will happen if ye touch me? I'll have the police here and you'll all go to jail."

This was what Sin had been working to avoid. Police coming here meant attention on who we were and what we were doing. There was no hiding anymore, no waiting. Burn at least would go to prison.

We had no choice, yet there was no fucking way we were letting this abusive fuck take her.

A figure cut in front of me. Burn flew at Jenkins, tackling him to the ground. The rest of us were right there behind him. I threw a fist at his face before he could connect his to my brother. Scar grabbed Cassie and carried her aside.

Sin stepped one huge boot on Jenkins' chest, pinning him down. I leaned over the bastard and rained another punch down on him, smashing his jaw. God, I'd missed a dirty fight.

He curled in a ball, clutching his face.

"He's ashes," Burn uttered, quietly but so deadly.

Our leader glanced his way then gripped Jenkins by the lapels and hauled him to his feet. "Listen up, you disgusting sack of shite. Set one foot near this place again, and I'll kill ye. Same if ye tell anyone what happened here. Ye got me?"

Jenkins glowered. "You're dead, all of ye."

With a wicked grin, Sin lifted the man by his throat. Jenkins flailed, his legs kicking. He choked out strangled gasps, clawing at the hand around his neck.

"I'm naw joking," Sin gritted out. "Your blood will be on my hands. Count this as your last warning."

He released him, and Jenkins stumbled down the road, sucking in air.

Cassie whimpered, and Burn dropped to his knees, bundling her in a hug.

"He needs to die," he said over her dark curls.

Sin watched the man go. "He will. Don't think for a second we're safe from him. Any of us. But killing him, or any of them, is a last resort. It means prison."

A crackling came from behind. At the hostel's entrance, our keeper sparked at her Taser, her heavy brow creased with anger lines.

"How dare ye," she spat.

Sin lowered his gaze at her.

This was a moment of reckoning. Her pretence of control over us had failed.

But her gaze was on me. "Ye, Ruin. I've heard all about the things ye get up to on the mainland. People have been asking after ye. Ye took my car, been driving around."

Twice, I'd done that, but Sin had done so, too. We maybe looked similar enough behind a windscreen. Not that I was telling her shite.

A horrible smile spread on her ugly face. "Whoring yourself out is my guess, ye dirty little slut. That's why people are trying to find ye. If you're making money, I want my share. You cost me today, so I'll have what I'm owed."

I opened my mouth to deny it. Fuck her and her assumptions. The whore accusation cut deep into a part of me which already ached.

Sin grabbed my shoulder and spoke directly into my ear, pressing the phone to my hands. "Don't let her get to ye. We've got this. Go inside and get her car keys. We'll keep her busy. Go help Thea."

Everything was coming to a head. Our enemies were closing in from all sides. Including unknown ones who had been asking after me.

But I didn't hesitate. Leaving my brothers to take on our keeper, I left on a mission to track down Theadora.

32

Thea

On Inverness's Church Street, I entered the Clansman pub, the place Henry had arranged to meet me. Music and laughter filled the space, busy on a Saturday night. Inside the door, a couple of guys from a group openly ogled me, their gazes taking in my black dress, heels, and my curls swept over one shoulder.

I couldn't share in the joy. My emotions had taken a beating.

Only days ago, in Struan's arms, I'd finally felt hopeful again. Things had shifted in my perspective. Dad had gone, and so had Granny, but my life was continuing. Answers would eventually come.

Yet the only place things felt good and right was when I was head-to-head with the boy I couldn't stop fighting. I'd wanted to talk. He'd turned it into sex. Then he gave me a bullshit reason for running again, deflecting our closeness with anger.

As he left, I'd reached an unforgivable conclusion.

I was in love with him.

Stupid, stupid girl.

A sharp ache had taken residence inside me, and I couldn't shift it. There would never be a point in which we met as equals and were able to let go of the bad. Logically, I knew that, but my heart wanted what it wanted.

He was dangerous, but I only felt safe when I was with him. He was angry, but I only felt calm when we were together. He quieted my demons by struggling with his own. And every inch of me came alive when we touched.

There was no going back for me now. I had to learn to live with this torment.

"Thea," Henry hollered.

I spotted him across the other side of the busy room and threaded my way through.

In his usual enthusiastic puppy-dog manner, Henry fell on me with a hug. "I haven't seen you in forever. I didn't think I would again, considering my family has been such a pain in your ass. How are you?" He held me at arm's length and ran his gaze over me, his grin turning into a leer. "Holy fuck. You look hot."

I didn't return his smile.

The black dress I'd worn tonight was battle armour. Bad-bitch attire that warned I was in control. It wasn't for him, or any other man. This was all for me.

The only reason I'd asked to see Henry was to have some kind of insight into how this evening was going to go down. It was 7:30 PM now, and I was supposed to be meeting his dad at nine. Who booked a business meeting at that time?

I didn't expect him to be an ally. I only knew Henry because our fathers were friends, so I couldn't rely on him.

"Let me grab you a glass of wine. You'll need it if you

have to sit through hours of paperwork with Dad."

"I'll get my own," I replied.

Leaving Henry at the table, I wound my way to the bar, catching a lucky break as the bar steward turned to take the next order. Her gaze set on me, and I leaned over to request my drink.

But as soon as the words were spoken from my lips, and the woman turned to pour the wine, I caught sight of someone deep in the crowd.

Dark hair, black t-shirt, a savage cut jaw.

I blinked, and he'd gone.

God, I was going crazy. I never had got to the bottom of how Struan was on the mainland when I saw him fetch medicine for the little girl, but he'd been in a hurry to get back. There was no way he was here, hours away from the islands.

My infatuation with him had turned into hallucinations. Great.

I paid my bill and found my way back to Henry's table.

"So," he said. "Catch me up with everything. How did your exams go? Pretty sure I had a few near misses."

I took a swig of the sweet, tart wine. "What's your dad up to?"

Henry's blond eyebrows dove together. "What do you mean?"

"I mean his business dealings. And how is that linked to my father? You told me that they were arguing, and that was the last day I saw him alive. Since then, nothing. The police aren't interested. All I know is he was in debt. Not long after, your dad threw that dinner for the old pervert, McInver. Tell me everything you know."

His smile died. "You don't think my dad had something to do with your dad's disappearance? He's cut up about it. They've been friends for years. I've never seen him so upset as when he realised your dad hadn't been heard of by anyone for months."

I didn't buy it. I didn't buy anything this family came out with.

I downed the rest of the wine and shook my head. "I'm not accusing him of anything. I'm just trying to paint a picture."

"Of what, exactly?"

"Of everything I don't know."

Henry pursed his lips. "Esme is pissed off with you. She really wanted you over for Christmas dinner."

"Esme came to my flat and told me I had to accept the abuse that McInver dealt out because all men were like that." I stared at my old friend, trying to see the truth in him. "Is that true? Are you the same?"

"No! How can you even say that?"

I slapped my hand down on the table, drawing the attention of a few curious drinkers. "Because you stood there and watched as it happened. You did nothing to stop him. I had to fight to get away, and only then did you decide to toss me your keys."

Henry hung his head. "Okay, fine. I should have said something. But it all happened so fast. I thought Dad had it."

I gave an incredulous laugh. "He doesn't deserve your loyalty. Do you see now why I'm asking these questions?"

For a long moment, Henry just watched me, his finger and thumb worrying his lower lip. Emotions battled in his expression. "I don't know what to think."

"I do." I leaned in, pinning him with my gaze. "Your dad is trying to con McInver into something, and I was bait. I don't know what the game is, but it doesn't take a genius to go from him being elderly and childless but having that huge mansion. What if my dad got in the way of that?"

Henry's hand now covered his mouth, and he said something I couldn't pick up.

"I can't hear you," I said.

He tore his hand away and pressed it as a fist to the table. "McInver is my mother's relative."

I stared, cogs turning in my mind.

Henry's mother was Charterman's second wife. He divorced Esme's mother to marry her within a couple of months of meeting the woman, Dad had once told me.

"You're related to him," I repeated.

"Yeah, but that doesn't mean I'm anything like him," Henry snapped. "I bear zero resemblance. He said that to my dad when we were there. And if you want my opinion on why you were invited, my guess is you were purely decorative. Dad wanted Esme, too, but she bailed. I don't mean this to sound creepy, but you're young and pretty, and what old man could resist you?"

"Resist me? Then that paid off."

"Fuck. I didn't mean that the way it came out. I'm sure Dad never expected him to grab you. He was probably caught up in the moment of trying to keep the old man sweet. Actually, I remember him muttering about how he regretted that the old man didn't recognise you. I guess he meant recognise that you weren't there to be pawed over. I know that doesn't excuse anything."

I touched my fingertips to my forehead, still in the dark about too many things. "That doesn't help me understand where my dad's gone, or why your dad has refused to meet me anywhere other than in his home. He's been holding my inheritance over me. Did he say anything to you about tonight?"

Behind Henry's head, about ten feet deep in the crowd, a man came into view, a shoulder to a pillar in the middle of the floor. His gaze fixed on me, and a whole-body shiver ran through me, chased by shock.

Struan. Here.

I hadn't imagined him.

With slow menace, Struan pointed at Henry then drew his finger over his own throat.

I almost laughed but gave him a tiny headshake then brought my attention back to Henry.

My old friend grimaced. "Sorry, but Dad told me to stay away tonight."

I released a breath in disbelief. "Do you realise how that sounds?"

"He wants to keep your business, I'm sure that's all it is. He wants to impress you and not get distracted in everything you need to talk about."

"Or he plans to smack me over the head and bury my body in the garden."

Henry bunched his hands into fists then stood, his lips twisted. He shook his head and extracted a pack of cigarettes from his pocket. "I need a minute. To think, all I wanted from tonight was to ask you out. You've changed, Thea."

He stormed off through the bar towards the exit, and I waited it out. In seconds, his seat was filled with a bigger, darker, far more menacing man.

Struan reclined in the chair and steepled his fingers.

All that heavy focus landed on me, and I resisted the urge to squirm. Instead, I let the sheer rush of being near him wash over me.

Neither of us spoke.

I mirrored his body language and sprawled back, mocking his confidence. Under the table, his knees bracketed mine, like he couldn't not touch me in some way.

After a beat, he tipped his chin at the direction Henry had gone. "Did he threaten ye?"

I gave a slow shake of my head. "What are you doing here?"

"You're in danger."

My irrational heart throbbed. "Doesn't leaving the island put you in danger?"

His gaze never left mine. "What does that matter? Lottie came to the hostel and told me where ye were going. When we were last together—"

"You decided that it was all or nothing," I supplied for him, the hurt too close to the surface. "Do you even know what I'm doing tonight?"

"Meeting with the lawyer. I need to tell ye about him."

"I already know what kind of man he is."

Struan's jaw tightened. "He hurt ye."

"He was part of it."

"He's a dead man. Ye should also know that Sin saw his picture. That bastard is our jailor."

I goggled at him, open-mouthed, my words gone.

It had taken all my courage, every bit of my self-control to bring myself here, but I'd believed only myself to be under threat. If this was true...

Struan's eyes gleamed with anger. "After Lottie gave us a name, we looked him up. Sin recognised him. He comes to the hostel and delivers beatings. He's the man keeping us there, but we don't know why."

My heart beat double time. Nausea crawled up my throat, and more pieces of the puzzle fitted together. Jenkins had mentioned Dad employing a land manager called Jones. I hadn't made the leap in my thoughts to turn that into Charterman managing the hostel. It made sense.

The world crowded in around me, too many coincidences and connections being made.

"Thea?" Henry arrived at the table and stared at Struan. Then he travelled round to my side and placed his fingers on my shoulders, his fingers digging in. "She's here with me, mate."

Instinctively, I shrank in on myself, the action too similar to the one his father had taken when I'd been in front of McInver.

Struan went deadly still, his steely gaze fixed on Henry. "Take your hands off her."

"Don't tell me—"

"Take your hands off her or I'll break every one of your fingers."

Henry released me, and I shuddered.

He shoved back his floppy blond hair and scowled at Struan. "Don't threaten me. You're crashing my date."

I recovered and twisted to him. "No, Henry. Did you seriously think this was a date? What the hell is wrong with you?"

Henry flicked a knowing look at me. "I'm just trying to get this guy to leave you alone."

Glaring at him, I pointed at Struan. "That guy is with me."

Though I didn't glance his way, I felt the shift in atmosphere coming from Struan. His movement at the table, how he sat taller and absorbed what I'd said.

The casual way his knee parted my legs.

Henry danced his gaze between us. "You and him? He's a...friend?"

I raised an eyebrow, not willing to give an answer I couldn't settle on myself.

"You never said you were seeing anyone." His puppy-dog personality was now all wolf.

I tilted my head. I didn't have to explain myself to him. After today, I was done with the Chartermans. "I appreciate you meeting me. I need to leave to get to the appointment with your dad."

Henry blinked, realisation in his eyes that he'd been dismissed. "I'll go with you."

"No, ye won't," Struan said, calm as anything.

Red flushed Henry's cheeks, and he tensed his jaw. "Whatever."

He turned to go, but I remembered something else I'd wanted to ask.

For a while now, I'd been carrying around the picture of my grandmother's lost love, as I'd begun thinking about him. The dark-haired, handsome boy whose photo she'd carefully stored, and who definitely wasn't my grandfather.

Grabbing my purse, I called him back. "Hold up. Do you have any idea who the man is in this picture?"

Henry scowled at the old print. "He's familiar. Looks like your friend here." He curled his lip at Struan. "God, wait. It's McInver, isn't it? Why do you have this?"

McInver?

"No reason," I spluttered.

Henry tossed the photo back to the table and left

without another word. Struan picked it up.

"I found that in my grandmother's home alongside money she'd hidden away," I explained slowly. "How would she know him? I don't understand. But Henry's right. The man is like you."

He shrugged and passed it back. "More like Sinclair, if ye ask me. Who is McInver?"

I shivered. "The old man who grabbed me between the legs and said he wanted to rape me."

Struan's nostrils flared, the light in his eyes dying and a new darkness taking hold. "Were ye being serious when ye said you're still going to see the lawyer?"

Fear shot along my nerve endings, but I wasn't going to cower. "Deadly. I've been avoiding this for months because I'm scared of him. I want it behind me. I need to hear what he has to say and face him down."

Beyond anything, I'd wanted someone to go with me. To be a witness, or to stand beside me and have my back. I'd been a fool in thinking Henry could be that person. But I had no one else. Lottie was stuck on the island. Jenna had moved out of our flat, Esme I didn't trust. I hadn't even considered my parents. Even if Dad had been here, I wasn't sure whose side he was on.

For a long moment, Struan watched me.

"Don't tell me not to go," I spoke quietly.

"Wasnae going to. Did I ever tell ye you're the bravest person I know?"

A startled laugh flew out of my lips. "I'm not brave. I'm scared out of my mind. Will you go with me?"

Struan stilled for a long second, then he nodded, the motion tight as if my request had hit him hard. "As if I'd let ye go alone. That wasn't why I hesitated. I've been waiting to see this man and to get answers from him. To take payment from him in blood. Sinclair suffered most at his hands. I'm trying to work out a way to capture the fucker and take him back to the island to let my brother have at him."

"Brother?" Somehow, I knew he didn't mean the term in any kind of casual sense.

"We think that's what we are. Fathered by the same person."

My lips parted, and a horrible, twisting thought soured my mind. Struan looked like McInver. Granny had kept that picture of him.

What if we were *both* related to the old man?

31

Struan

A couple of streets away from the bar, we climbed into Theadora's flashy ride, and she drove us out of central Inverness. I left our keeper's old Ford behind. If it got picked up and towed, I didn't give a fuck. In coming here, I'd left my brothers to handle the imploding situation on the island. Our old life and routine were dead.

Nothing was going to be the same after tonight.

Just the same as my world had been flipped by Theadora's casual words in the bar. She'd claimed me in front of the preppie douchebag she'd been with.

In some small way, I was hers.

In silence, Theadora navigated to a suburb with wide streets and bigger houses. She slowed the car outside a large, detached house. A lamp glowed over the doorway, and I travelled my gaze over the darkened windows and two cars in the driveway.

"This it?"

Theadora took a shaky breath. "It is."

We climbed out and advanced on the house. At the

front door, I banged on the wood.

Nothing happened.

I thumped again, and Theadora reached to press a bell.

A light sprang on in the hall. I stood taller, resisting the urge to put Theadora behind me.

The door swung open, and a woman appeared in the frame. She peered between us, not making eye contact. "What do ye want?"

Theadora blinked. "Hello, Mrs Charterman. I'm here to see your husband."

The woman shrugged stiffly. "He isn't here."

"We had an appointment."

"He was called away," she said in a flat tone.

"I don't understand. He's been asking for this meeting forever. He refused to have it anywhere else. Why isn't he here?"

The woman started to close the door.

"Wait," Theadora exclaimed. "I need to ask you some questions about your relative, McInver. Can we come in?"

Fright sprang into the woman's eyes. "Don't ask that of me. He's a monster. I won't go!"

With a burst of energy, she went to close the door, but it bounced off Thea's boot.

"I promise we're not trying to make you see him. But I need to ask if you know whether he had children. This is important."

The older woman hunched in on herself. "Why are you asking that? What do you know?"

"Did he father any children?" she demanded.

"He'll kill me if I say anything."

Thea snatched the picture from her bag, thrusting it

forward. "This is him, right?"

Mrs Charterman started, drawing back more. "Where did ye get that?"

"My grandmother had it."

"So ye think you're in for inheriting all that money? Ye won't! You're not his blood." With a shove, she pushed Thea aside and shut us out.

"Hey." I thumped on the door again.

Theadora pressed her fingertips to my arm. "Something weird is going on."

"Aye, it's me. I'm not meant to be here." I took a step back so I could see the windows. "Charterman, come out, come out, wherever ye are. We've come all this way to see ye."

Nothing moved, no curtain twitched.

Anger rippled through me. "Ye owe Theadora answers," I bellowed. "And I've got one or two things to say to ye."

Stooping, I picked up a rock from a flowerbed, adjusted it in my grip, then launched it at the windscreen of the bigger of the two cars on the drive.

Glass shattered, the crash loud in the damp night air.

"Hear that?" I bellowed. "I'll break every fucking window until ye show your ugly face, then I'll start on your house."

A few steps away, Theadora clasped her hands to her mouth, but she didn't try and stop me.

I grabbed another rock and launched it at a second pane, the splintering just as loud.

"Charterman," I yelled. "Ye fucking coward. Do ye only like us when we're restrained? Does it only work for ye to have us on our knees and blindfolded?"

From a neighbouring house, a window swung open. "Stop that. I've called the police," a man squeaked.

For fuck's sake.

"Why?" I bellowed back. "This arsehole deserves what's coming."

"You can't damage property like that," the neighbour replied and slammed the window shut.

Theadora curled her arm through mine. "We need to go. He obviously isn't going to come out, and if the police get here, they're going to arrest you."

"But he's in there. And he owes ye an explanation."

In the distance, sirens cut through the night.

Theadora's eyes widened. "You, too, but you won't get them if you're locked up."

Shite.

She towed me to her car.

I held out my hand. "Give me the keys."

"But…"

"Ever had to outrun the police?"

She hesitated, then dropped the keys into my palm and dove for the passenger side. Without further pause, I fell into the driver's seat, slid it back to fit my bulk, and gunned the engine.

With the lights off, I put the pedal to the metal and shot down the main road in the opposite direction to the wailing sirens. Adrenaline spread through me, lighting up all my senses, sending my pulse flying.

A few turnings down, I swung off into a side street, powering on.

For a couple of tense minutes, I navigated the Inverness suburbs, moving fast but putting as many twists and turns between us and the police. The sirens kept up a constant background wail.

My nerves jangled, but the rush took over me, my need to protect Theadora dominating.

We crept past the busier part of the small city, still keeping to the narrower roads, and only catching glimpses of the shops and bars at the ends of the roads. To get any speed up, I had to get us onto the major roads and out of town. But that meant coming out of hiding.

Near a junction with a main street, I pulled in behind a row of parked cars and killed the engine, watching the line of traffic filter down busier roads ahead.

My heartbeat thrummed.

A police cruiser stopped at the lights, two cops in the front, one on the radio. For a nerve-racking thirty seconds, they sat there, a menacing presence blocking our route to safety.

I slid down in my seat, my lass doing the same.

If they'd had a description of our car and came this way, we were screwed. There wasn't the space in the road to turn, and traffic was too thick to speed through. We were pinned down and trapped.

"Fuck," I muttered, starting our car once more.

My heart pounded, and Thea's hand found mine, our fingers interlacing.

"I'll say it was me who threw the rocks," she said quietly.

"No, ye won't."

"Why not? I have no criminal record, and they won't care so long as they can arrest someone."

"They'd take one look at the two of us and know the truth. Then we'd both be in trouble."

All of a sudden, their lights sprang on, and they hit

the siren. It blared out its warning, and the traffic stopped.

The police moved into the centre of the junction, blocking all other traffic. One of the officers sliced a glance down our quiet street.

Oh fuck. They'd found us.

Then they floored it and went straight ahead.

Theadora let out a gasp. "They didn't see us?"

I sat tall and threw the car into gear. "No idea how we got so lucky, but I'm not wasting it."

I got us going, out through the city centre, then to a bigger road taking us out of town. Every stop and start had me sweating, but the cops had gone.

We made it out undetected.

Eventually, we reached the unlit A9 heading south out of Inverness, passing open countryside. I let myself relax my death grip on the steering wheel.

Theadora peered behind us. "No one's following."

"We're lucky." I pulled the phone from my pocket and handed it over. "Call Lottie. I need to get a message to Sin."

She dipped her head and placed the call. "Do you think that's where Charterman has gone?"

I gave a tight nod.

The phone rang, and she put it to her ear. "Lottie, I'm with Struan. I'm going to put you on loudspeaker, hang on."

"Are ye okay?" Lottie spluttered.

"Just great. We're currently on the run from the police," Theadora said with a startled laugh. "I can't believe I said that."

Another voice sounded Lottie's end of the line. "I'm at the hostel. Sin wants to talk to you both. Going to switch to hands-free now."

After a rustling noise, Sin's deep voice came on the line. "Thank fuck. Ye found each other, then."

I didn't try to stop my grin. "Ye have no idea how relieved I am to hear your voice. I expected our keeper to have Tasered ye all to death."

Sin made a sound almost like a laugh. "Funny ye should say that. She did electrocute someone."

I stared at the phone. "Who?"

"Herself. She's dead."

Shock constricted my voice. "Holy fuck. Please tell me you're not joking."

"He isn't," Lottie added. "I heard shouting and came back right in time to see her touch her own leg with the Taser. There was a bang, and she dropped to the floor."

"The witch is dead," Burn shouted in the background.

Theadora and I exchanged a glance.

"We need to hide the body," Sin came back on the line. "If anyone finds her, they'll reach the wrong conclusions and assume we killed her. Particularly if Jenkins finds out."

I sucked in a breath. "We'll be back as soon as we can. In the meantime, keep an eye out and stay together. We tried to see Charterman tonight, but he wouldn't come out. Either he's already heading your way, or we've just given him a good reason to go to the island."

Ahead, the headlights picked up the sign for the Cairngorms National Park. This wasn't the most direct route back to the islands, but it avoided us getting arrested before we could return. We couldn't go back through Inverness.

"Got it. I'll keep everyone safe. See when ye get back."

We disconnected the call, and I shook my head, unable to accept what had happened.

"Everything just got ten times more complicated," I finally said. "Ye need to get away from me."

"I can't believe you just said that." Theadora twisted in her seat. "Are you seriously pushing me away right now? If you—"

The engine spluttered and cut out.

The car cruised on, but all the controls had gone.

I braked and pulled in to the verge of the deserted road. Then I tried the engine again. Nothing.

Theadora peeked at the dashboard. "This car used to break down on my dad all the time. I was expecting that to happen when I drove it up from London, but no, it saved it for now."

Climbing out, I popped the bonnet and yanked it open using my sleeve. Steam rose.

Theadora shone her phone's torch inside. "What's wrong with it?"

"I don't know, I'm no mechanic."

"Me neither. I've never looked inside an engine. I can't even think of anyone I can call to come help us."

This was a disaster. We couldn't stay here. If we were picked up, assuming the description of me and the car was out there, I'd be arrested. We'd be separated. No matter what I'd said, the thought sent panic spiralling through me.

In a rush, I remembered the one person I did know who could fix engines.

Taking out my phone, I went into the notes folder where I'd saved Max McRae's details from the flyer. Then I raised my gaze to my lass.

"That time I ran from the hostel, I stole Keep's car

and got as far as the Skye bridge but ran out of petrol. This man stopped and helped me. He said he was part of a mechanic outreach programme and that he lived in the Cairngorms. Do ye think I should call him?"

Theadora chewed over my words. My request to have her input, her permission. "Do it. We have no other option. It's not as if we can walk to safety. We're in the middle of nowhere. If he reports us to the police, they'd only eventually pick us up here anyway."

I placed the call. It rang a couple of times, then a voice answered.

"Hello?"

My heart thudded. I didn't trust anyone, but I had to trust him. "Max, it's Struan. Ye might remember me as joyrider."

After a beat, he laughed. "Shite. Never expected to hear your voice again."

"I need help."

His tone changed. "Talk to me."

"We've broken down on the road coming into the Cairngorms. I remember ye saying this is where ye lived. I need to get us out of here."

"Are ye in trouble?"

I didn't want to lie. "Aye. But for good reasons."

"Who's with ye?"

"My lass."

"Just the two of ye?" At my confirmation, he continued. "Give me a second." The phone went muffled while he spoke to someone else then came back. "Just checking in with my woman. Our bairn's fast asleep, and she's going to bed, so I'm good to come out."

"Ye have a bairn? You're my age," I spluttered.

Max snorted. "Didn't I tell ye I had a wild side? Now give me your location."

I did, hearing him clattering around his room.

"Sit tight and I'll be there soon." He hung up.

Leaving Thea and I alone in the dark.

I stuffed the phone in my back pocket and closed in on her. Desperation and a dose of fear had taken hold of me. A world of coincidences and the actions of fucked-up men needed to be laid out, torn apart, and made sense of, but I only had attention for the woman in front of me. "If I get arrested, call the guys."

"Of course I will."

Running my hands to the back of her thighs, I lifted her and placed her on the boot of the Jaguar. Then I fitted my mouth to hers and stole a kiss, swallowing her yelp of shock. Thea curled her legs around my waist, her sexy-as-fuck dress rucking up.

I wasn't sure I was thinking. Whether I'd meant to reassure her, or just myself, but sheer need dominated.

"Ye have no idea of my panic when I realised where ye were going tonight," I told her between hard pulls of her lips.

"How do you think I feel at the thought of the police taking you away?" she countered.

I gave no answer, instead closing my eyes to kiss her again. The only time I ever felt good, or whole, was when I had her pressed tight against me. When I could get lost in her lips.

Connected like this, I was able to forget everything other than her.

I was addicted to the way she responded to me. How she matched my moves and the little sounds she gave up.

Theadora and I could never work out long-term, but it lit me up that I could please her.

I wasn't enough for her. I could never give her everything she wanted. When I lived with Ma, I thought we were at rock bottom, then life had drop-kicked me ever farther behind. I had nothing. Not one thing to offer.

Back in her home on the island, Theadora had wanted to talk, and I'd stopped it. I didn't want to hear her carve up my heart by defining what we were. Reducing us from all that I felt to something smaller. Contained.

A dull ache spread down my sternum. It was better not to know.

With rising passion, she kissed me back, then pushed on my chest to break us apart. "We're not doing this."

"What?"

She brushed my hair from my eyes, gazing at me. "Sex."

"Why not? We're good at it."

Her lips curved in amusement. "I didn't know you thought that. It's all new to me, so I could be terrible."

"Are ye serious?" I grabbed her hand and brought it down to the outline of my dick, straining in my jeans. "If you're near me, I'm hard for ye. I've never felt anything like when I'm with ye."

Her lips parted. "Yet not five minutes ago, you were about to reject me. Again. If you're speaking the truth, I want you to ask me to be your girlfriend. I shouldn't have to settle for less."

Girlfriend? Impossible. But then Thea's fingers curled around my bulge, and a wave of heat stole my thoughts. I gripped the back of her head and kissed her again, our tongues sliding over each other's.

Then I stepped away and opened the back door of the car, on the side away from the road, and reclined on the seats.

Thea, for all her big words, followed.

34

Thea

My pulse thrummed in a fast beat, and I stared in the back seat of the car. Inside, in the barest light from tonight's moon, Struan opened his jeans.

"What are you doing?"

"Touch me." He freed his dick and pumped his shaft.

My body was awake and tingling with need. "Ask me to be your girlfriend."

He smirked. "Ask me with your hand around my dick."

"Asshole."

"Never claimed otherwise."

I'd never touched him like he wanted before, but I'd pictured it all too much and needed the memory to go with my imagination. My request was serious, but I was less set on the no-sex deal.

Kneeling on the seat, I reached in to curl my hand around his shaft. My breath caught.

He was so hard, his skin silky smooth over the steel length. At my boldness, he rolled his head back. "Tell me how that makes ye feel."

"How about the other way around. You describe it to me." Delicious heat stole over me, urgency in my veins. I squeezed lightly and pumped my fist.

"Like you're gracing me with a fucking favour I shouldn't get. How I want your hand, then your lips, then your cunt. In that order. Make me come."

Headlights curved down the road. I squeaked and withdrew my hands. But the lorry cruised on by, not slowing for us.

Struan growled. "Stop, and I'll fuck ye on the grass outside for any passerby to see."

I didn't know what was worse, the threat, or the thrill I got at the thought of him claiming me like that. Shuffling his jeans down more, I bobbed my head and licked at the end of his dick.

"Fuck," he muttered, the cockiness leaving him.

I sank my lips over his shaft, taking him inside my mouth.

Struan groaned but held still, letting me explore.

"You taste good." I gripped the base of him with my fist, pumping once.

"Ye feel amazing," he spoke on a heavy breath.

I ducked my head again and took more of him into my mouth, drawing my lips over my teeth. Then I glided up and down, adding suction.

This was all brand-new, but I wanted so badly to make him fall apart at my hands. It took me out of my head, too. Away from those feelings that I didn't want to face.

Slipping my hand between his legs, I cupped his balls, no room to work with, but it didn't seem to matter. Struan wound my hair around his fist, not taking over but showing me that he needed some part of the control of this.

Somehow, that delighted me. I sped up, more confident now. His breathing hitched, and his hips made small jerks, not gagging me but enough to show intent.

In the dark interior of the car, I slowly found out what he liked. Another set of headlights cruised by, the engine loud, but it didn't slow and, this time, I didn't stop.

A tight grip. Harder moves. I doled it out and he took it.

His dick swelled in my mouth, precum leaking. Struan cursed then drew me off him to bring my lips to his. Then he devoured me, fucking my mouth with his tongue.

"Need to be inside ye," he rasped.

I peered up and down the dark road. Right now, I didn't care if we were caught.

Struan's mechanic friend surely couldn't be here this fast, and any other person would just get an eyeful and move on.

Making a decision, I straddled him on the narrow seat, my black dress flowing over us both. Struan bought our mouths together again and reached between us to cup me at the apex of my legs, hooking a finger into my underwear. He ripped it away then sank two fingers deep into me.

With my mouth open on his, I gasped, my eyes closed.

"We need to be fast." He pressed a kiss to my cheek, pumping his fingers in and out of me. "Whenever ye want me, I'm yours. Is that enough? But right now, I just need to fuck ye and make us both happy."

"Whatever." I grabbed his dick and lined it up, barely giving him a second to remove his hand before sinking down.

Both of us groaned. All I could feel was him. Every other sense left me.

"Never get used to how good that feels." Struan swore.

I rose an inch then slammed down, surprising myself with my force. Then I changed the angle, experimenting until I found a slow, steady motion. Struan tightened his muscles, still holding off from grabbing me and taking over.

Again and again, I worked his dick, building pleasure, constrained by the narrow space and our clothes.

Struan reared up and yanked down the front of my dress, exposing my tits.

I didn't care, lost to sensation. Only needing to feel more.

With a hot tongue, he licked and sucked me, rolling my nipples until I mewled with pleasure and stuttered in my rhythm.

Struan growled out a warning. Then he clamped his hands on my waist and jacked his hips to pump in and out of me, the control now his.

I braced myself on his chest, at his mercy and loving it.

We were on a time limit, and urgency grew.

Struan's actions became an onslaught of desire, and he drove into me, pounding, every demand deeper. Faster. A surge ignited, electricity crackling between us.

I clamped down hard on him. He wrestled a hand between us and stroked my clit, once, twice.

I arched my back, chasing the electric coil of heat he was building. A fire stoked by his moves. Then I gasped, my orgasm catching alight. Struan let out a rough sound and pumped into me over and over, merciless as he pushed to the edge. Then he was falling, too. Deep inside me, he came.

The whole world slowed. My heart sped out of time. I couldn't catch a breath.

All I knew was intense pleasure. Happiness.

Only when we were connected like this did I believe we could have a future. Struan had so many barriers, but then again maybe I did, too. My feelings had hopped, skipped, and jumped the boundary.

Growing up, I'd witnessed my parents' terrible relationship, and I'd believed myself to be the problem. Every day, I'd worked harder to be the best daughter, never letting a grade slip and being the model of a dutiful child. That had got me nowhere. Unloved. It hadn't been worth the pain. They'd never been honest with me, let alone each other. Recognising that released a clamp from around my heart.

Now, I was in the middle of changing, but I had no idea into what.

I needed to stand alone.

I wanted to do that with Struan beside me.

Slumping down, I ran my arms around him, trembling with all we'd done.

"Ask me to be your girlfriend."

He drew in a breath, his jaw locking. "I can't."

"I don't want less."

Struan's gaze shuttered. "Fine. Fuck ye. Leave me. Find a guy with a car, a job, a room of his own. Ask him your motherfucking question."

"Is that what you want?"

Still half hard inside me, he glowered, nostrils flaring. "No, sweetheart. Date someone else, and I'll kill him. Ye belong to me. Every part of ye. Every orgasm. Mine."

I grinned, watching the tallest of his walls shake. Struan was full of anger and hate, but he didn't scare me.

I stooped and popped a kiss to the end of his nose, then climbed off him. "Because I'm your girlfriend. You just have to accept it then ask for real. And do you know what? You're mine, too." My legs trembled, and I stood from the car, collecting my bag before I paused at the door. "You should know, I'm in love with you. And that has nothing to do with possessions or anything else. It's just a fact."

Struan furrowed his brow, his angry breathing stalling.

He reached for me, but I danced back, heart pounding.

"Sorry, I need a second." I blew him a kiss and ducked away.

At the front of the car, I grabbed tissues and cleaned myself up, tossing them plus my ruined underwear into the bushes. When I was fixing my skirt, Struan stepped out into the night.

"Thea," he said slowly.

The roar of an engine came, followed by bright lights spilling over us, blinding after so long in the dark. I shielded my eyes as a truck pulled up. The door opened, lights dimmed, and a redheaded man stepped out, saving Struan from the awkward sentence he couldn't finish.

I could only hope that he found his own way to the truth, just like I had.

35

Struan

My moment to respond to Thea was gone. Over the rushing of my blood in my ears, Max said something and extended a hand for me to shake.

She'd told me she was in love with me.

"Thanks for coming out," I managed.

The mechanic shot a look to my lass.

"This is Theadora."

She waved then folded her arms. "Thank you for rescuing us. This is my car, but Struan was driving. It's died an untimely death."

Max set on bright lights from his rescue truck and poked around under the bonnet. "It just cut out, aye?"

I dragged my gaze off Thea. "Out of the blue."

"And was the brake heavy when ye bought yourself to a stop?"

"It was. I had to jam on it."

A few more minutes of messing around, and the mechanic came back to us. He scrubbed the heel of his hands into his red hair and blew out a breath. "It isn't great news.

This model is notorious for this kind of problem."

"What kind of problem?" Thea frowned at the engine.

"Crankshaft failure. Catastrophic."

She sighed. "Then it can't be fixed by the roadside?"

"Sorry. The best bet is to talk to your dealership. This isnae a cheap fix." He angled his head at her. "I already guessed it was your car before ye said. I know it's naw this guy's, after my run-in with that shitty grey Ford of his. Too big an upgrade."

I huffed a laugh, not taking offence.

"It's my dad's. Or it was."

Max's curious expression dropped. "Shite. Sorry. I don't know what to tell ye. Getting it back on the road means a lot of work."

Which we didn't have time for. I had to get back to my brothers.

Thea turned to me. "Is your car in Inverness? We can't exactly go back for it."

I shot a glance at the mechanic. "Aye, we can't."

Max rotated a tool in his hands. "Why?"

Done with lies and mistakes, I hauled in a breath. "Because I lost my head and smashed up some arsehole's car. Someone called the police, and they were chasing us. If they pick me up, I'll be charged, and I cannae afford to be locked away."

A low whistle was my answer. Max twisted his lips. "Who was the arsehole?"

Thea answered. "My dad's lawyer. He's holding my inheritance over me, but he's done a lot worse than that. If you're going to call the police, you'll be making a mistake. He deserved everything he got, and more."

For a beat, Max looked between us. I had no idea if

I'd made a mistake in contacting him or not, but that deed was done.

"I asked around about ye," Max said slowly.

A short buzz of panic passed through me. "Why?"

"Had a bad feeling about ye. After our run-in, I couldn't get your situation out of my head. It didnae make any sense. Not your ankle tracker, the fear I saw in ye, or the fact ye drove at breakneck speed to buy child's medicine. That got reported back to me by someone who saw ye in the village after I asked around. No one had heard of a youth offending place anywhere in the islands, which meant either you were lying or something strange was going on."

So that was who Keep had heard asking about me.

"I didn't lie," I spat.

"I believe ye. My family runs the mountain rescue from our estate, so we're used to searching for people. I had the idea of coming up to try and find ye." He moved in closer, his expression severe in the stark light from his truck. "If something bad is happening, you're not alone in it. I have men. We can help."

In a heartbeat, I wanted to trust him. That an outsider could help. But it wasn't just my life at stake. I had three brothers and a wee sister, too. If Burn left the island, he could go to jail. This wasn't my call to make, not alone.

A thrumming sound filled the air, a helicopter, sudden and loud.

Max scanned the skies and sought it out. The din grew, and we all watched as it moved on and away, lights flashing in the dark sky.

"One of ours," Max stated. "I'm naw on call tonight, but like I said, we're well-equipped for helping people out." He looked to Thea then back to me. "If ye both come with me, I'll find ye a bed for the night. A hot meal. We can try to sort out the car, but I'm pretty certain it will take more than tinkering to fix it. Alongside that, I'll introduce a couple of family members who are smarter than I am. Or, I can deliver ye wherever else ye want to go. Your choice, but the offer's there."

I set my gaze on my lass. After leaving her hanging, I wouldn't blame her for wanting out. She had no reason to keep her faith in me. In fact, the opposite. I'd let her down and led her astray.

A moment passed, and Thea summoned a smile. "That's a kind offer, but I don't think we're ready to take it. Plus there are others... What I mean is, it would be better if we returned to the island and worked things out for ourselves. If you could help us back to our boat, we'd be grateful."

Max nodded swiftly then gestured to the car. "I'll drive ye there now, then return to take your car into our garage. It can stay there until ye call me."

Thea took a moment to empty her belongings from the car, including a box of paperwork from the boot. We loaded into Max's breakdown truck, and he drove us through the night to Skye and up to the boat dock. There, we jumped out, and he followed, gazing down at the small boat.

"What island?" he asked.

During the drive, he'd told us a story of how he'd become a father at a young age and showed pictures of his wee redheaded daughter. He also talked about his role on the mountain rescue and how callouts and difficult situations were his family's bread and butter.

The more he spoke, the more I liked him. He was open and factual, and he had a helicopter pilot twin brother who'd gone to the same university as Thea. He didn't push me for more information but showed genuine interest in the tiny slices of my life I was willing to give up.

He felt like an ally when I'd only ever known people to be out for themselves.

Giving up the name of the place felt like a risk, but then almost everyone else there was a threat. It wouldn't matter if that number was added to.

"Torlum," I uttered.

Max nodded then raised a hand in farewell. "Ye have my number. Use it."

He drove away, and we boarded our boat for the long, silent journey back to the island.

I had no idea what we'd find there.

36

Struan

The grave spread out before me, a dark hole in the seeping ground. Deep, but empty of its occupant.

Sin threw out a final shovelful of earth and climbed out, dirt on his hands and face. After the trip back to Torlum, where Theadora had huddled at the front of the boat and neither of us had tried to talk, we'd arrived on the island at dawn. I'd expected her to return to her grandmother's house, but she kept with me as we snuck around the back of the village and out to the hostel.

"No sign of Charterman?" I asked.

Sin shook his head once. "Jenkins came back. Drunk this time, but we couldnae risk burying her while he was looking around. I started digging when he left."

"Where's the body?"

"On the floor of her office. We closed the blinds and wrapped her in her bedsheet." Discomfort flitted over his tight expression. "Will ye help me get her into the hole? The boys and Cassie are sleeping. I don't want them to see her again. It's fucking traumatising."

My stomach roiled, but I jerked my head in agreement then turned to Theadora. "Go inside the bunk room and make sure they don't come out."

She gave me a searching glance but entered the back door of the hostel. Sin and I rounded to the front. In the office, the lump that used to be our keeper laid on the floor, hidden under the white sheets. Disgust soured my mouth, and I focused on breathing through my mouth only.

Sin took one end of the sheet, and I the other.

Neither of us made eye contact beyond coordinating our lift. The sooner this was done, the better. Staggering outside, Keep's dead weight swinging between us, we peered around in the gloomy morning.

"Clear. Move fast," he ordered.

Pacing over the ground, we rounded the corner to the pit that Sin had dug, and without ceremony, lowered Keep inside.

Sin grabbed the shovel and cut into the pile of earth at the graveside, dragging in as much as possible. When he paused for breath, I took it from him and did the same. Inch by inch, the sheet containing our keeper disappeared.

A strange sense of an ending settled as we worked. As the eldest, it was up to us to handle this. To protect the others from memories that would torment them.

Hushed voices sounded at the doorway, and I raised my gaze to find Theadora, arms outstretched, trying to prevent Burn from emerging.

Both of them stopped, eyes glued to the pit at Sin's and my feet.

My youngest brother's mouth turned down. "I want my share. Don't treat me like a child."

I exchanged a glance with Sin then dipped my head. Theadora stepped aside, letting him out.

Burn marched over and snatched the shovel from me, then tossed mud into the grave. Scar appeared next and silently took over when Burn's energy waned.

Theadora disappeared back inside, leaving the four of us to the task.

Spadeful by spadeful, the pit was filled. When there was only a couple of inches left, Sin stopped us and indicated a pile of turf. He must have dug the grave quickly, but also carefully, considering how we'd conceal it after. We each lifted the lumps of grassy earth, wedging them onto the mud pile like a jigsaw puzzle.

"Fuck ye and your cruelty," Scar muttered, driving his heel down into one piece.

"Fuck ye and your willingness to sell children for sex," Burn added.

Sin looked between them, then stomped with one heavy boot. "Fuck ye for being a worthless human who could only cause pain in others."

All attention fell to me.

After everything she'd done, her physical and emotional abuses of all of us, I felt nothing. She'd locked me up. Electrocuted me. Stabbed me with a needle. I didn't care about her life or her death. I didn't give a shite if anyone wouldn't miss her.

Placing the last piece of turf down, I drove my weight into it. "Just fuck ye," I spat.

Then it was done. One enemy down and who knew how many others to go.

We tidied the ground, watering away the loose mud, before moving inside to take turns in the shower and clean ourselves up.

In the bunk room, Cassie slept on. Sin, water droplets still clinging to his shorn hair, summoned the rest of us to the corridor and closed the door so she wouldn't hear.

"First things first," he said and produced a set of keys from his pocket.

Grasping Burn's leg, he fitted a weird-shaped key to the tracker, and the device dropped away.

Silence fell across all of us. Moving quicker, he undid Scar's, mine, and finally his.

"I'll take off Cassie's when she wakes," he muttered.

I pressed my fingertips to the white flesh revealed underneath. That lump of plastic had sat there as a dead weight for over nine months. I'd got so used to it, it barely registered anymore.

Wild delight broke me out of the sombre mood from burying our keeper.

"This is... I mean..." Burn leapt to his feet and snatched his up. He marched around the corner, through the internal door, then a rush of cooler air met us. A noise of exertion followed, and he returned to us grinning. "Yeet-ed that fucker out onto the moor."

Scar barked a laugh and jumped up. Sin and I followed, traipsing to the back door. Then all three of us hurled the tracking devices as far as we could.

Returning to the corridor, we jostled each other, all grinning.

Leaning against the wall, Theadora watched us. "You can't stay here." Her gaze set on me, but she dragged it away to Sinclair. "Charterman is your jailor, right? You recognised him. Last night, we went to his house. He didn't answer, but I'm sure he knew we were there. Which means he knows Struan was off the island."

"He didn't come here," Sin answered slowly.

"Yet. Whatever he's into involved keeping you locked up. He has to intervene," she replied.

My mirth fell away. "She's right. We're sitting ducks here, just waiting for him."

Sin pressed his lips together. "We need to go to the mainland. But, I still need to bring him down, and I won't allow Burn to be taken to jail."

Burn's gaze darkened. "If he's coming here, we need to lie in wait for him. Besides, I have my own unfinished business, and I willnae leave until it's done."

Thea nodded. "This needs to end. But there are so many parts to it all, I can't make sense of it. I'm as tangled up in this as you all are. We'll go to my house. It's spacious enough for all of us, and he won't look for you there. At least not at first, so we'll have the advantage."

It wasn't entirely true that she was in as deep. Thea could cut ties altogether now, but instead, she was bringing us closer. Sticking with me. I openly stared at her, all kinds of shite rising in my dumb head.

Finally, I lifted my chin. "We'll go there and make a plan. Fill in the gaps."

"Share the intelligence, secure a base. After that, we mobilise," Sin added. "Let's go."

The door to the bunk room opened, and a tousle-haired lass peered out with big eyes, her blanket bundled around her and Thea's blue wool scarf around her neck. "Where are we going?"

Burn whooped and snatched her up in her blanket. "We're done with this place and going on an adventure."

"Am I staying with ye?" she asked.

"Of course ye are. We're a family now," Burn said.

Sin unclipped the tracker from her leg, and Cassie waggled her foot in glee.

I was stuck on the *family* comment. I'd got so far as thinking of the men as brothers, but beyond that, I'd no clue how we'd go on from here. Only that this had to come to an end.

Scar had been quiet through all of the decision-making. "Before we go, I have something to do." He wheeled away towards the hostel's reception.

The rest of us followed, Burn setting Cassie on her feet.

At the entrance to Keep's office, Scar booted the door, catching it on the rebound. With a low yell of rage, he lifted the chair and smacked it into the desk, splinters flying. Then he grabbed the laptop and hurled it against the wall, metal and plastic cracking apart.

The filing cabinet clattered to its side next, the drawers sliding out and jamming. Then Scar spun around to glare at all of us.

"Come the fuck on," he commanded.

With an animalistic howl, Burn joined him, and the two burst into our dead keeper's private rooms, smashing everything in their wake. Theadora held Cassie's hand and backed her away from the violence, saying something low and soothing to the little girl and offering her Keep's coffee mug to shatter.

Sin stooped to the trashed filing cabinet to collect the single stack of files contained within. Likewise, I picked up the broken laptop. Then the two of us went around every flat surface, door handle, and frame with clothes to remove fingerprints.

"Anything else in here that would identify us?" I asked him.

Sin gave a single shake of his head. "No. Unless someone DNA checks the mattresses, and why would they bother? It was very contained. Deniable, once they were done with us. I've been waiting for this moment for so long. We all needed to be here. I needed to know the extent of my family."

And now we had it. Five of us, almost free. But I didn't doubt the biggest battles were yet to come.

37

Charterman

The phone rang in my office, shrill and too loud in the early morning. I lifted my aching head from my desk, drool on the wood from where I'd slept and a discarded whisky bottle immediately ahead of my slumped arms.

My brain cells bled, but I forced my eyes to focus on the display.

Him.

I picked up the phone. "What?"

"You failed."

"What are you talking about?" I rubbed my eyes.

"The boys. You promised me this would be simple. Easy money, you claimed. The old man would lap up your illustrious company, and the boys would live out in obscurity. We should've just killed them from the start."

I winced at his raised voice, then small glimpses of the previous night eked back in. "Theadora failed. It wasn't my fault. Yesterday evening, I had a message from Henry saying Theadora had a picture of McInver and was asking questions. She came to my house with one of the boys. They smashed up my car."

I opened my laptop, clicking through to the tracker system employed on Torlum. All five signals showed a last position this morning in or near the hostel. The system had been off-line for an hour, but it often was. I breathed a sigh of relief. "He's back on Torlum."

A pregnant pause followed. "If they know about Mc-Inver, you've royally fucked up. There's only one way out of this now."

My hand gripping the phone trembled. "What?"

"You need to kill them," he uttered, deathly calm. "I did everything I had to do. I held up my end of the bargain. It's only a matter of time until they discover the whole truth. What will happen then?"

Everything would fall apart, but he didn't need me to say that. "How am I supposed to take them down by myself?" I spluttered.

"I don't give a damn. You own a gun, don't you? Go there, drain the lifeblood out of every last one of them, and only contact me when it's done."

The call disconnected, and I snatched up the whisky bottle and sucked down the dregs.

Everything was messed up. It wasn't fair that this fell to me. I could be caught, or injured.

What could I do? There was no way...

Wait.

I had resources. Other ways I could get close to them, particularly now I knew Theadora was in thick.

Taking up my phone, I drafted a message to the one of my children I'd always been able to rely on. The one who was as motivated as me when correctly encouraged.

They were two sides of a coin, my offspring. One held all the good, the other all the personality.

But before I hit send, another call came in.

I goggled at the screen, the alcohol I'd drunk blurring my vision.

McInver.

I hooted at my luck. The old bastard hadn't spoken to me, rejecting my calls since our visit to his house.

"Hello, McInver? It's so good to hear from you."

A pause, then his croaky voice came on the line. "Ye brought me her," he uttered. "I didnae realise, but ye brought me her and she was in my home. What must she think of me?"

He sobbed, and I sat taller, new life infusing me.

Of all the luck. Finally, he'd had the spark of recognition I'd dreamed about. The shakier of my plans might pay off yet.

"There, there," I chided. "It had been a long time. She wasn't sure you'd recognise her."

"I didn't! She slipped through my fingers. My lost love. My dear, sweet Rhona." Shuffling sounded, like he was rolling in his piles of money, Scrooge-style. "Ye have to bring her back," he demanded. "Bring her back and make her stay. I have a room for her, all set up. Locks and a bed. She willnae run from me again."

"Of course," I crooned, mentally revising my message to my child. "But it could be hard work, and I have other priorities..."

McInver let out an angry snarl. "Have whatever ye want. I'll sign your damn papers. Just bring her back. Do what it takes and deliver my woman to me."

He hung up, and I slumped back in my chair. Theadora, so like her dead grandmother, was ours. Or, rather, his.

She'd love her new home in his mansion, or maybe we'd all get lucky and he'd die of a heart attack from fucking her too much.

Throwing my head back, I laughed, and laughed, and laughed.

38

Struan

In Thea's grandmother's prim living room, the six of us sat or slumped on the furniture. In the corner, the television played quiet cartoons for Cassie.

We'd arrived in ones or twos, slinking across the back garden so the villagers didn't spot us. At the bay window, Burn watched the water, on the lookout for any boats.

Thea held the floor. "Let's start with the facts. You were all kidnapped and brought here." She sliced a glance at Cassie then dropped her voice. "Abused."

Sin folded his arms. "By Charterman, with agreement of and assistance by at least some of the locals. Lottie's father was my captor, and I was first here. The men who brought my brothers after were hired in, I assume, because I've never seen them again."

Thea dipped her head. "And the brothers thing?"

Rapid-fire, Sin gave his explanation of why he thought we were related.

"Right," Thea continued. "So all fingers point to Charterman being the ringleader. The question is why. Charterman and my dad were apparently in business together, though I don't know the details."

I drummed my fingers. "And your father has been missing since I was brought here."

"True. Another mystery. But I think this all ties back to McInver."

She explained the story of being taken to McInver's house, and how she thought Charterman wanted the old man's money for his side of the family. At the point she described her assault by the old man, though only implying the details for Cassie's sake, I leapt up and paced the room.

"Sorry that happened to ye," Sin said, the others echoing their regrets.

"Thank you. It was horrible. We can all see how Charterman is prepared to do anything to get what he wants."

"Which means were all in D-A-N-G-E-R," Scar spelled out, with a glance at our sister.

I stopped my pacing and made a sweeping gesture with my finger. "No one goes anywhere alone. We stay together."

Sin straightened from his lean on the wall. "Agreed. We need a game plan. But before that, back to the reason we're hidden away here. If Charterman is trying to get the old man's money, then we're in the way of that."

"Which means, what, that we might be entitled to it, too?" Scar asked.

There was only one horrible conclusion to be drawn. My skin crawled, but I forced out the words. "McInver is our father."

Expressions of disgust appeared on every face, but Thea produced the photograph from her bag.

"This is him," she said. "Henry recognised him."

"Fuck," Sin drawled. "We all look like him. Christ, I always wondered who my mother was so hung up over that she resented Burn's ma his whole life."

Burn drifted away from the window, moving in on the picture. "Because he was rich, aye? He trolled Scotland for women, knocking a few up. And we're the result. Ye said he lived in a big house?"

Thea widened her eyes. "Yes, which you're all in line to inherit. Holy heck."

She grabbed her phone and searched, then held up the picture. A mansion stared back at us. Something from a film, not real life.

"It's called the Great House. McInver lives there alone, and the place is massive. There's artwork and antiques everywhere," she explained. "Charterman is trying to stop you from taking your share. He wants it all for Henry."

"For himself, more like," I deadpanned.

Sin gazed at the screen. "There's nothing more motivating than money. Evidence in everything he was prepared to do to secure it."

A chill went through me. "Why didn't he just do away with us?" I dragged my finger over my throat. "He arranged to have us picked up, one by one, and brought here. What stopped him from throwing us in the sea?"

Burn hissed a warning, slicing his gaze at Cassie.

The little girl giggled at the cartoon's antics, thankfully not listening.

Sin scrubbed a hand over his shorn hair, his eyebrows beetled. "He didn't need to. None of us are important. No one came hunting us down after our abductions. Murder leaves a trail. Witnesses, if he couldnae do it all by himself. Bodies aren't easy to hide. Locking us away for a few years while he sweet talked the old man had to be a thousand times easier. He made sure none of us saw him, aside from the single glimpse I had. He had the means to hide us away. The place to take us. An accomplice. And that was the easiest solution."

Thea swallowed. "Which meant he and my father sat down and concocted this plan between them. Either that or Dad was coerced into it. Maybe my father stayed his hand."

"Whatever his role, it made him a liability," I murmured to her.

Thea's gaze touched mine. "You think Charterman got him out of the way?"

"Maybe."

A pulse of something strong passed between us, and she didn't drop the heavy eye contact. I still owed her answers.

Her words burned inside me.

Thea took a shuddering breath and snapped her focus back to the wider room. "They can't get away with it. If that man is your father, then you're entitled to inherit from him. It's the least we should aim for after all you've been through. But we need to be sure. We started with facts but we've gone into speculation."

Cold trickled in my veins. There was one easy way to do this, but it forced me to acknowledge something I hadn't wanted face. "My mother would know. She's the only one left alive. Maybe."

"And she's in prison," Sin placed his words carefully. "Which means someone could visit her, take the photograph, and confirm the story. From there, we have a case. Proof to back up the conspiracy. We need that if we're ever to live on the mainland again. Without it, we're a group of delinquents no one will believe. The islanders will lie about us. There's a body in a grave that incriminates us all. If we survive this island, we need all the evidence we can get."

"Incoming," Burn announced suddenly from his perch at the window. "Two boats, sailing in fast."

We moved to the bay window, peering out. Across the bright water, two boats powered through the waves, coming our way. They went out of sight behind the rise of the land, the harbour invisible from here.

"Do we think it's him?" I asked, my adrenaline picking up.

At my side, Sin stood taller. Of all the facts we'd covered, an older one had stuck in my mind. He'd suffered the worst at Charterman's hand and wanted his blood.

Yet Charterman's murder would only make us real criminals.

Burn fidgeted, flicking his lighter over and over. "It could just be fishermen or other islanders returning from a trip. The only way to be sure is for some of us to go out and scout."

"I'll go," Thea said.

"No," I spat. "No fucking chance."

She glowered at me, but Burn curled his hand around her shoulder.

"He's right. If the islanders know you're helping us, they could turn on ye," my youngest brother said. He tipped his head at Sin. "We'll go. We can fight them off if we need to."

Sin jerked his head in agreement, and the two of them snuck to the back door and left the house.

Scar sat with Cassie on the rug and chatted with her about the TV, but his worried gaze flicked repeatedly to the window.

Thea spared a searching glance for me. "I need to get changed."

"I'll come with ye."

She jogged up the stairs with me at her heels. From the shadows around Thea's bedroom window, I watched my brothers creep across the garden then down the wall that led to the road. Unless someone came looking, they'd be well concealed. The neighbouring houses were single-storey and not that close.

Still, panic built.

I traded out glances at Thea, swapping her dress for leggings and a shirt, with peeks at the grounds. My panic eased once I saw my brothers creep back again. We returned downstairs to meet them in the living room. Burn grinned, clearly enjoying the drama, and Scar leapt to his feet.

"Not Charterman," Sin announced. "A group of men took the road from the harbour, moving inland."

"Coming for us?" I asked.

"Hard to say. Their body language was relaxed, and they talked easily. Unless someone has been out to the hostel, there's no reason for the islanders to be up in arms."

"Unless Charterman told them to take us down," Scar pondered. "He knows Struan was on the mainland. If he checked the trackers or tried to call Keep, he'd have reason to send someone to look in on us."

Thea shivered. "If they're heading there now, it won't be long until they find it empty and call a search of the island. Do we run?"

Sin's expression twisted, choices tearing him in two. "If we leave in broad daylight, people at the dock will see us. We're too visible as a group. Even if we reach the boat, we'll be followed, or a nice police escort will be waiting at the other end."

"If it's just a couple of people, we'd be able to over-power them," Burn said.

"Aye, we could knock them out, but the moment someone finds them, or they wake, they'll call the cops."

"What will the police do?" I asked. "Wait for us at the ferry port in Uig? There are other places we could land the boat."

Sin considered this. "Does anyone here know the coast well enough to bring us in at a town or somewhere we can steal a car? No, me neither. If we're caught, Burn goes to jail. I will, too." He stared each of us down. "Keep's death is on me. If anyone needs to answer for it, all of ye will plead no knowledge."

"No fucking chance," I bit out. "Ye didnae kill her. It was her own fault."

He curled his lip. "No one will believe that. Plus, I'm pretty sure it's a crime not to report a death and to bury a body without authorisation."

I wheeled away and trod the faded rug. "Then what, we sit here and wait for them to find us?"

"They don't know we're here. So long as we're careful and stay out of sight, we can hide until dark. At least that way we can reach the mainland unseen." Sin turned to Thea. "Talk to Lottie. Find out if she knows what her da is doing."

Thea nodded and placed the call. It rang out, the answerphone picking up. She tapped out a message and sighed. "If her father is on the warpath, he could've taken her phone. He's done it before. I've said I need her opinion on a recipe, so to call me asap."

Sin glowered more and strode off, saying something about making food from the scant tinned supplies left in the cupboards and what we'd brought from the hostel.

I turned to my lass. There were multiple other things that we needed to do. Decisions to make, strategies to discuss. But I was stuck on the biggest one of all. Of the things Thea said about being mine despite the thousand and one ways that shouldn't be possible.

It hit into the darkest parts of me I'd wanted left covered.

"What?" She tilted her head.

I stepped into her space and tucked her hair behind her ear. Her expression softened, and her fingertips grazed my biceps. But if my woman thought this was a tender moment, she was deadly wrong.

Stooping, I threw her over my shoulder and carried her from the room, smirking as she cursed me.

39

Thea

Struan deposited me on my bed and took a few steps back, spearing his fingers into his hair. "Everything is fucked up, and the only thing I'm sure about is how much I want ye. Which means I need to do this shite." He gestured between us, touching his chest.

A thrill shot through my heart, and I hid my smile. "Correct."

He stared at me for a long minute as if I'd do the hard work for him. But I couldn't. I'd made my case, even if I'd caved almost immediately, and had to stand my ground.

"The only family I ever had was Ma. I never kept friends for long because we moved around, never had loving grandparents, no one. The longest real relationships I've ever had are with those arseholes downstairs, and ye."

I sat on my hands, urgency building inside me to hear his words.

Struan's gaze bounced from me to the floor. "No one ever told me that word ye said."

The love word? The one I'd spoken with no response.

I parted my lips in astonishment. "Not even your mother?"

"No. Probably because no one ever said it to her. She showed it in other ways but never said."

"You must miss her," I said softly.

He raised a shoulder. "She used to go away for days on end, off with some paying guy or another, and I never knew if she was coming back. Her leaving me was the pattern of my childhood."

His reaction to me telling him I was going... It all made sense now.

Struan continued, nervous energy rippling off him. "This is so fucked up, but the last night I saw her, she told me she was going to prison. She kept it secret, all of it, from going to court to her final days as a free woman, then she laid it on me. Know what I did? I ran. Immediately after, I was picked up and brought here."

"You can't be blamed for that reaction."

His gaze flicked up, filled with pain. "She used to tell me that if she ever served time, which was highly fucking likely because she did minor criminal shite often, she wouldn't be able to stand it. She told me she'd kill herself. When I left, I knew it would be the last time I saw her. Ever."

Oh God. "I'm sure she didn't mean it."

"Or she did. If we need a witness to all that went on, and that's happening now, she might not be around."

My brain sprinted over the problem. "I'll go and see her. If I explain who I am, she'll talk to me. She must miss you hard."

His blue eyes focused on me. "That wasn't my purpose in sharing this with ye. Aye, it's a problem to be tackled, but I wanted to work through it so I could explain myself.

I've treated ye badly, and ye need to know that I'm sorry. None of that is on ye. You're naw her. I was a fucking idiot for acting out. I have something else to say to ye that's nothing to do with that headfuck."

Butterflies took flight in my belly.

I'd wanted this so badly. For him to meet me in our emotional connection. To match me. I'd barely believed it a possibility.

With his hands on his hips, Struan stared at me. Then he swore and swore again.

Still, I didn't fill in the gaps. The words had to come from his lips.

On an angry breath, he dropped to his knees in front of me and gripped my jaw to hold my face before his.

"I'm in love with ye," he bit out.

Delight danced through me, chased by astonishment. In the middle of our stark situation, everything else paled to the power of his statement.

He loved me.

I wanted to laugh.

"For fuck's sake," he added, desperation in his tone. "Say it back."

"I love you, too," I said fast. "Does this mean you're asking me to be your girlfriend?"

He scowled. "No. That implies we're dating, which sounds temporary. I told ye, Theadora, from the start that ye are mine. I have nothing to offer ye—"

"You just gave me everything I needed."

I flung my arms around him and hugged him. For a moment, Struan froze, but then he hugged me back, taking in a deep breath and burying his face alongside mine.

This was all I'd ever wanted. Someone of my own.

Someone who loved me like I loved them. He pushed me, challenged me, thrilled me and I'd never imagined the depths of love I had for him could be possible. It was, and he shared it.

The atmosphere shifted from big emotion to something even more desperate.

I kissed him, sinking my feelings into that hot press of lips.

"Love," he muttered against my lips. "You're killing me, and I'm going to die happy."

Struan picked me up and carried me to the window, ducking to place me on my knees, my head just below the level of the glass.

From behind, he whispered in my ear. "Hands on the windowsill."

My whole body trembled, and I obeyed him, gripping the white painted wood.

He pulled my hair to one side and kissed my neck. "The door's closed, but sound travels in old houses. If ye don't want my brothers to hear, ye need to stay quiet. And if ye don't want to bring an attack down on the house, ye have to stay out of sight of anyone outside."

He kissed higher, directly under my ear. Simultaneously, he slid his arms down my body, fingertips grazing the swell of my breasts. At my waistband, he tugged down my cropped leggings, pulling them and my underwear off in one go, pausing only to remove my sandals.

"So beautiful." He ran his hands up my thighs, curving in to yank them wider apart.

Then his palm hit my ass cheek, a slap resounding.

I took in a shocked breath, and wetness pooled at my core. "Did you just spank me?"

"I did."

"Are you angry at me because you feel out of control?" I peeked around.

Struan stared at my backside, his head angled as if he was admiring the red handprint he'd no doubt left.

"I'm naw angry," he said slowly. "I just want to brand ye all over. Mark ye as mine."

I sucked in a breath, turning back to the glass. "Do it again and I'll slap your dick."

"Try it." He dipped his hand between my legs, landing at my wet centre. Coating his fingers in my arousal, he teased me, then drew them back until he reached my other hole. I held still, wary.

"I have this urge to claim every part of ye, too," Struan told me. "Here included."

He tested my back entrance, pressing the tip of one finger inside. I closed my eyes against the rush of desire. It was a strange sensation, yet another brand-new feeling, but I didn't hate it. Everything he tried pushed me to discover my sexuality.

Slowly, I rocked my hips.

Struan swore and withdrew his hand. A rustle came, and I gazed back to find him stripping. Then, in a fast move, he rolled onto his back and lifted me over him, settling me down on my knees above his face.

"Ride my mouth while I finger-fuck ye," he ordered from between my thighs.

I threw an anxious glance at the window and got into position with my pussy above his mouth. Struan strained to lick me, making me gasp out loud, but then took two handfuls of my hips and brought me down harder on to him.

"I'll suffocate you," I squeaked.

He rumbled a laugh. "No better way to go."

Undeniable need had me sinking lower, until Struan's tongue could get exactly where I wanted him. He licked me, groaning a deep sound of masculine pleasure. The hand at my backside swept lower, gathering wetness, then returned to my puckered entrance. He held me in place, then drifted the other hand underneath me.

Simultaneously, he pushed two fingers into my pussy and one into my ass.

I moaned in shock but didn't stop moving on his mouth. Struan shifted to my clit, rolling it with his tongue before sucking hard. He stretched both my entrances.

God, the onslaught of feeling was almost too much. I was at his mercy, too. If I raised myself up and off, I'd be in sight of anyone outside.

Which meant only accepting what he was doing to me.

He found a rhythm with his fingers, sliding in and out easily. I was so wet for him, so turned on by his words and actions. A throb started at my clit and echoed through my body. I released one hand from the windowsill to palm my breasts, thrusting down harder on Struan's face.

He growled between my legs, and I slipped my hand inside my shirt to pinch my nipple.

Tremors hit me inside, powerful and insistent.

I couldn't come. It was too quick. Impossible. My thighs trembled, and I grinded down, in pursuit of the too-good feeling.

Struan sucked harder, then used the edge of his teeth on my clit.

"Struan," I moaned.

His hands kept up their motion, the penetration stretching me, hitting me in so many pleasure centres at once. His stubble scratched my thighs. His fingers generated sparks.

I broke. Spasms hit me, and I gasped, dropping my head to the arm still stretched to the window ledge. Brilliant pleasure spread, spiking along my nerves. Under me, Struan kept his hands in action. Wringing every last drop of pleasure out of me.

The moment my climax ebbed, he drew out from under me. I breathed hard, barely conscious from the hard hit, but smiled as his body crushed against mine. On his knees behind me, Struan thrust inside, sinking home without hesitation.

My body yielded to him, the intrusion prolonging my orgasm. He jacked his hips, seating himself fully, then started a rhythm, one hand braced with mine against the windowsill.

Again, I accepted his demands. Loved it. Loved him.

Without pause, he pumped in and out, his pace going from demanding to punishing. I dropped my head to watch his steel-hard length disappearing into me, glistening. Ah God, that was hot.

Then he reached around to stroke my clit. There was no way I could come again. I wasn't sure I'd even finished from the first time. Yet that same weaving, spiralling sensation built.

Breathing hard, I pressed my face to his arm. In response, he landed hot, open-mouthed kisses to my back and shoulders.

Together, we were dynamite. Explosive. Perfect counterpoints. Him so big and male. Me more delicate in body but just as strong in mind.

Inside me, his dick pulsed, and I arched back to him.

"Come for me," Struan demanded.

He upped the pace then slapped me between the legs. Just as I'd threatened to do to him. Immediately, he pressed softer circles into my flesh, the shock and blood rush bringing me to the edge.

"Do that again," I ordered.

He did, the smack direct to my clit. Yet another orgasm detonated.

I gasped and splintered, coming so hard I could barely see. Behind, Struan surged, pounded into me a couple more times, then collapsed onto my back, pulsing inside me, his breathing as rough as my own.

My limbs lost their rigidity, and I was falling, but his arms were right there. Struan held me up, still in me. Joined so completely in love and lust, ruined together.

It took a long moment to catch our breaths.

But as I raised my head and opened my eyes, I found myself dead on with the window.

A figure the other side of the garden wall stared right back at me.

40

Thea

At the door, I held my breath and slowly opened it to the dusk. At my back, Struan gave off waves of menace, staring out into the gloomy garden.

A figure moved towards us.

Upstairs, I'd had the shock of my life spotting her. I'd cleaned up and dressed in a flash, then sprinted to get here before anyone else saw.

Lottie bolted up the path and flew through the entrance.

I shut us in, then fell on her in a hug. "I'm so glad you're here."

"Did anyone see ye coming?" Struan demanded.

She took a breath, her cheeks pink in the low light. "I don't think so. Most of the islanders are in a meeting."

Footsteps drummed in the hallway, and Sin and Burn burst into the kitchen. At the sight of Lottie, Sin's hostility dropped, something entirely new registering in his expression.

Wide-eyed, she stared at him for a moment, then dragged her gaze back to me. "I saw your message, but Da took my phone. I came as soon as I could."

From the way her attention sprang back to Sin, I could tell she wasn't expecting the men to be here, which could only be a good thing. If she didn't know, maybe the islanders didn't either. Linking her arm with mine, I drew her into the living room, and the men followed.

On the sofa, I turned to her. "Can we assume your father doesn't know the men have left the hostel?"

Lottie sucked in a breath. "They definitely don't, or about the dead woman. I overheard part of their meeting, and they are up in arms about being owed money. They're talking about challenging someone."

"The lawyer?" I asked.

She nodded. Then fear sprang into her vision again. "You're leaving, aren't ye? I mean, I'm glad that your nightmare is almost over, but this is it. You're all about to go."

"Hell yes," Burn said from his perch in the window, where he had returned to monitoring the sea. "Going, and never looking back. I hate this place. It's evil."

Lottie shrank in on herself. "It's worse than that. The island is beautiful, but there's a darkness here that's infected the people. Or maybe the people are the source. My father is the worst of them." She swallowed. "I'm glad you're going. Ye all need to get away as fast as ye can."

"Come with us."

I'd opened my mouth to say those words, but someone else had voiced them first.

Sin.

Lottie's lip trembled, her attention on the big man. "I can't. It's already going to be a battle for ye to get away.

They willnae want to give up their only collateral. If I'm along for the ride, Da will go ballistic. He'll never let me leave."

I snatched up her hand. "You're an adult. He can't keep you here."

"He can. But listen, I needed to warn ye that they are planning something. I don't know what, but I'll do whatever I can to help ye get away. Just expect a fight."

Sin swore and paced to the window, sticking to the shadows so he didn't create a silhouette. He glowered at Burn. "We'll leave the moment it's dark enough to hide out at sea. But if we get caught on the mainland, I will do everything I can to protect ye."

Burn raised a shoulder, his usually open expression more guarded now. "What does it matter? At least if I get jailed in a real prison, it'll have an end date. Just promise me you'll take care of our sister."

In a chair, the little lass slept, my scarf bundled around her. I'd never called out Struan on stealing it, but he'd caught a knowing look.

"What will ye go to jail for?" Lottie asked quietly. "You're so young. Surely it can't be that bad."

Burn smiled, but it was without humour. "I picked up a nasty habit of punishing bad people by means of fire. Ye know, just your average paedophile burning to death in his bed."

He was only now eighteen. I couldn't imagine the horrors that had driven him to such an act at an even younger age.

Lottie didn't break his gaze. "Sounds like it couldn't have happened to a more fitting person."

Burn lifted his chin, then turned again to watch outside.

I felt the weight of attention on me and peered around to find Sin watching me.

"As the landowner, I thought ye could make a declaration that the hostel was valid, and Burn had served his time."

I winced. "Pretty sure that won't work."

"Aye, I gave up on the idea once I'd thought it through."

Struan started on an explanation about the mechanic guy who'd helped us, and how he ran the mountain rescue, but Lottie stood, gesturing for me to go with her. In the hallway, she perched on the bottom stair, and I sat with her.

"Is there anything else I can do?" she asked.

"I don't think so. The best-case scenario is that we get off the island and the men can get to their father to claim an inheritance. Money solves a lot of problems, including paying off people if we need to."

Quickly, I filled her in on all we'd discovered on McInver and our assumptions on the reason they'd been imprisoned here.

Lottie hugged me. "Ye love him, don't ye? Struan, I mean. I can't imagine ye voluntarily walking back into that old pervert's house otherwise."

"I'd do anything for him. And I'm not afraid of McInver, more angry than anything. There are still so many parts of this mystery that I don't understand."

"Like what?"

"Why Granny had McInver's photo, why he went on a spree of getting women pregnant around Scotland, and how Charterman knew enough about it to be able to track each child down. And the last one, the little girl. She's only six, which means seven years ago, the old bastard was still doing it. Presumably after that, he became decrepit."

"Give me your phone." She held her hand out.

I handed it over, and Lottie tapped in a number. "I'm going to talk to Annis. Don't worry, she's not on the island right now, and I know she doesn't have much to do with the other people who live here. But she'd know, I'm sure. Her mother was good friends with your granny."

The line rang, and a voice answered, barely audible to me. Lottie rattled out a question, then told Annis she was putting her on loudspeaker so I could hear the answer.

"Thea, I don't like to dredge up old gossip, but my mother used to speak about this. It's a small island, and chat a favourite currency for some. Before your grandmother married your grandfather, she had an infamous love affair with the man of the name Lottie just mentioned. He was very wealthy and would take her to the mainland and drive her around in expensive cars. She was very beautiful, just like ye. He was a handsome devil, too. Every lass's head was turned by him, but then something happened. Your grandmother broke things off with him. My mother implied he'd been improper with her, which nowadays probably means he tried to force her into something she didn't want."

I took a long inhale. "Poor Granny. That sounds exactly like him."

Annis continued. "She went on to marry your grandfather, and two years later had your dad, so all's well that ended well. But not for the man she jilted. He used to haunt her, claiming he'd never let her go. Apparently, he even showed up at her wedding and threatened her groom, but that might have been Ma embellishing the story a wee bit."

She chatted on, describing how lovely my grandparents' wedding had been, but I was making connections previously invisible to me. Thank God I knew I wasn't related to him, as otherwise I'd be thinking his resentfulness was the same as Dad's. Like father like son, twisted up over the one who got away.

Another point became clear. Henry was wrong. Charterman hadn't invited me to that dinner purely as decoration. I looked like my grandmother. He was trying… What?

"I think I was bait," I whispered.

Lottie shot her gaze to me, then thanked Annis and hung up the call.

"He took me there to offer me up to McInver in my grandmother's place," I said on a breath. "The old man is losing his marbles. I bet he hoped he'd think I was her."

"Why, though? What if McInver suddenly decided to give it all to ye?"

"He wouldn't. He thinks women are decorative or whores. Charterman knew that. He wants Henry to be declared the heir. It's so obvious to me now. It was all desperate manipulation."

"Then ye were meant to charm McInver so he'd be content after years of suffering. So he'd write a will and Charterman, via his son, would get everything," Lottie breathed. "He hurt ye for that."

"I'll kill him for touching ye," a voice came from the door. Struan leaned on the frame, his features flat in the dim light.

I gazed at him, the strength of the connection between us so powerful. Love was a dangerous force. Wonderful when reciprocated, deadly when it kindled hate. "I almost pity McInver. He'd been so in love but couldn't get over it after."

"He doesn't deserve your pity, sweetheart. He made his choices."

I released a gasp. "It all makes sense now. Twenty-one years ago, when he started his campaign of sleeping with women and getting them pregnant, that's when my grandfather died. What if he'd waited for her all that time but she'd refused him again? It sent him on a spiral."

"Or he'd always been an abuser of women. But by then, he just didn't give a shite."

Sin appeared behind him, and with a single quiet saying of her name, pulled Lottie aside into the kitchen.

I set my gaze back on Struan. He held so still I wasn't sure he was breathing.

"What if I'm like him? Obsessive."

"Just tell me you love me," I replied.

"I fucking love ye. So much it hurts. Everywhere."

"I love you, too, so it's okay to be obsessed with each other. You are nothing like him and never will be."

In my hands, my phone buzzed, Esme's name on the screen again. She'd messaged several times, but I hadn't read or replied to any of them. Multiple new messages spilled in.

Esme: My dad has been ranting about you. Henry is being weird, too. Please tell me you're safe.

Esme: I keep thinking about how I should've done more to support you. It was wrong saying that we should behave differently to accommodate horrible men.

Esme: I want to be a better friend. Please let me help.

I held it up for Struan to see, and an idea sprang into

my mind. "I don't trust her, but what if we use her? Ask her to go to the jail on our behalf. I don't have anyone else I can send, and we need to know."

"If Ma's still alive. Not a bad idea. I know she wouldn't take my call."

I exhaled hard, hating his resigned tone. "Sorry."

He shrugged. "It's fine. If she hasn't done away with herself, get Ma to ID him. It'll stop us making a mistake if we go there and challenge him. Actually, I'm naw sure I care. Even if he is our da, I don't want his money."

"What about for your brothers and sister? They'd be set for life. You could give your mother whatever she wanted when she's free."

He pressed his lips together in an unhappy grimace. "Let's get off this island first. Send your fake friend later."

I tapped out a holding reply, ignoring her requests to speak now. Then I twisted my phone in my fingers, lost in my head for a moment.

"What is it?" Struan asked.

I exhaled and gave up my thoughts. "If we're right about all this, it's because the generations that came before us treated us like we weren't worth the truth. You were all targeted and imprisoned in the name of greed. My parents were a living lie, with their relationship a failure from the start, and then my dad got himself in trouble, signed over the island to me, and vanished without a word."

"Maybe he was trying to protect ye from losing this place. Considering what happened with your ma leaving and whatever he was planning."

"Perhaps. But why not say anything?"

He tongued his cheek, keeping his opinion to himself.

I filled in the blank. "Because he wanted to but

couldn't. He ran out of time. Is that what you think? That he was killed by Charterman, or maybe a debt collector? It makes sense. He left everything behind apart from his phone and wallet. Stuff he'd have with him if he was just stepping out for a moment. He really is gone, isn't he?"

"I'm sorry." He took his turn now in apologising for things neither of us should.

"If ever I have children," I said, "I'll only tell them the truth."

Struan's gaze slid down my body, and he prowled to me, forcing me to lie back on the staircase as he covered my body with his. Instant heat flashed through me.

"I never thought I'd want kids, but the thought of ye being pregnant with my bairn is a real fucking turn-on."

He kissed me, his hand sliding under my head to protect me from the step. Sinking into the cradle of my hips, he rested his weight without crushing me.

"Maybe in ten years," I whispered between hot presses of our mouths. "For now, upstairs."

Then I was in his arms and being carried away to finish what we'd started.

41

Lottie

In the dark kitchen, I hopped onto the counter and crossed my ankles, waiting for Sin to speak. I should be scared of this man. At six and a half feet tall, he had thick muscles and a twisted smile that could drive fear into the hearts of his enemies. Who knew what secrets he hid behind that impenetrable exterior.

Well, perhaps I was a little afraid.

He strode a few steps away, then wheeled around, fingertips raking over his shorn hair. His dark-eyed gaze bored into mine. "Find a way to leave."

I couldn't. Not now, not like this.

"No," I said softly.

This was Sin's weakness. With my chubby cheeks and belly rolls, I couldn't pretend to myself that he wanted me. No, he *pitied* me. He was a protector. I saw it in everything he did for his brothers and sister.

I'd been caught in that net, and it was too hard to break out.

I adored him.

I'd follow him to the ends of the earth, but in doing so, I'd bring down the wrath of my father on his broad shoulders. Da wouldn't give me up. Not without a fight to the death. He refused to let Ma go, even though their marriage had long ago disintegrated to dust. I had no hope.

His expression darkened all the more, and he moved in on me, raising a hand.

I flinched, the response automatic.

Sin froze, just about to tuck my hair behind my ear. A muscle in his jaw ticked. "He hits ye," he gritted out.

"Don't all fathers beat their daughters?"

"No, they don't."

He was so close now, I was grateful the sun had set and he couldn't look too closely, because he couldn't fail to see my anguish. The wrench as my poor lonely heart tore in two. If he knew, I'd activate that protector mode even more. I felt it to my bones.

I ducked my head, breaking our eye contact, and pushed his chest to get him to back off.

Sin didn't budge.

"I have to go," I told him. "Tell Thea I'll call her when I get my phone back. I'll do everything I can to warn ye if I hear anything more."

Still, he didn't move. Purposefully, Sin placed his hands on my knees and pulled them apart, inserting his body to the gap. Then he rested his forehead on mine.

I couldn't breathe.

Our lips were an inch apart.

"Thoughts of ye torture me, Violet Hunter. When I thought Struan had taken your first kiss, I wanted to kill him. "

"Why?" I whispered, no other thought in my head

than this moment.

"Hands behind your back."

Instantly, I did as ordered, twisting my fingers together at the base of my spine.

Sin grunted approval then, tipping up my face with his fingers, pressed his lips to mine. In shock, I went utterly still. I'd dreamed about this so many times, but my imagination could never match the reality. The complete sensory overload.

And still I wasn't moving.

Sin didn't stop. He nudged harder against me, encouraging me to move with him. I did, and he surged, hunger in the way he took me over. His fingers speared into my hair. His big body warmed mine.

For a blissful second, I kissed him back, lust and deep satisfaction washing me in rainbows of light. Who knew it could be like this? That my whole body would feel so... alive. So full of potential. Ready to map to his.

If he wanted, he could take my virginity on the countertop, and I'd let him. Tear open my clothes. Meld our bodies.

A shout came from deep inside the house. "The boats!"

Sin broke our kiss, breathing hard. For a moment, he just stared at me, then swore and charged out of the kitchen.

I didn't wait to find out what had happened. If the action was starting, I had to be far away from here. Slipping out the back door, I fled.

42

Struan

Thundering down the stairs, Theadora's hand gripped in mine, I burst into the lounge. At the windows, my brothers stared out at the dusk, the sunset a blood-red flare on the horizon.

"What the fuck is going on?" I demanded.

"The boats from the harbour. Every one has been taken out," Scar answered.

In a line across the sea, a chain of lights bobbed.

"They led them out and tied them off to a buoy. I need to go check from the road, but I bet there isn't a single one left," he added.

Sin cursed and strode across the room. "I'll go with ye."

The two disappeared, and I stared at the view. Every fishing boat, rowing boats, even the fucking canoes had been taken out to sea, the islander responsible paddling back in on a single-seater.

Waves tossed them, the ocean as angry as me.

"Without a boat, we can't get off the island," Cassie

said from under Burn's arm.

He patted her hair. "We'll find a way," he promised, his gaze finding me.

Fuck. Frustration built in me. Lottie had warned us that they wouldn't let us go, but we'd played it safe. And now we were stuck.

A few minutes on, Scar and Sin returned.

"No boats," Sin confirmed. "The dock is empty."

"Then they know we're about to leave," I stated. Energy replaced my anger. "We can get to where they've moored those boats on our surfboards. Thea can go with me, and Cassie can go on Burn's. We can paddle out."

"It's a risk. There's a storm rising." Sin glowered at the window.

Rain spat, hitting the glass.

"And? We can't sit here with no way out. We're just waiting for them to find us, and they've made a move. We need to go," I bit out.

"Fuck it. You're right. We have no other choice," he decided. "Grab a bag for dry clothes and any other essentials. We're heading out now."

We mobilised, each snatching up a few possessions. At the front door, I swung it open, letting the night air rush in.

A group of men crossed the road.

Behind, more came, sticks in hand. A mob. Here for us.

Thea cried in dismay, and my heart shrank.

"Back," I uttered in a growl to the others.

"No use hiding. We've seen ye now," the first man called.

I slammed the door, turning to my family in the now

pitch-black hall. "Through the kitchen. Run."

We half fell through the big house to reach the rear exit. Sin peered from the window, an arm out to hold us off, then let out an angry snarl. "They're all around us."

Thumping came at the front door, echoing through the rooms.

"We have ye surrounded," a man called. "Don't even think about trying to get away."

My family congregated at the base of the stairs, close together.

Sin turned to Thea. "There's no basement, correct? No other way out than the two exits they are covering?"

"None." She wrapped her arms around herself, features silvered in the faint light.

Sin and I exchanged a look, and his expression drove fear through me. We were trapped here. They could do any number of things to get us out. Bust down the door and pick us off. Smoke us out.

Burn the place.

"Listen," the man shouted again. "We all want the same thing. Open the door so we can talk."

I wheeled around and ran at the door, smacking the palm of my hand to the wood. "You're a few burning torches away from being a bad film. Leave us the fuck alone."

"That's Hunter, Violet's father," Sin spat.

"I'll spell it out for ye," Hunter continued. "We have the power here. One phone call from me, and the police will come and cart the lot of ye away. Try to get off the island, and they'll be waiting at every dock. We all have stories about ye bunch of degenerates. Stealing, vandalism, defiling our daughters. Mine will happily back up the claim."

"Ye lying sack of shite. What do ye want from us?" I blasted back.

"Give us Jones and we'll go. All we want is him."

"Which of us is Jones?" Burn asked quietly.

No one answered.

Thea took in a rush of breath. "I bet it's a fake name, and not for one of us."

"Ye mean for Charterman?" I asked.

She nodded. "Why would he give his real one when he came here as the land manager running a secret jail?"

"Do ye mean the land manager?" I called back.

"Aye. Him, or the other. They owe us money."

"If ye mean our keeper, she left the island yesterday," I lied through my teeth.

"No. Augustus Stewart."

Stillness descended. I stared at Thea.

"My dad?" she said slowly. "They know he's missing. He didn't go to the funeral, I talked to people there. They sympathised."

The man outside hammered again. "We put up with this for too long, and they made us promises. I want my money. We know Theadora is in there. If he won't come, we'll take her instead. The rest of ye can go."

I left the door and went to her, pulling her into my arms. "Over my dead body," I muttered. "What are our options? How do we get out?"

Sin rubbed his jaw. "If we get Charterman back, we could have a chance. I wouldn't trust that baying group of inbreds as far as I could throw them, but it might provide the distraction we need. Either way, we need help."

"Charterman wants me," Thea said. "His daughter messaged another warning. He's looking for me. If I call him—"

"Ye are not offering yourself as a sacrifice," I snapped.

She huddled into me. "We have no other way out of this. We can't get out without a fight, and there's too many of them. If Charterman is willing to come here to pick me up, the villagers can grab him before he gets anywhere near me."

"The man isn't stupid. There's no way he's just going to moor a boat in that empty dock then wander into a trap."

Sin leaned in. "Which is why we need to be clever about this. He wants Thea, the villagers want him, we just need off this island. Talk to me again about the guy from the mountain rescue who helped ye."

Max McRae. He'd already been on my mind. I was so used to being alone, but I'd found family now. Maybe I could ask for help and get it.

Slowly, we pieced together a plan.

43

Max McRae

In the operations room of the hangar, I stared up at one of the giant maps we had on the walls. This evening, we'd assembled at the mountain rescue headquarters, but our callout had been cancelled almost as soon as it started. The missing person reported in unharmed, so dispatch stood us down.

I was buzzing with energy and ready to go.

Most of the rest of the crew had gone home, leaving me, my brother, and a couple of other men.

"There." I placed a finger on the island of Torlum.

Maddock, my twin, joined me and squinted at the wee landmass. "I thought you'd chilled out about this since ye met the guy again."

I twisted my lips. "No. Everything about that setup is bothering me. Whatever happened to that lad, it isn't good Now I know there's a lass involved, too. A whole group of them if I'm to believe him. Something is really fucked up on this island. Check this." I held up my phone. "He sent me a text earlier that read, 'Shit is going down. Can I tru you?' But nothing since. There's no chance I'll relax unt hear back."

Where we lived, in the middle of the Cairngorms National Park, we were surrounded by family. My uncles owned the land for miles around. We operated the mountain rescue service, and I had been born with the instincts for saving others.

I knew from the moment I met Struan that he was in trouble.

Getting the call to help him at the roadside had both set my mind at rest and piqued my interest all the more.

Maddock's gaze drifted from the island down across the central Highlands, and I knew his helicopter pilot's mind was calculating the distance. Fuel needed. Timings. "No harm in taking a run up there," he offered. "Gabe could do with some night-time winch training."

Across the room, Gabe, another of our pilots, raised his head. "We heading out?"

My phone buzzed in my hand. On-screen, the name gave me a jolt of recognition. Joyrider.

I held it up. "Fuck. It's him."

I read the text, wide-eyed at what the lad had been through in the past few hours, and my energy turned to pure focus.

In ten minutes, we had mobilised and were in the air, all of us infected with the same energy and discussing the tactics that had been trained into us. My uncle Gordain, who owned the hangar, joined us, a full crew kitted up and ready for a rescue.

I'd been right about everything, but for Struan, things had become infinitely worse.

If we didn't get there soon, it could be too late.

Thea

At the end of the dock, I shivered, huddling into myself against the biting wind. Ahead, the black sea churned, waves pounding each other, the distant boats clattering where they were chained far away.

Behind, the string of lights illuminated the empty harbour bays and concrete slope. No lights shone in the village. Every other person hid, waiting their chance.

I was the lamb to the slaughter, but I'd convinced the locals to let me do it, then slipped away before Struan could stop me. My father had facilitated his imprisonment. Coordinated to create this hell. I needed to undo his crime and set everyone free.

However tonight ended up, I'd done everything I could to make things right.

An engine sound broke through my consciousness. Beyond that, a chopping noise was fainter still. Struan's friend with the helicopter crew, I hoped. But though they'd agreed to come out, they didn't know this place. There was a chance they couldn't get here in time, or find us. Or still be willing to help when they saw exactly what was going down.

Through the sea spray and gloom, a brightly lit boat appeared.

The ferry. The small passenger-only one Struan had been brought here on.

My heart skittered.

It neared, and I struggled to see who was on board. It appeared empty, but then a figure moved at the controls. Charterman. How the heck did he get a ferry? It clicked. He had someone there paid off, too. He'd brought the boys here under their noses.

By degrees, the boat neared.

"Come on," I muttered, flexing my fingers, then forced an upset expression and waved.

It surged closer until it was fifty feet from my lonely position. Then Charterman threw the engine into reverse, stalled it, and powered down.

He left the cabin and appeared on deck.

Dread washed through me. This wasn't the plan. On the phone, he'd jumped at the chance to come and collect me. I'd fake-cried and told him I'd made mistakes. Needed his help. Would do whatever he asked.

We all knew why he wanted to capture me. At one point, I'd been crucial to his goal of convincing McInver to hand over his money, and I'd taken the chance that that was still in play. That Charterman intended to let the old man do whatever he wanted with me in the name of my poor dead grandmother. I had to trust that his desperation lived on.

So why was he stopping? We were so close.

"Theadora," he shouted with an evil smile. "So good

to see you."

I gasped, leaning forward. "I've been trying to see you for months. Please. I need your help. Get me away from here."

I had to play the game and cool my temper, but the past year had changed me beyond recognition. I'd been meek and mild, quiet and obedient, and it had got me nowhere. It had hurt people. Ones I loved. Now, I was the avenging angel, ready to bring down this man who thought he could harm others for his own gain.

Acting the part took every bit of my focus.

Charterman held the ferry's rail and tilted his head.

"I'm begging you. Come and get me," I shouted against the wind. "I made a mistake. Everything has gone wrong. I want you to fix it for me."

All we needed was for his boat to reach the land, then the islanders could rush him and take him away. He'd unknowingly gifted us the vessel we could then use to leave. He'd be delivered his fate, we'd get on with our lives, assuming they didn't set the police on the men.

And yet Charterman didn't return to the cabin. "Where's your boyfriend?"

"He isn't my boyfriend," I lied.

In the back of my mind, when I'd thought this out, I'd known Charterman feared Struan. That he'd probably hidden from us when we visited his house. But still, he'd agreed to come.

At the last hurdle, he was faltering.

"Jump," he called with a sneer.

My blood iced over. "What?"

"You heard. Swim to me."

The dark water swirled beneath my feet, splashing at

the dock, salt in the air. The distance I could handle, but this wasn't the plan. If I swam to the boat and climbed on, he couldn't be captured.

The whole idea fell to pieces in front of my eyes.

"I can't swim," I said in a desperate surge of inspiration.

"Nonsense. I've seen you swim in this very sea when you were a flat-chested prepubescent unfuckable thing. Jump in and swim to me, Theadora. Your transport is waiting."

It was true, I'd learned to swim here. The sea didn't scare me.

My hatred and fear surged and crested with a new idea. Something so high-risk but possible when all other avenues had failed.

If I couldn't get Charterman onto the island, I had to get him off that boat. This was my only chance.

Steeling myself for the cold, I toed out of my shoes and dragged my light sweater over my head.

Then I pushed off the dock and dived into the churning water.

Instantly, seawater rushed over my head, obliterating my senses. But I pushed through it and surfaced with a gasp. Throwing one arm in front of the other, I tore through the water, waves threatening to drag me under.

Halfway to the boat, I stopped. "Help!"

Water rushed over my head, and I doggy-paddled to stay afloat and shouted louder. "Help me!"

Through vision blurred with salty tears, I spotted Charterman leaning over the rail, gaze fixed on me.

"Swim harder," he urged.

"Can't. I'm drowning." I made a show of splashing

around, submerging again.

Under the water, a kind of peacefulness reigned. It was hard to believe I was here and that I'd done this. Ran from Struan so he couldn't stop me. Made this recompense happen.

I wafted my hands to keep myself below the surface, my hair floating around me like a mermaid's. The brine on my lips stung, and I kept my eyes tight closed, waiting it out until the right moment.

A distant splash made it through to my consciousness.

My lungs burned, and I shot to the surface once more and sucked in air.

Scrubbing my eyes, I found the boat and stared. *Empty.*

Holy shit. My plan worked. Charterman must be in the water, too. Tossed by the current, I swung my head around, trying to see a dark shape moving towards me.

But there was nothing. Nothing but more waves.

With increasing desperation, I pushed up in the water, straining to see.

A hand snatched at my throat. Charterman was right in front of me, features twisted in hatred and purpose.

"Your father should've taught you your place," he screamed. "He promised me a docile little bitch, able to keep this godforsaken place from his debt collectors so no one would come prying while he hid away, and what did I get? A devious hellcat. Decades, I planned this! Married into the family. Gave him an heir. All I needed was for you to do my bidding. You will not ruin my life."

For all his ranting, I was caught up on the bit about Dad. He hid away? Implying he was still alive? With an anguished gasp, I kicked out and connected with Charterman's gut.

He gurgled, and I rushed back.

In utter fear, I powered through the waves. He was so close and had moved so fast. I sensed him catching up with me, my skin crawling.

Clawed nails grasped my ankle, yanking me back.

I screamed and kicked at him, taking a mouthful of seawater. Almost choking, I swallowed it down and stifled my need to breathe, and my spasms from the water in my lungs.

This wasn't how I was going to die. Not at his hands. Not within the reach of this dark place.

Underwater, I kicked again, succeeding in dislodging his slippery grip. Now, I didn't hesitate. Swimming deeper, I drove energy into my arms and legs and put as much distance between us as I could in the inky-black sea. I might've been a strong swimmer, but I wasn't muscular. My limbs quickly burned from overexertion.

Going under saved me. Nothing touched me. No hand snatched out to take hold.

When I could stand it no longer, I burst up to the surface and silently hacked, breathing and choking and clearing the seawater so I could take in precious air.

Yet I couldn't wait. In the brief seconds I'd taken to stop myself dying, he could've seen me. Be closing in again. I scrubbed at my eyes, wrenching my sodden hair aside.

Then shock stole my panic.

I was right next to the ferry.

The boat dipped, lights swinging. The huge metal hull so close.

With a final burst of energy, I scrambled to grab the pitching ledge. Hauling myself onto the deck, I forced myself to my feet. At the door to the cabin, I fell inside and gawked at the controls. I'd driven a boat numerous times, but this was on a different scale. There was a wheel instead of a tiller. A screen with colourful circles.

For a moment, it overwhelmed me, and I sobbed.

No. I had this. The clutch and throttle, I understood. At least I could get it moving. Trembling and weak, I powered up the engine. If I could throw it in reverse, and the big boat obeyed me, I'd get away from the land.

I couldn't see Charterman in the water now. For all I knew, he could be creeping up behind me.

But if he wasn't, he'd have nowhere to go other than onto the island. Or drown.

A laugh tried to wrench from my exhausted lungs, and I set a hand on the clutch to engage the engine. But then I spotted a figure at the end of the dock, standing exactly where I'd been.

The person paused for a second, raising their face so I got a clear view of them.

Struan. Panicked. Features tight in fear.

He must have seen me dive in then fought the islanders to get through.

In a rush, he threw himself into the waves.

Then a hand closed over my mouth and a person snatched me from behind.

45

Struan

Pulling myself through the cold water, I swam out, desperate to find Thea. The faint figure bobbed in the water, an arm waving, and I put my head down and powered through the sea to reach her.

"Help," the person hollered.

I was six feet away when realisation clicked.

That wasn't her voice. It was *him*.

Anger consumed me. After everything this bastard had done, all I wanted was to drown him here and now. His death was so close I could almost taste it.

But I had to find Thea.

Farther out in the water, the big ferryboat's engines growled, and I swung around to seek it out. A figure moved on board. He'd brought backup. Probably his evil son.

A wave hit the side of my head, half drowning me. Then I caught a glimpse of the face in the cabin.

Thea? Shite. I couldn't be sure.

Salt stung my eyes, but as I swiped at them, I finally got a clear view. Fuck me, she was at the controls.

A right hook drove into my skull.

Blindsided, I dropped like a stone under the surface of the ocean. My lips opened on instinct, and water rushed in.

Pain throbbed in my head, and saltwater rinsed my mouth. For a long moment, blackness stole my thoughts. The urge to succumb too easy. My whole life had been a series of fuck-ups. From my birth, fathered by that man who I wanted to kill as much as I never wanted to meet, to Ma's problems and jail time, to being brought here. The evil ran deep. Not just in the island but in everyone connected with it, too. Charterman, who'd used it as a jail. The corrupted villagers. McInver who'd haunted the place after being dumped by Thea's grandmother.

Anger gave me back my strength.

Thea gave me purpose. She fucking loved me. I was not going to die on her.

Surging up again, I cleared my lungs and clenched my fists. Charterman was swimming away, towards the boat Thea had taken control of. I couldn't let him reach it.

I pursued him, giving over all my strength to the chase. After a few powerful pulls, I was on him, and I grasped his shoulder, ducking him down.

Charterman thrashed to dislodge me. I smirked at the fucker, seawater in my eyes. Then I drove my fist into his nose. Even in the dark, the faint light still showed me the red that poured from his skull.

Screaming, he switched direction and swam towards the shore. Catching him was child's play, and I threw another punch, suddenly realising my feet could touch the bottom. We'd come in so shallow, adjacent to the dock, that the concrete expanse that led up to the road was just ahead of us.

I found my footing and drove fist after fist into his evil face.

My knuckles cracked, stinging with the salt, but still I kept up my attack. He'd hurt so many people. He deserved nothing but a painful death.

And he wasn't moving now. On his back in the water, Charterman stared unseeing at the night sky.

I'd killed him.

Shite. His death was meant to be at Sin's hands, not mine. Too late for that now.

Better it be on my conscience than his. After what he'd done to Thea, I was glad.

Dark figures left the shadows of the wall and moved down the slope. The villagers, coming for their man.

I released the grip I had on his soggy shirt and backed away, losing contact with the ground. My brothers and sister were still in the house—I'd burst past our guards the moment I saw Thea in danger. But I couldn't go to them. I had to reach my lass.

Overhead, lights flashed, and chopping cut through the air.

I'd picked up the sounds of the helicopter coming in. I could only hope it was my friend and not the cops.

Twisting back into the sea, I dove for the boat.

46

Sin

In the front garden of Thea's house, I stood in a face-off with Hunter. After Thea dove into the water and Struan raced to help her, the rest of us sprinted outside, only to be pinned down by the villagers. Scar held our little sister in his arms, and I stood before them, protecting them.

Hunter had dispatched a group to bring Charterman in, but neither of us budged.

Fury swirled inside me, crimson red and hot. This man beat his daughter. Terrified her. Yet she wouldn't leave with me.

Fuck her for her secrets. For rejecting me with no explanation.

I couldn't take her from him. Not if I was going to get the rest of my family away.

But I'd return for Violet.

I'd raze the fucking place to the ground and take her to safety. Then I'd walk away and forget I ever obsessed over the lass.

The ear-splitting whirring of rotor blades and a downdraught broke our stare off, bright lights illuminating us all. Across the road, on a rise above the harbour, a helicopter touched down.

The moment it settled, three men in jumpsuits leapt out.

Struan's friends had stepped up. I could only hope they'd believe us and take our side.

"What's this?" Hunter snapped out. "Who the fuck are ye? Get off my island," he shouted to the approaching men.

"Gordain McRae," the older of the men identified himself. "Someone tell me what's going on here."

"Hey, McRae." I raised my hand, drawing the man's attention. "Struan's my brother. He called ye, aye?"

A younger man pushed past and closed in on me, his gaze leaping over us. "I'm Max. Where is he?"

At his question, I cast my gaze over the sea. On the brightly lit ferry, the figure helped another on board, then they hugged. If I didn't know it was Thea and Struan, I'd have assumed they were fighting.

I breathed a sigh of relief. "On that boat with his lass. Please get us the fuck out of here."

"Now wait a second," Hunter started.

On the road, another group of villagers carried a lifeless body between them. Charterman. Hunter followed my gaze then hissed a warning, and they sped away, others following.

The mountain rescue men exchanged a glance between them.

The older man, Gordain, gestured to me. "Tell me how to feel about what I just saw."

"That we're next if we don't get out of here."

"Grab your things. You're coming with us."

Hunter grimaced. "I'll ask again, who the fuck are ye? Not police, I'd know because I've called them. These boys are going to prison as soon as they get here."

Bile rose in my throat. "Ye wanted Charterman, we delivered him. You've kept us here under false imprisonment, and you're threatening us with the cops?"

His eyes glittered with anger. "What good is Charterman to us dead? Someone is going to pay what we're owed."

Gordain McRae stared him down. "If ye have called the police, what are ye going to tell them when they arrive? That you've enabled the trafficking and abuse of young men on your watch? A wee lass, too," he added, his eyes widening a fraction as Scar stepped around me holding Cassie.

"This is none of your business, outsider." Hunter's face reddened. "This is my land, by rights. No one is coming here and telling me what to do. Leave."

Gordain let a grin spread. He crossed the ground until he was at my side, then separated me from Hunter. Taking another stride, he pushed the islander back by the sheer force of his presence. The men behind Hunter shuffled with him, their expressions fearful. Another man moved with Gordain, having his back.

Whoever these people were, the McRaes, I envied them. I wanted this for my family. The readiness to defend each other and do what was right. I would guard mine until the end of my life.

Gordain said something too low for me to hear, but Hunter stiffened, fright in his beady eyes. Resistance curled his lip, but Gordain held his ground.

Max rounded on us. "Heli. Now."

We didn't hesitate. Struan and Theadora had got away, at least out into the ocean. The rest of us needed to escape, too. With the rotor blades still whirring, the noise level deafened me, but I guided Scar and Cassie inside the helicopter, nodding to the pilot at the controls who looked a lot like Max.

No one else followed.

I was one brother short.

"Where's Burn?" I scanned the ground. He wasn't in the road or in the front garden.

The pilot gave us headsets and guided the others to sit down and buckle in. I crouched on the door, still searching, but now able to hear the others.

"He was right behind me," I said.

"I didn't see him slip away, but I bet I know where he's gone," Scar choked. "He filled his lighter at Thea's house. Remember the thing he said he wanted to do most before he left?"

"Burn down the bad guy's house," Cassie chirped.

I closed my eyes, desperation rinsing away the relief of being rescued.

We were so close.

The mountain rescue men backed up to the helicopter, still arguing with the villagers.

I made a decision. I couldn't leave Burn here alone. The others could go to safety, but I had to stay.

Removing my headset, I handed it to Scar with a meaningful look. One of the rescuers jumped up front with the pilot, and Gordain and Max stood in front of me.

"I can't go. One of us is missing," I shouted to them.

Gordain pressed his lips together. "Shite is about to go

down," he mouthed, air swirling around us.

I knew it, and knew my chances of ever leaving this place again were next to nothing, but I wouldn't leave Burn—Jamieson—behind to die alone.

"We need to leave," he yelled back.

This was it, my decision point.

All around us, the islanders drew closer. If they made a grab for the helicopter or tried to board it, all was lost. No one was getting away unscathed.

"Thank ye for saving my family." I clapped the two rescuers on the shoulder, then stepped away.

"No," Cassie screamed after me, her little voice making it through the din.

I eyed the ring of men around us. To get through, I'd have to fight them, then run to find my brother. This was going to hurt. I primed my muscles, ready for the pain.

A gap formed, giving me a glimpse of the moor behind Thea's grandmother's home.

The dark heart of the island.

A neon-orange light bobbed in the murk.

I stared at it, willing my eyes not to be deceiving me.

Orange was Burn's surfing light's colour. His sign of safety in the black seas. The way we could always find each other.

Holy fuck. The light grew nearer until I could make out my brother himself. Smirking, he charged the ring of men, knocking two aside before diving for me. Receiving him in a tackle-hug, I half threw him into the helicopter's cabin then clambered in after myself.

One of the McRaes locked us in.

The pilot got us into the air.

"I didn't run." Burn pawed my arm. "He grabbed me.

But look at him now."

At the edge of the village, fire tore through Jenkins' house, scaling the walls.

Breathless, I stared down as we left the dark island behind.

47

Thea

On the deck of the ferry, Struan dragged me into his arms and touched his forehead to mine. "I thought I'd lost ye. What the fuck were ye doing, jumping into the water like that?"

"It was the only way to get him off the boat. I had to do it." I threw my arms around him, his clothes soaking wet against mine, his body hard, his grip on me so fierce.

Safe. He'd made it. My poor heart could barely handle the strain of him being in the black sea.

"Thea?" a voice came from the cabin doorway.

A violent shiver ran through me.

The moment I saw Struan dive into the water, I'd had the second fright of my life. Esme, here on the boat. She'd spun me around, burst into tears, and hugged me. Since then, she'd been talking non stop about our friendship and how much she loved me and wanted to help. It was an echo of the flurry of text messages she'd sent.

"Who the hell are ye?" Struan pushed me behind him.

Under us, the boat gently bobbed. The roar of the

helicopter got louder over the island.

Esme wrapped a curl of blonde hair in her fingers. "I'm her friend. I'd never have let her jump in the sea."

Ducking under his arm, I pressed a hand to Struan's chest. "This is Esme, Charterman's daughter. The friend I was telling you about. He made her come with him but she's on our side. Esme, this is Struan."

She stared at him, strange emotion flitting over her features. He glowered back.

"Where's my father?" she asked him. "I saw people at the water's edge. Where did he go?"

Around my shoulders, Struan's arm tightened. He ignored Esme entirely and turned to me, fever in his moves. "We need to get out of here. Sail to the mainland."

"I can get the ferry going," I said. "Docking it will be harder."

"Then we'll get near to land and swim in. Better that way as the police could be waiting, assuming Charterman stole this boat. First, I need to know that Max can get my family away."

Esme took a step closer, still staring at Struan. "Did you hurt my dad? He told me about you. He might've been a bastard but he was never wrong about people. Thea, you can't trust this man."

Struan launched past her, drawing me along with him. Inside the cabin, he stood over the controls. "How do we get on the radio? Can we talk to the heli?"

I paused to remember the small amount of boating knowledge I had. "If we go to an open channel, we can hail them."

"Do it." He swung a glance at the door, to where Esme loomed.

"Thea," she tried again. "Please, we can't take him with us."

Hostility rippled up inside me. I cared about Esme, even if she'd been a terrible friend. It was all the influence of her dad. But I couldn't hear her talk about Struan like that. "You know nothing about him. He's been a prisoner for months. Your father put him there. My whole plan was to get him off this island."

Her features twisted and she took a step closer. "Why was he imprisoned in the first place, though? He's a bad man. He killed his own mother."

Struan snorted and picked up the radio, his back to her.

"He didn't," I gritted out. "That's a lie." Clearly her father hadn't shared what he'd told me in the water.

"But it isn't," Esme insisted. "Just listen to me."

"Max," Struan barked into the handset. "Max McRae. Can ye hear me? It's Struan on the boat. Talk to me."

"Your father too," Esme said slowly. Purposefully. Her gaze never leaving Struan. "Did you wonder where he'd gone? Dad revealed to me the real truth, not the lie about him having an affair. The boys on the island found Augustus there and killed him. You see what I'm trying to tell you? How can you go anywhere with this man when he's a murderer? We need to get rid of him."

Struan shook his head in what looked like disbelief and braced himself against the movement of the boat. A voice came over the radio in his hand.

"Struan? This is Maddock, Max's brother. We have your family. Do ye need us to lift ye from the boat?"

"He didn't kill my dad," I half-whispered. "How could you say that?"

"Because it's true. Think about it. Augustus vanished when your man arrived on the island. It's because they took him. He and his criminal friends. Your boyfriend took your dad's life and you're trying to protect him."

"You're delusional," I stuttered.

She didn't stop, instead inching closer. "All this time, my family has tried to protect you. But you just won't fall in line. You need to listen to me now. I'm trying to save you and you're ruining everything."

"Fucking lunatic. This has gone far enough." Struan turned.

Rage glittered in Esme's eyes. She reached for something behind her, concealing her hand at her back. "You won't win."

"Thea, get behind me," Struan snapped. He lifted the radio to his mouth. "Maddock, aye, we need help. Now. There's a third person on the boat—"

Thrust out of sight, I couldn't see what happened next. The awful escalation of Esme's rant. But I witnessed the outcome. The deadly, terrifying result.

A deafening scream filled the cabin.

Blood droplets hit the metal riveted wall.

All we'd fought for had been ruined.

Epilogue

Augustus Stewart

In the village hall, Charterman's empty vessel of a body spread out before me. The islanders had carried him in and dumped him, muttering about how he was dead and they needed to hide the body from incomers.

How dare he die on me. I kicked his swollen, unseeing head.

Useless fool.

I'd been stuck on this island for most of a year. I'd hidden out, even signed my inheritance over to my daughter, protecting it, and our secret, from debt collectors that were chasing me through no fault of my own. Yes, my part of the plan had been neatly executed.

Bitter resentment soured my tongue.

And for what? Now I had his half of the bargain to uphold, too. This dumb fuck had failed me for a last time.

A gurgle came from his blue lips, spit bubbles forming, and I snatched a cushion from the piano chair and slammed it onto his face. His hands clawed weakly at me, and his legs jerked.

Holding the cushion down, I smothered the last of the life out of him.

Then he was finally still.

I had to leave before I was found and went the same way as my ex-business partner.

My daughter's new friends would pay for all they'd done. Sinclair most of all.

He was the reason for it all, and he had to die. For my pain. For his mother's actions.

My darkest sin.

The End.

Want to read a bonus epilogue for Struan and Thea? Get his take on their power's-out, dark-house steamy scene here.
http://jolievines.com/extras

Order Sin and Lottie's high stakes romance here.
http://mybook.to/DarkSin

ACKNOWLEDGEMENTS

As always, first of all, I want to thank you, my lovely reader, for picking up Ruin.

I'm glad you took a chance on my new series, and hugs for making it way back here to read my waffle too!

This book has been my passion project for the longest time, and I'd dreamed about the opening scene of the handcuffed, bloodied man on the boat for months before I was able to write it. I found myself constantly distracted by Struan and Thea's story. How deeply their lives crossed. The magnetism between them.

Phew, what a twisty turny path.

Struan is very different to my usual brand of hero. His expectations are darker, his past murky, and his actions dubious. He was so much fun to discover, and made a great match for Thea. She had a shell to break out of and a world to take on. The lives of the other boys were likewise enthralling to uncover.

There's more drama to come with Sin and Lottie. I can't wait to unleash their push-and-pull on the world. Things won't be easy, particularly when it comes to trust, but the draw between them will burn up the pages.

Thanks also go to the team around the book. Elle Thorpe and Zoe Ashwood, my close writer friends who play pivotal roles in every book I create. Sara Massery and Shellie Maddison who beta read and hunt down all the errors and plot holes. Emmy Ellis who edits and plays a guessing game of whodunnit with each mystery. Natasha Snow for the cover, and Cleo Moran for the promotional graphics.

A big hug goes to Liz Parker, my PA who runs my Facebook reader group (please stop by!), ARC and Street team, and is my right arm. If you've ever won swag or bought merchandise from me, Liz is fulfilling the orders (or reminding me if it's my job). She's the best.

I'm highly grateful to my team who read, review, and share my stories, and to every reader who does the same.

Lastly, to my husband and son who are the centre of my world. They've supported me through twenty books, until writing has becoming part of the foundation of our lives.

Onto the next book!

Jolie <3

P.s. you can add yourself to my newsletter here
https://www.jolievines.com/newsletter

ALSO BY JOLIE VINES

Dark Island Scots series

1) Ruin

2) Sin

3) Scar

4) Burn

Standalones

Cocky Kilt:

a Cocky Hero Club Novel

Race You:

An Office-Based Enemies-to-Lovers Romance

Fight For Us:

a Second-Chance Military Romantic Suspense

Visit and follow my Amazon page for all new releases

https://amazon.com/author/jolievines

Add yourself to my insider list to make sure you don't miss my publishing news

https://www.jolievines.com/newsletter

ABOUT THE AUTHOR

JOLIE VINES is a romance author who lives in the UK with her husband and son.

Jolie loves her heroes to be one-woman guys.

Whether they are a brooding pilot (Gordain in Hero), a wrongfully imprisoned rich boy (Sebastian in Lion Heart), or a tormented twin (Max in Betrayed), they will adore their heroine until the end of time.

Her favourite pastime is wrecking emotions, then making up for it by giving her imaginary friends deep and meaningful happily ever afters.

Have you found all of Jolie's Scots?

Visit her page on Amazon and join her ever active Fall Hard Facebook group.